A
GREAT
DELIVERANCE

A
Great
Deliverance

ELIZABETH
GEORGE

BANTAM BOOKS
TORONTO • NEW YORK • LONDON • SYDNEY • AUCKLAND

A GREAT DELIVERANCE
A Bantam Book / June 1988

BOMC offers recordings and compact discs, cassettes
and records. For information and catalog write to
BOMR, Camp Hill, PA 17012.

Book Design by Jaye Zimet.

Library of Congress Cataloging-in-Publication Data

George, Elizabeth.
A great deliverance.

I. Title.
PS3557.E478G74   1988   813'.54   87-47906
ISBN 0-553-05244-6

Published simultaneously in the United States and Canada

---

*Bantam Books are published by Bantam Books, a division of
Bantam Doubleday Dell Publishing Group, Inc. Its trademark, consisting of the words "Bantam Books" and the por-
trayal of a rooster, is Registered in U.S. Patent and Trademark
Office and in other countries. Marca Registrada. Bantam Books,
666 Fifth Avenue, New York, New York 10103.*

PRINTED IN THE UNITED STATES OF AMERICA

For Natalie
in celebration of the growth of the spirit
and the triumph of the soul

AND HE SAID, Ye have taken away my gods which I made, and the priest and ye are gone away; and what have I more?

Judges 19:24

AUTHOR'S NOTE

IF ONE CAN acknowledge an area of the world for existing and thus being a source of inspiration, I would acknowledge the tremendous and changing beauties of Yorkshire, England, that so much became the heart of this book.

I am grateful to the people who have read and criticised the rough drafts of all my work: Sheila Hillinger, Julie Mayer, Paul Berger, Susan Berner, Steve Mitchell, and Cathy Stephany.

I thank my parents and husband for their patience and support, Dr. H. M. Upton for his generous input, and especially Deborah Schneider and Kate Miciak for their willingness to take a chance on someone unknown.

And of course, Don Martin, whose annual injunctions against my addressing him in writing ultimately became the spur that so decisively pricked the sides of my intent.

A
Great
Deliverance

1

IT WAS A solecism of the very worst kind. He sneezed loudly, wetly, and quite unforgivably into the woman's face. He'd been holding it back for three-quarters of an hour, fighting it off as if it were Henry Tudor's vanguard in the Battle of Bosworth. But at last he'd surrendered. And after the act, to make matters worse, he immediately began to snuffle.

The woman stared. She was exactly the type whose presence always reduced him to blithering idiocy. At least six feet tall, dressed in that wonderfully insouciant mismatch of clothing so characteristic of the British upper classes, she was ageless, time-less, and she peered at him through razor blue eyes, the sort that must have reduced many a parlourmaid to tears forty years ago. She had to be well over sixty, possibly closer to eighty, but one could never tell. She sat bolt upright in her seat, hands clasped in her lap, a finishing-school posture which made no concessions towards comfort.

And she stared. First at his Roman collar, then at his unde-niably dripping nose.

Do forgive, darling. A thousand apologies. Let's not allow a little faux pax like a sneeze to come between such a friendship as ours. He was always so amusing when engaged in mental conversations. It was only aloud that everything became a terrible muddle.

He snuffled again. Again she stared. Why on earth was she travelling second class? She'd swept into the carriage in Doncaster, like a creaking Salome with rather more than seven veils to her ensemble, and for the remainder of the trip she'd alternated between imbibing the railway's foul-smelling tepid coffee and staring at him with a disapproval that shouted Church of England at every available opportunity.

And then came the sneeze. Unimpeachably correct behaviour from Doncaster to London might have somehow excused his Roman Catholicism to her. But alas, the sneeze condemned him forever.

"I . . . ah . . . that is . . . if you'll excuse . . ." It was simply no good. His handkerchief was deep within his pocket. To reach it he would have to loosen his grasp on the battered attaché case in his lap, and that was unthinkable. She would just have to understand. *We aren't talking about a breach of etiquette here, madam. We are talking about MURDER.* Upon that thought, he snuffled with self-righteous vigour.

Hearing this, the woman sat even more correctly in her seat, every fibre of her body straining to project disapproval. Her glance said it all. It was a chronicle of her thoughts, and he could read each one: Pitiful little man. Pathetic. Not a day under seventy-five and looking positively every second of it. And so very much what one would expect of a Catholic priest: a face with three separate nicks from a poor job at shaving; a crumb of morning toast embedded in the corner of his mouth; shiny black suit mended at elbows and cuffs; squashed hat rimmed with dust. And that dreadful case in his lap! Ever since Doncaster, he had been acting as if she'd boarded the train with the deliberate intention of snatching it from him and hurling herself out the window. Lord!

The woman sighed and turned away from him as if seeking salvation. But none was apparent. His nose continued to dribble until the slowing of the train announced that they were finally approaching their journey's end.

She stood and scourged him with a final look. "At *last* I understand what you Catholics mean by purgatory," she hissed and swept down the aisle to the door.

"Oh dear," muttered Father Hart. "Oh dear, I suppose I really *have ...*" But she was gone. The train had come to a complete halt under the vaulted ceiling of the London station. It was time to do what he had come to the city to do.

He looked about to make sure that he was in possession of all his belongings, a pointless operation since he had brought nothing with him from Yorkshire save the single attaché case that had as yet not left his grip. He squinted out the window at the vast expanse of King's Cross Station.

He had been more prepared for a station like Victoria—or at least the Victoria he remembered from his youth—with its comforting old brick walls, its stalls and buskers, these latter always staying one step ahead of the metropolitan police. But King's Cross was something altogether different: long stretches of tiled floor, seductive advertisements hanging from the ceiling, newsagents, tobacconists, hamburger shops. And all the people—many more than he had expected—in queues for tickets, gobbling down hurried snacks as they raced for trains, arguing, laughing, and kissing goodbye. Every race, every colour. It was all so different. He wasn't sure he could bear the noise and confusion.

"Getting out, Father, or planning to stop t' night?"

Startled, Father Hart looked up into the ruddy face of the porter who had helped him find his seat earlier that morning upon the train's departure from York. It was a pleasant, north country face with the winds of the moors etched upon it in a hundred separate blood vessels that rode and broke near the surface of his skin.

His eyes were flinty blue, quick and perceptive. And Father Hart felt them like a touch as they slid in a friendly but querying movement from his face to the attché case. Tightening his fingers round the handle, he stiffened his body, hoping for resolution and getting an excruciating cramp in his left foot instead. He moaned as the pain balled hotly to its zenith.

The porter spoke anxiously. "Maybe you oughtn't be travellin' alone. Sure you don't need no help, like?"

He did, of *course* he did. But no one could help. He couldn't help himself.

"No, no. I'm off this very moment. And you've been more than kind. My seat, you know. The initial confusion."

The porter waved his words away. "Don't mind that. There's

lots of folks don't realise them tickets means reserved. No harm done, was there?"

"No. I suppose . . ." Father Hart drew in a quick, sustaining breath. Down the aisle, out the door, find the tube, he told himself. None of that could be as insurmountable as it seemed. He shuffled towards the exit. His case, clutched two-handed upon his stomach, bounced with each step.

Behind him, the porter spoke. " 'Ere, Father, the door's a bit much. I'll see to 't."

He allowed the man space to get past him in the aisle. Already two surly-looking railway cleaners were squeezing in the rear door, rubbish sacks over their shoulders, ready to prepare the train for its return trip to York. They were Pakistani, and although they spoke English, Father Hart found that he couldn't understand a single word beneath the obfuscation of their accents.

The realisation filled him with dread. What was he doing here in the nation's capital where the inhabitants were foreigners who looked at him with cloudy, hostile eyes and immigrant faces? What paltry good could he hope to do? What silliness was this? *Who* would ever believe—

"Need some help, Father?"

Father Hart finally moved decisively. "No. Fine. Simply fine."

He negotiated the steps, felt the concrete platform beneath his feet, heard the calling of pigeons high in the vaulted ceiling of the station. He began to make his distracted way down the platform towards the exit and Euston Road.

Behind him again he heard the porter. "Someone meeting you? Know where you're going? Where you off to now?"

The priest straightened his shoulders. He waved a goodbye. "Scotland Yard," he replied firmly.

St. Pancras Station, directly across the street from King's Cross, was such an architectural antithesis of the latter that Father Hart stood for several moments simply staring at its neo-Gothic magnificence. The clamour of traffic on Euston Road and the malodourous belching of two diesel-fueled lorries at the pavement's edge faded into insignificance. He was a bit of an architecture buff, and this particular building was architecture gone wild.

"Good heavens, that's wonderful," he murmured, tilting his head to have a better view of the railroad station's peaks and valleys. "A bit of a cleaning and she'd be a regular palace." He looked about absently, as if he would stop the next passerby and give a discourse on the evils that generations of coal fires had wrought upon the old building. "Now, I wonder who . . ."

The two-note siren of a police van howled suddenly down Caledonian Road, shrieking through the intersection onto Euston. It brought the priest back to reality. He shook himself mentally, part in irritation but another, greater part in fear. His mind was wandering daily now. And that signalled the end, didn't it? He swallowed a gagging lump of terror and sought new determination. His eyes fell upon the scream of a headline across the morning paper propped up on a nearby newsstand. He stepped toward it curiously. Ripper Strikes at Vauxhall Station!

Ripper! He shrank from the words, cast a look about, and then gave himself over to one quick paragraph from the story, skimming it rapidly lest a closer perusal betray an interest in morbidity unseemly in a man of the cloth. Words, not sentences, caught his sight. *Slashed . . . semi-nude bodies . . . arteries . . . severed . . . victims male . . .*

He shivered. His fingers went to his throat and he considered its true vulnerability. Even a Roman collar was no certain protection from the knife of a killer. It would seek. It would plunge.

The thought was shattering. He staggered back from the newsstand, and mercifully saw the underground sign a mere thirty feet away. It jogged his memory.

He groped in his pocket for a map of the city's underground system and spent a moment painstakingly perusing its crinkled surface. "The circle line to St. James's Park," he told himself. And then again with more authority, "The circle line to St. James's Park. The circle line to St. James's Park."

Like a Gregorian chant, he repeated the sentence as he descended the stairs. He maintained its metre and rhythm up to the ticket window and did not cease until he had placed himself squarely on the train. There he glanced at the other occupants of the car, found two elderly ladies watching him with unveiled avidity, and ducked his head. "So confusing," he explained, trying out a timid smile of friendship. "One gets so turned about."

"All *kinds* is what I'm tellin' you, Pammy," the younger of the two women declared to her companion. She shot a look of practiced, chilling contempt at the cleric. "Disguised as *anything*, I hear." Keeping her watery eyes on the confused priest, she dragged her withered friend to her feet, clung to the poles near the door, and urged her out loudly at the very next stop.

Father Hart watched their departure with resignation. No blaming them, he thought. One couldn't trust. Not ever. Not really. And that's what he'd come to London to say: that it wasn't the truth. It only looked like the truth. A body, a girl, and a bloody axe. But it wasn't the truth. He *had* to convince them, and . . . Oh Lord, he had so little talent for this. But God was on his side. He held onto that thought. *What I'm doing is right, what I'm doing is right, what I'm doing is right.* Replacing the other, this new chant took him right to the doors of New Scotland Yard.

"So damned if we don't have another Kerridge-Nies confrontation on our hands," Superintendent Malcolm Webberly concluded. He paused to light a thick cigar that immediately permeated the air with a nasty pall of smoke.

"Christ in heaven, Malcolm, open a window if you insist on smoking that thing," his companion replied. As chief superintendent, Sir David Hillier was Webberly's superior, but he liked to let his men run their individual divisions in their own way. He himself would never dream of launching such an olfactory assault so shortly before an interview, but Malcolm's ways were not his own and they had never been proven ineffectual. He moved his chair to escape the worst of the fumes and let his eyes take in the worst of the office.

Hillier wondered how Malcolm ever managed his department as efficiently as he did, given his bent for chaos. Files and photographs and reports and books covered every surface. There were empty coffee cups and overfull ashtrays and even a pair of ancient running shoes high on a shelf. Just as Webberly intended, the room looked and smelled like the disordered digs of an undergraduate: cramped, friendly, and fusty. Only an unmade bed was missing. It was the sort of place that made gathering, lingering, and talking easy, that bred camaraderie among men who had to work as a team. Clever Malcolm, Hillier thought. Five or six times shrewder than his ordinary, stoop-shouldered, overplump looks would indicate.

Webberly pushed himself away from his desk and played about with the window, grunting and straining with the latch before finally forcing it open. "Sorry, David. I always forget." He sat back down at his desk, surveyed its litter with a melancholy gaze, and said, "What I didn't need was this right now." He ran one hand back through his sparse hair. Ginger once, it was now mostly grey.

"Trouble at home?" Hillier asked carefully, eyes fixed on his gold signet ring. It was a difficult question for both of them since he and Webberly were married to sisters, a fact that most of the Yard knew nothing about, one of which the two men themselves rarely spoke.

Their relationship was one of those quirks of fate in which two men find themselves locked together in a number of ways which are generally better not discussed between them. Hillier's career had mirrored his marriage. Both were successful, deeply satisfying. His wife was perfection: a rock of devotion, an intellectual companion, a loving mother, a sexual delight. He admitted that she was the very centre of his existence, that his three children were merely tangential objects, pleasant and diverting, but nothing at all of real importance compared to Laura. He turned to her—his first thought in the morning, his last thought at night—for virtually every need in his life. And she met each one.

For Webberly it was different: a career that was, like the man, plodding along, one not brilliant but cautious, filled with countless successes for which he rarely took credit, for Webberly simply was not the political animal he needed to be to succeed at the Yard. Thus, no knighthood loomed seductively on his professional horizon, and this was what had put the enormous strain upon the Webberly marriage.

Knowing that her younger sister was *Lady* Hillier clawed at the fabric of Frances Webberly's life. It had turned her from a shy but complacent middle-class housewife to a social climber of the pushiest kind. Dinner parties, cocktail parties, dreary buffets which they could ill afford were given for people in whom they had no interest, all of them part of what Frances perceived as her husband's climb to the top. And to them all the Hilliers faithfully went, Laura out of sad loyalty to a sister with whom she no longer lovingly communicated and Hillier himself to protect Webberly as best he could from the piercingly cruel comments Frances often made publicly about her husband's lacklustre career. Lady Macbeth incarnate, Hillier thought with a shudder.

"No, not there," Webberly was responding. "It's merely that I thought I'd got Nies and Kerridge sorted out years ago. To have a confrontation crop up again between them is disconcerting."

How typical of Malcolm to take responsibility for the foibles of others, Hillier thought. "Refresh my memory on their last fray," he said. "It was a Yorkshire situation, wasn't it? Gypsies involved in a murder?"

Webberly nodded. "Nies heads up the Richmond police." He sighed heavily, forgetting for a moment to blow the smoke from his cigar towards the open window. Hillier strained not to cough. Webberly loosened his necktie a fraction and absently fingered the frayed collar of his white shirt. "An old gypsy woman was killed up there three years ago. Nies runs a tight CID. His men are meticulous, accurate to the last detail. They conducted an investigation and arrested the old crone's son-in-law. It was an apparent dispute over the ownership of a garnet necklace."

"Garnets? Were they stolen?"

Webberly shook his head, tapping his cigar against a dented tin ashtray on his desk. The action dislodged debris from previous cigars, which drifted like dust to mingle with papers and manila folders. "No. The necklace had been given to them by Edmund Hanston-Smith."

Hillier sat forward in his chair. "Hanston-Smith?"

"Yes, you're remembering it now, aren't you? But that case was after all this. The man arrested for the old woman's murder—Romaniv, I think his name was—had a wife. About twenty-five years old and beautiful in the way only those women can be: dark, olive-skinned, exotic."

"More than a bit enticing to a man like Hanston-Smith?"

"In truth. She got him to believe that Romaniv was innocent.

It took a few weeks—Romaniv hadn't come up before the assizes yet. She convinced Hanston-Smith that the case needed to be reopened. She swore that they were only being persecuted because of their gypsy blood, that Romaniv had been with her the entire night in question."

"I imagine her charms made that easy to believe."

Webberly's mouth quirked. He stubbed out the tip of his cigar in the ashtray and clasped his freckled hands over his stomach. They effectively hid the stain on his waistcoat. "From the later testimony of Hanston-Smith's valet, the good Mrs. Romaniv had no trouble keeping even a man of sixty-two more than busy for one entire night. You'll recall that Hanston-Smith was a man of some considerable political influence and wealth. It was no difficult matter for him to convince the Yorkshire constabulary to become involved. So Reuben Kerridge—he's still Yorkshire's chief constable in spite of all that happened—ordered Nies' investigation reopened. And to make matters worse, he ordered Romaniv released."

"How did Nies react?"

"Kerridge is his superior officer, after all. What could he do? Nies was wild with anger, but he released Romaniv and ordered his men to begin again."

"It would seem that releasing Romaniv, while making his wife happy, would bring a premature end to Hanston-Smith's joy," Hillier noted.

"Well, of course, Mrs. Romaniv felt duty-bound to thank Hanston-Smith in the manner to which he'd become so accustomed. She slept with him one last time—wore the poor bloke out until the wee hours of the morning, if I have the story straight—and then let Romaniv into the house." Webberly looked up at a sharp knock on the door. "The rest, as they say, is a bit of bloody history. The pair murdered Hanston-Smith, took everything they could carry, got to Scarborough, and were out of the country before dawn."

"And Nies' reaction?"

"Demanded Kerridge's immediate resignation." The knock sounded again. Webberly ignored it. "He didn't get it, however. But Nies' mouth has been watering like the devil for it ever since."

"And here we are back with them again, you say."

A third knock, much more insistent. Webberly called entrance to Bertie Edwards, the Met's head of forensics, who entered the room in his usual brisk manner, scribbling on his clipboard and speaking to it at the same time. To Edwards, the clipboard was as human as most men's secretaries.

"Severe contusion on the right temple," he was announcing happily, "followed by the main laceration to the carotid artery. No identification, no money, stripped down to the underclothes. It's the Railway Ripper, all right." He finished writing with a flourish.

Hillier surveyed the little man with profound distaste. "Christ, these Fleet Street appellations. We're going to be haunted by Whitechapel till the end of time."

"Is this the Waterloo corpse?" Webberly asked.

Edwards glanced at Hillier, his face an open book in which he considered whether he should argue the merits of nameless killers being dubbed something—anything—for the sake of public awareness. He apparently rejected that line of communication, for he wiped at his forehead with the sleeve of his lab coat and turned to his immediate superior.

"Waterloo." He nodded. "Number eleven. We've not quite finished Vauxhall yet. Both are typical of the Ripper victims we've seen. Transient types. Broken nails. Dirty. Badly cut hair. Body lice as well. King's Cross is still the only one out of sync, and that's the bloody devil after all these weeks. No ID. No missing-person's call on him yet. I can't make it out." He scratched his head with the end of his pen. "Want the Waterloo snap? I've brought it."

Webberly waved towards the wall on which were already posted the photographs of the twelve recent murder victims, all of them killed in an identical manner in or near London train stations. Thirteen murders now in just over five weeks. The papers were screaming for an arrest. As if he were oblivious to this, Edwards whistled airily between his teeth and rooted on Webberly's desk for a drawing pin. He carried the latest victim to the wall.

"Not a bad shot." He stepped back to admire his work. "Sewed him up quite nice."

"Jesus!" Hillier exploded. "You're a ghoul, man! At least have the decency to remove that filthy coat when you come here! Have you no sense at all? We've women on these floors!"

Edwards wore the guise of patient attention, but his eyes flicked over the chief superintendent and lingered longest on the fleshy neck that hung over his collar and on the thick hair that Hillier liked to have called leonine. Edwards shrugged at Webberly in mutual understanding. "Quite the gent, he is," he commented before leaving the room.

"Sack him!" Hillier shouted as the door shut behind the pathologist.

Webberly laughed. "Have a sherry, David," he said. "It's in the cabinet behind you. We none of us ought to be here on a Saturday."

Two sherries considerably palliated Hillier's irritation with the pathologist. He was standing before Webberly's display wall, staring morosely at the thirteen photographs.

"This is one hell of a mess," he noted sourly. "Victoria, King's Cross, Waterloo, Liverpool, Blackfriars, Paddington. God *damn* it, man, why can't he at least be alphabetical!"

"Maniacs often lack that little organisational touch," Webberly responded placidly.

"Five of these victims don't even have *names*, for God's sake," Hillier complained.

"ID is always removed, so are money and clothes. If there's no missing-person report filed, we start with prints. You know how long something like that takes, David. We're doing our best."

Hillier turned around. The one thing he knew for a certainty was that Malcolm would always do his absolute best and would quietly remain in the background when the kudos were given. "Sorry. Was I frothing?"

"A bit."

"As usual. So this new Nies-Kerridge squabble? What's it all about?"

Webberly glanced at his watch. "Another Yorkshire murder being disputed, no less. They're sending someone down with the data. A priest."

"A *priest*? Christ—what kind of case is this?"

Webberly shrugged. "Evidently he's the only third party that Nies and Kerridge could agree upon to bring us the information."

"Why's that?"

"Seems he found the body."

2

HILLIER WALKED TO the office window. Afternoon sunlight shafted across his face, detailing lines that spoke of too many late nights, highlighting puffy pink flesh that spoke of too much rich food and port. "By God, this is irregular. Has Kerridge gone quite mad?"

"Nies has certainly been claiming that for years."

"But to have the first person on the scene . . . and not even a member of the force! What can the man be thinking?"

"That a priest is the only person they both can trust." Webberly glanced at his watch again. "He should be here within the hour, in fact. That's why I asked you to come down."

"To hear this priest's story? That's certainly not your style."

Webberly shook his head slowly. He had come to the tricky part. "Not to hear the story. Actually, to hear the plan."

"I'm intrigued." Hillier went to pour himself another sherry and held the bottle towards his friend, who shook his head. He returned to his seat and crossed one leg over the other, careful not to destroy the razor crease in his beautifully tailored trousers. "The plan?" he prompted.

Webberly poked at a stack of files on his desk. "I'd like Lynley on this."

Hillier cocked an eyebrow. "Lynley and Nies for a second go-round? Haven't we had trouble enough in that quarter, Malcolm? Besides, Lynley's not on rota this weekend."

"That can be dealt with." Webberly hesitated. He watched the other man. "You're letting me hang here, David," he said at last.

Hillier smiled. "Forgive me. I was waiting to see how you were going to ask for her."

"Damn you," Webberly cursed softly. "You know me too well by half."

"Let's say I know you're too fair for your own good. Let me advise you on this, Malcolm. Leave Havers where you put her."

Webberly winced and swiped at a nonexistent fly. "It grates on my conscience."

"Don't be a bloody fool. Don't be worse than that—don't be a sentimental fool. Barbara Havers proved herself incapable of getting along with a single DI for her entire tenure in CID. She's been back in uniform these past eight months and doing a better job there. Leave her."

"I didn't try her with Lynley."

"You didn't try her with the Prince of Wales either! It's not your responsibility to keep moving detective sergeants around until they find a little niche in which they can grow old happily. It's your responsibility to see that the flaming job gets done. And *no* job got done with Havers on it. Admit it!"

"I think she's learned from the experience."

"Learned what? That being a truculent pigheaded little bitch is not likely to advance her up the ranks?"

Webberly let Hillier's words scathe the air between them. "Well," he said finally, "that was always the problem, wasn't it?"

Hillier recognised the sound of defeat in his friend's voice. That was indeed the problem: advancing through the ranks. God, what an ignorant thing to say. "Forgive me, Malcolm." He quickly finished his sherry, an act that gave him something to do other than look at his brother-in-law's face. "You deserve my job. We both know it, don't we?"

"Don't be absurd."

But Hillier stood. "I'll put a call out for Havers."

* * *

Detective Sergeant Barbara Havers tugged the door of the super's office shut, walked stiffly past his secretary, and made her way into the corridor. She was white with rage.

God! God, how dare they! She pushed her way past a clerk, not bothering to stop when the folders he was carrying slipped from his grasp and scattered. She marched right through them. Who did they think they were dealing with? Did they think she was so stupid she couldn't see the ploy? God damn them! God *damn* them!

She blinked, telling herself that there would be no tears, that she would not cry, that she would not react. The sign LADIES appeared miraculously in front of her and she ducked inside. No one was present. Here, it was cool. Had it really been so hot in Webberly's office? Or had it been her outrage? She fumbled at her necktie, jerked it loose, and stumbled over to the basin. The cold water gushed out of the tap beneath her fumbling fingers, sending a spray onto her uniform skirt and across her white blouse. That did it. She looked at herself in the mirror and burst into tears.

"You cow," she sneered. "You stupid, ugly cow!" She was not a woman easily given to tears, so they were hot and bitter, tasting strange and feeling stranger as they coursed down her cheeks, making unattractive rivulets across what was an extremely plain, extremely pug-like face.

"You're a real sight, Barbara," she upbraided her reflection. "You're an absolute vision!" Sobbing, she twisted away from the basin, resting her head against the cool tile of the wall.

At thirty years old, Barbara Havers was a decidedly unattractive woman, but a woman who appeared to be doing everything possible to make herself so. Fine, shiny hair the colour of pinewood might have been suitably styled for the shape of her face. But instead, she wore it cut bluntly at an unforgivable length just below her ears as if a too-small bowl had been placed upon her head for a model. She used no make-up. Heavy, unplucked eyebrows drew attention to the smallness of her eyes rather than to their fine intelligence. A thin mouth, never heightened in any way by colour, was pressed permanently into a disapproving frown. The entire effect was that of a woman stubby, sturdy, and entirely unapproachable.

So they've given you the golden boy, she thought. What a

treat for you, Barb! After eight miserable months, they bring you back from the street "for another chance"—and all the while it's Lynley!

"I will not," she muttered. "I will *not* do it! I will not work with that sodding little fop!"

She pushed herself away from the wall and returned to the basin. She ran cold water into it carefully this time, bending to bathe her hot face and scrub away the incriminating sign of her tears.

"I'd like to give you another opportunity in CID," Webberly had said. He'd been fingering a letter opener on his desk, but she'd noticed the Ripper photos on the walls and her heart had soared. To be on the Ripper! *Oh God, yes! When do I start? Is it with MacPherson?*

"It's a peculiar case involving a girl up in Yorkshire." *Oh, so it's not the Ripper. But still, it's a case. A girl, you say? Of course I can help. Is it Stewart, then? He's an old hand in Yorkshire. We'd work well together. I know we would.*

"In fact, I'm expecting to receive the information in about three-quarters of an hour. I'll need you here then, if you're interested, that is." *If I'm interested! Three-quarters of an hour gives me time to change. Have a bite to eat. Get back here. Then be on the late train to York. Will we meet up there? Shall I see about a car?*

"I'll need you to pop round to Chelsea before then, I'm afraid."

The conversation ground to a sudden halt. "To Chelsea, sir?" What on earth had Chelsea to do with all this?

"Yes," Webberly said easily, dropping the letter opener onto the general clutter on his desk. "You'll be working with Inspector Lynley, and unfortunately we've got to pull him out of the St. James wedding in Chelsea." He glanced at his watch. "The wedding was at eleven, so no doubt they're well into the reception by now. We've been trying to raise him on the phone, but apparently it's been left off the hook." He looked up in time to see the shock on her face. "Something wrong, Sergeant?"

"Inspector Lynley?" She saw it all at once, the reason they needed her, the reason why no one else would really quite do.

"Yes, Lynley. Is there a problem?"

"No, no problem at all." And then, as an afterthought, "Sir."

Webberly's shrewd eyes evaluated her response. "Good. I'm glad to hear it. There's a lot you might learn from working with Lynley." Still the eyes watched, gauging her reaction. "Try to be back here as fast as you can." He gave his attention back to the papers on his desk. She was dismissed.

Barbara looked at herself in the mirror and fumbled in the pocket of her skirt for a comb. Lynley. She tugged the plastic through her hair mercilessly, dragging it against her scalp, abrading the skin, welcoming the pain. *Lynley!* It was only too obvious why they'd brought her back out of uniform. They wanted Lynley on the case. But they needed a woman as well. And every person on Victoria Street knew that there wasn't a female in CID who was safe near Lynley. He'd slept his way through department and division, leaving a trail of the discarded behind him. He had the reputation of a racehorse put out to stud and, from all the tales told, the endurance as well. She angrily shoved the comb back into her pocket.

So, how does it feel, she demanded of her reflection, to be the one lucky woman whose virtue is quite secure in the presence of the almighty Lynley? No wandering hands while our Barb's in the car! No confidential dinners to "go over our notes." No invitations to Cornwall to "think the case out." No fear here, Barb. God knows that you're safe with Lynley. In her five years working in the same division with the man, she was certain he'd managed to avoid so much as saying her name, let alone having a single second's foul contact with her. As if a grammar school background and a working-class accent were social diseases that might infect him if he were not scrupulously careful to keep himself clear of them.

She left the room and stalked down the corridor towards the lift. Was there *anyone* in all of New Scotland Yard whom she hated more than she hated Lynley? He was a miraculous combination of every single thing that she thoroughly despised: educated at Eton, a first in history at Oxford, a public school voice, and a bloody family tree that had its roots somewhere just this side of the Battle of Hastings. Upper class. Bright. And so damnably charming that she couldn't understand why every criminal in the city simply didn't surrender to accommodate him.

His whole reason for working at the Yard was a joke, a flaming little myth that she didn't believe for a moment. He wanted to be useful, to make a contribution. He preferred a career in London to life on the estate. What a ruddy good laugh!

The lift doors opened and she punched furiously for the garage. And hadn't his career been convenient and sweet, purchased lock, stock, and barrel with the family funds? He bought his way right into his current position and he'd be a Commissioner before he was through. God knew inheriting that precious title hadn't hurt his chances for success one bit. He'd gone from sergeant to inspector in record time straight away. Everyone knew why.

She headed for her car, a rusty Mini in the far corner of the garage. How nice to be rich, to be titled like Lynley, to work only for a lark, and then to swing home to the Belgravia townhouse, or better yet fly to the Cornish estate. With butlers and maids and cooks and valets.

And think of it, Barb: picture yourself in the presence of such greatness. What shall you do? Shall you swoon or vomit first?

She flung her handbag into the rear seat of the Mini, slammed the door, and started the car with a sputter and roar. The wheels squealed on the pavement as she ascended the ramp, nodded brusquely towards the officer on guard in the kiosk, and headed for the street.

The light weekend traffic made getting from Victoria Street to the Embankment a manoeuvre of a few minutes only, and, once there, the mild breeze of the October afternoon cooled her temper, calmed her nerves, and coaxed her into forgetting her indignation. It was a pleasant drive, really, to the St. James house.

Barbara liked Simon Allcourt-St. James, had liked him from the first time she had met him ten years ago when she was a nervous twenty-year-old probationary police constable all too aware of being a woman in a closely guarded man's world where women police were still called Wopsies after a few drinks. And she'd been called worse than that—she knew it. Damn them all to hell. To them, any woman who aspired to CID was a bona fide freak and made to feel that way. But to St. James, two years her senior, she had been an acceptable colleague, even a friend.

St. James was now an independent forensic scientist, but he

had begun his career at the Yard. By his twenty-fourth birthday, he was the very best of the scene-of-crime men, quick, observant, intuitive. He could have gone in any direction: investigations, pathology, administration, anywhere. But it had all ended one night eight years ago on a drive with Lynley, a wild junket through the back roads of Surrey. They had both been drunk— St. James was always prompt to admit this fact. But everyone knew that it was Lynley who had been driving that night, Lynley who had lost control on a curve, Lynley who had walked away without a scratch while his childhood friend, St. James, had emerged a cripple. And although he could have continued his career at the Yard, St. James had instead retired to a family house in Chelsea, where for the next four years he had lived like a recluse. Score that to old Lynley, she thought sourly.

She couldn't believe that St. James had actually maintained his friendship with the man. But he had, and something, some sort of quirky situation, had cemented their relationship nearly five years ago and had brought St. James back into the field where he belonged. Score *that*, she thought reluctantly, to Lynley as well.

She pulled the Mini into an available space on Lawrence Street and walked back along Lordship Place towards Cheyne Row. Not far from the river, it was an area of the city where elaborate white plaster and woodwork decorated deep umber brick buildings and black paint restored the wrought iron at windows and balconies. In keeping with the village that Chelsea once had been, the streets were narrow, metamorphosed into bright autumn tunnels by massive sycamores and elms. St. James' house stood on a corner, and as she passed by the high brick wall that fenced in the garden, Barbara heard the sounds of the party in progress. A voice was raised in a toast. Shouts of approval followed applause. An old oak door in the wall was closed, but that was just as well. Dressed as she was, she hardly wanted to burst into the festivities as if she were making an arrest.

She rounded the corner to find the front door of the tall, old house open to the late afternoon sun. The sound of laughter floated towards her, the pure tones of silver and china, the popping of champagne, and somewhere in the garden the music of violin and flute. There were flowers everywhere, right out onto the front steps where the balustrades were twined with white and pink roses that filled the air with a heady perfume. Even the balconies above held potted convolvuli that tumbled trumpet-shaped flowers in a riot of colours over the edge.

Barbara drew in a breath and mounted the steps. There was no point to knocking, for although several guests near the door gave her inquisitive glances as she hesitated outside in her ill-fitting uniform, they strolled back towards the garden without speaking to her, and it soon became apparent that if she wanted to find Lynley, she would have to barge right into the wedding reception to do so. The thought made her more than a little bit ill.

She was about to retreat cravenly back to her car to retrieve an old mackintosh that would at least cover up her clothes—too tight in the hips and straining the material at shoulder and neck—when the sounds of footsteps and laughter close by directed her attention to the stairway in the hall. A woman was descending, calling over her shoulder to someone who remained on the floor above.

"Just the two of us are going. You must come as well and we'll make a party of it, Sid." She turned, saw Barbara, and stopped where she was, one hand on the banister. It was very nearly a pose, for she was the kind of woman who could manage to make yards of haphazardly arranged teal-coloured silk look like the very latest word in haute couture. She was not particularly tall, but very slender, with a fall of chestnut hair framing a perfect, oval face. From the dozens of times she had been to fetch Lynley from the Yard, Barbara recognised her at once. She was Lynley's longest-running mistress and St. James' lab assistant, Lady Helen Clyde. Lady Helen completed her descent and crossed the hall to the door. So confident, Barbara noted, so completely self-possessed.

"I've the most dreadful feeling that you've come for Tommy," she said immediately, extending her hand. "Hello. I'm Helen Clyde."

Barbara introduced herself, surprised at the firmness of the woman's grip. Her hands were thin, very cool to the touch. "He's wanted at the Yard."

"Poor man. How miserable. How damnably unfair." Lady Helen spoke more to herself than to the other woman, for she suddenly shot Barbara an apologetic smile. "But it's not your fault, is it? Come, he's just this way."

Without waiting for a reply, she moved down the hallway to the garden door, giving Barbara no choice but to follow. However, at her first glimpse of the cluster of linen-covered tables at which fashionably clad guests chatted and laughed, Barbara stepped quickly back into the dimly lit hall. Her fingers wandered up to her neck.

Lady Helen paused, her dark eyes reflective. "Shall I search Tommy out for you?" she offered with another quick smile. "It's a crush out there, isn't it?"

"Thank you," Barbara replied stiffly and watched her walk across the lawn to a group standing in merry conversation round a tall man who managed to look as if somehow he'd been born wearing morning clothes.

Lady Helen touched his arm and said a few words. The man looked towards the house, revealing a face that bore the unmistakable stamp of aristocracy. It was a Greek sculpture sort of face, unaccountably timeless. He brushed his blond hair back from his forehead, placed his champagne glass on a table nearby, and, after exchanging a quip with one of his friends, came towards the house with Lady Helen at his side.

From the safety of the shadows, Barbara watched Lynley's approach. His movements were graceful, fluid, like a cat's. He was the handsomest man she had ever seen. She loathed him.

"Sergeant Havers." He nodded when they joined her. "I'm not on call this weekend." Barbara read the implication clearly: *You're interrupting me, Havers.*

"Webberly sent me, sir. Ring him if you like." She didn't look at him directly as she replied but rather focused her eyes somewhere just over his left shoulder.

"But surely he *knows* that today's the wedding, Tommy," Lady Helen protested mildly.

Lynley let out his breath in a puff of anger. "Damn and blast, of course he knows." He glanced out at the lawn, then sharply back to Barbara. "Is this Ripper business? I'd been told that John Stewart would join MacPherson."

"It's business in the North as far as I know. Some girl's involved." Barbara thought he'd appreciate that piece of information. Some spice to the case, just the way he liked it: a tart for dessert. She waited for him to demand the particulars that, no doubt, were first and foremost on his mind: age, marital status, and measurements of the damsel whose distress he was only too willing to alleviate.

His eyes narrowed. "In the North?"

Lady Helen laughed regretfully. "Well, there go our plans to go dancing tonight, Tommy darling, and I was just persuading Sidney to come as well."

"I suppose it can't be helped," Lynley replied. But he moved abruptly from the shadows into the light, and both the tightness of the movement and the play of a repressed reaction on his face told Barbara how irritated he really was.

Lady Helen evidently saw this as well, for she spoke again cheerfully. "Of course, Sid and I *could* easily go dancing alone. With androgyny the rage, no doubt one of us might be taken for a man no matter how we dress. Or there's Jeffrey Cusick. We could telephone him." It was somehow a personal joke between them and it had its desired effect, for Lynley relaxed into a smile. He followed it with a dry chuckle.

"Cusick? My God, these *are* desperate times."

"Oh, you may laugh," Lady Helen replied and did so herself, "but he took us to Royal Ascot when you were far too busily engaged in some bloodthirsty murder watch at St. Pancras Station. Cambridge men, you see, have all sorts of fine qualities."

Lynley laughed outright. "Among which is the tendency to look like a penguin when formally dressed."

"You dreadful creature!" Lady Helen gave her attention to Barbara. "May I at least offer you some lovely crab salad before you drag Tommy back to the Yard? Years ago, I was served the most terrifying egg sandwich there. If the food's not improved, this may be your last chance to eat well today."

Barbara glanced at her watch. She sensed an undercurrent of urgency in Lynley and knew quite well that he wanted her to accept the invitation so that he'd have a few more minutes with his friends before being called back to duty. She wasn't about to accommodate him. "There's a meeting in twenty minutes, I'm afraid."

Lady Helen sighed. "Well, that's hardly enough time to do it the justice it deserves. Shall I wait for you, Tommy, or shall I phone Jeffrey?"

"Don't do that," Lynley responded. "Your father would never forgive you for putting your future into the hands of Cambridge."

She smiled. "Very well. If you're off, then, let me fetch the bride and groom to bid you farewell."

His face altered swiftly. "No. Helen. I . . . just make my excuses."

A look passed between them, something said without being said. "You must see them, Tommy," Lady Helen murmured. There was another pause, a compromise being sought. "I'll tell them you're waiting in the study." She left quickly, giving Lynley no chance to respond.

He uttered something inaudible under his breath, following Lady Helen with his eyes as she wove back through the crowd. "Have you brought a car?" he asked Barbara suddenly and started down the hall, away from the celebration.

Nonplussed, she followed. "A Mini. You're not exactly dressed for its splendour."

"I'll adjust, I'm sure. Chameleon-like. What colour is it?"

She was puzzled by the query, an ill-concealed attempt to make conversation as they walked to the front of the house. "Mostly rust, I'm afraid."

"My favourite." He held open a door and motioned her into a dark room.

"I'll just wait in the car, sir. I've left it—"

"Stay here, Sergeant." It was a command.

Reluctantly, she preceded him. The curtains had been drawn; the only light came from the door which they had opened. But Barbara could see it was a man's room, richly panelled in dark oak and filled with shelves of books, well-used furniture, and an atmosphere redolent of comfortable old leather and the fragrance of scotch.

Lynley gravitated absently to a wall that was covered with framed photographs and stood there quietly, his eyes on a portrait that was central to the display. It had been taken in a cemetery, and the man who was its subject bent to touch the inscription on a tombstone whose carving had long since been obliterated by time. The skillful composition of the piece directed the viewer's eyes not to the awkward leg brace that distorted the man's posture but to the piercing interest that lit his gaunt face. Studying the picture, Lynley seemed to have forgotten her presence.

The moment, Barbara decided, was probably as good as any to give him the news.

"I'm off the street," she announced bluntly. "That's why I've come, if you're wondering."

He turned slowly towards her. "Back in CID?" he asked. "Good for you, Barbara."

"But not for you."

"What do you mean?"

"Well, someone's got to tell you, since Webberly obviously hasn't. Congratulations: you're stuck with me." She waited to see his look of surprise. When it was evident that none was forthcoming, she pushed on. "Of course, it's damned awkward having me assigned to you—don't think I don't know it. I can't figure out *what* Webberly wants." She was stumbling on, barely hearing her own words, uncertain whether she was trying to forestall or provoke his inevitable reaction: the sharp explosion of anger, the movement to the telephone to demand an explanation, or, worse, the icy politeness that would last until he got the superintendent behind closed doors. "All that I can think is that there's no one else available or that I've got some sort of wonderful latent talent that only Webberly knows of. Or maybe it's a bit of a practical joke." She laughed, a little too loudly.

"Or perhaps you're the best for the job," Lynley finished. "What do you know about the case?"

"I . . . nothing. Only that—"

"Tommy?" They swung around at the sound of the voice, the single word spoken as if on a breath. The bride stood in the doorway, a spray of flowers in one hand and others tucked into the tumble of coppery hair that fell round her shoulders and down her back. Backlit from the hallway, she looked in her ivory dress as if she were surrounded entirely by a cloud, a Titian creation come to life. "Helen tells me you're leaving . . . ?"

Lynley appeared to have nothing to say. He felt in his pockets, brought out a gold cigarette case, opened it, and then snapped it shut with a flash of annoyance. During this operation, the bride watched him, the flowers in her hand trembling momentarily.

"It's the Yard, Deb," Lynley finally answered. "I have to go."

She watched him without speaking, fingering a pendant she wore at her throat. Not until he met her eyes did she reply. "What a disappointment for everyone. It's not an emergency, I hope. Simon told me last night that you might be reassigned to the Ripper case."

"No. Just a meeting."

"Ah." She looked as if she might say something more—indeed, she began to do so—but instead she turned to Barbara with a friendly smile. "I'm Deborah St. James."

Lynley rubbed his forehead. "Lord, I *am* sorry." Mechanically, he completed the introduction. "Where's Simon?"

"He was right behind me, but I think Dad caught him. He's absolutely terrified to let us off on our own, certain I'll never take care of Simon well enough." Her laughter bubbled up. "Perhaps I should have considered the problems of marrying a man my father is so inordinately fond of. 'The electrodes,' he keeps lecturing me. 'You mustn't forget to see to his leg every morning.' I think he's told me that ten times today."

"I imagine it was all you could do to keep him from going on the honeymoon as well."

"Well, of course, they've not been apart for more than a day since . . ." She stopped suddenly, awkwardly. Their eyes met. She bit the inside of her lip and an ugly flush stained her cheeks.

There was an immediate, anxious silence between them, the kind in which the most telling sort of communication exists in body language and tension in the air. It was finally—mercifully, Barbara decided—broken by the sound of slow, painfully uneven footsteps in the hall, awkward harbinger of Deborah's husband.

"I see that you've come to capture Tommy." St. James paused in the doorway but continued to speak quietly, as was his habit, to direct attention away from his disability and put others at ease in his presence. "That's a strange twist on tradition, Barbara. Time was when the brides were kidnapped, not the best man."

He was, Barbara decided, very much Hephaestus to Lynley's Apollo. Aside from his eyes, the satin blue of a highland sky, and his hands, the sensitive tools of an artist, Simon Allcourt-St. James was singularly unattractive. His hair was dark, unruly with curls, and haphazardly cut in a way that did nothing to make it manageable. His face was a combination of aquilinity and angles, harsh in repose, forbidding in anger, yet vibrant with good nature when softened by his smile. He was sapling thin, but not sapling sturdy, a man who had known too much pain and sorrow at far too young an age.

Barbara smiled as he joined them, her first genuine smile of the entire afternoon. "But even best men are generally not kidnapped to New Scotland Yard. How are you, Simon?"

"Fine. Or so my father-in-law continues to tell me. Lucky as well. It seems he saw it all from the beginning. He knew it directly the day of her birth. You've been introduced to Deborah?"

"Only just now."

"And we can keep you no longer?"

"Webberly's called a meeting," Lynley put in. "You know how that is."

"How I do. Then we won't ask you to stay. We're off ourselves in a very little while. Helen has the address if anything should come up."

"Don't give a thought to that." Lynley paused as if he were not quite sure what to do next. "My warmest congratulations, St. James," he settled on saying.

"Thank you," the other man replied. He nodded to Barbara, touched his bride's shoulder lightly, and left the room.

How odd, Barbara thought. They didn't even shake hands.

"Will you go to the Yard dressed like that?" Deborah asked Lynley.

He looked at his clothes ruefully. "Anything to keep up my reputation as a rake." They laughed together. It was a warm communication that died as suddenly as it had risen. From it grew yet another little silence.

"Well," Lynley began.

"I'd a speech all planned," Deborah said quickly, looking down at her flowers. They trembled once again in her hand and a shower of baby's breath fell to the floor. She raised her head. "Something . . . it was just the kind of thing Helen might say. Talk about my childhood, Dad, this house. You know the sort of thing. Witty and clever. But I'm absolutely pathetic at that sort of thing. Quite out of my depth. A hopeless incompetent." She looked down again to see that a very small dachshund had come into the study and carried in its jaws a woman's sequined handbag. The dog placed the bag at Deborah's satin-shod feet, supremely confident that the offering had merit. A tail wagged in the friendliest fashion. "Oh no! *Peach!*" Laughing, Deborah bent to retrieve the purloined article, but when she straightened, her green eyes glittered with tears. "Thank you, Tommy. For everything. Really. For it all."

"The best, Deb," he said lightly in reply. He went to her, hugged her quickly to him, and brushed a kiss against her hair.

And it came to Barbara, as she stood there watching, that for some reason St. James had left the two of them together precisely so that Lynley could do just that.

3

THE BODY HAD no head. That single, grisly detail was the most prominent feature of the police photographs that were being passed among the three CID officers gathered at the circular table in the Scotland Yard office.

Father Hart looked nervously from one face to the next, and he fingered the tiny silver rosary in his pocket. It had been blessed by Pius XII in 1952. Not an individual audience, of course. One could never hope for that. But certainly that trembling, numinous hand making the sign of the cross over two thousand reverential pilgrims counted for a powerful sort of something. Eyes closed, he'd held the rosary high above his head as if somehow that would allow the Pope's blessing to strike it more potently.

He was well on his way into the third decade of the sorrowful mysteries when the tall, blond man spoke.

" 'What a blow was there given,' " he murmured, and Father Hart looked his way.

Was he a policeman? Father Hart couldn't understand why the man was dressed so formally, but now, upon hearing the words, he looked at him hopefully. "Ah, Shakespeare. Yes. Just the very thing somehow." The big man with the awful cigar looked at him blankly. Father Hart cleared his throat and watched them continue to scrutinise the pictures.

He'd been with them for nearly a quarter of an hour and in that time barely a word had been exchanged. A cigar had been lit by the older man, the woman had twice bitten off something she'd intended to say, and nothing more had occurred until that line from Shakespeare.

The woman tapped her fingers restlessly on the top of the table. *She* at least was some sort of police person. Father Hart knew that by the uniform she wore. But she seemed so entirely unpleasant with her tiny, shifting eyes and her grim little mouth. She would never do. Not what he needed. Not what Roberta needed. What should he say?

The horrid photographs continued to be passed among them. Father Hart did not need to see them. He knew far too well what they captured. He'd been there first, and it was all so unspeakably engraved on his mind. William Teys sprawled out on his side—all six feet four of him—in a ghastly, quasi-fetal position, right arm extended as if he'd been reaching for something, left arm curled into his stomach, knees drawn up halfway to his chest, and where the head had been . . . There was simply nothing. Like Cloten himself. But no Imogen there to awaken in horror by his side. Just Roberta. And those terrifying words: "I did it. I'm not sorry."

The head had rolled into a mound of sodden hay in a corner of the stall. And when he'd seen it . . . Oh God, the stealthy eyes of a barn rat glittered in the cavity—quite small, of course—but the quivering grey snout was brilliant with blood and the tiny paws dug! *Our Father, who art in heaven . . . Our Father, who art in heaven . . . Oh, there's more, there's more and I can't remember it now!*

"Father Hart." The blond man in the morning coat had removed his reading spectacles and had taken from his pocket a gold cigarette case. "Do you smoke?"

"I . . . yes, thank you." The priest snatched quickly at the case so that the others might not see how his hand trembled. The man passed the case to the woman, who shook her head sharply in refusal. A silver lighter was produced. It all took a few moments, blessed time to allow him to gather together his fragmented thoughts.

The blond man relaxed in his chair and studied a long line of photographs that had been posted on one of the walls of the office.

"Why did you go to the farm that day, Father Hart?" he asked quietly, his eyes moving from one picture to the next.

Father Hart squinted myopically across the room. Were those pictures of suspects? he wondered hopefully. Had Scotland Yard seen fit to begin pursuing this malevolent beast already? He couldn't tell, wasn't even certain from this distance that the photographs were of people at all.

"It was Sunday," he replied as if that would somehow say everything.

The blond man turned his head at that. Surprisingly, his eyes were an engaging brown. "Were you in the habit of going to Teys' farm on Sundays? For dinner or something?"

"Oh ... I ... excuse me, I thought the report, you see ..." This would never do. Father Hart sucked eagerly at the cigarette. He looked at his fingers. The nicotine stains climbed past every joint. No wonder he'd been offered one. He shouldn't have forgotten his own, should have bought a pack back at King's Cross. But there was so very much then. ... He puffed hungrily at the tobacco.

"Father Hart?" the older man said. He was obviously the blond's superior. They'd all been introduced but he'd stupidly forgotten their names. The woman's he knew: Havers. Sergeant, by her garments. But the other two had slipped his mind. He gazed at their grave faces in mounting panic.

"I'm sorry. You asked ... ?"

"Did you go to Teys' farm every Sunday?"

Father Hart made a determined effort to think clearly, chronologically, systematically for once. His fingers sought the rosary in his pocket. The cross dug into his thumb. He could feel the tiny corpus stretched out in agony. *Oh Lord, to die that way.* "No," he answered in a rush. "William is ... was our precentor. Such a wonderful basso profundo. He could make the church ring with sound and I ..." Father Hart took a ragged breath to put himself back on the track. "He'd not come to Mass that morning, nor had Roberta. I was concerned. The Teys never miss Mass. So I went to the farm."

The cigar smoker squinted at him through the pungent smoke. "Do you do that for all your parishioners? Must certainly keep them in line if you do."

Father Hart had smoked his cigarette down to the filter. There was nothing for it but to stub it out. The blond man did the same although his was not half-smoked. He brought out the case and offered another. Again the silver lighter appeared; the flame caught, produced the smoke that seared his throat, soothed his nerves, numbed his lungs.

"Well, it was mostly because Olivia was concerned."

A glance at the report. "Olivia Odell?"

Father Hart nodded eagerly. "She and William Teys, you see, had just become engaged. The announcement was to be made at a small tea that afternoon. She'd rung him several times after Mass but got nothing. So she came to me."

"Why didn't she go out there herself?"

"She wanted to, of course. But there was Bridie and the duck. He'd got lost somehow, the usual family crisis, and she couldn't be settled down until he was recovered."

The three others glanced at one another warily. The priest reddened. How *absurd* it all sounded! He plunged on. "You see, Bridie is Olivia's little girl. She has a pet duck. Well, not really a pet, not in the actual sense." How could he explain all of it to them, all the twists and turns of their village life?

The blond man spoke, kindly. "So while Olivia and Bridie were looking for the duck, you went out to the farm."

"That's so exactly right. Thank you." Father Hart smiled gratefully.

"Tell us what happened when you arrived."

"I went to the house first, but no one was there. The door wasn't locked and I remember thinking that was strange. William always locked everything tight as a drum if he went out. He was peculiar that way. Insisted I do the same with the church if I wasn't about. Even when the choir practised on Wednesdays, he never once left until every person was gone and I'd seen to the doors. That's the way he was."

"I imagine his unlocked house gave you a bit of a turn," the blond man said.

"It did, really. Even at one o'clock in the afternoon. So, when I couldn't raise anyone with a knock . . ." he looked at them all apologetically, "I suppose I walked right in."

"Anything peculiar inside?"

"Nothing at all. It was perfectly clean, as it always was. There was, however . . ." His eyes shifted to the window. How to explain?

"Yes?"

"The candles had burned down."

"Have they no electricity?"

Father Hart looked at them earnestly. "These are votive candles. They were always lit. Always. Twenty-four hours a day."

"For a shrine, you mean?"

"Yes, that's exactly what it is. A shrine," he agreed immediately and hurried on. "When I saw that, I knew at once something was wrong. Neither William nor Roberta would ever have let the candles go out. So I went through the house. And from there, out to the barn."

"And there . . . ?"

What was there really left to report? The chilling tranquility had told him at once. Outside, in the near pasture, the bleating of sheep and the cry of birds spoke of sanity and peace. But in the barn, the absolute quiet was the core of diablerie. Even from the door, the rich cloying smell of pooled blood had reached him, over the mixed odours of manure and grain and rotting hay. It had drawn him forward with seductive, unavoidable hands.

Roberta had been sitting on an overturned pail in one of the stalls, a big girl born of her father's stock, used to the labour of a farm. She was motionless, staring not at the headless monstrosity that lay at her feet but at the opposite wall and at the cracks that mapped its surface.

"Roberta?" he had called urgently. He felt sickness rising from stomach to throat and his bowels loosening.

There was no response, not a breath, not a movement. Just the sight of her broad back, her sturdy legs curled beneath her, the axe at her side. And then over her shoulder, he'd seen the body clearly for the first time.

"I did it. I'm not sorry," the only thing she'd said.

Father Hart squeezed his eyes shut against the memory. "I went at once to the house and rang Gabriel."

For a moment Lynley believed that the priest was talking about the archangel himself. The odd little man did seem a bit in touch with other worlds as he sat there painfully struggling through his story.

"Gabriel?" Webberly asked incredulously. Lynley could tell that the super's patience was wearing thin. He fingered through the report for some indication of the name and found it quickly enough.

"Gabriel Langston. Village constable," he said. "And I take it, Father, that Constable Langston phoned the Richmond police at once?"

The priest nodded. He looked warily at Lynley's cigarette case and the other man opened it and offered another round. Havers refused and the priest was about to do so as well until Lynley took one himself. His throat felt raw, but he knew they'd never get to the end of the story unless the cleric was supplied with nicotine, and it appeared that he needed a companion in his vice. Lynley swallowed uncomfortably, longed for a whisky, lit up again, and let the cigarette burn itself to nothing in the ashtray.

"Police came down from Richmond. It was all very quick. It was . . . they took Roberta."

"Well, what could you expect? She admitted to the crime." Havers had spoken. She'd risen from her seat and wandered to the window. Her voice clearly informed them that in her opinion they were wasting their time with this foolish old man, that they ought to be barrelling towards the North at this very moment.

"Lots of people admit to crimes," Webberly said, motioning her back to her seat. "I've had twenty-five confessions to the Ripper killings so far."

"I just wanted to point out—"

"That can come later."

"Roberta didn't kill her father," the priest went on as if the other two had not spoken. "It's just not possible."

"But family crimes happen," Lynley said gently.

"Not when there's whiskers."

To the priest's bizarre comment—so obviously logical and satisfactory to himself—no one made a response. No one spoke at all or looked particularly at anyone else. There was a lengthy, unendurable pause in the proceedings, broken by Webberly, who pushed away from the table. "*Jesus*," he muttered. "I'm terribly sorry, but . . ." He stalked to a cabinet at the corner of the room and pulled out three bottles. "Whisky, sherry, or brandy?" he asked the others.

Lynley sent a prayer of thanksgiving to Bacchus. "Whisky," he replied.

"Havers?"

"Nothing for me," she said primly. "I'm on duty."

"Yes, of course. Father, what'll it be?"

"Oh, a sherry would be only too—"

"Sherry it is." Webberly tossed back a small, neat whisky before pouring again and returning to the table.

They all stared meditatively into their glasses, as if each wondered who'd be the first to ask the question. Lynley finally did so, his throat newly soothed by the fragrant single malt. "Ah . . . whiskers?" he prompted.

Father Hart looked down at the papers spread out on the table. "Isn't it in the report?" he asked plaintively. "About the dog?"

"Yes, it does mention the dog."

"That was Whiskers," the priest explained, and sanity was restored.

There was collective relief. "It was dead in the stall with Teys," Lynley noted aloud.

"Yes, don't you see? That's why we all of us know Roberta's innocent. Aside from the fact that she was devoted to her father, there's Whiskers to consider. She would *never* hurt Whiskers." Father Hart eagerly sought out the words to explain. "He was a farm dog, part of the family since Roberta was five. He was retired, of course, a bit blind, but one just doesn't put down dogs like that. Everyone in the village knew Whiskers. He was a bit of a pet to all of us. He'd wander down of an afternoon to Nigel Parrish's house on the common, have a bit of a lie in the sun whilst Nigel played the organ (he's our organist at church, you see). Or sometimes he'd have his tea at Olivia's."

"Got on with the duck, did he?" Webberly asked, straight-faced.

"Oh, famously!" Father Hart beamed. "Whiskers got on with us all. And when Roberta was out and about, he followed her everywhere. That's why, when they took Roberta, I had to do something. And here I am."

"Yes, indeed, here you are," Webberly concluded. "You've

been more than helpful, Father. I believe Inspector Lynley and
Sergeant Havers have all that they need for now." He got to his
feet and opened the door of his office. "Harriman?"

The Morse-like tapping of word processor keys stopped. A
chair scraped on the floor. Webberly's secretary popped into the
room.

Dorothea Harriman bore a modest resemblance to the Princess of Wales, which she emphasised to a disconcerting degree
by tinting her sculptured hair the approximate shade of sunlight
on wheat and refusing to wear her spectacles in the presence of
anyone likely to comment upon the Spencerian shape of her nose
and chin. She was eager to advance, swept up in her "c'reer," as
she monosyllabically called it. She was intelligent enough to
make a success of her job and would most likely do so, especially
if she could bring herself to renounce her distracting manner of
dress, which everyone referred to as Parody Princess. Today she
was wearing what looked like a drop-waisted pink ball gown that
had been shortened for everyday wear. It was utterly hideous.

"Yes, Superintendent?" she asked. In spite of threats and im-
precations, Harriman insisted upon calling every employee at the
Yard by his or her full title.

Webberly turned to the priest. "Are you staying in London,
Father, or returning to Yorkshire?"

"I'm on the late train back. Confessions were this afternoon,
you see, and as I wasn't there, I *did* promise to have them until
eleven tonight."

"Of course." Webberly nodded. "Call a cab for Father Hart,"
he told Harriman.

"Oh, but I haven't enough—"

Webberly held up a restraining hand. "It's on the Yard, Father."

On the Yard. The priest mouthed the words, coloured with
pleasure at the implication of brotherhood and acceptance behind
them. He allowed the superintendent's secretary to shepherd him
from the room.

"What do you drink when you *do* drink, Sergeant Havers?"
Webberly asked when the Father Hart had gone.

"Tonic water, sir," she replied.

"Right," he muttered and opened the door again. "Harriman," he barked, "find a bottle of Schweppes for Sergeant Havers. . . . Don't pretend you haven't the slightest idea where to get one. Just *get* one." He slammed the door, went to the cabinet, and brought out the bottle of whisky.

Lynley rubbed his forehead and pressed tightly at both sides of his eyes. "God, what a headache," he murmured. "Have either of you any aspirin?"

"I do," Havers replied crisply and rooted through her handbag for a small tin. She tossed it across the table to him. "Take as many as you like, Inspector."

Webberly regarded them both thoughtfully. He wondered, not for the first time, if this partnership of two such antipodal personalities had even the ghost of a chance for success. Havers was like a hedgehog, curling herself into a protective ball of thistle at the least provocation. Yet underneath that prickly exterior of hers was a fine, probing mind. What was left to question was whether Thomas Lynley was the right combination of patience and congeniality to encourage that mind to overcome the wrangling of the termagant personality that had made it impossible for Havers to work in successful partnership with anyone else.

"Sorry to take you out of the wedding, Lynley, but there was no other way. This is the second run-in Nies and Kerridge have had up North. The first one was a disaster: Nies was right all along, and crisis ensued. I thought," he fingered the rim of his glass and chose his words carefully, "that your presence might serve to remind Nies that he can sometimes be wrong."

Webberly watched carefully for a reaction from the younger man—a stiffening of muscles, a movement of the head, a flicker behind the eyelids. But there was nothing to betray him. It was no particular secret among his superior officers at the Yard that Lynley's single run-in with Nies nearly five years before in Richmond had resulted in his own arrest. And however premature and ultimately spurious that arrest had been, it was the only black mark on an otherwise admirable record of service, a denigration that Lynley would have to live with for the rest of his career.

"It's fine, sir," Lynley replied easily. "I understand."

A knock on the door announced Miss Harriman's successful

quest for the Schweppes, which she placed triumphantly on the table in front of Sergeant Havers. She glanced at the clock. Its hands were nearing six.

"As this isn't a regularly scheduled workday, Superintendent," she began, "I thought I might—"

"Yes, yes, go on home." Webberly waved.

"Oh no, it isn't that at all," Harriman said sweetly. "But I think in Regulation Sixty-five-A regarding compensatory time . . ."

"Take Monday and I'll break your arm, Harriman," Webberly said with equivalent sweetness. "Not in the middle of this Ripper business."

"Wouldn't think of it, sir. Shall I just put it on the tick? Regulation Sixty-five-C indicates that—"

"Put it *anywhere*, Harriman."

She smiled understandingly at him. "Absolutely, Superintendent." The door closed behind her.

"Did that vixen wink at you as she left the room, Lynley?" Webberly demanded.

"I didn't notice, sir."

It was half past eight when they began gathering together the papers from the table in Webberly's office. Darkness had fallen and the fluorescent lighting did nothing to hide the room's genial air of disarray. If anything, it was worse now than it had been before, with the additional files from the North spread out on the table and an acrid cirrus of cigarette and cigar smoke that, in conjunction with the mixed scents of whisky and sherry, produced the effect of being in a rather down-at-heel gentlemen's club.

Barbara noticed the deep lines of exhaustion that were drawn on Lynley's face and judged that the aspirin had done him little good. He had gone to the wall of Ripper photographs and was inspecting them, moving from one to the next. As she watched, he lifted a hand to one of them—it was the King's Cross victim, she noted needlessly—and traced a finger along the crude incision that the Ripper's knife had made.

" 'Death closes all,' " he murmured. "He's black and white, flesh with no resilience. Who could ever recognise a living man from this?"

"Or from this, for that matter," Webberly responded. He brusquely gestured to the photographs that Father Hart had brought.

Lynley rejoined them. He stood near Barbara but was, she well knew, oblivious of her. She watched the expressions pass quickly across his face as he sorted through the photographs one last time: revulsion, disbelief, pity. His features were so easy to read that she wondered how he ever managed to conduct a successful investigation without giving everything away to a suspect. But he did it all the time. She knew his record of success, the string of follow-up convictions. He was the golden boy in more ways than one.

"We'll head up there in the morning, then," he said to the superintendent. He picked up a manila envelope and tucked all the materials inside.

Webberly was examining a train schedule which he had unearthed from the jumble on his desk. "Take the eight forty-five."

Lynley groaned. "Have a bit of mercy, sir. I'd like at least the next ten hours to get rid of this migraine."

"Then the nine-thirty. And no later than that." Webberly glanced round his office one last time as he shrugged into a tweed overcoat. Like his other clothing, it was becoming threadbare in spots, and a small patch was worked poorly into the left lapel where, no doubt, cigar ash had done its worst. "Report in on Tuesday," he said as he left.

The superintendent's absence seemed to rejuvenate Lynley at once, Barbara noted, for he moved with amazing alacrity of spirit to the telephone the moment the man was gone. He dialled a number, tapped his fingers rhythmically against the desk top, and peered at the face of the clock. After nearly a minute, his face lit with a smile.

"You *did* wait, old duck," he said into the phone. "Have you broken it off with Jeffrey Cusick at last? . . . Ha! I knew it, Helen. I've told you repeatedly that a barrister can't possibly make you happy. Did the reception end well? . . . He *did*? Oh Lord, what a scene that must have been. Has Andrew ever cried in his life? . . . Poor St. James. Was he absolutely slain with mortification? . . . Well, it's the champagne does it, you know. Did Sidney recover? . . . Yes, well, she did look for a while as if she'd get a bit maudlin at the end. She's never made a secret of it that Simon's

her favourite brother. . . . Of course dancing's still on. We promised ourselves, didn't we? . . . Can you give me, say, an hour or
so? . . . Hmm, *what* was that? . . . Helen! My God, what a naughty
little girl!" He laughed and dropped the phone back onto its
cradle. "Still here, Sergeant?" he asked when he turned from the
desk.

"You've no car, sir," she replied stonily. "I thought I'd wait
to see if you needed a ride home."

"That's awfully good of you, but we've all been kept here long
enough for one evening, and I'm sure you've far better things to
do on a Saturday night than see me home. I'll catch a cab." He
bent over Webberly's desk for a moment, writing quickly on a
piece of paper. "This is my address," he said, handing it to her.
"Be there at seven tomorrow morning, will you? That should
give us some time to make more sense of all this before we head
to Yorkshire. Good evening, then." He left the room.

Barbara looked down at the paper in her hand, at the hand-
writing which even in a hurry still managed to be an elegant
scrawl. She studied it for more than a minute before she ripped
it into tiny pieces and tossed them into the rubbish. She knew
quite well where Thomas Lynley lived.

The guilt began on the Uxbridge Road. It always did. Tonight
it was worse when she saw that the travel agency was closed,
preventing her from gathering the material on Greece as she'd
promised. Empress Tours. Where had they ever come up with a
name like that for such a grubby little shop where people sat
behind plastic-topped desks that were painted to look as if they
were wood? She slowed the car, peering through the dirty windscreen to look for signs of life. The owners lived above the shop.
Perhaps if she banged on the door a bit, she could rouse them.
No, it was too ridiculous. Mum was no more going to Greece
than to the moon; she'd just have to wait for the brochures a bit
longer.

Still, she'd passed at least a dozen agencies in the city today.
Why hadn't she stopped? What else did Mum have to live for but
those silly little dreams? Overcome with the need to compensate
in some way for her failure, Barbara pulled the car over in front

of Patel's Grocery, a ramshackle affair of green paint, rusting shelves, and precariously stacked crates from which emanated that peculiar blend of odours that comes from vegetables not quite as fresh as they ought to be. Patel was still open, at least. Leave it to him never to miss a chance to make ten pence.

"Barbara!" He greeted her from inside the shop as she bent over the boxed fall fruit on the pavement outside. Mostly apples. A few late peaches shipped in from Spain. "Whassa doin' out so late?"

He couldn't imagine her having a date, of course. No one could. She couldn't herself. "Had to work late, Mr. Patel," she replied. "How much for the peaches?"

"Eighty-five a pound, but for you, pretty face, we say eighty."

She picked out six. He weighed them, wrapped them, and handed them over. "I was seeing your father today."

She looked up quickly and caught the guard dropping over Mr. Patel's darkface like a mask when he saw her expression. "Was he behaving himself?" she asked casually, shouldering her handbag.

"My goodness, yes. He *always* behaves!" Mr. Patel took her money, counted it twice carefully, and dropped it into his register. "You take care now, Barbara. Men see a nice girl like you and—"

"Yes, I'll take care," Barbara interrupted. She tossed the peaches onto the front seat of the car. *Nice girl like you, Barb. You take care. Keep those legs crossed. Virtue like yours is definitely easy to lose, and a woman fallen is fallen forever.* She laughed bitterly, jerked the car into gear, and pulled out onto the road.

In Acton there were two potential areas of residence, simply called by inhabitants the right and wrong streets. It was as if a dividing line split the suburb arbitrarily, condemning one set of residents while it elevated others.

On the right streets of Acton, pristine brick houses boasted woodwork which always sparkled admirably in the morning sun in a multiplicity of colours. Roses grew in abundance there. Fuchsias flourished in hanging pots. Children played games on unlittered pavements and in patchwork gardens. Snow kissed gabled roofs in peaks of meringue in the winter, while in summer tall elms made green tunnels through which families strolled in the perfumed evening light. There was never an argument in the right streets of Acton, never loud music, the smell of cooking fish, or fists raised in a fight. It was sheer perfection, the single ocean on which every family's boat of dreams sailed placidly forward. But things were much different as close as a single street away.

People liked to say that the wrong streets of Acton got the heat of the day and that's why things were so different there. It was as if an enormous hand had swept down from the sky and jumbled up houses and avenues and people so that everything was always just a bit out of sorts. No one worked quite so hard on appearances: houses sagged moodily into decay. Gardens once planted were soon ignored, then forgotten altogether and left to fend for themselves. Children played noisily on the dirty pavements, disruptive games that frequently brought mothers to doorways, shrieking for peace from the din. The winter wind spit through poorly sealed windows and summer brought rain that leaked through the roofs. People in the wrong streets didn't think much about being anywhere else, for to think of being elsewhere was to think of hope. And hope was dead in the wrong part of Acton.

Barbara drove there now, turning the Mini in on a street lined with cars that were rusting like her own. Neither garden nor fence fronted her own house, but rather a pavement-hard patch of dirt on which she parked her little car.

Next door, Mrs. Gustafson was playing BBC-1. Since she was nearly deaf, the entire neighbourhood was nightly regaled with the doings of her favourite television heroes. Across the street, the Kirbys were engaging in their usual preintercourse argument while their four children ignored them as best they could by throwing dirt clods at an indifferent cat that watched from a nearby first-floor window sill.

Barbara sighed, groped for her front door key, and went into her house. It was chicken and peas. She could smell it at once, like a gust of foul breath.

"That you, lovey?" her mother's voice called. "Bit late, aren't you, dear? Out with some friends?"

What a laugh! "Working, Mum. I'm back on CID."

Her mother shuffled to the door of the sitting room. Like Barbara, she was short, but terribly thin, as if a long illness had ravaged her body and taken it sinew by sinew on a march towards the grave. "CID?" she asked, her voice growing querulous. "Oh must you, Barbara? You know how I feel about that, my lovey." As she spoke, she raised a skeletal hand to her thin hair in a characteristic, nervous gesture. Her overlarge eyes were puffy and rimmed with red, as if she had spent the day weeping.

"Brought you some peaches," Barbara responded, gesturing with the sack. "The travel agent was closed, I'm afraid. I even banged on the door to get them down from above, but they must've gone out."

Diverted from the thought of CID, Mrs. Havers' face changed, lighting with a dusty glow. She caught at the fabric of her shabby housedress and held it bunched in one hand, as if containing excitement. "Oh, that doesn't matter at all. *Wait* till you see. Go in the kitchen and I'll be right there. Your dinner's still warm."

Barbara walked past the sitting room, wincing at the chatter of the television and the fusty smell of a chamber too long kept closed. The kitchen, fetid with the odour of tough, broiled chicken and anaemic peas, was little better. She looked gloomily at the plate on the table, touched her finger to the withered flesh of the fowl. It was stone cold, as slippery and puckered as something kept preserved in formaldehyde for forensic examination. Fat had congealed round its edges, and a single, rancid dab of butter had failed to melt on peas that looked as if they had had their last warming in a former decade.

Wonderful, she thought. Could the "lovely crab salad" have even come close to this epicurean splendour? She looked for the daily paper and found it, as always, on the seat of one of the wobbly kitchen chairs. She grabbed the front section, opened it to the middle, and deposited her dinner on the smiling face of the Duchess of Kent.

"Lovey, you've not thrown away your nice dinner!"

Damn! Barbara turned to see her mother's stricken face, lips working in rejection, lines drawn in deep grooves down to her chin, pale blue eyes filled with tears. She clutched an artificial leather album to her bony chest.

"Caught me, Mum." Barbara forced a smile, putting an arm round the woman's bird-like shoulders and leading her to the table. "I had a bite at the Yard, so I wasn't hungry. Should I have saved it for you or Dad?"

Mrs. Havers blinked quickly. The relief on her face was pathetic. "I . . . I suppose not. No, of course not. We wouldn't want chicken and peas two nights in a row, would we?" She laughed gently and laid her album on the table. "*Dad* got me Greece," she announced.

"Did he?" *So that's what he was doing out of the cage.* "All by himself?" Barbara asked casually.

Her mother looked away, fingering the edges of her album, picking nervously at the artificial gold leaf. She gave a sudden movement, a quick, brilliant smile, and pulled out a chair. "Sit here, lovey, let me show you how we went."

The album was opened. Previous trips through Italy, France, Turkey—now there was a bizarre one—and Peru were flipped through quickly until they arrived at the newest section, devoted to Greece.

"Now, here's the hotel we stayed at in Corfu. Do you see how it's just right there on the bay? We could have gone down to Kanoni to a newer one, but I liked the view, didn't you, lovey?"

Barbara's eyes smarted. She refused to submit. *How long will it take? Will it never end?*

"You've not answered me, Barbara." Her mother's voice quivered with anxiety. "I did work so hard on the trip all today. Having the view was better than the new hotel in Kanoni, wasn't it, lovey?"

"Much better, Mum." Barbara forced the words out and got to her feet. "I've got a case tomorrow. Can we do Greece later?" *Would she understand?*

"What sort of case?"

"It's a . . . bit of a problem with a family in Yorkshire. I'll be gone a few days. Can you manage, do you think, or shall I ask Mrs. Gustafson to come and stay?" *Wonderful thought, the deaf leading the mad.*

"Mrs. Gustafson?" Her mother closed the album and drew herself stiffly upright. "I think not, my lovey. Dad and I can manage on our own. We always have, you know. Except that short time when Tony . . ."

The room was unbearably, stiflingly hot. *Oh God,* Barbara thought, *just a wisp of air. Just this once. For a moment.* She went to the back door, which led out to the weed-choked garden.

"Where're you going?" her mother asked quickly, that familiar note of hysteria creeping into her voice. "There's nothing out there! You mustn't go outside after dark!"

Barbara picked up the discarded chicken dinner. "Rubbish, Mum. I won't be a moment. You can wait by the door and see I'm all right."

"But I . . . By the door?"

"If you like."

"No, I mustn't be by the door. We'll leave it open just a bit, though. You can shout if you need me."

"That sounds the plan, Mum." She picked up the package and went hurriedly out into the night.

A few minutes. She breathed the cool air, listened to the familiar neighbourhood sounds, and felt in her pocket for a crumpled pack of Players. She shook one out, lit it, and gazed up at the sky.

What had started the seductive descent into madness? It was Tony, of course. Bright, freckle-faced imp. Fresh, spring air in the constant darkness of winter. *Watchme, watchme, Barbie! I can do anything!* Chemistry sets and rugger balls. Cricket on the common and tag in the afternoon. And horribly, stupidly chasing a ball right onto the Uxbridge Road.

But he didn't die from that. Just a stay in hospital. A persistent fever, a peculiar rash. And a lingering, etiolating kiss from leukemia. The wonderful, delicious irony of it all: go in with a broken leg, come out with leukemia.

It had taken him four agonising years to die. Four years for them to make this descent into madness.

"Lovey?" The voice was tremulous.

"Right here, Mum. Just looking at the sky." Barbara crushed her cigarette out on the rock-hard ground and walked back inside.

4

DEBORAH ST. JAMES braked the car to a halt on a breath of laughter and turned to her husband. "Simon, have you never been told you're quite the world's worst navigator?"

He smiled and closed the road atlas. "Never once. But have a heart. Consider the fog."

She looked out the windscreen at the large, dark building that loomed in front of them. "Poor excuse for not being able to read a road map, if you ask me. Are we at the right place? It doesn't look as if a soul's waited up for us."

"I shouldn't be surprised. I told them we'd arrive at nine and now it's . . ." he peered at his watch in the weak interior light of the car, "good God, it's half past eleven." She heard the laughter in his voice. "Are you for it, my love? Shall we spend our wedding night in the car?"

"Teenagers grappling hotly in the backseat, do you mean?" She tossed her long hair back with a shake of her head. "Hmm, it *is* a thought. But I'm afraid in that case you should have hired something larger than an Escort. No, Simon, there's nothing for it, I'm afraid, but banging on the doors and rousing someone. But *you* shall make all our excuses." She stepped out into the chilly night air, taking a moment to study the building before her.

It was a pre-Elizabethan structure by initial design, but one which had undergone a number of Jacobean changes that added to its air of rakish whimsicality. Mullioned windows winked in the moonlight that filtered through the wispy fog which had settled on the moors and was now drifting down into the dales. Walls were covered with Virginia creeper, its leaves burning the old stone to rich russet. Chimneys germinated upon the roof in a helter-skelter pattern of capricious warts against the night sky. There was a contumacy about the building that denied the very existence of the twentieth century, and this quality spread to the grounds that surrounded it.

Here enormous English oaks stretched out their branches over lawns where statuary, encircled by flowers, interrupted the flow of the land. Pathways meandered into the woods beyond the house with a beckoning, siren charm. In the absolute stillness, the play of water from a fountain nearby and the cry of a lamb from a distant farm were the only auditory concomitants to the whisper of the breeze that soughed through the night. They might have been Richard and Anne, home to Middleham at last.

Deborah turned back to the car. Her husband had opened his door and was watching her, waiting in his usual patient fashion for her photographer's reaction to the beauty of the place. "It's wonderful," she said. "Thank you, my love."

He lifted his braced left leg from the car, dropped it with a thump onto the drive, and extended his hand. With a practised movement, Deborah helped him to his feet. "I feel as if we've been going round in circles for hours," St. James remarked, stretching.

"That's because we *have*," she teased. " 'Just two hours from the station, Deborah. A *wonderful* drive.' "

He laughed softly. "Well, it was, love. Admit it."

"Absolutely. The third time I saw Rievaulx Abbey, I was positively enchanted." She glanced at the forbidding oak door before them. "Shall we try it then?"

They crunched across the gravel drive to the dark recess into which the door was set. A pitted wooden bench was tipped drunkenly against the wall next to it, and two enormous urns stood on either side. With the perversity of plants, one urn held a burgeoning beauty of flowers while the other was home to a with-ering colony of geraniums whose dried leaves fluttered raspingly to the ground as Deborah and her husband passed.

St. James applied some considerable strength to the large brass fixture that hung in the centre of the door. Silence greeted its fading echoes. "There's a bell as well," Deborah noticed. "Have a go with that."

The ringing far back in the deepest reaches of the house im-mediately roused what sounded like an entire pack of hounds into furious howling. "Well, that's certainly done it," St. James laughed.

"Dammit, Casper! Jason! S'only the bell, you devils!" Pitched very much like a man's but with the unmistakable cadence of a country woman born and bred, a raucous voice shouted brisk reprovals behind the door. "Down with you! Out! Get back t'the kitchen." A pause, followed by some desperate scuffling. "No, blast you! Out in the back! Why, you blackguard fiends! Give me my slips! Damn your eyes!" With that, a bolt shrieked back from the inside of the door, which was pulled briskly open. A barefooted woman hopped back and forth on the icy stones of the entry, her frizzy grey hair flying about her shoulders in bursts of electricity. "Mr. Allcourt-St. James," she said without pream-ble. "Come in with you both. Damn!" She removed the woollen shawl she had thrown about her shoulders and dropped it to the floor, where it immediately became a rug for her feet. She tugged the edges of a voluminous, crimson dressing gown more closely round her and, the moment the others entered, energetically slammed home the door. "There, that's better, thank God." She laughed, a bellow both, ungoverned and unrefined. "Pardon me, both. I'm generally not so awfully Emily Brontë. Did you get lost?"

"Extensively," St. James admitted. "This is my wife, Deborah, Mrs. Burton-Thomas," he added.

"You must be frozen solid," their hostess noted. "Well, we'll take care of that soon enough. Let's get out of here and into the oak hall. I've a nice fire there. Danny!" she shouted over her left shoulder. Then, "Come, it's just this way. Danny!"

They followed her through the old, stone-flagged room. White walled, dark beamed, it was bone-chillingly cold, with recessed windows uncovered by curtains, a single black refectory table in the centre of the floor, and a large unlit fireplace sinking deep into the far wall. Above it hung an assortment of firearms and oddly peaked military helmets. Mrs. Burton-Thomas nodded as St. James and Deborah gave their attention to these.

"Oh yes, Cromwell's Roundheads were here," she said. "They had a nice bite out of Keldale Hall for a stretch of ten months in the Civil War. Sixteen forty-four," she added darkly, as if expecting them to commit to memory the year of infamy in the history of the Burton-Thomas clan. "But we rid ourselves of them just as soon as we could. Blackguard devils, the lot!"

She led them through the shadows of a darkened dining room and from there to a long, richly panelled chamber where scarlet curtains were drawn across embrasured windows and a coal fire roared in the grate. "Well, Lord, where's she got herself to?" Mrs. Burton-Thomas muttered and went to the door through which they'd just come. "Danny!" That brought a responding running of footsteps, and a tousle-haired girl of about nineteen appeared in the doorway.

"Sorry!" the newcomer laughed. "Got your slips, though." She tossed these to the woman, who caught them deftly. "Chewed a bit here and there, I'm afraid."

"Thanks, pet. Will you fetch some brandy for our guests? That dreadful Watson man finished off a good third of a decanter before he staggered off to bed tonight. It's gone dry and there's more in the cellar. Will you see to it?"

As the girl went to do so, Mrs. Burton-Thomas examined her slippers, frowning at a hole newly chewed in one heel. She muttered beneath her breath, put the slippers back on her feet, and replaced the shawl—which she had been using as a sort of earthbound flying carpet in their progress through the house—on her shoulders.

"Please do sit down. Didn't want to light the fire in your room till you arrived, so we'll have a bit of a chat whilst it heats up. Bloody cold for October, isn't it? Early winter, they say."

The cellar was obviously closer than the word itself implied, for within moments, young Danny returned with a fresh bottle of brandy. She opened and decanted it at a Hepplewhite table which stood under a portrait of some glowering, hawk-featured

Burton-Thomas ancestor, then returned to them with a tray on which three brandy glasses and a decanter sparkled.

"Shall I see to the room, Auntie?" she asked.

"Please. Get Eddie for the luggage. And *do* apologise to that American couple if they're wandering about wondering what all the uproar is, will you?" Mrs. Burton-Thomas poured three healthy drinks as the girl left the room once again. "Ah, but they came here for atmosphere, and by God, I can dish it up in spades!" She laughed uproariously and threw down her drink in a single gulp. "I cultivate colour," Mrs. Burton-Thomas admitted gleefully, pouring herself another. "Give them a bit of the old eccentric, and you'll make every guidebook from Frommer to Ronay."

The woman's appearance served as complete verification of this last statement. She was a combination of stately home and gothic horror: imposingly tall, with a man's broad shoulders, she moved with a loose-limbed indifference to the priceless furniture with which the room was filled. She had the hands of a labourer, the ankles of a dancer, and the face of an aging Valkyrie. Her eyes were blue, deep-sunken above cheekbones jutting across her face. She had a hook-shaped nose that with the passage of years had grown more pronounced, so that now in the uncertain light of the room, it seemed to be casting a shadow upon her entire upper lip. She looked about sixty-five years old, but age to Mrs. Burton-Thomas was obviously a very relative matter.

"Well," she was looking them over, "hungry at all? You did miss dinner by about . . ." a glance cast towards the grandfather clock ticking sonorously against a far wall, "two hours."

"Hungry, my love?" St. James asked Deborah. His eyes, Deborah saw, were alive with amusement.

"Ah . . . no, not a bit." She turned to Mrs. Burton-Thomas. "You've others staying here then?"

"Just one American couple. You'll see them at breakfast. You know the sort. Polyester and showy gold chains. God-awful diamond ring on the man's little finger. Kept me howlingly entertained last night with a discourse on dentistry. Wanted me to have my teeth sealed, it seems. The very latest thing." Mrs. Burton-Thomas shuddered and downed another drink. "Bit Egyptian-sounding. Something for posterity, you know. Or was it to prevent cavities?" She shrugged with grand indifference. "Haven't the slightest. What *is* this fixation Americans all have with their teeth, I ask you? All straight and shiny. Well, God! Crooked teeth give a face a bit of *dash*, I say." She poked ineffectually at the fire, sending a shower of sparks out onto the rug, then stomped on these with terrific energy. "Well, delighted *you're* here, is all I can say. Not that Grandpapa isn't still doing flip-flops in the grave at my opening the place up to the tourist trade. But it was that or the bleeding National Trust." She winked at them over the rim of her glass. "And pardon me for saying so, but this sort of life is ever so roaringly more amusing."

There was a clearing of the throat from the direction of the doorway, where a boy stood awkwardly in plaid flannel pyjamas, an antique smoking jacket several sizes too large belted clumsily round his slender waist. It gave his appearance an anachronistic panache. He carried a pair of crutches in his hands.

"What is it, Eddie?" Mrs. Burton-Thomas asked impatiently. "You've done the luggage, haven't you?"

"These're in the boot, Auntie," he responded. "Shall I do 'em as well?"

"Of course, you ninny!" He turned and scurried from her sight. She shook her head darkly. "I'm a martyr to my family. An absolute religious martyr. Well, come now, little ones, let me show you to your room. You must be dropping with fatigue. No, no, bring the brandy with you."

They followed her back through the dining room to the stone hall and from there through another doorway that took them to the stairway. Polished, uncarpeted oak stairs led to the upper regions of the house, swathed in deep shadows. "Baronial stairway," Mrs. Burton-Thomas informed them, slapping her hand on its thick wood railing. "Don't even *make* these dandies anymore. Come, it's just this way."

In the upper hall, she led them down a dimly lit corridor in which ancestral portraits battled with three Flemish tapestries. Mrs. Burton-Thomas nodded moodily towards the latter. "Simply must move them. God knows they've been hanging there since 1822, but no one could ever convince Great-grandmama that these things look better from a bit of a distance. Tradition. You understand. I battle it everywhere. Here we are, little ones." She threw open a door. "I shall leave you here. All the mod cons. But you'll find them, no doubt." With that she was gone, dressing gown flapping round her ankles, slippers slapping comfortingly upon the floor.

A tumble of coals upon the hearth welcomed them into the bedroom. It was, Deborah thought as she entered, the most beautiful room she had ever seen. Oak panelled, with the beguiling faces of two Gainsborough women smiling down from either end, it embraced them with centuries' old welcome and grace. Small table lamps with rose shades put forth a diffused radiance that burnished the mahogany of the enormous four-poster. A looming wardrobe cast an elongated shadow against one wall, and a dressing table held an array of crystal atomisers and silver-backed brushes. At one of the windows stood a cabriole-legged table on which an arrangement of lilies had been placed. Deborah walked to this and touched her fingers to the fluted edge of one ivory flower.

"There's a card," she said, pulled it off and read it. Her eyes filled with tears. She turned to her husband. He had gone to the hearth and lowered himself into an overstuffed chair that sat to one side of it. He was watching her as he so often did, with that familiar reserve, the only communication coming from his eyes. "Thank you, Simon," she whispered. She tucked the card back into the flowers, swallowed an emotion she couldn't define, and forced herself to speak lightly. "How did you ever find this place?"

"Do you like it?" he asked in answer.

"You couldn't possibly have chosen anything more wonderful. And you know it, don't you?"

He didn't reply. A knock at the door, and he looked at her, a smile dancing round the corners of his mouth, his expression plainly saying: *What's next!* "Come in," he called.

It was the girl, Danny, a pile of blankets in her arms. "Sorry. Forgot these. There's an eiderdown already, but Auntie thinks the world's as cold as herself." She walked into the room with an air of friendly proprietorship. "Eddie get your things in?" she asked, opening the wardrobe and plopping the blankets unceremoniously inside. "He's just a *bit* thick, you know. Got to excuse him." She studied herself in the wavy mirror on the inside of the wardrobe door, fingered a few wandering hairs just a bit more out of place than they'd been before, and caught them watching her. "Now you'd best beware of the baby's cry," she pronounced solemnly. It was as if she'd spoken exactly on cue. The hounds would surely howl next.

"The baby's cry? Have the Americans a child with them?" Deborah asked.

Danny's dark eyes widened. She looked from woman to man. "You don't know? Has no one ever told you?"

Deborah saw from the girl's behaviour that they were soon to be enlightened, for Danny wiped her hands prefatorily down the sides of her dress, glanced from one end of the room to the other for unwanted listeners, and walked to the window. In spite of the cold, she unfastened the latch and swung it open. "Has no one told you about *that*?" she asked dramatically, gesturing out into the night.

There was nothing for it but to see what "that" was. Deborah and St. James joined Danny at the window, where, in the distance, the skeletal walls of a ruined building rose through the fog.

"Keldale Abbey," Danny intoned and settled right in next to the fire for a confidential chat. "That's where the cry of the baby comes from, not from here."

St. James pulled the window closed, drew across the heavy curtains, and led Deborah back to the fire. She curled up on the floor next to his chair, warming herself, allowing the fire to tingle against her skin.

"A ghost baby, I take it?" she said to Danny.

"An absolute one that I heard myself. You'll hear it as well. Wait and see."

"Ghosts always have legends attached," St. James noted.

Glad you asked, Danny's posture replied as she wriggled back into her chair. "As does this," she said solemnly. "Keldale was Royalist, you know, during the war." She spoke as though the late seventeenth century were only a week removed. "Loyal t' the last man of 'em t' the King. The village of Keldale, down the road a mile. You've seen it?"

St. James chuckled. "We should have, but I'm afraid we came in from a . . . different direction."

"The scenic route," Deborah added.

Danny chose to ignore the diversion. "Well," she went on, "was towards the end of t' war. And old blackguard devil

Cromwell"—obviously Danny had learned her history at her auntie's knee—"got word that the Lords o' the North were planning an uprising. So he swept through the dales one last, grand time, taking manor houses, ruining castles, destroying Royalist villages. Keldale's well hidden."

"So we discovered," St. James put in.

The girl nodded earnestly. "But days in advance the village got word that the murd'rous Roundheads was coming. 'Twasn't the *village* that old Cromwell wanted, but the villagers themselves, all o' them that was loyal t' King Charlie."

"To kill them, of course," Deborah prompted as the girl paused in her story to catch her breath.

"T' kill every last one!" she declared. "When word came that Cromwell was looking for the Kel, the village got a plan together. They'd move every stick, every stitch, every soul t' the grounds o' the abbey. So when the Roundheads arrived, there'd be Keldale, all right, but not a soul in her."

"Rather an ambitious plan," St. James remarked.

"An' it worked!" Danny replied proudly. Her pretty eyes danced above rosy cheeks, but she lowered her voice. " 'Cept for the baby!" She inched forward in her chair; obviously they had reached the climax of the tale. "The Roundheads arrived. 'Twas just as the villagers hoped. 'Twas deserted, and silent with a heavy fog. And throughout all the village, not a soul, not a stitch, not a living creature. And then"—Danny's swift glance made certain her audience was with her—"a baby began t' cry in the abbey where all the villagers were. Ah God!" She clutched her lovely bosom. "The terror! For they'd escaped Cromwell only t' be betrayed by a babe! The mother hushed the baby by offering her breast. But 'twas no good. The wee baby cried and cried. They were desperate in terror that the dogs from the village would begin t' howl with the noise and Cromwell would find them. So they hushed the poor child. An' they *smothered* it!"

"Good heavens!" Deborah murmured. She edged closer to her husband's chair. "Just the sort of story one longs to hear on a wedding night, isn't it?"

"Ah, but you *must* know." Danny's expression was fervent. "For the sound of the babe is *terrible* luck 'less you know what t' do."

"Wear garlic?" St. James asked. "Sleep with a crucifix clutched in one's hand?"

Deborah punched him lightly on the knee. "*I* want to know. I insist upon knowing. Shall I have my life blighted because I've married a cynic? Tell me what to do, Danny, should I hear the baby."

Gravely, Danny nodded. " 'Tis always a' night when the baby cries from the abbey grounds. You must sleep on your right side, your husband on his left. An' you must hold on t' one another close till the wailing stops."

"That's interesting," St. James acknowledged. "Sort of an animated amulet. May we hope that this baby cries often?"

"Not terrible often. But I . . ." She swallowed and suddenly they saw that this was no amusing legend for love-struck honeymooners, for to her the fear and the story were real. "But I heard i' myself some three years back! 'Tis not something I'll soon forget!" She got to her feet. "You'll remember what t' do? You'll not forget?"

"We'll not forget," Deborah reassured the girl as she vanished from the room.

They were quiet at her departure. Deborah rested her head against St. James' knee. His long, thin fingers moved gently through her hair, smoothing the curly mass back from her face. She looked up at him.

"I'm afraid, Simon. I didn't think I would be, not once this last year, but I am." She saw in his eyes that he understood. Of *course* he did. Had she ever truly doubted that he would?

"So am I," he replied. "Every moment today I felt just a little bit mad with terror. I never wanted to lose myself, not to you, not to anyone in fact. But there it is. It happened." He smiled. "You invaded my heart with a little Cromwellian force of your own that I couldn't resist, Deborah, and I find now that rather than lose myself, the true terror is that I might somehow lose you." He touched the pendant he'd given her that morning, nestling in the hollow of her throat. It was a small gold swan, so long between them a symbol of commitment: choosing once, choosing for life. His eyes moved from it back to her own. "Don't be afraid," he whispered gently.

"Make love to me then."

"With great pleasure."

* * *

Jimmy Havers had little pig's eyes that darted round the room when he was nervous. He might feel as if he were putting on the bravura performance of a lifetime, lying his way grandly out of everything from an accusation of petty larceny to being caught in flagrante delicto, but the reality was that his eyes betrayed him every time, as they were doing now.

"Didn't know if you'd be home in time to get your Mum the Greece stuff, so Jim went out himself, girl." It was his habit to speak of himself in the third person. It allowed him to evade responsibility for virtually any unpleasantness that cropped up in his life. Like this one now. *No, I didn't go to the turf accountant. Didn't pick up snuff, either. If it was done at all, was Jimmy that done it, not me.*

Barbara watched her father's eyes dance their way round the sitting room. God, what a grim little death pit it was: a ten-by-fifteen-foot room whose windows were permanently sealed shut by years of filth and grime, crammed with that wonderful three-piece suite so essential to delicate living, but this one a creation that had billed itself as "artificial horsehair" thirty-five years ago when even real horsehair was a hideous concept of comfort. The walls were papered with a maddening design of interlocking rosebuds that simpered their way to the ceiling. Racing magazines overflowed from tables onto the floor and argued there with the fifteen simulated leather albums that assiduously documented every inch, every mile of her mother's breakdown. And through it all Tony smiled and smiled and smiled.

A corner of the room held his shrine. The last picture of him before his illness—a distorted, unfocused little boy kicking a football into a temporary goal net set up in a garden that had once leapt with flowers—was enlarged to beyond life-size proportions. On either side, suitably framed in mock oak, hung every school report he had ever done, every note of praise from every teacher he'd had, and—God, have mercy on us all—given pride of place, the certificate of his death. Beneath this, an arrangement of plastic flowers did obeisance, a rather dusty obeisance considering the state of the room itself.

The television blared, as it always did, from the opposite corner, placed there "so Tony can watch it as well." His favourite shows still played regularly to him, frozen in time, as if nothing had happened, as if nothing had changed. While the windows and doors were closed and locked, chained and barred to hold out the truth of that August afternoon and the Uxbridge Road.

Barbara strode across the room and switched off the set.

"Hey, girl, Jim was watching that!" her father protested.

She faced him. My God, he was a pig. When was the last time he'd had a bath? She could smell him from here—the sweat; the body oils that collected in his hair, on his neck, behind the creases of his ears; the unwashed clothing.

"Mr. Patel told me you were by," she said, sitting down on the horrible couch. It prickled against her skin.

The eyes flicked around. From the dead television to the plastic flowers to the obscene roses scaling the wall. "Jim went to Patel's, sure." He nodded.

He grinned at his daughter. His teeth were badly stained, and along the gumline Barbara saw the liquid building within his mouth. The coffee tin was by his chair, inexpertly hidden by a racing form. She knew he wanted her to look away for a moment so that he'd have time to do his business without getting caught. She refused to play along.

"Spit it out, Dad," she said patiently. "There's no use swallowing it and making yourself sick, is there?" Barbara watched her father's body sag in relief as he reached for the tin and spat the snuff-induced, brown slime from his mouth.

He wiped himself off with a stained handkerchief, coughed into it heavily, and adjusted the tubes that fed the oxygen into his nose. Mournfully, he looked at his daughter for tenderness and found none. So his eyes quickly shifted and began their slither round the room.

Barbara watched him thoughtfully. Why wouldn't he die? she wondered. He'd spent the last ten years decaying by degrees; why not one big jump into black oblivion? He'd like that. No more gasping for breath, no more emphysema. No more need for snuff to soothe his addiction. Just emptiness, nothingness, nothing at all.

"You'll get cancer, Dad," she said. "You know that, don't you?"

" 'Ey, Jim's okay, Barb. Don't you worry, girl."

"Can't you think of Mum? What would happen if you had to go into hospital again?" *Like Tony.* It hung unspoken in the air. "Shall I speak to Mr. Patel? I don't want to have to do that, but I shall, you know, if you persist in this business with snuff."

"Patel gave Jim the idea in the first place," her father protested. His voice was a whine. "After you told him to cut off Jim's fags."

"You know I did that for your own good. You can't smoke round an oxygen tank. The doctors told you that."

"But Patel said snuff was okay for Jim."

"Mr. Patel is *not* a doctor. Now, give me the snuff." She held out her hand for it.

"But Jim wants—"

"No argument, Dad. Give me the snuff."

He swallowed. Twice. Hard. His eyes darted here and there. "Got to have something, Barbie," he whimpered.

She winced at the name. Only Tony had called her that. On her father's lips it was a malediction. Nonetheless, she moved to him, put her hand on his shoulder, and forced herself to touch his unwashed hair. "Dad, try to understand. It's Mum we have to consider. Without you, she would never survive. So we've got to keep you healthy and fit. Don't you see? Mum . . . loves you so much."

Was there a glimmer there at that? Did they still see each other in this little hell they so richly deserved, or was the fog too thick?

He gave a choked sob. A dirty hand went into his pocket and the small, round tin was produced. "Jim don't mean no harm, Barbie," he said as he handed the tin to his daughter. His eyes slid from her face to the shrine, to the plastic flowers in their plastic vases beneath it. She went to them at once, dumped out the flowers, and confiscated the additional three tins of snuff hidden there.

"I'll speak to Mr. Patel in the morning," she said coldly and walked out of the room.

Of *course* it would be Eaton Terrace. Eaton Place was simply too, too Belgravia, and Lynley would never stoop to ostentation.

Besides, this was just the city townhouse. Howenstow—the Cornish estate—was where the Lynleys really hung their hats.

Barbara stood looking at the elegant white building. How enchantingly clean everything was in Belgravia, she thought. How upper-class chic. It was the only area in the city where people would consent to live in converted stables and boast about it to all their friends!

We're in Belgravia now. Did we mention it! Oh, do stop by for tea! It's nothing much. Just three hundred thousand pounds, but we like to think of it as such an investment. Five rooms. With the sweetest little cobblestone street that you've ever seen. Do say you'll be here at half past four. You'll recognise the place. I've planted begonias in every window box.

Barbara mounted the spotless marble steps and, with a scornful shake of her head, noted the small Asherton coat of arms beneath the brass light fixture. *Armigerous, Lynley! No converted stable for you.*

She lifted her hand to press the bell but stopped herself and turned to survey the street. Since yesterday there had been no time to consider her position. Her initial meeting with Webberly, fetching Lynley from the wedding, and the subsequent meeting at Scotland Yard with the peculiar little priest had all followed so swiftly that there had been no moment in which she could sort out her feelings and devise a strategy for surviving this new apprenticeship.

True, Lynley had not been as appalled at the assignment as she had thought he would be, certainly not as appalled and outraged as she herself had been. But then his mind had been occupied with other matters: the wedding of his friend and, no doubt, his late-night assignation with Lady Helen Clyde. Now, with some time to reflect upon it, he would surely allow her to feel the full brunt of his irritation at being saddled with such a pariah as herself.

So what to do? Here it was at last, the opportunity she had been waiting for—hoping for, praying for—the chance to prove herself in CID once and for all. It was the chance to make up for the arguments, the slips of the tongue, the impetuous decisions, the foolish mistakes of the past ten years.

"There's a lot you might learn from working with Lynley."

Webberly's words returned to her, and she knotted her brow. What could she possibly learn from Lynley? The right wine to order with dinner, a few dance steps, how to dazzle a roomful of people with engaging conversation? *What* could she learn from Lynley?

Nothing, of course. But she knew too well that he represented her only chance of being reassigned to CID. So, as she stood on his fine doorstep, she considered thoughtfully her best approach to getting along with the man.

It would have to be complete cooperation, she decided. She would offer no suggestions, would agree with every thought he had, with every statement he made.

Survive, she told herself, and turned and pressed the bell.

She had been expecting a buxom, uniformed, pert little maid to answer her ring, so she was surprised. For Lynley himself opened the door, a piece of toast in one hand, slippers on his feet, and his reading spectacles perched on the end of his aristocratic nose.

"Ah, Havers," he said, looking over them at her, "you're early. Excellent."

He led the way to the back of the house and into an airy morning room, fresh with white wainscoting, pale green walls, and an unusually restrained Adams ceiling. French doors at one end were undraped to allow a view of a late-blooming garden, and breakfast was laid out in silver serving dishes along an ornate walnut sideboard. The room smelled invitingly of warm bread and bacon, and in answer to the odour, Barbara felt her stomach rumble hollowly. She pressed her arm against it and tried not to think of her own morning's fare of a single overboiled egg and toast. The dining table was laid for two, a number that momentarily surprised Barbara until she remembered Lynley's evening rendezvous with Lady Helen Clyde. Her ladyship was no doubt at this moment still in his bed, unused to rising before half past ten.

"Do help yourself." Lynley motioned absently towards the sideboard with his fork and gathered up a few sheets of the police report that lay in haphazard fashion among the china. "There isn't a person I know who can't think better while eating. But avoid the kippers. They seem a bit off."

"No, thank you," she replied politely. "I've eaten, sir."

"Not even a sausage? They, at least, are remarkably good. Do you find that the butchers are finally having a whack at putting more pork than meal into sausages these days? It's refreshing, to say the least. Nearly five decades after World War II and we're finally coming off rationing." He picked up a teapot. Like everything else on the table, it was antique bone china, no doubt part of the man's family history. "What about something to drink? I have to warn you, I'm addicted to Lapsang Souchong tea. Helen claims that it tastes like dirty socks."

"I . . . I could do with a cuppa. Thank you, sir."

"Good," he declared. "Have some and tell me what you think."

She was adding a lump of sugar to the brew when the front bell rang again. Footsteps came running up a stairway in the back. "I'll get it, my lord," a woman's voice called. It was a Cornish accent. "Sorry about the last time. The baby and all."

"It's the croup, Nancy," Lynley murmured to himself. "Take the poor child to the doctor."

The sound of a woman's voice floated down the hall. *"Breakfast?"* A lighthearted laugh. "What a propitious arrival I've effected, Nancy. He'll never believe it's purely coincidental." Upon her last sentence Lady Helen breezed into the room and paralysed Barbara into a moment of breath-catching, ice-sheathed despair.

They were wearing identical suits. But while Lady Helen's had obviously been cut by the designer himself to fit her figure, Barbara's own was off-the-rack, a through-the-looking-glass chain store copy with rucked seams and altered hemline to prove it. Only the differing colours might possibly save her from complete humiliation, she thought. She grasped her teacup but lacked the will to lift it to her lips.

Lady Helen paused only fractionally at the sight of the policewoman. "I'm in a mess," she said frankly. "Thank God you're here as well, Sergeant, for I've a terrible feeling it'll take three heads to see me clear of the muddle I've made for myself." That said, she deposited a large shopping bag on the nearest chair and went directly to the sideboard, where she began browsing through the covered dishes as if food alone were sufficient to see her through her dilemma.

"Muddle?" Lynley asked. He glanced at Barbara. "How do you like the Lapsang?"

Her lips felt stiff. "It's very nice, sir."

"*Not* that awful tea again!" Lady Helen groaned. "Really, Tommy. You're a man without mercy."

"Had I known you were coming, I'd hardly have been so remiss as to serve it twice in one week," Lynley replied pointedly.

Unoffended, she laughed. "Isn't he piqued, Sergeant? From the way he talks, you'd think I was here every morning, eating him out of house and home."

"There *is* yesterday, Helen."

"You vicious man." She turned her attention back to the sideboard. "These kippers smell appalling. Did Nancy bring them up in her suitcase?" She joined them at the table with a plate piled high with a gastronomic argument of eggs and mushrooms, grilled tomatoes and bacon. "What's she doing here, by the way? Why isn't she at Howenstow? Where's Denton this morning?"

Lynley sipped his tea, his eyes on the report on the table before him. "As I'll be out of town, I've given Denton the next few days off," he replied absently. "No need for him to come with me."

A crisp piece of bacon halted in mid-air. Lady Helen stared. "You're joking, of course. Tell me you're joking, darling."

"I'm perfectly capable of getting along without my valet. I'm not totally incompetent, Helen."

"But that's not what I mean!" Lady Helen drank a mouthful of the Lapsang Souchong, grimaced at the taste, and set down the cup. "It's Caroline. She's gone off on holiday for this entire week. You don't think . . . Tommy, if she's run off with Denton, I'll be absolutely lost. No"—this as he was about to speak—"I know what you're going to say. They have every right to their personal lives. I agree completely. But we simply must come to some sort of compromise over this—you and I—because if they get married and live with you—"

"Then you and I shall get married as well," Lynley replied placidly. "And we'll be as happy as hedgehogs, the four of us."

"You think it's amusing, don't you? But just look at me. One morning without Caroline in the flat and I'm a complete disaster. Surely you don't think this is an ensemble that *she* would approve of?"

Lynley regarded the ensemble in question. Barbara didn't need to do so. The vision of Lady Helen was branded into her mind: a smartly tailored burgundy suit, silk blouse, and a mauve scarf that cascaded down to a trim waist.

"What's wrong with it?" Lynley asked. "It looks fine to me. In fact, considering the hour"—he glanced at his pocket watch —"I'd say you're almost too sartorially splendid."

Lady Helen turned to Barbara in exasperation. "Isn't that every bit just like a man, Sergeant? I end up this morning looking like an overripe strawberry and he murmurs 'looks fine to me' and buries his nose in a murder file."

"Far better that than assist you with your clothing for the next few days." Lynley nodded at the ignored shopping bag that had toppled over and now spilled a few assorted pieces of material onto the floor. "Is that why you've come?"

Lady Helen pulled the bag towards her. "I only wish it were that simple," she sighed. "But it's worse by far than the Denton-Caroline affair—we've not finished with that, by the way—and I'm at a total loss. I've mixed up Simon's bullet holes."

Barbara was beginning to feel as if she'd walked into something designed by Wilde. Surely at any moment Lane would enter stage left with the cucumber sandwiches.

"Simon's bullet holes?" Lynley, more accustomed to Lady Helen's pirouettes of thought, was patient.

"*You* know. We were working on the patterns of blood splattering based on trajectory, angle, and calibre. You remember that, don't you?"

"The piece to be presented next month?"

"The very one. Simon had left it all organised for me in the lab. I was supposed to run off the preliminary set of data, attach them to the cloth, and set up the lab for the final study. But I—"

"Mixed up the cloths," Lynley finished. "St. James *will* go on about that, Helen. What do you propose to do?"

She looked forlornly down at the samples that she had dumped unceremoniously onto the floor. "Of course, I'm not hopelessly ignorant in the matter. After four years in the laboratory, at least I recognise the twenty-two calibre and can easily find the forty-five and the shotgun. But as to the others . . . and even worse, as to which blood pattern goes with each trajectory . . ."

"It's a muddle," Lynley finished.

"In a word," she agreed. "So I thought I'd pop by this morning to see if perhaps we could sort it all out."

Lynley leaned down and fingered his way through the pile of material. "Can't be done, old duck. Sorry, but you've hours of work here and we've a train to catch."

"Then whatever shall I say to Simon? He's been working on this for ages."

Lynley pondered the question. "There's one thing . . ."

"What?"

"Professor Abrams at Chelsea Institute. Do you know him?" When she shook her head, he went on. "He and Simon both have testified as expert witnesses. They did in the Melton case only last year. They know each other. Perhaps he'd help. I could phone him for you before I leave."

"*Would* you, Tommy? I'd be so grateful. I'd do anything for you."

He lifted an eyebrow. "Surely not the thing to say to a man over breakfast."

She laughed engagingly. "Even the dishes! I'd even give up Caroline if it came to that."

"And Jeffrey Cusick?"

"Even Jeffrey. Poor man. Traded for bullet holes without a second thought."

"All right then. I'll see to it as soon as we've finished our breakfast. I take it that we *may* now finish our breakfast?"

"Oh yes, of course." She dug happily into her plate while Lynley put on his spectacles and looked at his papers once more. "What kind of case is it that has you two rushing off so early in the morning?" Lady Helen asked Barbara, pouring herself a second cup of tea, which she sugared and creamed with a liberal hand.

"A decapitation."

"That sounds particularly grim. Are you travelling far?"

"Up to Yorkshire."

The teacup was suspended and then lowered carefully to the saucer beneath. Lady Helen's eyes moved to Lynley, regarding him for a moment before she spoke. "Where in Yorkshire, Tommy?" she asked impassively.

Lynley read a few lines. "A place called . . . here it is, Keldale. Do you know it?"

There was a minute pause. Lady Helen considered the question. Her eyes were on her tea, and although her face was without expression, a pulse began to beat in the vein at her throat. She looked up but the smile she offered did not touch her eyes. "Keldale? Not at all."

5

LYNLEY TOSSED DOWN his newspaper and considered Barbara Havers. There was no need to do so surreptitiously, for she was bent over the glaucous-hued Formica train table between them, perusing the Keldale murder report. He gave momentary, idle consideration to the depths to which British Rail was sinking with its current colour scheme designed to take maximum wear with minimum upkeep, but then his thoughts returned to the officer opposite him.

He knew about Havers. Everyone did. She'd failed miserably through her first tenure in CID, swiftly alienating MacPherson, Stewart, and Hale, three of the easiest DIs with whom one could ever hope to work. MacPherson especially, with his rolling highland humour and his paternal approach, should have been a mentor *extraordinaire* for someone like Havers. The man was a virtual teddy bear. Had *any* DS ever failed to work successfully at his side? Only Havers.

Lynley remembered the day of Webberly's decision to put her back in uniform. Everyone had known it was coming, of course. It had been coming for months. But no one had been quite prepared for the woman's reaction.

"If I was lah-dee-dah Eton, you'd be keeping me," she'd shouted in Webberly's office in a broken voice loud enough for the entire floor to hear. "If I'd a cheque-book large enough and a title on my name and a willingness to screw everything in sight—woman, man, child, or animal—I'd be *quite* good enough for your precious department!"

At the mention of Eton, three heads had swivelled in Lynley's direction. By the end of the diatribe, a quick cessation of workday noise indicated to him that every person within range of vision was looking his way. He'd been standing at a cabinet, rooting about for the file on that miserable little worm Harry Nelson but found that his fingers had suddenly become clumsy. Of course, he really didn't need the file. Not exactly at the moment. Indeed, he couldn't stand there forever; he had to turn, to go back to his desk.

He made himself do it, made himself say quite lightly, "Good Lord, I *always* draw the line at animals," and made himself walk casually across the room.

Nervous, uncomfortable laughter greeted his remark. Then Webberly's door slammed and Havers stormed wildly down the corridor. Her mouth was twisted with rage, her face blotched and mottled with tears that she wiped off savagely with the sleeve of her coat. Lynley felt the entire force of her hatred wash over him as her eyes met his and her lips curled in contempt. It was like being struck by an illness for which there was no cure.

A moment later, MacPherson lumbered by his desk, tossed down the file on Harry Nelson, and said, "Ye're a class act, laddie," in his amiable rumble. But still, it had taken at least ten minutes for his hands to stop shaking so that he could dial the phone for Helen.

"Lunch, old duck?" he had asked her.

She could tell. She could hear it at once. "Absolutely, Tommy. Simon's been forcing me all morning to look at the most hideous hair samples imaginable—did you know that scalp actually *comes off* when you pull out someone's hair, darling?—and somehow lunch seems just the very thing. Shall we say the Connaught?"

Blessed Helen. God, what a wonderful anchor she'd been in his life this past year! Lynley pushed the thought from his mind and returned to his study of Havers. She reminded him just a bit of a turtle. Especially this morning when Helen had come into the room. The poor wretch had absolutely frozen, muttered less than ten words, and retreated right into her shell. What bizarre behaviour! As if she had something to fear from Helen! He felt in his pockets for his cigarette case and lighter.

Sergeant Havers glanced up at his movement, then returned to her report, her face impassive. She doesn't smoke or drink, Lynley thought and smiled wryly. *Well, get used to it, Sergeant. I'm not at all a man who neglects his vices. Not in the past year, at least.*

He'd never quite been able to comprehend the woman's remarkable antipathy towards him. There was, if one thought about it, the entire ridiculous subject of class—and God knows he'd taken a fair share of ribbing once his colleagues discovered he'd inherited a title. Yet after a week or two of their mocking bows and fanfares whenever he entered a room, the title had simply ceased to be an issue at all. But not for Havers, who seemed to hear the orotund words *Eighth Earl of Asherton* booming out every time he walked anywhere near her, something he'd scrupulously avoided doing since she'd been returned to uniform.

He sighed. And here they were now together. What was it exactly that Webberly had in mind in establishing this grotesque alliance of theirs? The super was by far the most intelligent man he'd ever run across at the Yard, so this quixotic little partnership hadn't come out of nowhere. He looked out the rain-splattered window. *If I can only determine which one of us is Sancho Panza, we'll get on famously.* He laughed.

Sergeant Havers looked up curiously but said nothing. Lynley smiled. "Just looking for windmills," he told her.

They were drinking the railway's Styrofoam coffee from its Styrofoam cups when Sergeant Havers tentatively brought up the question of the axe.

"No prints on it at all," she observed.

"It does seem odd, doesn't it?" Lynley replied. He winced at the taste of the liquid and shoved the cup aside. "Kill your dog, kill your father, sit there waiting for the police to arrive, but wipe the axe handle clean of your fingerprints? It doesn't follow."

"Why do you think she killed the dog, Inspector?"

"To silence it."

"I suppose so," she agreed reluctantly.

Lynley saw that she wanted to say something more. "What do *you* think?"

"I . . . It's nothing. You're probably quite right, sir."

"But you have another idea. Let's hear it." Havers was eying him warily. "Sergeant?" he prompted.

She cleared her throat. "I was only thinking that she really wouldn't need to silence it. I mean . . . it was *her* dog. Why would it bark at her? I could be wrong, but it seems that it would bark at an intruder and an intruder would want to silence it."

Lynley studied the tips of his steepled fingers. " 'The curious incident of the dog in the night-time,' " he murmured. "It *would* bark at a girl it knew if she were killing her father," he argued.

"But . . . I was thinking, sir." Havers nervously pushed her clipped hair behind her ears, a gesture that made her more unattractive than ever. "Doesn't it look as if the dog were killed first?" She leafed through the papers that she had replaced in the folder and took out one of the photographs. "Teys' body has collapsed right over the dog."

Lynley examined the picture. "Yes, of course. But she could have arranged it."

Havers' sharp little eyes widened in surprise. "I don't think she could, sir. Not really."

"Why not?"

"Teys was six feet four inches tall." She clumsily pulled out more of the report. "He weighed . . . here it is, fourteen and one-half stone. I can't see this Roberta slinging round fourteen and one-half stone of dead weight just to arrange a crime scene. Especially if she intended to confess immediately after. It doesn't seem possible. Besides, the body had no head, so you'd think there'd be a bit of blood on the walls if she'd slung it about. But there wasn't."

"Score a point for you, Sergeant," Lynley said, pulling his reading spectacles out of his pocket. "I think I agree. Here, let me have a look at that." She handed him the entire file. "Time of death was put at between ten and midnight," he said, more to himself than to her. "Had chicken and peas for dinner. Something wrong, Sergeant?"

"Nothing, sir. Someone walked over my grave."

A charming expression. "Ah." He read on. "And barbiturates in the blood." He looked up, his brow furrowed, and stared sightlessly at Sergeant Havers over the tops of his spectacles. "Somehow one never thinks of a man like that needing sleeping pills. There he is, putting in a hard day's work on a farm, out in that wonderful fresh air of the dales. He eats a hearty dinner and just drops off to sleep by the fire. Bucolic bliss. So why sleeping pills?"

"It looks as if he'd only just taken them."

"Obviously. One hardly expects him to have somnambulated his way out to the barn."

She froze at once at his tone, retreated back into her shell. "I only meant—"

"Excuse me," Lynley interrupted quickly. "I was joking. I do sometimes. It relieves the tension. You'll have to try to get used to it."

"Of course, sir," she replied with deliberate courtesy.

The man accosted them as they walked over the pedestrian bridge towards the exit. He was extremely thin, anaemic-looking, obviously someone who was victim to at least a thousand different kinds of stomach problems that were the bane of his existence. Even as he approached them, he popped a tablet into his mouth and began chewing upon it with furious determination.

"Superintendent Nies," Lynley remarked affably. "Have you come all the way from Richmond to meet us? That's quite a drive for you."

"Sixty bloody miles, so let's get it straight right from the top, Inspector," Nies snapped. He'd stopped dead in front of them, blocking their way to the stairs that would lead them down to the departures platform and out of the station. "I don't want you here. This is Kerridge's goddamned game and I've *nothing* to do with it. You want anything, you get it from Newby Wiske, not from Richmond. Is that perfectly clear? I don't want to see you. I don't want to hear from you. If you've come up here with a personal vendetta in mind, Inspector, then just shove it up your arse right now. Got it? I've no time for poncey schoolboys itching for a pretty scratch of revenge."

There was a moment of silence. Watching Nies' dyspeptic

face, Barbara wondered if anyone ever spoke to Lord Asherton in such a colourful manner on his Cornish estate.

"Sergeant Havers," Lynley said mildly, "I don't believe you've ever been introduced to Chief Superintendent Nies of the Richmond police force."

She had never seen a man driven to a loss so swiftly, done with an impeccable show of manners. "Nice to meet you, sir," she said dutifully.

"Damn you to hell, Lynley," Nies snarled. "Just stay out of my way." With that, he turned on his heel and pushed his way through the crowd towards the exit.

"Nicely done, Sergeant." Lynley's voice was serene. His eyes searched through the swarm of humanity in the terminal. It was nearly noon, and the usual bustle of York's station was intensified by the lunch hour as people took the opportunity to purchase tickets, to argue car hire prices with the station agents, to meet loved ones who had timed arrivals to fit into the schedules of a working world. Lynley found the person he was looking for, said, "Ah, I see Denton up ahead," and raised his hand in acknowledgement to a young man who was approaching them.

Denton had just come out of the cafeteria, caught in the midst of a meal. He was chewing, swallowing, and wiping his mouth with a paper napkin as he dodged through the crowd. He additionally managed to comb his thick dark hair neatly, straighten his necktie, and give a quick glance at his shoes, all before reaching them.

"Good trip, my lord?" he asked, handing Lynley a set of keys. "The car's just outside." He smiled pleasantly, but Barbara saw that he avoided Lynley's eyes.

Lynley gazed at his valet critically. "Caroline," he said.

Denton's round, grey eyes grew immediately rounder. "Caroline, my lord?" he repeated innocently. His cherubic face became, if possible, even more cherubic. He flicked a nervous glance back in the direction from which he'd just come.

"Don't 'Caroline, my lord?' me. We've a few things to straighten up here before you go off on this holiday of yours. This is Sergeant Havers, by the way."

Denton gulped and nodded quickly at Barbara. "Pleased, Sergeant," he said and turned his eyes back to Lynley. "My lord?"

"Stop being so obsequious. You don't do it at home and in public it makes my skin positively crawl with embarrassment." Impatient, Lynley shifted his black overnight case from one hand to the other.

"Sorry." Denton sighed and dropped the pose. "Caroline's in the cafeteria. I've a cottage lined up in Robin Hood's Bay."

"What a romantic you are," Lynley observed drily. "Spare me the details. Just tell her to phone Lady Helen and reassure her you're not off to Gretna Green. Will you do that, Denton?"

The young man grinned. "Will do. In a tic."

"Thank you." Lynley reached into his pocket and from his wallet extracted a credit card. He handed it to the man. "Don't get any ideas," he warned. "I want *only* the car on this. Is that clear?"

"Absolutely," Denton replied crisply. He glanced over his shoulder to the cafeteria, where a pretty young woman had come outside and was watching them. She was as fashionably dressed and as fashionably coiffured as Lady Helen Clyde herself always was. Practically her clone if it came down to it, Barbara thought sourly and wondered if it was a requirement of the job: hand-maiden to the youngest daughter of an earl, just like someone stepping out of the nineteenth century. The only real difference between Caroline and her ladyship was a minor lack of self-assurance evidenced by Caroline's grip upon her handbag: a two-fisted clinging to the handles as if it were to be used as a defensive weapon.

Denton spoke. "Shall I be off then?"

"Be off," Lynley responded, and added as the man scurried back in the direction he had come, "Take some care, will you?"

"Not a fear, my lord. Not a fear," was the swift reply.

Lynley watched him disappear into the crowd, the young woman on his arm. He turned to Barbara. "I think that's the last interruption," he said. "Let's be on our way."

With that, he led her out onto Station Road and directly up to a sleek, silver Bentley.

"I—have—got—the—*poop*," Hank Watson said confiden-tially from the next table. "The—straight—certified—verified—

poop!" Satisfied that he had the undivided attention of the others in the dining room, he went on. "About the baby-in-the-abbey story. JoJo-bean and I had the straight, certified from Angelina this morning."

St. James looked at his wife. "More coffee, Deborah?" he asked politely. When she demurred, he poured some for himself and gave his attention back to the other couple.

Hank and JoJo Watson hadn't wasted much time becoming elbow-rubbing intimates of the only other guests at Keldale Hall. Mrs. Burton-Thomas had seen to that by seating them at adjoining tables in the hall's immense dining room. She hadn't bothered with introductions. She knew quite well there would be no need. The beautiful bolection mouldings of the room's panelled walls, the Sheraton sideboard, and the William and Mary chairs became entirely lost to the American couple's interest once St. James and Deborah entered the room.

"Hank, hon, maybe they don't want to hear about the baby in the abbey." JoJo fingered her gold chain, from which were hanging a veritable excrescence of trinkets. *#1 Mom, Applepie,* and *Sugarbean* danced alongside a Mercedes-Benz symbol, a diminutive spoon, and a minuscule Eiffel Tower.

"Hellsapoppin they don't!" was Hank's riposte. "You just *ask* them, Bean."

JoJo rolled her eyes in apology at the other couple. "Hank's charmed with England. Just really charmed," she explained.

"Love it." Hank nodded. "If I could just get some toast that's h-o-t, the place'd be perfect. Why in heck d'you people eat your toast cold?"

"I've always thought it was a cultural deficiency," St. James responded.

Hank brayed appreciatively, his mouth open wide to display a row of startlingly white teeth. "Cultural deficiency! That's good! That's real good! Hear that, Bean? Cultural deficiency!" Hank always repeated any remark that made him laugh. Somehow, it gave him a certain authorship over it. "Now, back to the abbey." He was also not easily diverted.

"Hank," his wife murmured. She was a bit like a rabbit, exophthalmic, with a little upturned nose that continually twitched and flexed on her face as if she were not quite used to the air she breathed.

"Loosen up, Bean," her husband urged. "These people here are the salt—of—the—earth."

"I think I *will* have more coffee, Simon," Deborah said.

Her husband poured, met her eyes, and said, "Milk, dear?"

"Yes, please."

"H-o-t milk for the coffee!" Hank remarked, seeing a new avenue in which to demonstrate his considerable verbal flexibility. "Now that's something else I just haven't got used to. Hey! Here's Angelina now!"

The said young girl—obviously by her physical resemblance to Danny yet another member of the curiouser and curiouser Burton-Thomas clan—was carrying a large tray into the dining room with intense concentration. She was not as pretty as Danny: a plump little red hen of a girl whose scrubbed cheeks and rough hands made her look as if she'd be more at home on a farm than attempting to be part of her family's eccentric establishment. She bobbed a nervous good morning, avoiding their eyes, and awkwardly distributed breakfast, gnawing her bottom lip miserably as she did so.

"Shy little thing," Hank observed loudly, squashing a square of toast into the center of his fried egg. "But she gave us the true poop last night after dinner. Now you've heard about that baby, right?"

Deborah and St. James looked at each other, deciding which one of them would take up the conversational ball. It was tossed to Deborah. "Yes, indeed we did," she replied. "Crying from the abbey. Danny told us about it just after we arrived."

"Ha! Bet she did," Hank said obscurely, and then to make sure his meaning was clear, added, "Nice little piece. You know. Likes the attention."

"Hank . . ." his wife murmured into her porridge. Her hair was very short, strawberry blonde, and the tips of her ears, showing through it, had become quite red.

"JoJo-bean, these people are not d-u-m," Hank replied. "They know the score." He waved a fork at the other two. A piece of sausage was poised perilously on the prongs. "You gotta excuse the Bean," he explained. "You'd think living in Laguna Beach'd make a swinger outa her, wouldn't you? You familiar with Laguna Beach, California?" No pause for an answer. "It is the finest place in the world to live, no offence to you here, of course.

JoJo-bean and I've lived there for—how long is it now, pretty face? Twenty-two years?—and she still blushes, I tell you, when she sees two queers getting personal! 'JoJo,' I tell her, 'there—is—no—use getting hot and bothered about queers.' " He lowered his voice. "We got them coming out our verified *ears* in Laguna," he confided.

St. James could not bring himself to look at Deborah. "I beg your pardon?" he asked, unsure if he had correctly heard the unusual, gymnastic pun.

"*Queers*, man! Faggots! Ho-mo-sex-shuls. By the certified, verified millions in Laguna! They all want to live there! Now, as to the abbey." Hank paused to slurp gustily at his coffee. "Seems the real story is that Danny and her you-know-what used to meet at the abbey on a regular basis. You know what I mean. For a little clutch-and-feel. And on the night in question some three years back they've just decided it's time to consecrate the relationship. You follow me?"

"Completely," St. James replied. He studiously avoided Deborah's eyes.

"Now, Danny, see, is a little leery of this. After all, being a virgin on the wedding night's a *puh-retty* big item to let go of, don't you agree? 'Specially in this neck of the woods. And if little Danny lets this fella have his way . . . well, there's no backward road, is there?" He awaited St. James' response.

"I should imagine not."

Hank nodded sagely. "So, as her sister Angelina tells it—"

"She was there?" St. James asked incredulously.

Hank spent a moment guffawing at the thought, banging his spoon with tympanic delight on the top of the table. "You're a card, fella!" He directed his attention to Deborah. "He always like this?"

"Always," she replied promptly.

"That's great! Well, back to the abbey."

Of course, Deborah and St. James' exchanged looks replied.

"So here's this fella with Danny." Hank painted the scene in the air with his knife and fork. "The gun is loaded and the trigger cocked. When all of a sudden comes this baby wailing fit to beat the band! Can you see it? Huh, *can* you?"

"In detail," St. James replied.

"Well, these two hear that baby and think it's the worda God himself. They get outa that abbey so fast that you'd think the devil was chasing them. And *that*, my friends, put an end to *that*."

"To the baby crying, do you mean?" Deborah asked. "Oh, Simon, I was hoping we'd hear it tonight. Or perhaps even this afternoon. Warding off evil turned out to be so much more rewarding than I expected it to be."

Minx, his look said.

"*Not* to the crying baby," Hank instructed. "To the you-know-what between Danny and whoever he was. Who the hell *was* he, anyway, Bean?"

"A weird name. Ezra somebody."

Hank nodded. "Well, anyway, Danny comes back to the hall here with a case of the who-ha's that just won't quit. Wants to confess her sins and go right to the Lord. So they call the local priest in. It is *ex—or—cism* time!"

"For the abbey, the hall, or Danny?" St. James enquired.

"All *three*, fella! So this priest comes rushing down and does the bit with the holy water, goes on to the abbey, *and—*" He stopped completely, his face lit with joy, his eyes alive with delight: a master storyteller with the audience tearing and clawing to hear every last syllable.

"More coffee, Deborah?"

"Thank you, no."

"And what do you *think*?" Hank demanded.

St. James considered the question. He felt his wife's foot nudge his good leg. "What?" he dutifully responded.

"Damn if there wasn't a *real* baby there. A newborn with the cord still attached. Couldn't be more than a couple hours old. Deader'n a door knocker by the time the old priest got there. Exposure, they say."

"How dreadful." Deborah's face paled. "What a horrible thing!"

Hank nodded solemnly. "You're talking horrible, just think of poor Ezra! Bet he couldn't you-know-what for another two years!"

"Whose baby was it?"

Hank shrugged. He turned his attention to his now-cold breakfast. Clearly, the juicier elements of the story were the only ones that he had pursued.

"No one knows," JoJo answered. "They buried it in the

churchyard in the village. With the funniest epitaph on the poor little grave. I can't recall it, offhand. You'll have to go see it."

"They're newlyweds, Bean," Hank put in with a broad wink at St. James. "I bet they got plenty m-o-r-e on their minds than traipsing through graveyards."

Obviously, Lynley favoured the Russians. They'd begun with Rachmaninoff, moved to Rimsky-Korsakov, and were now slam-banging their way through the cannonades of the *1812* Overture.

"There. Did you notice it?" he asked her, once the music had crashed to its finale. "One of the cymbalists was just a counter-beat behind. But it's my only bone of contention with that particular recording of *1812*." He flipped the stereo off.

Barbara noticed for the first time that he wore absolutely no jewellery—no crested signet ring, no expensive wrist watch to flash gold richly when it caught the light. For some reason, that fact was as distracting to her as an unsightly display of opulent ornamentation would have been.

"I didn't catch it. Sorry. I don't know a lot about music." Did he really expect her—with her background—to be able to converse with him about classical music?

"I don't know much about it either," he admitted ingenuously. "I just listen to it a great deal. I'm afraid I'm one of those ignoramuses who say, 'I don't know a thing about it, but I know what I like.' "

She listened to his words with surprise. The man had a first in history, an Oxford education. Why in the world would he ever apply the word *ignoramus* to himself? Unless, of course, it was designed to put her at ease with a liberal dose of charm, something he was capable of doing quite well. It was effortless for him, as easy as breathing.

"I must have developed my liking for it during the very last part of my father's illness. It was always playing in the house when I could get away to see him." He paused, removed the tape, and the silence in the car became every bit as loud as the music had been, but far more disconcerting. It was some moments before he spoke again, and when he did, it was to pick up the thread of his original thought. "He simply wasted away to nothing. So much pain." He cleared his throat. "My mother wouldn't consider putting him into hospital. Even towards the end when it would have been so much easier on her, she wouldn't hear of it. She sat with him hour after hour, day and night, and watched him die by degrees. I think it was music that kept them both sane those last weeks." He kept his eyes on the road. "She held his hand and listened to Tchaikovsky. In the end he couldn't even speak. I've always liked to think the music did his speaking for him."

It was suddenly crucial to stop the direction the conversation was taking. Barbara gripped the stiff edges of the folded roadmap with dry, hot fingers and searched for another subject.

"You know that bloke Nies, don't you?" It blurted out badly, all too obviously an ill-concealed attempt to digress. She shot a wary look at him.

His eyes narrowed, but otherwise he gave no immediate reaction to the question. One hand merely dropped from the steering wheel. For a moment, Barbara thought, ridiculously, that he intended to use it to silence her, but he simply chose another tape at random and slid it into the stereo. He did not, however, turn the unit on. She stared out at the passing countryside, mortified.

"I'm surprised you don't know about it," he finally said.

"Know about what?"

He looked at her then. He appeared to be trying to read her face for insolence or sarcasm or perhaps a need to wound. Apparently satisfied with what he saw, he returned his eyes to the road.

"Just about five years ago, my brother-in-law, Edward Davenport, was murdered in his home north of Richmond. Superintendent Nies saw fit to arrest me. It wasn't a long ordeal, just a matter of a few days. But quite long enough." A glance at her again, a self-deprecatory smile. "You've not heard that story, Sergeant? It's nasty enough to make good cocktail party gossip."

"I . . . no . . . no, I'd not heard it. And anyway, I don't go to cocktail parties." She turned blindly to the window. "I should guess the turn-off is near. Perhaps three miles," she said uselessly.

She was shaken to the core. She could not have said why, did not want to think about it, and forced herself to study the scenery, refusing to be caught up in any further conversation with the man. Concentration on the land became imperative, and as she gave herself over to it, the country began its process of seduction upon her, for she was so used to the frenetic pace of London and the desperate grime of her neighbourhood in Acton that Yorkshire came as a bit of a shock.

The countryside was a thousand different shades of green, from the patchwork quilts of the cultivated land to the desolation of the open moors. The road dipped through dales where forests protected spotless villages and then climbed switchbacked curves to take them again up to the open land where the North Sea wind blew unforgivingly across heather and furze. Here, the only life belonged to the sheep. They wandered free and unfenced, unfettered by the ancient dry stone walls that constructed boundaries for their fellows in the dales below.

There were contradictions everywhere. In the cultivated areas, life burgeoned from every cranny and hedgerow, a thick vegetation that in another season would produce the mixed beauties of cow parsley, campion, vetch, and foxglove. It was an area where transportation was delayed while two dogs expertly herded a flock of plump sheep across pasture, down hillside, and along the road for a two-mile stroll into the centre of a village, directed only by the whistling of the shepherd who followed, his fate and the fate of the animals he owned left to the skill of the running dogs. And then suddenly, the plants, villages, magnificent oaks, elms, and chestnuts—this truly insubstantial pageant—faded to nothing in the glory of the moors.

Here, the cerulean sky exploded with clouds. It swept down to meet the rough, unconquered land. Earth and air: there was nothing else, save the sapient presence of the black-faced sheep, stalwart denizens of this lonely place.

"It's beautiful, isn't it?" Lynley asked after some minutes. "In spite of everything that's happened to me here, I still love Yorkshire. I think it's the loneliness here. The complete desolation."

Again Barbara resisted the confidence, the implicit message behind the words that here was a man who could understand. "It's very nice, sir. Not like anything I've ever seen. I think this is our turn."

The road to Keldale switched back and forth, taking them to

the deepest section of the dale. Moments after the turn, the woods closed in on them. Trees arched over the road, ferns grew thickly at its sides. They came to the village the way that Cromwell had come, and they found it as he had: deserted.

The ringing of St. Catherine's church bells told them immediately why there was no sign of life in the village. Upon the cessation of what Lynley was beginning to believe was surely Sayers' nine tailors, the church doors opened and the ancient building spewed forth its tiny congregation.

"At last," he murmured. He stood leaning against the car, thoughtfully surveying the village. He'd parked in front of Keldale Lodge, a trim little hostelry, heavily hung with ivy and multi-paned windows, from which he had a sweeping view in four directions. Taking it in, he concluded that there couldn't possibly have been a more unlikely spot on earth for a murder.

To the north was the narrow high street, flanked by grey stone buildings with tiled roofs and white woodwork containing the requisite elements for comfortable village life: a shoebox-sized post office; a nondescript greengrocer's; a shop advertising Lyons cakes on a rusty yellow sign and looking like the purveyor of everything from motor oil to baby food; a Wesleyan chapel wedged with delightful incongruity between Sarah's Tea Room and Sinji's Beauty Shoppe ("Pretty Curls Make Lovely Girls"). The pavement on either side of the street was raised only slightly off the road, and water pooled in front of doorways from the morning's rainfall. But the sky was clear now, and the air was so fresh that Lynley could taste its purity.

To the west, a road called Bishop Furthing led off towards farmland, enclosed on either side by the ubiquitous dry stone walls of the district. On its corner stood a tree-shaded cottage with a front door only steps from the street. It had an enclosed garden to one side from which the excited yelping of small dogs burst forth at regular intervals, as if someone were playing with them, rough and tumble. The building itself was labelled as inconspicuously as possible with the single word POLICE, blue letters on a white sign that stuck out from a window. Home of the archangel Gabriel, Lynley concluded, suppressing a smile.

To the south, two roads veered off from an overgrown two-bench common: Keldale Abbey Road, ostensibly leading to the same, and over the humped bridge that spanned the lazy movement of the River Kel, Church Street, with St. Catherine's built on a hillock on the corner. It, too, was surrounded by a low, stone wall, and imbedded into this was a World War I memorial plaque, the sombre commonality of every village in the nation.

To the east was the road down which they had wended their way to this bit of Yorkshire heaven. It had been deserted earlier, but now the bent form of a woman trudged up the incline, a scarf tucked into her black coat. Shod in heavy brogues and dazzling blue ankle socks, she carried a mesh bag over one arm. It dangled there limply, empty. On a Sunday afternoon, there was little hope of filling it with foodstuffs purchased at the grocer's, for everything was locked up tight, and even if it were not, she was heading in the wrong direction to be making a purchase: out of the village, back up towards the moors. A farmwife, perhaps, having made some delivery.

The village was surrounded by woods, by the upward slope of meadow, by the feeling of absolute security and peace. Once St. Catherine's bells ceased ringing, the birds took up, tittering from rooftops and trees. Somewhere, a fire had been lit and wood-smoke, just the ghost of its fragrance, was like a whisper in the air. It was hard to believe that three weeks past, a mile out of town, a man had been decapitated by his only daughter.

"Inspector Lynley? I hope I haven't kept you waiting long. I always lock up during church since there's no one else to watch the place. I'm Stepha Odell. I own the lodge."

At the sound of the voice, Lynley turned from his inspection of the village, but at the sight of her, his polite introduction died on his lips.

A tall, shapely woman—perhaps forty years old—stood before him. She was dressed for church in grey linen, a well-cut dress with a white collar. The rest of her was black: shoes, belt, handbag, and hat. Except for her hair, which was coppery red and fell to her shoulders. She was stunning.

He found his voice. "Thomas Lynley," he said idiotically. "This is Sergeant Havers."

"Do come in." Stepha Odell's voice was warm and pleasant.

"I've your rooms ready. You'll find us a quiet inn at this time of year."

There was a chill in the building they entered, an atmosphere produced by thick walls and stone floors. These were covered with a faded Axminster carpet. She led them into a tiny reception area, moving with a swift, unconscious grace, and produced an oversized register for them to sign. "You've been told I only do breakfast, haven't you?" she asked earnestly, as if satisfying hunger were the uppermost thing on his mind at this moment.

Do I look that desperate? "We'll manage, Mrs. Odell," Lynley said. *Tricky move, old boy. Transparent as hell.* Havers stood mute at his side, her face without expression.

"Miss," their hostess replied. "Stepha really. You can get meals at the Dove and Whistle on St. Chad's Lane or at the Holy Grail. Or if you want something special, there's Keldale Hall."

"The Holy Grail?"

She smiled. "The pub across from St. Catherine's."

"That name must certainly propitiate the abstinent gods."

"At least it does Father Hart. But he's been known to tip a pint or two in an evening there. Shall I show you your rooms?"

Without waiting for an answer, she led them up the crooked stairs, displaying, Lynley noted, a remarkably pretty pair of ankles above which rose an even prettier pair of legs. "You'll find us glad to have you in the village, Inspector," she stated as she opened the door to the first room and then with a gesture of her hand indicated the room next door with the unspoken message that it was up to them to decide who stayed where.

"That's helpful. I'm glad to hear it."

"We've none of us anything against Gabriel, you see. But he's not been a popular man round here since they carted Roberta off to the asylum."

6

LYNLEY WAS POSITIVELY white with rage, but there was not the slightest indication of that emotion in his voice. Barbara watched his performance on the telephone with grudging admiration. A virtuoso, she admitted.

"The name of the admitting psychiatrist? . . . There wasn't one? What a fascinating procedure. Then upon whose authority . . . When exactly did you expect me to stumble upon this information, Superintendent, since you've conveniently left it out of the report? . . . No, you've got things backwards, I'm afraid. You don't move a suspect to an institution without formal paperwork. . . . It's unfortunate that your police matron is on holiday, but you find a replacement. You don't move a nineteen-year-old girl into a mental hospital for the simple reason that she refuses to speak to anyone."

Barbara wondered if he would allow himself to explode, if he would show even a crack in that well-tailored Savile Row armour of his.

"I'm afraid that bathing daily is not the preeminent indication of unshakable sanity, either. . . . Don't pull rank on me, Superintendent. If this is any indication of the manner in which you've handled this case, there's no wonder to me that Kerridge is after your skin. . . . Who's her solicitor? . . . Shouldn't you be getting her one yourself, then? . . . Don't tell me what you have no intention of doing. I've been brought in on this case and henceforth it shall be conducted correctly. Am I being quite clear? Now please listen carefully. You have exactly two hours to get everything to me in Keldale: every warrant, every paper, every deposition, every note that was taken by every officer on this case. Do you understand? Two hours . . . Webberly. W-e-b-b-e-r-l-y. Phone him then and have done with it." Stone-faced, Lynley handed the telephone back to Stepha Odell.

She replaced it behind the reception counter and ran a finger along the receiver several times before looking up. "Should I have said nothing?" she asked, a trace of anxiety in her voice. "I don't want to cause trouble between you and your superiors."

Lynley flipped open his pocket watch and checked the time. "Nies is not my superior. And yes, you should have told me. Thank you for doing so. You saved me a needless trip to Richmond that no doubt Nies was longing to force me to make."

Stepha didn't pretend to understand. Instead, she gestured vaguely to a door on their right. "I . . . May I offer you a drink, Inspector? You as well, Sergeant? We've got a real ale that, as Nigel Parrish is fond of saying, 'sets you to rights.' Come this way.

She led them into a typical English country inn lounge, whose air was heavy with the scent of a recent fire. The room had been cleverly designed with enough home-like qualities to keep residents comfortable while maintaining a formal enough atmosphere to keep villagers out. There were a variety of plump, chintz-covered couches and chairs decorated with petit point pillows; tables spread out in no particular arrangement were maple, well used and ringed on their tops where too many glasses had been placed on the wood without protection; the carpet was a floral design, patchy with darker colours in some sections where furniture had recently been moved; suitably tedious prints hung on the walls: riding to hounds, a day at Newmarket, a view of the village. But behind the bar at the far side of the room and over the fireplace were two watercolours that displayed a distinctive talent and remarkable taste. Both were views of a ruined abbey.

Lynley wandered to one of these as Stepha worked behind the bar. "This is lovely," he remarked. "A local artist?"

"A young man named Ezra Farmington does them," she replied. "They're of our abbey. Those two are how he paid for his board here one autumn. He lives in the village permanently now."

Barbara watched the redheaded woman deftly work the taps and scoop the foam from the churning brew that was developing a life of its own in the glass. Stepha laughed in a breathless, charming way when the foam slipped over the side and onto her hand, and she unconsciously raised her fingers to her lips to lick the residue. Barbara idly wondered how long it would take Lynley to get her into bed.

"Sergeant?" Stepha asked. "An ale for you as well?"

"Tonic water, if you have it," Barbara replied. She looked out the window. On the common, the old priest who had been to see them in London was having an anxious conversation with another man. From the gesturing and pointing at the silver Bentley, the news of their arrival was apparently the topic of the village. A woman crossed from the bridge to join them. She was wispy-looking, an effect produced by a dress too gauzy for the season and by baby-fine hair which the smallest air current ruffled. She rubbed her arms for warmth, and, rather than joining in the conversation of the two men, she merely listened as if waiting for one or the other of them to walk off. In a moment, the priest said a few final words and meandered back towards the church. The other two remained standing together. Their conversation went in fits and starts, with the man saying something with a quick look at the woman and then away and the woman replying briefly. There were long silences in which the woman looked at the bank of the river next to the common and the man focused his attention on the lodge—or perhaps the car in front of it. Someone was significantly interested in the arrival of the police, Barbara decided.

"A tonic water and an ale," Stepha was saying as she placed both glasses on the bar. "It's a home brew, my father's recipe. We call it Odell's. You must tell me what you think of it, Inspector."

It was a rich, brown liquid shot through with gold. "Has a bit of a kick, doesn't it?" Lynley said when he tasted it. "Are you sure you won't have one, Havers?"

"Just the tonic water, thank you, sir."

He joined her at the couch in front of which he had earlier spilled out the contents of the report on the Teys murder and had icily flipped through every paper looking for the explanation of Roberta Teys' placement in Barnstingham Mental Asylum. There had been none. That had set him off on the telephone to Richmond. Now he began to go through the paperwork again, stacking things in categorical fashion. From the bar, Stepha Odell watched them with friendly interest, sipping an ale that she'd poured for herself.

"We've got the original warrants, the forensics report, the signed depositions, the photographs." Lynley fingered the materials as he named them. He looked up at Barbara. "No keys to the farmhouse. *Damn* the man."

"Richard has a set of those if you need them," Stepha said quickly, as if hoping to make up for her remark about Roberta that had set Lynley off on a collision course with the Richmond police in the first place. "Richard Gibson. He was . . . is William Teys' nephew. He lives in the council cottages on St. Chad's Lane. It's just off the high street."

Lynley looked up. "How does he come to have keys to the farmhouse?"

"Having arrested Roberta . . . well, I suppose they just gave them to Richard. He's to inherit it anyway once the estate's all settled," she added. "In William's will. I suppose he's seeing to the place in the meantime. Someone must."

"He's to inherit? How was Roberta treated in the will?"

Stepha gave the bar a thoughtful sweep with a cloth. "It was fixed between Richard and William that the farm would go to Richard. It was a sensible arrangement. He works there with William. . . . Worked there," she corrected herself, "ever since he returned to Keldale two years ago. Once they got over their row about Roberta, it all worked out to everyone's advantage. William had someone to help him, Richard had a job and a future, and Roberta had a place to live for life."

"Sergeant." Lynley nodded at her notebook, which was lying unused next to her tonic water. "If you would please . . ."

Stepha flushed as she saw Barbara reach for her pen. "Is this an interview then?" she asked, flashing an anxious smile. "I don't know how much I can help you, Inspector."

"Tell us about the row and Roberta."

She came round the bar and joined them, pulling a comfortable, cushioned chair to the other side of the table. She sat down, tucking her legs to one side, and glanced at the stack of photographs in front of her. She looked away quickly.

"I'll tell you what I can, but it isn't much. Olivia's the one who can tell you more."

"Olivia Odell . . . your . . ."

"Sister-in-law. My brother Paul's widow." Stepha placed her glass of ale on the table and used the same movement to cover the photographs with a pile of forensic reports. "If you don't mind . . ."

"Sorry," Lynley said quickly. "We get so used to looking at horrors like that that we become immune." He replaced it all in the folder. "Why did they have a row about Roberta?"

"Olivia told me later—she was with them at the Dove and Whistle when it happened—that it was all due to the way Roberta looks." She fingered her glass, made a pattern of lace on the moisture of its surface. "Richard's from Keldale, you see, but he'd been gone a good few years trying his luck with barley in the fens. He'd married down there, had two children as well. When the farming didn't work out, he returned to the Kel." She smiled at them. "They say that the Kel never lets one go easily, and that was the case for Richard. He was gone for eight or nine years and, when he returned, he was quite a bit shocked to see the change in Roberta."

"You said it was all due to the way she looks?"

"She didn't always look as she does now. She was always a big girl, of course, even at eight when Richard left. But she was never . . ." Stepha hesitated, clearly searching delicately for the right word, for a euphemism that would be factual at the same time as it was noncommittal.

"Obese," Barbara finished. *Like a cow.*

"Yes," Stepha went on gratefully. "Richard had always been great friends with Roberta, for all he's twelve years her senior. And to come back and find his cousin so sadly deteriorated— physically, I mean, she was much the same otherwise—was a terrible shock to him. He blamed William for ignoring the girl. Said she had done it to herself to try to get his attention. William raged at that. Olivia said she'd never seen him so angry. Poor man, there'd been problems enough in his life without an accusation like that from his own nephew. But they got it sorted out. Richard apologised the very next day. William wouldn't take Roberta to a doctor—he wouldn't bend that far—but Olivia found a diet for the girl, and from that time on, all went well."

"Until three weeks ago," Lynley observed.

"If you choose to believe that Roberta killed her father, then yes, it all went well until three weeks back. But I don't believe she killed him. Not for one *blessed* moment."

Lynley looked surprised at the force behind her words. "Why not?"

"Because aside from Richard—who heaven knows has enough trouble just dealing with that family of his own—William was all that Roberta had. Besides her reading and dreams, there was only her father."

"She'd no friends her own age? No other girls nearby on the farms or in the village?"

Stepha shook her head. "She kept to herself. When she wasn't working on the farm with her father, mostly she read. She was here every day for the *Guardian*, in fact, for years on end. They never did take a paper on the farm, so she'd come every afternoon once everyone'd seen it and we'd let her take it home with her. I think she'd read every book of her mother's in the house, all of Marsha Fitzalan's, and the newspaper was the only thing left for her. We've no lending library, you see." She frowned down at the glass in her hands. "She stopped looking at the paper a few years back, though. When my brother died. I couldn't help thinking . . ." Her grey-blue eyes darkened. "That perhaps Roberta was in love with Paul. After he died four years ago, we saw nothing of the girl for quite some time. And she never came again to ask for the *Guardian*."

If a village as small as Keldale could even have an undesirable area out of which residents aspired to escape, St. Chad's Lane would have been that spot. It was more like an alley than a street, an unpaved thoroughfare to nowhere, having the one distinction of a pub on the corner. This was the Dove and Whistle, its doors and woodwork painted a blinding shade of purple, itself looking very much as if it wished it could have had the good fortune to be settled somewhere—anywhere—else.

Richard Gibson and his brood lived in the last attached house in this lane, a pinched stone building with chipped window sashes and a front door that had once been painted royal blue but now was fading to a decided grey. This stood open to the late afternoon, mindless of the rapidly dropping temperature in the dale, and from within the confines of the tiny house came the noise of a family quarrelling passionately.

"God damn you, *do* something with him, then. He's your son as well. Jesus Christ! You'd think he was a miraculous little version of virgin birth from all the interest you take in his up-bringing!" It was a woman speaking, a shrieking that sounded as if at any moment it would choose hysteria or cachinnation as a second line of attack.

A man's voice rumbled in answer, indistinguishable in the general uproar.

"Oh, it *will* be better then? That's a fine laugh, Dick. When you've the whole bleeding farm to use as an excuse? Just like last night! You couldn't wait to get there, could you? So don't tell me about the farm! We'll *never* see you then when you've five hundred acres to hide in!"

Lynley rapped sharply with the rust-grimed knocker on the open door, and the scene froze before them.

With a plate on his knee, obviously attempting to eat some sort of utterly unappetising afternoon meal, a man sat on a sagging couch in a cramped sitting room while in front of him a woman stood, her arm upraised, a hairbrush in her hand. Both stared at the unexpected visitors.

"You've caught us at our very best moment. It was straight to bed next," Richard Gibson said.

The Gibsons were a portrait of contrasts: the man was enormous, nearly six and a half feet, with black hair, swarthy skin, and sardonic, brown eyes. He was bull-necked, with the thick limbs of a labourer. His wife, on the other hand, was a scrap of a blonde, sharp-featured and, at the moment, white to the lips with rage. But there was an electricity in the air between them that gave credence to what the man had said. Here was a relationship where every argument and discussion was merely a skirmish before the major battle of who would be master between the sheets. And the answer to that, judging from what Lynley and Havers could see before them, was clearly a toss-up.

Shooting a final, smouldering look at her husband that spoke of desire as much as rage, Madeline Gibson left the room, slamming the kitchen door behind her. The big man chuckled when she was gone.

"Eight stone of tiger," he commented, getting to his feet. "One hell of a woman." He extended a large paw. "Richard Gibson," he said genially. "You must be Scotland Yard." When Lynley had made the introductions, Gibson went on. "Sundays are always the worst round here." He jerked his head towards the kitchen, from which a steady wailing indicated the state of the relationship between mother and what sounded like fourteen children. "Roberta used to help out. But we're without her now. Of course, you know that. That's why you've come." He hospitably indicated two antiquated chairs that were belching stuffing onto the floor. Lynley and Havers picked their way across the room to them, avoiding broken toys, scattered newspapers, and at least three plates of half-consumed food that lay on the bare floor. Somewhere, a glass of milk had been left too long in the room, for its sour smell overcame even the other odours of poorly cooked food and plumbing gone bad.

"You've inherited the farm, Mr. Gibson," Lynley began. "Will you move there soon?"

"It can't be soon enough for me. I'm not sure my marriage can survive another month of this place." Gibson toed his plate away from the couch. A scrawny cat slid out of nowhere, sniffed at the dried bread and pungent sardines, and rejected the offering by attempting to bury it. Gibson watched the animal, his face amused.

"You've lived here several years, haven't you?"

"Two to be exact. Two years, four months, and two days, to be even more precise. I could probably get it down to the hours as well, but you get the idea."

"I couldn't help overhearing the fact that your wife doesn't seem to be enthused about the Teys farm."

Gibson laughed. "You're well bred, Inspector Lynley. I like that sort of thing when the police come calling." He ran his hands through his thick hair, looked at the floor beneath his feet, and found a bottle of ale that, in the general confusion, had become positioned precariously against the side of the couch. He picked it up and drained it before going on, wiping his mouth on the back of his hand. It was the gesture of a man used to taking his meals out in the fields. "No. Madeline wants the fens again. She wants the open spaces, the water and the sky. But I can't give that to her. So I've got to give her what I can." Gibson's eyes flicked over Sergeant Havers, who kept her head bent over her notebook. "Sound like the words of a man who would kill his uncle, don't they?" he asked pleasantly.

Hank finally caught up with them in the novices' room. St. James looked up from kissing his wife—her skin smelled intoxicatingly of lilies, her fingers moved silkily through his hair, her murmured "my love" against his mouth fired his blood—and there was the American, grinning wickedly down at them from his perch on the wall of the day room.

"Cotcha." Hank winked.

St. James contemplated murder. Deborah gasped in surprise. Hank hopped down, unbidden, to join them. "Hey, Bean," he shouted. "Found the lovebirds in here."

JoJo Watson appeared only moments later, struggling through the doorway in the ruined abbey, teetering dangerously on high heels. Round her neck, as a complement to the chains and trinkets, hung an Instamatic camera.

"Taking some shots," Hank said in explanation, nodding towards the camera. "A few minutes more and we'd've had a few sweet ones-a you!" He snorted with laughter, slapping St. James affectionately on the shoulder. "Don't blame you a bit, fella! If she belonged to me, I couldn't keep my mitts off her." He gave brief attention to his wife. "Dammit, Bean, be careful, woman! Break your neck in this place." He turned back to the other two and noticed Deborah's equipment—camera case, tripod, discarded lenses. "Hey, you taking shots, too? Got sidetracked, huh? That's honeymooners for you. Come on down here, Bean. Join the party."

"Back from Richmond so soon?" St. James finally managed

to ask with strangled courtesy. Deborah, he noted, was surreptitiously trying to straighten her clothes. Her eyes met his, full of laughter and mischief, alive with desire. What in God's name were the Americans doing here *now*?

"Well," Hank admitted as JoJo reached them at last, "I gotta tell you, fella, Richmond wasn't quite everything that you promised it'd be. Not that we didn't get a bang outa the drive. Whatsay, JoJo-bean? Didn't we love it?"

"Hank loves driving on the wrong side of the road," JoJo explained. Her nose twitched. Her eyes caught the exchange of looks between the two younger people. "Hank, why don't we take a nice, long walk toward Bishop Furthing Road? Wouldn't that be a sweet way to end the afternoon?" She put her bejewelled hand on her husband's arm, attempting to draw him out onto the abbey grounds.

"Hellsapoppin, no," Hank answered pleasantly. "I have done e-n-u-f-f *walking* on this trip to last me a lifetime." He cocked his head at St. James shrewdly. "That was some m-a-p you gave us, fella! If the Bean here wasn't so fast at reading road signs, we'd be in Edinburgh by now." He pronounced it Ed-in-berg. "Well, there's no harm done, is there? We got here in time to show you the death hole itself."

There was nothing for it but to go along. "Death hole?" Deborah enquired. She had knelt and was replacing her equipment —forgotten for a few moments in the lovely blue of Simon's eyes—in its case.

"The baby, remember?" Hank said patiently. "Although considering what you two's up to in here, I can see the baby story didn't exactly scare the livin' hell outa you, did it?" He winked lasciviously.

"Ah, the baby," St. James responded. He picked up Deborah's case.

"Now I got your interest!" Hank approved. "I could tell at first you mighta been a little peeved at me popping in on you like that. But now I got you, I can tell."

"Yes, indeed," Deborah responded, but her thoughts were elsewhere. Curious, how it had all happened in a moment. She loved him, had loved him from her childhood. But in a dizzying lightning bolt moment of time, she'd realized that it had changed somehow, becoming quite different between them from what it had been before. He'd all of a sudden become not that gentle Simon whose tender presence had filled her heart with joy but a whip-bodied lover whose very look aroused her. Good heavens, Deborah, you've become quite silly with lust, she thought.

St. James heard his wife's bubble of laughter. "Deborah?" he asked.

Hank nudged him in the ribs with a knowing elbow. "Don't worry about the bride," he confided. "They're all shy at first." He strutted on ahead like Stanley with Livingston in sight, pointing out areas of interest to his wife with a "Catch that, Bean. Get it in the lens!"

"Sorry, my love," St. James murmured as they followed the progress of the other two through the ruined day room, across court and warming house and into the cloister. "I thought I had him taken care of until midnight at least. Five minutes more and I'm afraid he would have caught me getting you into some truly serious trouble."

"What a thought!" she laughed. "Oh, Simon, what if he had! He would have shouted, 'Get it in the lens, Bean!' and our love life might have been destroyed forever!" Her eyes danced and sparkled. Her hair gleamed brightly in the afternoon sun, blowing about her throat and shoulders carelessly.

St. James drew in a sharp breath. It was like a pain. "I don't think so," he said evenly.

The death hole was in what remained of the vestry. This was no more than a narrow roofless hallway, overgrown with grass and wildflowers, just beyond the south transept of the ancient church. Here, a series of four arched recesses lined the wall, and it was to these that Hank pointed with ghoulish drama.

"In one-a *them*," he announced. "Get it in the lens, Bean." He tromped through the grass and posed toothily. "Seems this was the place where the monks kept their church duds. Sorta a cupboard or something. And on the night in question, the baby was plopped right in and left to die. Pretty sickening when you think about it, huh?" He bounced back to their sides. "Just the right size for a kid, though," he added thoughtfully. "Like a what-daya-call-it? Sacrificial offering."

"I'm not sure the Cistercian monks were in that line of business," St. James commented. "And human sacrifices have been out of fashion for a good number of years."

"Well, whatdaya think, then? Whose baby was it?"

"I couldn't even begin to guess," St. James replied, knowing full well the theory was forthcoming.

"Then lemme tell you how it happened, because the Bean and I figgered it out the first day. Didn't we, Bean?" A wait for the woman to nod her head loyally. "Come on over here. Lemme show you two lovebirds a thing or two."

Hank led them through the south transept, across the uneven paving of the presbytery, and out onto the abbey grounds through a gap in the wall. "There you have it!" He pointed triumphantly to a narrow track that led to the north through the woods.

"I see indeed," St. James replied.

"Got it figgered out too?"

"Ah, no."

Hank hooted. "Sure you don't. That's 'cause you haven't thought it through like me 'n' the Bean have, right, Sugarplum?" Sugarplum nodded mournfully, moving her bunny eyes from St. James to Deborah in silent contrition. "Gypsies!" her spouse went on. "Okay, okay, I admit it. Bean and I didn't get the full handle on this till we saw them today. You know who I mean. Those trailers parked on the side-a the road. Well, we figgered out that there musta been some-a the same here that night. It had to be a baby-a theirs."

"I understand gypsies are inordinately fond of their children," St. James noted drily.

"Well, not-a *this* kid, anyway," Hank replied, undeterred. "So get the pitcher here, fella. Danny and Ezra are over there somewhere"—he waved vaguely in the direction from which they had come—"getting ready for the plunge, you know? And tippy-toeing along this path comes some old crone with a kid."

"Old crone?"

"Well sure, don't you see it?"

" 'Ditch-delivered,' no doubt," St. James said.

"Ditch-who?" Hank shrugged off the literary allusion like lint from his coat. "The old crone looks around, right and left," Hank demonstrated, "and slips into the abbey. Looks around for a deposit box and bingo, Bob's-yer-uncle."

"It certainly is an interesting theory," Deborah put in. "But I always feel just a bit sorry for the gypsies. They seem to get blamed for everything, don't they?"

"*That*, little bride, brings me right on up to theory number two."

JoJo-bean blinked her apologies.

Gembler Farm was in excellent condition, a fact unsurprising since Richard Gibson had continued to work it throughout the three weeks since his uncle's death. Opening the well-oiled gates that hung between two stone posts, Lynley and Havers entered and surveyed it.

It would be quite an inheritance. To their left stood the farmhouse, an old building constructed from the common brown bricks of the district, with freshly painted white woodwork and frail clematis conscientiously trimmed and trellised over windows and door. It was set back from Gembler Road, and a well-tended garden, fenced to keep out the sheep, separated the two. Next to the house was a low outbuilding, and, forming another side to the quadrangle that comprised the yard, the barn loomed to their right.

Like the house, it was constructed of brick with a heavily tiled roof. It was two floors high, with gaping windows on the second floor through which the tops of ladders could be seen. Dutch doors were used on the ground level of the barn, for this was a building for tools and animals only. Vehicles would be kept in the outbuilding to the far side of the house.

They walked across the well-swept yard, and Lynley inserted a key into the rusting lock that hung on the barn door. It swung noiselessly open. Inside, it was eerily still, dim, musty, and overcold, too much the place where a man had met a violent end.

"Quiet," Havers observed. She hesitated at the door while Lynley entered.

"Hmm," he responded from the third stall. "Expect that's due to the sheep."

"Sir?"

He looked up at her from where he had squatted on the pock-marked stone floor. She was quite pale. "Sheep, Sergeant," he said. "They're in the upper meadow, remember? That's why it's so quiet. Have a look here, will you?" Seeing that she was reluctant to approach, he added, "You were right."

She came forward at that and passed her eyes over the stall. At the far end was heaped a mouldy pile of hay. To the centre was a not overlarge pool of dried blood—brown, not red. There was nothing else.

"Right, sir?" Havers asked.

"Dead on the button, if you'll pardon the expression. Not a drop of blood on the walls. I don't think we had any body-slinging here. No crime-scene arrangement done after the fact. Nice thinking, Havers." He looked up in time to see the surprise on her face.

She reddened in confusion. "Thank you, sir."

He stood up and directed his attention back to the stall. The overturned bucket upon which Roberta had been sitting when the priest found her was still in its place. The hay into which the head had rolled remained untouched. The pool of dried blood had scraping marks from the forensic team and the axe was gone, but otherwise everything remained as it had been originally photographed. Except for the bodies. *The bodies.* Good God. Feeling like the fool Nies intended him to be, Lynley gaped numbly at the outer edge of the stain where a heelprint matted several black and white hairs into the coagulated blood. He swung to Havers.

"The *dog*," he said.

"Inspector?"

"Havers, what in God's name did Nies do with the dog?"

Her eyes went to the same heelprint, saw the same hairs. "It was in the report, wasn't it?"

"It *wasn't*," he replied with a muttered curse and knew that he was going to have to drag every scrap of information out of Nies as if he were a surgeon probing for shrapnel. It would be absolute hell. "Let's look at the house," he said grimly.

They entered as the family would, through an enclosed porch-like hallway in which old coats and mackintoshes hung on pegs and workboots stood beneath a single-plank bench along the wall. The house had gone unheated for three weeks, so the air was tomb-like. A car rumbled past on Gembler Road, but the sound was muffled and distant.

The hall took them immediately into the kitchen. It was a large room, with a red linoleum floor, dark ash cabinets, and brilliantly white appliances that looked as if they were still polished daily. Nothing whatsoever was out of place. Not a dish was out of a single cupboard; not a crumb lay on a single work top; not a stain marred the surface of the white, cast iron sink. In the centre of the room stood a worktable of unpainted pine, its top scarred with the slashings of thousands of knives cutting thousands of vegetables, with the discolouration of generations of cooking.

"No wonder Gibson is eager for the place," Lynley remarked as he looked it over. "Certainly a far cry from St. Chad's Lane."

"Did you believe him, sir?" Havers asked.

Lynley paused in his inspection of the cupboards. "That he was in bed with his wife when Teys was killed? Considering the nature of their relationship, it's a credible alibi, wouldn't you say?"

"I . . . I suppose so, sir."

He glanced at her. "But you don't believe it."

"It's only that . . . well, she looked like she was lying. Like she was angry with him as well. Or maybe angry with us."

Lynley considered Havers' statement. Madeline Gibson had indeed spoken to them grudgingly, spitting the words out with barely a glance of corroboration at her husband. For his part, the farmer had smoked stolidly during her recitation, a blank expression of disinterest on his face but, unmistakably, a lurking touch of amusement behind his dark eyes. "There's something not quite right there, I'll agree. Let's go through here."

They went through a heavy door into the dining room, where a mahogany table was covered with clean, cream-coloured lace. On it, yellow roses in a vase had long since died, weeping petals onto the fret of the cloth. A matching sideboard stood to one side with a silver epergne placed in its exact centre, as if someone with a measuring tool had made certain it was equidistant from each end. A china cabinet held a beautiful collection of dishes obviously unused by the inhabitants of the house. They were antique Belleek pieces, each one stacked or tilted or turned in some way to display it best. As in the kitchen, nothing was out of place. Save for the flowers, they might have been wandering through a museum.

It was across the hall from the dining room, however, where they first found signs of the life of the house. For here in the sitting room the Teys had kept their shrine.

Havers preceded Lynley into the room, but at the sight she cried out involuntarily, and stepped back quickly, one arm raised as if to ward off a blow.

"Something wrong, Sergeant?" Lynley inspected the room to see what had startled her, observing nothing but furniture and a collection of photographs in one corner.

"Excuse me. I think . . ." She produced an unnatural grimace to pass for a smile. "Sorry, sir. I . . . I think I must be hungry or something. A little light-headed. I'm fine." She walked to the corner of the room in which the photographs hung, before which the candles rested, underneath which the flowers died. "This must be the mother," she said. "Quite a tribute."

Lynley joined her at a three-cornered table that backed into the wall. "Beautiful girl," he replied softly, studying the pictures. "She really wasn't much more than that, was she? Look at the wedding picture. She looks as if she were ten years old! Such a little creature."

It was unspoken between them. How had she produced a cow like Roberta?

"Don't you think it's a bit . . ." Havers paused and he glanced at her. She clasped her hands stiffly behind her. "I mean, if he was planning to marry Olivia, sir."

Lynley set down what was obviously the final portrait of the woman. She looked about twenty-four: a fresh, smiling face; golden freckles sprinkled across the bridge of her nose; long, gleaming blonde hair tied back and curled. Beguiling. He stepped back from the collection.

"It's as if Teys established a new religion in the corner of this room," he said. "Macabre, wouldn't you agree?"

"I . . ." She tore her eyes from the picture. "Yes, sir."

Lynley turned his attention to the rest of the room. Everyday living had gone on in it. There were a comfortably worn couch, several chairs, a rack holding numerous magazines, a television set, and a woman's escritoire. Lynley opened this. Neatly stacked stationery, a tin of postage stamps, three unpaid bills. He glanced at them: a chemist's receipt for Teys' sleeping pills, the electricity, the telephone. He looked at the last, but there was nothing of interest. No long distance calls. Everything neat and clean.

Beyond the sitting room was a small library-office and they opened the door to this, looked at each other in surprise, and walked into the room. Three of the four walls had shelves that climbed to the ceiling, and every shelf was littered with books. Books stacked. Books piled. Books falling loosely to one side. Books standing up at rigid attention. Books everywhere.

"But Stepha Odell said—"

"That there was no lending library so Roberta came for the newspaper," Lynley finished. "She'd read all of her own books—how was *that* possible?—and all of Marsha Fitzalan's. Who, by the way, is Marsha Fitzalan?"

"Schoolteacher," Havers responded. "She lives on St. Chad's Lane. Next door to the Gibsons."

"Thank you," Lynley murmured, inspecting the shelves. He put on his spectacles. "Hmm. A bit of everything. But heavily into the Brontës, weren't they?"

Havers joined him. "Austen," she read, "Dickens, bit of Lawrence. They went in for the classics." She pulled down *Pride and Prejudice* and opened it. *Tessa's!* was scrawled childishly across the flyleaf. This same declaration was in Dickens and Shakespeare, two Norton anthologies, and all the Brontës.

Lynley moved to a book stand that was fixed underneath the room's only window. It was the kind used for large dictionaries, but on its top rested an immense, illuminated Bible. He ran his fingers down the page to which the book was open. " 'I am Joseph your brother, whom ye sold into Egypt,' " he read. " 'Now therefore be not grieved, nor angry with yourselves, that ye sold me hither. For God did send me before you to preserve life. For these two years hath the famine been in the land: and yet there are five years, in the which there shall neither be earing nor harvest. And God sent me before you to preserve you a posterity in the earth, and to save your lives by a great deliverance.' " He looked up at Havers.

"I'll never understand why he forgave his brothers," she said. "After what they'd done to him, they deserved to die."

The bitterness behind her words burned. He closed the book

slowly, marking the place with a scrap of paper from the desk. "But he had something they needed."

"Food," she scoffed.

He removed his spectacles. "I don't think it had anything at all to do with food. Not really," he noted. "What's above stairs?"

The second floor of the house was simple: four bedrooms, lavatory, bathroom, all opening off a central, square landing illuminated by a skylight of opaque glass. An obvious modernisation to the house, this last architectural feature gave the effect of being in a greenhouse. Not altogether unpleasant, but unusual on a farm.

The room on their right appeared to be a guest room. A neatly made, pink-counterpaned bed, a rather smallish affair considering the size of the house's occupants, stood against one wall on a rug printed with a design of roses and ferns. It was obviously quite old, and the once brilliant reds and greens were muted now, bleeding one into the other in a soothing rust. The walls were hung with paper on which tiny flowers—daisies and marigolds —sprinkled down. On the bedside table a small lamp stood upon a circle of lace. The chest of drawers held nothing, as did the wardrobe.

"Reminds me of a room in an inn," Lynley remarked.

Barbara noted the view from the window: an uninteresting panorama of the barn and the yard. "Looks as if no one's ever used it."

Lynley was examining the counterpane across the bed. He pulled it back to reveal a badly stained mattress and a yellowing pillow. "No guests expected here. Odd to leave a bed unmade, wouldn't you say?"

"Not at all. Why put sheets on it if it's never going to be used?"

"Except that—"

"Look, shall I go on to the next room, Inspector?" Barbara asked impatiently. The house was oppressing her.

Lynley glanced up at the tone of her voice. He drew the counterpane back over the bed exactly as it had been placed before and sat on the edge. "What is it, Barbara?" he asked.

"Nothing," she replied, but she heard the edge of panic in her voice. "I'd just like to get on with it. This room obviously hasn't been used in years. Why examine every inch of it like Sherlock Holmes, as if the murderer were going to pop out of the floorboards?"

He didn't reply at once, so the shrillness of her voice seemed to linger in the room long after she had spoken. "What's wrong?" he repeated. "May I help?" His eyes were on her, dark with their concern, so infinitely kind. It would indeed be easy—

"There's nothing wrong!" she exploded. "I just don't want to have to follow you around like a spaniel dog. I don't know what you expect of me. I feel like an idiot. I've a *brain*, goddammit! Give me something to do!"

He got to his feet, his eyes still on her. "Why don't you go across the landing and deal with the next room," he suggested.

She opened her mouth to say more, decided against it, and left him, pausing for a moment in the greenish light of the landing. She could hear her own breathing, harsh and loud, and knew he must be able to hear it as well.

That damnable shrine! The farm itself was bad enough with its ghastly lifelessness, but the shrine had completely unnerved her. It had been set up in the very finest corner of the room. With a view of the garden, Barbara thought weakly. Tony has the telly and she has the damn garden!

What had Lynley called it? A religion. Yes, sweet Jesus! A temple to Tony! She compelled her breathing to return to normal, crossed the landing, and went into the next room.

That's torn it, Barb, she told herself. What happened to agreement, to obedience, to cooperation? How will you feel back in uniform next week?

She looked about furiously, her lips quivering in disgust. Well, who bloody well cared? After all, it was a preordained failure. Had she really expected this to be a success?

She crossed the room to the window and fumbled with the latch. What had he said? *What is it? May I help?* The insanity was that for just a moment, she had actually thought about talking to him, about telling him everything there was to tell. But, of course, it was unthinkable. No one could help, least of all Lynley.

She unlocked the window, threw it open to feel the fresh air on her burning cheeks, then turned back, determined to do her job.

This was Roberta's room, neat like the other, but with a lived-in air about it. A large four-poster was covered by a quilt, a patchwork affair with a bright, cheerful design of sun, clouds, and rainbow on a sapphire background sky. Clothes hung in the wardrobe. Sturdy shoes—work shoes, walking shoes, slippers—stood lined beneath them. There were a dressing table with a wavy cheval glass, and a chest of drawers on which a framed photograph lay, face down, as if it had toppled over. Barbara glanced at it curiously. Mother, father, and a newborn Roberta in the father's arms. But the picture itself, slightly distended, was crowded into its frame as if it didn't quite fit. She turned the frame in her hands and prised off the backing.

She was correct in her guess. The photograph *had* been too large for the purchased frame, so it had been folded back. Unfolded, the picture was very much different, for to the left of the father, hands clasped behind her, stood the mirror image of the baby's mother, a smaller version, certainly, but undoubtedly the offspring of Tessa Teys.

Barbara was about to call out to Lynley when he came to the door, a photograph album in his hands. He paused as if trying to decide how to get their relationship back in order.

"I've found the strangest thing, Sergeant," he said.

"As have I," she replied, as determined as he to forget her outburst. They exchanged their items.

"Yours explains mine, I dare say," Lynley remarked.

She gave curious attention to the open pages of the album. It was a pictorial family record, the kind that documents weddings and births, Christmas, Easter, and birthdays. But every picture that had more than one child in it had been cut up in some way, oddly defaced, so that pictures had central slices missing or wedges cut into them, and the size of the family was systematically reduced in every one. The effect was chilling.

"A sister of Tessa's, I'd say," Lynley observed.

"Perhaps her first child," Barbara offered.

"Surely she's too old to be a first child unless Tessa produced her when she was a child herself." He set the frame down, slipped the photograph into his pocket, and turned his attention to the drawers. "Ah," he said, "at least we know why Roberta was so anxious for the *Guardian*. She's lined her drawers with it. And . . . Havers, look at this." From the bottom drawer, beneath a pile of worn jerseys, he pulled something which had been placed face down, hidden. "The mystery girl once again."

Barbara looked at the photograph he handed to her. It was the same girl, but older this time, a teenager. She and Roberta were standing in the snow in St. Catherine's churchyard, both grinning at the camera. The older girl had her hands on Roberta's shoulders, pulling her back against her. She had bent over—although certainly not far, for Roberta was nearly as tall as she—and had pressed her cheek to the other girl's. Her dark gold hair touched Roberta's brown curls. In front of them, with Roberta's hand clutched into his fur, was a border collie who looked very much as if he were grinning as well. Whiskers.

"Roberta doesn't look half bad there," Barbara said, handing the picture to Lynley. "Big, but not fat."

"Then this must have been taken sometime before Gibson left. Remember what Stepha said? She'd not been fat then, not until Richard was gone." He pocketed the additional photograph and looked round the room. "Anything else?" he asked.

"Clothes in the wardrobe. Nothing much of interest." As he had done in the other room, she drew back the quilt from the bed. Unlike the other, however, this bed was made, and its fresh, laundered linen gave off the scent of jasmine. But underneath it, as if the jasmine were incense subtly burning to hide the odour of cannabis, was the cloying smell of something more. Barbara looked at Lynley. "Do you—"

"Absolutely," he replied. "Help me pull off the mattress."

She did so, covering her mouth and nose when the stench filled the room and they saw what lay beneath the old mattress. The boxspring covering had been cut away in the far corner of the bed, and resting within was a storehouse of food. Rotting fruit, bread grey with mould, biscuits and candy, pastries half-eaten, bags of crisps.

"Oh, Jesus," Barbara murmured. It was more prayer than ex-clamation and, in spite of the catalogue of gruesome sights she had seen as a member of the force, her stomach heaved uneasily and she backed away. "Sorry," she gasped with a shaky laugh. "Bit of a surprise."

Lynley dropped the mattress back into place. His face was expressionless. "It's sabotage," he said to himself.

"Sir?"

"Stepha said something about a diet."

As Barbara had done before, Lynley walked to the window. Evening was drawing on, and in a fading patch of the dying light he withdrew the photographs from his coat pocket and examined them. He stood motionless, perhaps in the hope that an uninterrupted, undisturbed study of the two girls would tell him who killed William Teys and why, and what a storehouse of rotting food had to do with anything. Watching him, Barbara was struck by how a trick of light falling across hair, cheek, and brow made him look vastly younger than his thirty-two years. And yet nothing altered or obscured the man's intelligence or the wit behind his eyes, not even the shadows. The only noise in the room was his breathing, steady and calm, very sure. He turned, found her watching him, and began to speak.

She stopped him. "*Well*," she said forcefully, pushing her hair behind her ears in a pugnacious gesture, "see anything else in the other rooms?"

"Just a box of old keys in the wardrobe and a veritable museum of Tessa," he replied. "Clothing, photographs, locks of hair. Among Teys' own things, of course." He replaced the photographs in his pocket. "I wonder if Olivia Odell knew what she was in for."

They had walked the three-quarters of a mile from the village down Gembler Road to the Teys' farm. As they returned, Lynley began to wish that he had driven his car. It was not so much concern that darkness had fallen but a longing for music to distract him. Without it, he found himself glancing at the woman walking wordlessly at his side, and he reluctantly considered what he had heard about her.

"One angry vairgin," MacPherson had said. "What she needs is a faer toss i' the hay." Then he roared with laughter and lifted his pint in his big, bear's grasp. "But no' *me*, laddies. I'll not test *those* waters. I leave tha' plaisure to a young'r man!"

But MacPherson was wrong, Lynley thought. There was no question of angry virginity here. It was something else.

This wasn't Havers' first murder investigation, so he could not understand her reaction to the farm: her initial reluctance to enter the barn, her strange behaviour in the sitting room, her inexplicable outburst upstairs.

For the second time he wondered what on earth Webberly had in mind in creating their partnership, but he found he was too weary to attempt an explanation.

The lights of the Dove and Whistle came in sight upon the final curve of the road. "Let's get something to eat," he said.

"Roast chicken," the proprietor announced. "It's our Sunday night dinner. Get you some up quick if you have a seat in the lounge."

The Dove and Whistle was doing a brisk evening's business. In the public bar, which had fallen into stillness upon their entrance, a pall of cigarette smoke hung like a heavy rain cloud over the room. Farmers gathered in conversation in a corner, their mud-encrusted boots placed on rungs of ladder-backed chairs, two younger men played a boisterous game of darts near a door marked TOILETS, while a group of middle-aged women compared the Sunday evening remnants of Saturday's crimps and curls, courtesy of Sinji's Beauty Shoppe. The bar itself was surrounded by patrons, most of whom were joking with the girl who worked the taps behind it.

She was clearly the village anomaly. Jet black hair rose out of her scalp in spikes, her eyes were heavily outlined in purple, and her clothes were nighttime-in-Soho explicit: short black leather skirt, white plunging blouse, black lace stockings with holes held together by safety pins, black laced shoes of the sort that grandmothers wear. Each of her ears—pierced four times—wore the dubious decoration of a line of stud earrings, except for the bottom right hole, which sported a feather dangling to her shoulder.

"Fancies herself a rock singer," the publican said, following their glance. "She's m' daughter, but I try not to let the word out often." He thumped a pint of ale on the wobbly table in front of Lynley, gave a tonic water to Barbara, and grinned. "Hannah!"

he shouted back into the public bar. "Stop making a spectacle of yourself, girl! Y're driving every man present insane with lust!" He winked at them wickedly.

"Oh Dad!" she laughed. The others did as well.

"Tell him off, Hannah!" somebody called. And another, "What's the poor bloke ever known about style?"

"Style, is it?" the publican called back cheerfully. "She's a cheap one to dress, all right. But she's running through my fortune buying gunk for her hair."

"How d'you keep them spikes up, Han?"

"Got scared in the abbey, I'd say."

"Heard the baby howl, did you, Han?"

Laughter. A playful swing at the speaker. The statement made: *See, we're all friends here.* Barbara wondered if they'd rehearsed the whole thing.

She and Lynley were the only occupants of the lounge, and once the door closed behind the publican, she longed for the noise of the public bar again, but Lynley was speaking.

"She must have been a compulsive eater."

"Who murdered her father because he put her on a diet?" It slipped out before Barbara could stop herself. Sarcasm was rich in her voice.

"Who obviously did a lot of eating in secret," Lynley went on. His own voice was unperturbed.

"Well, it doesn't look that way to me," she argued. She was pushing him, and she knew it. It was defensive and stupid. But she couldn't help it.

"What does it look like to you?"

"That food's been forgotten. Who knows how long it's been there?"

"I think we can agree that it's been there three weeks and that any food that's left out for three weeks is likely to spoil."

"All right, I'll accept that," Barbara said. "But not the compulsive eating."

"Why not?"

"Because you can't *prove* it, dammit!"

He ticked off items on his fingers. "We have two rotting apples, three black bananas, something that at one time might have been a ripe pear, a loaf of bread, sixteen biscuits, three half-eaten pastries, and three bags of crisps. Now you tell *me* what we have here, Sergeant."

"I've no idea," she replied.

"Then if you've no idea, perhaps you'll consider mine." He paused. "Barbara—"

She knew at once from his tone that she had to stop him. He couldn't, he wouldn't understand. "I'm sorry, Inspector," she said swiftly. "I got spooked at the farm and I . . . I've jumped all over you for it ever since. I . . . I'm sorry."

He appeared to be taken aback. "All right. Let's start again, shall we?"

The publican approached and plopped two plates down onto the table. "Chicken and peas," he announced proudly.

Barbara got up and stumbled from the room.

7

"NO! EZRA, STOP! I can't!"

With a deliberately unstifled curse, Ezra Farmington lifted himself off the struggling girl beneath him, swung to the edge of the bed, and sat there, fighting for breath and composure, his entire body—but most particularly, he noticed sardonically, his head—throbbing. He lowered this to his hands, burying his fingers in honey-coloured hair. Now she would cry, he thought. "All right, all *right!*" he said and added savagely, "I'm not a rapist, for God's sake!"

She did begin to cry at that, a fist at her mouth, dry hot sobs erupting from deep within her. He reached for the lamp. "No!" Her voice stopped him.

"Danny," he said, trying to speak calmly but aware that he was forcing words out between clenched teeth. He couldn't look at her.

"I'm sorry!" she wept.

It was all too familiar. It couldn't go on. "This is ridiculous, you know." He reached for his watch, saw from the luminous dial that it was nearly eight, and put it on. He began to dress.

At that, the crying increased. A hand reached for him, touched his naked back. He flinched. The sobbing continued. He picked up the rest of his clothes, left the room, went into the lavatory, and, after dressing, stared morosely at his reflection in the dusky mirror while his watch ticked away five minutes.

When he returned, the weeping had stopped. She still lay on the bed, her ivory body shimmering in the moonlight, and stared at the ceiling. Her hair was darkness; the rest of her was light. His artist's eyes travelled the length of her: the curve of cheek, the fullness of breast, the swelling of hip, the softness of thigh. An objective study in black and white, translated quickly to canvas. It was an exercise he often engaged in, one which disassociated mind from body, something he most particularly wanted to do right now. His eyes fell on the curling triangle of darkness. Objectivity shot out the window.

"For God's sake, get dressed," he snapped. "Am I supposed to stand here staring at you as retribution?"

"You know why 'tis," she whispered. She made no other move. "You know why."

"That I do," he replied. He stayed across the room by the lavatory door. It was safer there. A few feet closer and he'd be on her again, and there'd be no stopping it. He felt his jaw tighten, felt every muscle coil with a life of its own. "You don't lose a chance to remind me."

Danny sat up, swung on him. "Why should I?" she shouted. "You know wha' you did!"

"Be quiet! Do you want Fitzalan to report back to your aunt? Have *some* sense, won't you?"

"Why should I? When did you?"

"If you won't let it go, then what's the point, Danny? Why see me at all?"

"You c'n ask *that*? Even now? When everyone knows?"

He crossed his arms in front of him, steeling himself to the sight of her. Her hair was tangled round her shoulders; her lips were parted; her cheeks were wet with tears, glistening in the dull light. Her breasts . . . He forced his eyes to remain on her face.

"You know what happened. We've been over it a thousand times. Going over it a thousand times more won't change the past. If you can't let it go, then we've got to stop seeing each other."

More tears welled up and spilled down her cheeks. He hated

to see her cry. It made him want to cross the room and crush her in his arms, but what was the use? It would only begin again and end in disaster.

"No." She was still crying, but her voice was low. She hung her head. "I don' want that."

"Then what do you want? I need to know because I know very well what *I* want, Danny, and if we both don't want the same thing, then there's really no use, is there?" He was struggling to summon up control but what little he had was vanishing quickly. He thought he might actually cry with frustration.

"I want you," she whispered.

Oh God, that cuts it. That really does. "You don't want that," he replied miserably. "Because even if you did, and even if you had me, at every juncture you'd throw the past in my face. And I can't bear that, Danny. I've had *enough.*" To his horror, his voice caught on the last word.

Her head flew up. "I'm sorry," she whispered. She slipped off the bed and came across the room, her body sculpted by moonlight. He looked away. Her smooth fingers found their way to his cheek, across it, into his hair. "I never do think o' your pain," she said. "Only my own. I'm so *sorry*, Ezra."

He drove his gaze to the wall, the ceiling, the square of night sky beyond the window. If he met her eyes, he knew he was lost.

"Ezra?" Her voice was like a caress in the darkness. She smoothed back his hair, took a step closer.

He could smell her musky fragrance, feel the tips of her breasts sear his chest. Her hand dropped to his shoulder and pulled him closer. "Don't you think," she continued, "we *both* have t' forgive?"

It was finally too much. There was nowhere else to look. His last sane thought was: *Better lost than alone.*

Nigel Parrish waited until they returned from the lounge to the public bar. He was still sitting in his usual corner, taking his time about nursing a Courvoisier, when they finished their meal.

He regarded them with the kind of interest he usually reserved for the village inhabitants, quite as if they were going to be around for the next few years. They were certainly worth the time and consideration, he decided, for they were so deliciously bizarre a couple.

The man's dressed absolutely to kill, Nigel thought and chuckled inwardly at his tasteless pun. Charcoal suit, hand-tailored and fairly shrieking Savile Row, gold pocket watch looped across waistcoat, Burberry tossed casually onto the back of a chair—why is it that people with the money to buy Burberries always toss them about without a second thought?—shoes polished to a sombre, unscuffed shine. *This* was Scotland Yard?

Somehow the woman was more what he had in mind. She was short and dumpy, sort of a walking rubbish-bin type. She wore a wrinkled, stained suit that fitted her badly. Entirely the wrong colour for her as well, Nigel noted. *Baby blue's a lovely colour, but not on you, dumpling.* Her blouse was yellow and did distressing things to her sallow complexion, not to mention the fact that it was very badly tucked in all around. And the shoes! Sensible brogues were what one would expect of the police and indeed she wore them. But with blue tights to match the suit? Lord, what a vision the poor woman was. He clucked his disapproval and got to his feet.

He sauntered over to the table they had chosen near the door. "Scotland Yard?" he began chattily, without introduction. "Has anyone told you about Ezra?"

As he lifted his head to look at the newcomer Lynley's first thought was, *No, but I should guess you're about to.* A man stood there, brandy glass in hand, obviously waiting for an invitation to sit. When Sergeant Havers automatically opened her notebook, he considered himself a member of their party and pulled out a chair.

"Nigel Parrish," he introduced himself.

The organist, Lynley recalled. He guessed that the man was somewhere in his forties, and he was blessed with features that middle age enhanced. Thinning brown hair, touched by grey at the temples, was combed neatly off an intelligent brow; a firm, straight nose gave Parrish's face distinction; a strong jaw and chin were indications of strength. He was slender, not particularly tall, and striking rather than handsome.

"Ezra?" Lynley prompted him.

Parrish's brown eyes darted from person to person in the room, as if he were waiting for someone to enter. "Farmington. Our resident artist. Doesn't every village have a resident artist, poet, novelist, or something? I thought that was a virtual requirement of country life." Parrish shrugged narrow shoulders. "Ezra's ours. Watercolours. The occasional oil. Not bad, actually. He even sells some of them in a gallery in London. He used to come here for just a month or so each year, but he's become one of us now." He smiled down at his drink. "Dear, *dear* Ezra," he mused.

Lynley was not about to be played like a fish on the line. "What is it you'd like us to know about Ezra Farmington, Mr. Parrish?"

Parrish's startled glance betrayed that he hadn't quite been expecting so direct an approach. "Aside from the fact that he's just the teeniest bit of a village Lothario, there's what happened on the Teys' place that you ought to know."

Lynley found Ezra's romantic inclinations to be neither here nor there, although obviously they were of interest to Parrish. "What happened on the Teys' place?" he asked, ignoring the other dangling line.

"Well . . ." Parrish warmed to his topic but a sad glance at his empty glass cooled the fires of the story.

"Sergeant," Lynley said tonelessly, his eyes on the other man, "would you get Mr. Parrish another—"

"Courvoisier," Parrish said with a smile.

"And one for me."

Havers obediently left the table. "Nothing for her?" Nigel asked, face wrinkled with concern.

"She doesn't drink."

"What a bore!" When Havers returned, Parrish treated her to a sympathetic smile, took a genteel sip of the cognac, and settled down to his story. "As to Ezra," he said, leaning into the table confidentially, "it was a nasty little scene. The only reason I know about it is that I was out that way. Whiskers, you see."

Lynley had gone in this direction once before. "The musical dog."

"Pardon?"

"Father Hart told us that Whiskers liked to lie on the common and listen to you play the organ."

Parrish laughed. "Isn't it the absolute devil? I practise my fingers to the bone, dear ones, and my most enthusiastic audience is a farm dog." His words dealt with the matter in a lambent fashion—as if nothing on earth could really be more amusing. Yet Lynley could see it was a brittle performance, a facade made frangible by the force of a current of bitterness that ran, swift and sure, just beneath the surface. Parrish was working at joviality and rather too industriously.

"Well, there you have it," he continued. He turned the snifter in his hands, admiring the variety of colours that the cognac produced as it caught the light. "A virtual Sahara of musical appreciation in the village. In fact, the only reason I play at St. Catherine's on Sundays is to please myself. God knows no one else can tell a fugue from a scherzo. D'you know that St. Catherine's has the finest organ in Yorkshire? Typical, isn't it? I'm sure Rome purchased it personally to keep the RCs in control in Keldale. I'm C of E, myself."

"And Farmington?" Lynley asked.

"Ezra? I don't think Ezra's religious at all. Except," seeing no amused appreciation on Lynley's face, "what you probably mean is what do I have to say about Ezra."

"You've certainly read me, Mr. Parrish."

"Ezra." Parrish smiled and took a drink, perhaps for courage, perhaps for solace. It was difficult to tell. He lowered his voice momentarily, however, and as he did so, a brief glimmer of the real man emerged, brooding and moody. But the chatty gossip replaced him almost at once. "Let me see, loves, it must have been about a month ago when William Teys ran Ezra off the farm."

"Was he trespassing?"

"Absolutely. But according to Ezra, he has some sort of 'artistic licence' that allows him to trespass everywhere. And I do mean *everywhere*. He was doing what he calls 'light studies' of High Kel Moor. Your basic Rouen Cathedral sort of thing. Start a new picture every fifteen minutes."

"I'm familiar with Monet."

"Then you know what I mean. Well, the only way—let's say the quickest way—up to High Kel Moor is right through the woods behind Gembler Farm. And the way to the woods—"

"Was across Teys' land," Lynley finished.

"Exactly. I was trotting along the road with Whiskers in tow. He'd put in his usual appearance on the common and, as it seemed late to let the old boy find his own way home, I was taking him there myself. I had hoped our darling Stepha might be willing to do the job in her Mini, but she was nowhere to be found. So I had to drag the old thing out there on these poor, stiff legs."

"You don't own a car?"

"Not one that runs with any reliability, I'm afraid. Anyway, I got to the farm and there they were, right in the road having the most god-awful row I've ever seen. There was William in his jimjams—"

"Excuse me?"

"His *pyjamas*, Inspector. Or was it his dressing gown?" Parrish squinted at the ceiling and considered his own question. "It was his dressing gown. I remember thinking, 'Lord, what hairy legs old William has,' when I saw him. Quite like a gorilla."

"I see."

"And Ezra was standing there, shouting at him, waving his arms, and cursing in ways that must have made poor sainted William's hair stand on end. The dog got hot into the action and took *quite* a piece out of Ezra's trousers. While he was doing that, William ripped three of Ezra's precious watercolours into shreds and dumped the rest of the portfolio right onto the verge. It was dreadful." Parrish looked down as he concluded his story, a mournful note to his voice, but when he lifted his head, his eyes said clearly that Ezra had got what he'd long deserved.

Lynley watched Sergeant Havers climb the stairs and disappear from view. He rubbed his temples and walked into the lounge, where a light at the far end of the room illuminated the bent head of Stepha Odell. She looked up from her book at his footsteps.

"Have we kept you up to lock the door?" Lynley asked. "I'm terribly sorry."

She smiled and stetched her arms languidly over her head. "Not at all," she replied pleasantly. "I was nodding a bit over my novel, however."

"What are you reading?"

"A cheap romance." She laughed easily and got to her feet, which, he noticed, were bare. She had changed from her grey church dress into a simple tweed skirt and sweater. A single freshwater pearl on a silver chain hung between her breasts. "It's my way of escaping. Everyone always lives happily ever after in a romance novel." He remained where he was, near the door. "How do you escape, Inspector?"

"I don't, I'm afraid."

"Then what do you do about the shadows in your life?"

"The shadows?"

"Chasing murderers down. It can't be a pleasant job. Why do you do it?"

There was the question, he admitted, and knew the answer. *It's penance, Stepha, an expiation for sins committed that you couldn't understand.* "I never stopped to think about it."

"Ah." She nodded thoughtfully and let it go. "Well, you've a package that's come. Brought by a rather nasty man from Richmond. He wouldn't give me his name, but he smelled like a large digestive tablet."

An apt description of Nies, Lynley thought, as she went behind the bar. He followed. She had evidently been working in the lounge in the late afternoon, for the room was scented richly with beeswax and the yeasty smell of ale. That combination took him right back to Cornwall, a ten-year-old boy hurriedly wolfing down pasties in the kitchen of the Trefallen farm. Such delicacies they were to him, meat and onions folded into a flaky shell, fruit forbidden and unheard of in the formal dining room of Howenstow. "Common," his father would snort contemptuously. And indeed they were, which was why he loved them.

Stepha placed a large envelope on the counter. "Here it is. Will you join me for a nightcap?"

"Thank you. I'd like that."

She smiled. He noticed how it curved her cheeks, how the tiny lines round her eyes seemed to vanish. "Good. Sit down then. You look exhausted."

He went to one of the couches and opened the envelope. Nies had made no effort to put the material in any sort of order. There were three notebooks of information, some additional photographs of Roberta, forensic reports identical to the ones he already had, and nothing whatsoever on Whiskers.

Stepha Odell placed a glass on the table and sat opposite him, drawing her legs up into the seat of the chair.

"What happened to Whiskers?" Lynley asked himself. "Why is there nothing about that dog?"

"Gabriel knows," Stepha responded.

For a moment he thought it was some sort of village expression until he recalled the constable's name. "Constable Langston?"

She nodded, sipping her drink. Her fingers on the glass were long and slender, unencumbered by rings. "He buried Whiskers."

"Where?"

She shrugged a shoulder and pushed her hair back off her face. Unlike the ugliness of the gesture by Havers, in Stepha it was a lovely movement, chasing shadows away. "I'm not sure. I expect it was somewhere on the farm."

"But why was no forensic study done on the dog?" Lynley mused.

"I suppose they didn't need one. They could see how the poor thing died."

"How?"

"His throat was slit, Inspector."

He fumbled back through the material, looking for the pictures. No wonder he had failed to see it before. Teys' body, sprawled right over the dog's corpse, obscured the view. He considered the photograph.

"You see the problem now, don't you?"

"What do you mean?"

"Can you imagine Roberta slitting Whiskers' throat?" An expression of distaste passed across Stepha's face. "It's impossible. I'm sorry, but it's just impossible. Beyond that, no weapon was ever found. Surely she didn't slit the poor animal's throat with an axe!"

As she spoke, Lynley found himself beginning to wonder for the first time exactly who the real target of the crime had been: William Teys or his dog.

Suppose a robbery had been in the works, he thought. The dog would need to be silenced. He was old, certainly incapable of attacking someone, but well enough able to make a din if a foreign presence were found in his territory. So the dog would have to be dealt with. But perhaps not quickly enough, so that when Teys rushed out to the barn to see what the yelping was all about, he would have to be dealt with as well. Perhaps, thought Lynley, we have no premeditated murder here, but a crime of an entirely different nature.

"Stepha," he said thoughtfully. He reached in his pocket. "Who is this?" He handed her the photograph that he and Havers had found in Roberta's chest of drawers.

"Where on earth did you get this?"

"In Roberta's bedroom. Who is it?"

"It's Gillian Teys, Roberta's sister." She tapped the photograph lightly for emphasis, studying it as she spoke. "Roberta must have kept this well hidden from William."

"Why?"

"Because after Gillian ran off, she was dead to William. He threw away her clothes, got rid of her books, and even destroyed every picture that she was in. Burnt her birth certificate as well as everything else in a great bonfire right in the middle of the yard. How on earth," she asked, more to herself than to him, her eyes on the photograph, "did Roberta manage to save this?"

"More importantly perhaps, why did she save it?"

"That's easy enough. Roberta adored Gillian. God knows why. Gillian was the great disaster in the family. She turned out quite wild. She drank and swore and ran around like mad, having the time of her life, off to a party in Whitby one night, out with some hellion God-knows-where the next. Picking up men and giving them a run for their money. Then one night, some eleven years ago, she left. And she never came back."

Lynley caught the word. "Left? Or disappeared?"

Stepha's body backed into the chair. One of her hands rose to her throat, but she stopped the gesture as if it were betraying her. "Left," she said firmly.

He went along. "Why?"

"I imagine because she was at odds with William. He was fairly straitlaced and Gillian was nothing if not after a good time. But Richard—her cousin—could probably tell you more. The two of them were rather thick before he left for the fens." Stepha got to her feet, stretched, and walked to the door, where she paused.

"Inspector," she said slowly. Lynley looked up from the photograph, half-expecting her to say more about Gillian Teys. She hesitated. "Would you like . . . anything else tonight?"

The light from the reception area behind her cast a glow upon her hair. Her skin looked smooth and lovely. Her eyes were kind. It would be so easy. An hour of bliss. Impassioned acceptance. A simple, longed-for forgetting. "No, thank you, Stepha," he made himself say.

The River Kel was a peaceful tributary unlike many of the rivers that debouched frantically from the hillsides down into the dales. Silently, it wended its way through Keldale, flowing past the ruined abbey on its way to the sea. It loved the village, treating it well, seldom overflowing in destruction. It welcomed the lodge to exist on its banks, splashed greetings onto the village common, and listened to the lives of the people who lived in the houses built at its very edge.

Olivia Odell had one of these houses, across the bridge from the lodge, with a sweeping view of the common and of St. Catherine's Church. It was the finest home in the village, with a lovely front garden and a lawn that sloped down to the river.

It was still early morning when Lynley and Havers pushed open the gate, but the steady wailing of a child, coming from behind the house, told them that the inhabitants were already up and about. They followed the grief-stricken ululation to its source.

On the back steps of the house sat the youthful mourner. She was huddled in a ball of woe, head bent to her knees, a crumpled magazine photograph beneath her grubby shoes. To her left sat her audience, a solemn male mallard who watched her sympathetically. Upon her head was the ostensible source of her grief, for she'd cut her hair—or rather somebody had—and had plastered it onto her skull with grease. It once had been red and, from the look of the locks escaping their confinement, decidedly curly. But now, giving off the malodourous waft of cheap pomade, it was nothing but dreadful to behold.

Havers and Lynley exchanged a look. "Good morning," the inspector said pleasantly. "You must be Bridie."

The child looked up, grabbing the photograph and clutching it to her chest in a motherly gesture. The duck merely blinked.

"What's wrong?" Lynley asked kindly.

Bridie's defiant posture was completely deflated at the gentle sound of the tall man's voice. "I cut my hair!" she wailed. "I saved my money to go to Sinji's but she said she couldn't make my hair go this way and she wouldn't cut it so I cut it myself and now look at me and Mummy's crying as well. I tried to straighten it all out with this stuff of Hannah's but it'll never come right!" She hiccupped pathetically on the last word.

Lynley nodded. "I see. It does look a bit awful, Bridie. Exactly what sort of effect were you going after?" He quailed inwardly at the thought of Hannah's black spikes.

"This!" She waved the photograph at him, wailing anew.

He took it from her and looked at the smiling, smooth coiffured semblance of the Princess of Wales, elegant in black evening gown and diamonds, not a hair out of place. "Of *course*," he muttered.

Bereft of her picture, Bridie took comfort in the presence of her duck, slinging an arm round him and pulling him to her side. "*You* don't care, Dougal, *do* you?" she demanded of the bird. In reply, Dougal blinked and investigated Bridie's hair for its edible propensities.

"Dougal the Duck?" Lynley enquired.

"Angus McDougal McDuck," Bridie responded. The formal introduction made, she wiped her nose on the sleeve of her tattered pullover and looked fearfully over her shoulder at the closed door behind her. A single tear rolled down her cheek as she went on. "An' he's hungry. But I can't go inside to get his food. All I got's these marshmallows. They're all right for a treat, but his real food's inside and I can't go in."

"Why not?"

" 'Cause Mummy said she didn't want to see me again till I'd done something about my hair and I don't know what to do!" The child began to cry again, real tears of anguish. Dougal would apparently starve—an unlikely prospect, considering his size—unless some quick thinking were applied to the situation.

It appeared, however, that a plan of attack would be unnecessary, for at that moment the back door was jerked open angrily.

Olivia Odell took one look at her daughter—her second only that day—and burst into tears.

"I can't believe you would do it! I just can't believe it! Get in the house and wash your hair!" Her voice rose higher with each word, climbing the peak to hysteria.

"But Dougal—"

"Take Dougal with you," the woman said, weeping. "But do as I say!" The duck was scooped into nine-year-old arms and the two offenders disappeared. Olivia tugged a tissue from the pocket of her cardigan, blew her nose, and smiled shakily at the two adults. "What a dreadful scene," she said. But as she spoke she began to cry again and walked into the kitchen, leaving them standing at the open back door. She stumbled to the table and buried her face in her hands.

Lynley and Havers looked at each other and, decision made, entered the house.

Unlike Gembler Farm, there was not the slightest doubt that this house was lived in. The kitchen was in total disarray: the stove top cluttered with pots and pans, appliances gaping open to be cleaned, flowers waiting to be put into water, dishes piled in the sink. The floor was sticky under their feet, the walls badly needed paint, and the entire room reeked with the charcoal bouquet of burnt toast. The offending source of this odour was lying on a plate, a sodden black lump that looked as if it had been hastily extinguished by a cup of tea.

Beyond the kitchen, what little they could see of the sitting room indicated that its condition was much the same. Housekeeping was certainly not Olivia Odell's strong point. Neither was child rearing, if the morning's confrontation were any indication.

"She's out of my control!" Olivia wept. "Nine years old and she's out of my control!" She tore the tissue to shreds, looked dazedly about for another, and, seeing none, cried harder still.

Lynley removed a handkerchief from his pocket. "Take this," he offered.

"Ta," she responded. "Oh my God, what a morning!" She blew her nose, dried her eyes, ran her fingers through her brown hair, and looked at her reflection in the toaster. She moaned when she saw herself, and her bloodshot brown eyes filled again but didn't spill over. "I look fifty years old. Wouldn't Paul have laughed!" And then disjointedly, "She wants to look like the Princess of Wales."

"So she showed us," Lynley responded impassively. He drew a chair out from the table, picked the newspapers off of it, and sat down. After a pause, Havers did likewise.

"Why?" Olivia asked, directing the question more to the ceiling than to her companions. "What have I done that my daughter believes the key to happiness is to look exactly like the Princess of Wales?" she squeezed her fingers into her forehead. "William would have known what to do. What a *mess* I am without him."

Wishing to avoid a fresh onslaught of tears, Lynley spoke quickly to divert her. "Little girls always have someone they admire, don't they?"

"Yes," Olivia said. "Oh yes, how true that is." She'd begun twisting his handkerchief into an appalling little rope. Lynley winced as he saw it mangled. "But I never seem to have the right thing to say to the child. Everything I try seems to end in hysterics. William always knew what to say and do. Whenever he was here, everything went smoothly. But the moment he was gone, we'd begin to fight like cats and dogs! And now he's really gone! What's to become of us?" She didn't wait for an answer. "It's her *hair*. She *hates* having red hair. She's hated it ever since she learned to speak. I can't understand it. Why is a nine-year-old girl so damned passionate about her hair!"

"Redheads," Lynley noted, "are generally passionate about everything."

"Oh, that's it! That's it! Stepha's quite the same. You'd think Bridie was her clone, not her niece." She drew in a breath and sat up in her chair. Footsteps came running down the hall. "Lord, give me strength," Olivia murmured.

Bridie entered the room, a towel wrapped precariously round her head, her pullover—which she hadn't bothered to remove in her haste to obey her mother's instructions—thoroughly soaked round her shoulders and down most of her back. She was followed by her duck, who walked like a seaman, with a peculiar rolling gait.

"He's crippled," Bridie announced, noticing Lynley's inspection of the fowl. "When he swims, he jus' goes round in a big circle, so I don't let him swim unless I'm there. We took him swimming lots last summer, though. In the river. We made a dam just outside and he had ever so much fun. He'd plunk himself in the water and go round and round. Huh, Dougal?" The mallard blinked his agreement and searched on the floor for something to eat.

"Here, let me see you, MacBride," her mother said. The daughter came forward, the towel was removed, the damage was surveyed. Olivia's eyes welled with tears again above her daughter's head. She bit her lip.

"Looks like it just needs a bit of a trim," Lynley interposed hastily. "What do you think, Sergeant?"

"A trim ought to do it," Havers agreed.

"I think the thing to do, Bridie, is to give up on the Princess of Wales idea. Now," Lynley added as the child's bottom lip trembled, "you've got to remember that your hair is curly. Hers is quite straight. And when Sinji told you that she couldn't make it go in that style, she was telling you the truth."

"But she's so pretty," Bridie protested. Tears threatened once again.

"She is. Absolutely. But it would be a fairly strange world if every woman were exactly like her, wouldn't it? Believe me, there are many women who are very pretty and look nothing like her."

"There are?" Bridie gave a longing glance to the crumpled photograph again. A large smear of grease was sitting on the Princess' nose.

"You can believe the inspector when he says that, Bridie," Havers added, and her tone implied the rest: *He's a bit of an expert on the subject.*

Bridie looked from woman to man, sensing undercurrents that she didn't understand. "Well," she announced, "I s'pose I got to feed Dougal."

The duck, at least, looked as if he approved.

The Odell sitting room was only a slight improvement over the kitchen. It was hard to believe that one woman and one child could produce such disarray. Clothes lay piled over chairs as if mother and daughter were in the process of moving; knickknacks perched in unlikely positions on the edges of tables and window sills; an ironing board was set up in what looked like permanent residence; an upright piano spat sheet music onto the floor. It was havoc, with dust so thick that it gave the air flavour.

Olivia appeared to be unaware of the mess as she absently gestured them towards seats, but she looked about as she took her own and sighed in unembarrassed resignation. "It's usually not this bad. I've been . . . it's been . . ." She cleared her throat and shook her head as if to get her thoughts in order. Once again the fingers went through the wispy, windblown-looking hair. It was a girlish gesture, oddly incongruous in a woman who so plainly was no longer a girl. She had paper-fine skin and delicate features, but the ageing process was not dealing with her kindly. She was lined and, although thin, her flesh lacked resiliency, as if she had lost too much weight too quickly. Bones jutted from her cheeks and wrists.

"You know," she said suddenly, "when Paul died, it wasn't this bad. I can't come to grips with what's happened to me over William."

"The suddenness," Lynley offered. "The shock."

She nodded. "Perhaps you're right. My husband Paul was ill for several years. I had time to prepare myself. And Bridie, of course, was too young to understand. But William . . ." She made an effort at control, fixing her eyes on the wall, sitting up tall. "William was such a presence in our lives, such a strength. I think we both started to depend on him and then he was gone. But it's selfish of me to be reacting like this. How can I be so awful when there's Bobba to consider?"

"Roberta?"

She glanced at him, then away. "She always came here with William."

"What was she like?"

"Very quiet. Very nice. Not an attractive girl. Heavy, you know. But she was always very good to Bridie."

"Her weight caused a problem between Richard Gibson and his uncle, though, didn't it?"

Olivia's brow furrowed. "A problem? How do you mean?"

"Their argument over it. At the Dove and Whistle. Will you tell us about it?"

"Oh *that*. Stepha must have told you. But that has nothing to do with William's death." This as she saw Sergeant Havers write a few lines in her notebook.

"One can never be sure. Will you tell us about it?"

A hand fluttered up as if in protest but resettled in her lap. "Richard hadn't been back from the fens for long. He ran into us at the Dove and Whistle. There were words. Silly. Over in a minute. That's all." She smiled vaguely.

"What sort of words?"

"It really had nothing to do with Roberta initially. We were all sitting together at a table and William, I'm afraid, made a comment about Hannah. The barmaid. Have you seen her?"

"Last night."

"Then you know she looks . . . different. William didn't at all approve of her, nor of the way her father deals with her. You know—as if he's just amused by it all. So William said something about it. Something like, 'Why her dad lets her walk about looking like a tart is a mystery to me.' That sort of thing. Nothing really serious. Richard was just a bit in his cups. He'd a terrible set of scratches on his face, so I think he'd been at it with his wife as well. His mood was foul. He said something about not being such a fool as to judge by appearances, that—as I recall— an angel could be wearing a streetwalker's guise and the sweetest blonde-headed little face could hide a whore."

"And William took that to mean what?"

She produced a tired smile. "As a reference to Gillian, his older daughter. Rather immediately, I'm afraid. He demanded to know what Richard meant by his remark. Richard and Gilly had been great friends, you see. I think—to avoid having to explain —Richard sidetracked onto Roberta."

"How?"

"As an example of not judging by appearances. Of course, it went on from there. Richard demanded to know why Roberta had been allowed to get into such an unattractive state. In turn, William demanded to know what he had meant by his insinuation about Gilly. Richard demanded that William answer. William demanded that Richard answer. You know the sort of thing."

"And then?"

She laughed. It was a tittering sound, like that of a trapped bird. "I thought they might fight. Richard said no child of his would ever be allowed to eat her way into an early grave and that William ought to be ashamed of the job he'd done as a father. William became so angry that he said something about Richard being ashamed of the job he was doing as a husband. He made a ... well, a bit of a crude reference to Madeline going unsatisfied—she's Richard's wife, have you met her?—and frankly just when I thought Richard might truly hit his uncle, instead he just laughed. He said something about being a fool to waste his time worrying about Roberta and left us."

"That was all?"

"Yes."

"What do you suppose Richard meant?"

"By being a fool?" As if seeing the direction his question was taking her, she frowned. "You want me to say that he felt he was being a fool because if Roberta died, he'd get the farm."

"Is that what he meant?"

"No, of course not. William rewrote his will shortly after Richard returned from the fens. Richard knew very well that the farm had been left to him, not to Roberta."

"But if you and William married then the will would most likely have been rewritten once again. Isn't that true?"

Clearly, she saw the trap. "Yes but ... I know what you're thinking. It was to Richard's advantage that William should die before we could marry. But isn't that always the case when there's an inheritance involved? And people don't generally kill one another just because they're to inherit something in a will."

"On the contrary, Mrs. Odell," Lynley objected politely, "people do it all the time."

"That wasn't the case here. I just think ... well, that Richard's not very happy. And unhappy people say lots of things that they really don't mean and do lots of things that they wouldn't otherwise do just to try to forget their unhappiness, don't they?"

Neither Lynley nor Havers replied at once. Olivia moved restlessly in her chair. Outside, Bridie's voice rose as she called to her duck.

"Did Roberta know about this conversation?" Lynley asked.

"If she did, she never mentioned it. When she was here, she mostly talked—in that low-voiced way of hers—about the wedding. I think she was eager for William and me to marry. To have a sister in Bridie. To have what she once had with Gillian. She missed her sister dreadfully. I don't believe she ever got over Gillian's running away." Her nervous fingers found a loose thread on the hem of her skirt, and she twisted it compulsively until it broke. Then she looked at it mutely, as if wondering how it came to be wrapped round her finger. "Bobba—that's what William always called her, and we did as well—would take Bridie off so that William and I could have time alone. She and Bridie and Whiskers and that duck would go off together. Can you imagine what they looked like?" She smiled and smoothed the creases in her skirt. "They'd go to the river, across the common, or down to the abbey for a picnic. The four of them. And then William and I would be able to talk."

"What did you talk about?"

"Tessa, mostly. Of course, it was a problem, but the last time he was here—the day of his death—he said it had finally been overcome."

"I'm not certain that I understand," Lynley remarked. "What kind of a problem? Emotional, you mean? An unwillingness to come to terms with her death?"

Olivia had been looking out the window, but she turned to them upon the last word. *"Death?"* she asked, perplexed. "Tessa's not dead, Inspector. She deserted William a short time after Roberta was born. He'd hired a detective to find her so that he could have their marriage annulled by the Church, and Saturday afternoon he came to tell me she'd been found at last."

"York," the man said. "And I'm not obligated to tell you anything more. I've yet to be paid for my services, you know."

Lynley gripped the telephone in his hand. He could feel the anger burning in his chest. "How does a court order sound?" he asked pleasantly.

"Listen here, old chap, don't try to pull that kind of shit on me—"

"Mr. Houseman, may I remind you that, in spite of what you may think, you are *not* part of a Dashiell Hammett novel." Lynley could just picture the man, feet up on his desk, a bottle of bourbon in the filing drawer, a gun tossed from hand to hand as he balanced the telephone receiver on his shoulder. He wasn't too far from the truth.

Harry Houseman looked out the grimy window of his office above Jackie's Barber Shop in Richmond's Trinity Church Square. A light rain was falling, not enough to clean off his window, just enough to emphasise its filth. What a dreary day, he thought. He'd intended to spend it on a drive to the coast—a little lady in Whitby was only too eager to do some serious private investigating with him—but this kind of weather didn't put him in the mood. And God knows he needed to be in the mood more and more these days before anything happened in the land down under. He grinned, showing a badly capped front tooth. It added a piratical dimension to his otherwise mundane appearance: dull brown hair, muddy-coloured eyes, cadaverous skin, and the incongruity of full, sensual lips.

He played with a well-chewed pencil on the top of his scarred desk. His eyes caught the thin-lipped glance of his wife's shrewish face peering moodily out at him from the photograph nearby. He reached out with his pencil and toppled it over, face down.

"I'm sure we can reach some sort of mutual agreement," Houseman said into the phone. "Let me see. Miss Doalson?" A suitable pause for dramatic effect. "Do I have time today to . . . Well, cancel *that*. It can certainly wait until I see . . ." Back to the phone. "What did you say your name was?"

"We aren't going to see each other," Lynley responded patiently. "You're going to give me the address in York and that's going to be the end of our relationship."

"Oh, I don't see how I can—"

"Certainly you do." Lynley's voice was steel. "Because, as you said, you haven't been paid yet. And in order for you ever to get paid once the estate is settled—which may, incidentally, take years if we don't get to the bottom of this—you're going to have to give me Tessa Teys' address."

A pause for consideration. "What is that, Miss Doalson?" the infuriating voice asked in saccharine tones. "On the other line? Well, put him off, will you?" A martyred sigh. "I can see, Inspector, that you're not an easy man to deal with. We all have to make a living, you know."

"Believe me, I know," Lynley replied curtly. "The address?"

"I'll just have to find it in my files. May I give you a ring in . . . say an hour or so?"

"No."

"Well, good *God*, man—"

"I'm on my way to Richmond."

"No, no, that won't be necessary. Just wait a moment, old chap." Houseman leaned back in his chair, eying the grey sky for a minute. He reached over to his dented filing cabinet, opening and closing a few drawers for effect. "What's that, Miss Doalson?" he called. "No, put her off till tomorrow, will you? I don't care if she's weeping *buckets*, sweetheart, I don't have time to spend with her today." He picked the scrap of memo paper off his desk. "Ah, *here* it is, Inspector," he said and gave Lynley the address. "But don't expect her to welcome you with open arms, will you?"

"I don't particularly care how she welcomes me, Mr. Houseman. Good—"

"Oh, but you ought to, Inspector. Just a bit, you know. Hubby went mad when he heard the news. Thought he'd strangle *me* right on the spot, so God knows what he'll do when Scotland Yard shows up. He's one of those scholarly types, big words and thick specs. But trust me, Inspector, that man is deep. There's an animal inside him."

Lynley's eyes narrowed. It was a cast upon the waters, an expert manoeuvre. He wanted to swim past it but admitted defeat. "What are you talking about? What news did he hear?"

"The news about hubby number one, of course."

"What are you trying to tell me, Houseman?"

"That Tessa Teys is a bigamist, old boy," Houseman finished with delight. "Married up with number two without seeing to the formal bye-byes to our William. Can you imagine her surprise when I popped up on her doorstep?"

The house wasn't at all what he had expected. Women who desert husband and children should somehow end up in tenement buildings pungent with the odours of garlic and urine. They should daily subdue a bucking, quarrelsome conscience with liberal applications of soporific gin. They should be faded and worn, their looks quite destroyed by the ravages of shame. Whatever they should be, Lynley was certain they shouldn't be Tessa Teys Mowrey.

He'd parked in front of the house, and they stared at it silently until Havers finally spoke. "Not exactly gone downhill, has she?" she asked.

They'd found it easily, a new, middle-class neighbourhood a few miles from the city centre, the kind of place where houses have numbers as well as coy little names. The Mowreys' home was called Jorvik View. It was the concrete reality of every mediocre dream: a facade of brick covered the poured-block construction; red tiles swept up to form steep gables; white-curtained bay windows showed off sitting and dining rooms on either side of a polished front door. A single-car, attached garage was topped by a white iron-fenced roof terrace, and a door opened onto this from the upper floor of the house. It was on this terrace that they had their first glimpse of Tessa.

She came out of the door, blonde hair blowing lightly in the breeze, to water potted plants: spider chrysanthemums, dahlias, and marigolds that made an autumn wall of colour against the white iron. She saw the Bentley and hesitated, watering can poised in midair, appearing every bit in the late morning light as if Renoir had captured her by surprise.

And she looked, Lynley noted grimly, not a day older than her photograph taken nineteen years before and religiously enshrined at Gembler Farm.

"So much for the wages of sin," he muttered.

8

"MAYBE THERE'S A portrait in the attic," Havers replied.
Lynley glanced at her in surprise. Thus far today, she
had been so markedly diligent about behaving appropri-
ately, about cooperating completely and promptly with his every
order, that to hear her break away from that and say something
amusing was a bit of a shock. A nice one, in fact. "Honours to
you, Sergeant," he chuckled. "Let's see what Mrs. Mowrey has
to say."

She met them at the front door, looking from one to the other
in confusion and—was it veiled just behind the eyes?—a touch
of fear. "Good morning," she said. Down from the roof terrace,
she looked at least more like a woman approaching middle age.
But the hair was still sunny-blonde, the figure slight, the skin
lightly freckled and virtually unlined.

Lynley showed her his warrant card. "Scotland Yard CID. May
we come in, Mrs. Mowrey?"

She looked from Lynley to Havers' grim face and back again.
"Of course." Her voice was quite even, polite and warm. But
there was a hesitation, a rigidity in her movements, that suggested strong emotion withheld.

She led them to the left, through an open door that took them
into the sitting room, where she gestured wordlessly at the fur-

niture, beckoning them to sit. It was a well-furnished, tasteful room, with pieces of a modern design, pine and walnut that mingled with subdued autumn colours. A clock was ticking somewhere, light and rapid like a racing pulse. Here was none of the riotous disorder of Olivia Odell nor the mechanical precision of Gembler Farm. Rather, this room was obviously the gathering place for a congenial family, with informal photographs displayed, souvenirs of trips, and a stack of boxed games and cards shelved among books.

Tessa Mowrey chose a chair in the farthest corner where the light was weakest. She sat down on its edge, her back upright, her legs crossed, her hands folded in her lap. She wore a plain gold wedding band. She didn't ask why Scotland Yard had come calling. Rather, she followed Lynley with her eyes as he walked to the mantel and took note of the photographs that were its display.

"Your children?" he asked. There were two of them, a girl and a boy, pictures taken on a family holiday in St. Ives. He recognised the familiar sweep of the bay, the grey and white buildings on the shore, and the assortment of boats left beached at low tide.

"Yes," she responded. She volunteered nothing else. Quiescent, she awaited the inevitable. The silence continued. Lynley allowed it to do so. Eventually, sheer nervousness compelled her to go on.

"Has Russell telephoned you?" There was an edge of despair in her voice. It was dull-sounding, as if she'd experienced the full range of grief and there was nothing left in her, no depth of emotion to plummet further. "I thought he might. Of course, it's been three weeks. I'd begun to hope he was only punishing me till we sorted everything out." She stirred uneasily when Sergeant Havers took out her notebook. "Oh, must you?" she asked faintly.

"I'm afraid so," Lynley replied.

"Then I'll tell you everything. It's best." She looked down at her hands and tightened their grip on each other.

Odd, Lynley thought, how as members of the same species we inevitably rely on the same set of gestures for our nonverbal signals of distress. A hand raised to the throat, arms cradling the body protectively, a quick adjustment of clothing, a flinching to ward off a psychic blow. Tessa, he saw, was gathering strength now to get through this ordeal, as if one hand could give the other a transfusion of courage through the simple expedient of fingers intertwined. It seemed to work. She looked up, her expression defiant.

"I had just turned sixteen when I married him. Can you understand what it's like to be married to a man eighteen years older than yourself when you're only sixteen? Of course you can't. No one can. Not even Russell."

"You didn't want to stay on in school?"

"I'd planned to. But I'd left school to help on the farm for a few weeks when Dad's back went bad. It was only a temporary arrangement. I was supposed to return in a month. Marsha Fitzalan gave me work to do so that I wouldn't fall behind. But I fell behind, and there was William."

"How do you mean?"

"He'd come to buy a ram from Dad. I took him out to see it. William was . . . very handsome. I was romantic. He was Heathcliff come to claim Cathy at last, as far as I was concerned."

"Surely your father had some concern about his sixteen-year-old daughter wanting to marry? And to marry a man so much older than herself?"

"He did. Mother as well. But I was stubborn, and William was responsible, respectable, and strong. I think they believed that if they didn't let me marry him, I would turn out wild and go desperately bad in one way or another. So they gave their consent, and we married."

"What happened to the marriage?"

"What *does* a sixteen-year-old girl know about marriage, Inspector?" she asked in answer. "I wasn't even certain how babies got themselves born when I married William. You'd think a farm girl would have a bit more sense, but you have to remember that I spent most of my free time with the Brontës. Charlotte, Anne, and Emily were always a bit vague when it came down to the details. But I found out quickly enough. Gillian was born before my seventeenth birthday. William was thrilled. He adored her. It was as if his life began the moment he saw Gilly."

"Yet a number of years passed before you had a second child."

"That's because Gilly changed everything between us."

"How?"

"Somehow she—this tiny, fragile baby—made William discover religion and nothing was quite the same after that."

"I've somehow got the impression he was always religious."

"Oh no. Not till Gillian. It was as if he couldn't quite be a good enough father, as if he had to purify his soul to be worthy of a child."

"How did he do it?"

She laughed shortly at the memory, but the sound was regretful and unamused. "The Bible, confession, daily communion. Within a year of our marriage, he became the backbone of St. Catherine's and a devoted father."

"And there you were, a teenager, trying to live with a baby and a saint."

"That's exactly what it was like. Except that I didn't have to worry so much about the baby. I wasn't quite good enough to care for William's child. Or perhaps not holy enough because, at any rate, he mostly cared for her himself."

"What did you do?"

"I retreated to my books." She had sat nearly motionless through the initial part of their conversation, but now she moved restlessly, getting up and pacing across the room to look out the bay window where York Minster loomed in the distance. But instead of the cathedral, Lynley guessed that Tessa saw the past. "I dreamt that William would become Mr. Darcy. I dreamt that Mr. Knightley would sweep me off my feet. I hoped that any day I might meet Edward Rochester if I only believed enough that my dreams were real." She crossed her arms in front of her as if that could ward off the pain of that time. "I wanted desperately to be loved. How I wanted to be loved! Can you possibly understand that, Inspector?"

"Who couldn't understand?" Lynley replied.

"I thought that if we had a second child, we would each have someone special to love. So I . . . I seduced William back to our bed."

"Back?"

"Oh yes, back. He'd left me shortly after Gilly was born and had begun to sleep elsewhere. On the couch, in the sewing room, anywhere but with me."

"Why?"

"He used as an excuse the fact that Gilly's birth had been so hard on me. He didn't want me to become pregnant and go through the torture again."

"There are contraceptives—"

"William's Catholic, Inspector. There are no contraceptives." She turned from the window to face them again. The light bled colour from her cheeks, effaced eyebrows and lashes, and deepened the creases from nose to mouth. If she sensed this, she made no move to avoid it. Rather, she remained, as if willing to allow her age to be exposed. She went on.

"But I really think, looking back on it, that it was sex, not conception, that frightened William. At any rate, I got him back to my bed eventually. And eight years after Gilly, Roberta was born."

"If you had what you wanted—a second baby to love—why did you leave?"

"Because it began again. All of it. She wasn't mine any more than Gillian had been. I loved my little girls, but I wasn't allowed near them, not the way I wanted to be. I had nothing." Although her voice quavered on the last word, she drew herself in, cradling her body tighter, and found control. "All I had once again was Darcy. My books."

"So you left."

"I woke up one morning just a few weeks after Roberta was born and I knew that if I stayed I would shrivel to nothing. I was nearly twenty-five. I had two children I wasn't allowed to love and a husband who had begun to consult the Bible before dressing in the morning. I looked out the window, saw the trail leading to High Kel Moor, and knew I would leave that day."

"Didn't he try to stop you?"

"No. Of course, I wanted him to. But he didn't. I walked out of the door and out of his life, carrying just one valise and thirty-four pounds. I came to York."

"He never came to see you? Never tried to follow you?"

She shook her head. "I never told him where I was. I just

ceased to exist. But I'd ceased to exist so many years before for
William that what did it matter."

"Why didn't you divorce him?"

"Because I never intended to marry again. I came to York
longing for an education, not a husband. I planned to work for a
while, to save money, to go to London or even emigrate to the
States. But six weeks after I arrived in York, everything changed.
I met Russell Mowrey."

"How did you meet?"

She smiled at the memory. "They'd fenced off part of the city
when they began the Viking digs."

"Yes, I recall that."

"Russell was a graduate student from London. He was part of
the excavation team. I'd stuck my head through a bit of a hole
in the fence to have a look at the work. And there was Russell.
His first words to me were, 'Jesus, a Norse goddess!' and then he
blushed to the roots of his hair. I think I fell in love with him
then. He was twenty-six years old. He wore spectacles that kept
slipping down his nose, absolutely filthy trousers, and a university jersey. When he walked over to speak to me, he slipped in
the mud and fell directly onto his bottom."

"Not much of a Darcy," Lynley said kindly.

"No. So much more. We were married four weeks later."

"Why didn't you tell him about William?"

She knotted her brows, appeared to be searching for words
that would enable them to understand. "Russell was an innocent. He had such . . . such an image of me. He saw me as a
kind of Viking princess, a snow queen. How could I tell him I
had two children and a husband that I'd left on a farm in the
dales?"

"What would have changed if he'd known?"

"Nothing, I suppose. But at the time, I believed *everything*
would have. I believed that he wouldn't want me if he knew,
that he wouldn't be willing to wait for me through a divorce. I'd
been looking for love, Inspector. And finally, here it was. Could
I take a chance that it might escape me?"

"But you're only two hours from Keldale here. Were you never
worried that William might one day show up in your life? Even
as a chance encounter on the street?"

"William never left the dales. Not once in the years that I knew him. He had everything there: his children, his religion, his farm. Why on earth would he ever come to York? Besides, I thought at first that we'd go to London. Russell's family is there. I'd no idea that he'd want to settle here. But here we stayed. We had Rebecca five years later. Then William eighteen months after that."

"*William!*"

"You can imagine how I felt when Russell wanted to call him William. It's his father's name. What could I do but agree?"

"And you've been here, then, for nineteen years?"

"Yes," she replied. "First in a small flat in the city centre, then a row house near Bishopthorpe Road, and last year we bought this house. We'd . . . saved for so long. Russell worked two jobs and I've my job at the museum as well. We've been," she blinked back her first tears, "so happy. God, so happy. Until now. You've come for me, haven't you? Or have you brought me word?"

"No one's told you? You haven't read about it?"

"Read about it? Has something . . . He isn't . . ." Tessa looked from Lynley to Havers. It was obvious that she saw something in their faces, for her own face flashed fear before she went on. "The night Russell left, he was terribly angry. I thought that if only I said nothing, did nothing, it would work itself out. He'd come home and—"

Lynley suddenly understood that they were talking about two entirely different things. "Mrs. Mowrey," he said, "do you not know about your husband?"

Her eyes widened, growing dark with apprehension. "Russell," she whispered. "He left that Saturday the investigator found me. Three weeks ago. He's not been home since."

"Mrs. Mowrey," Lynley said carefully, "William Teys was murdered three weeks ago. On Saturday night between ten and midnight. Your daughter Roberta was charged with the crime."

If they had thought she might faint, they were wrong. She stared at them without speaking for nearly a minute, then turned back to the window. "Rebecca will be home soon," she said tonelessly. "She comes home for lunch. She'll ask about her father. She does every day. She knows something's wrong, but I've managed to keep most of it from her." A trembling hand touched her cheek. "I know Russell's gone to London. I haven't phoned his family because, of course, I didn't want them to know anything was wrong. But I know he's gone to them in London. I *know*."

"Do you have a photograph of your husband?" Lynley asked. "His family's London address?"

She swung on him. "He wouldn't!" she cried passionately. "This is a man who has *never* lifted his hand to strike one of his own children! He was angry—yes, I've said that—but his anger was with *me*, not with William! He wouldn't have gone, he couldn't have—" She began to cry, horribly, shedding what were probably her first tears in three agonising weeks. Pressing her forehead against the window glass, she wept bitterly, as if she would never be consoled.

Havers got to her feet and left the room. Good God, where is she going? Lynley wondered, half-expecting a repeat of her disappearing act in the pub last night. But she returned moments later with a pitcher of orange juice and a glass.

"Thank you, Barbara," he said.

She nodded, shot him a diffident smile, and poured the woman a glass of the liquid.

Tessa Mowrey took it but rather than drink, she clutched it as if it were a talisman. "Rebecca mustn't see me like this. I've got to pull myself together. Must be stronger than this." She saw the glass in her hand, took a sip, and grimaced. "I can't abide tinned orange juice. Why do I have it in the house? Oh, Russell says that it's not that bad. I suppose it isn't, really." When she turned back to Lynley, she looked, he saw, every single day of her forty-three years. "He did not kill William."

"That's what everyone in Keldale says of Roberta."

She flinched. "I don't think of her as my daughter. I'm sorry. I never knew her."

"She's been placed in a mental asylum, Mrs. Mowrey. When William was found, she claimed to have killed him."

"Then if she's *admitted* to the crime, why have you come to see me? If she says she killed William then certainly Russell . . ."

Her voice drifted off. It was as if she had suddenly heard her own words and realised how eager she was to trade daughter for husband.

He could hardly blame her. Lynley thought of the barn stall, the ornate Bible, the photograph albums, the cool silence of the melancholy house. "Did you never see Gillian again?" he asked abruptly, waiting for a sign, the smallest indication that Tessa knew of Gillian's disappearance. There was none.

"Never."

"She never contacted you in any way?"

"Of course not. Even if she'd wanted to, William wouldn't have allowed it, I'm sure."

Probably not, thought Lynley. But once she ran off, once she cut the ties with her father, why had she not sought her mother then?

"Religious fanatic," Havers declared decisively. She shoved her hair back behind her ears and gave her attention to the photograph she held. "But *this* one's not half bad. She did okay on her second time round. Too bad she didn't bother with a divorce." Russell Mowrey smiled up at her from the photograph Tessa had given them. He was a nice-looking man in a three-piece suit, wife on his arm. Easter Sunday. Havers put it in the manila folder and gave herself back to the passing scenery. "At least we know why Gillian left."

"Because of the father's religion?"

"That's the way I see it," Havers replied. "Obviously, a combination of that and the second baby. There she'd been, for eight years the centre of her father's life—Mum doesn't appear to have counted for much—when all of a sudden a new baby arrives. It's supposed to be Mummy's, but Dad doesn't trust Mummy to do right by her children, so he takes this one over as well. Mummy leaves and Gillian follows."

"Not exactly, Havers. She waited eight years to go wherever she went."

"Well, you can't expect her to have run off when she was eight years old! She bided her time, probably hating little Roberta every second for stealing her dad."

"That doesn't make sense. First you say that Gillian left because she couldn't abide her father's religious fanaticism. Then you say she left because she'd lost his love to Roberta. Now what is it? She either loves him and wants to be his favourite again, or she can't abide his religious devotion and feels she has to escape. You can't have it both ways."

"It's not black and white!" Havers protested loudly. "These things never are!"

Lynley glanced at her, amazed by the affront in her voice. Her stubby features looked like paste. "Barbara—"

"I'm sorry! Dammit! I'm doing it all over again! Why do I bother? I'm no *good* at this. I *always* do it. I never—"

"Barbara," he interrupted firmly.

She stared straight ahead. "Yes, sir?"

"We're discussing the case, not arguing before a bar of justice. It's fine to have an opinion. I want you to, in fact. I've always found it extremely helpful to talk a case over with someone." But it was more than that, really. It was arguing, laughing, hearing the sweet voice say *Oh, you think you're right, Tommy, but I shall prove you wrong!* He felt loneliness settle on him like a cold, wet shroud.

Havers moved restlessly in her seat. With no music playing, the tension was screaming to be heard.

"I don't know what it is," she said at last. "I get into the fray and forget what I'm doing."

"I understand." He let the matter drop, his eyes following the meandering pattern that the stone walls made on the hillside across the dale from the road on which they travelled.

He thought about Tessa. He knew that he was trying to understand her and that he was ill-equipped to do so. Nothing in his life of Cornwall and Howenstow, of Oxford and Belgravia, even of Scotland Yard, explained the paucity of experience of life on a remote farm that would drive a girl of sixteen to believe that her only future lay in immediate marriage. And yet surely that was the foundation of what had happened. No romantic interpretation of the facts at hand—no reflections upon Heathcliff, no matter how apt—could hide the real explanation. The drudgery and sheer ennui of those weeks when she had been forced to stay home and help out had made an otherwise simple Yorkshire farmer look arresting by comparison. Thus, she merely moved from one trap into another. Married at sixteen, a mother before her seventeenth birthday. Wouldn't any woman have wanted to escape such a life? Yet, if that was the case, why marry again in such a hurry?

Havers broke into his thoughts. An underlying note of urgency in her voice made Lynley glance at her curiously. Tiny beads of sweat stood out on her forehead. She swallowed noisily. "What I can't see is the . . . Tessa's shrine. The woman walks out on him—not that she didn't appear to have every right to—and he sets up a virtual Taj Mahal of photographs in a corner of the sitting room."

It suddenly dawned on Lynley. "How do we know *William* set up the shrine?"

Havers came to her own quick terms with the knowledge. "Either of the girls could have done it," she responded.

"Who do you imagine?"

"It had to be Gillian."

"As a bit of revenge? A little daily reminder to William that Mummy'd run off? A little knife inserted between the ribs since he'd started to favour Roberta?"

"Bet on it, sir," Havers agreed.

They drove on for several miles before Lynley spoke again. "She could have done it, Havers. Something tells me she was desperate enough."

"Tessa, d'you mean?"

"Russell was gone that night. She says she took aspirin and went directly to bed, but no one can verify it. She could have gone to Keldale."

"Why kill the dog?"

"He wouldn't have known her. He wasn't there nineteen years ago. Who was Tessa to him? A stranger."

"But decapitate her first husband?" Havers frowned. "Would have been easier to divorce him, I'd think."

"No. Not for a Catholic."

"Even so, Russell's a better candidate if you ask me. Who knows where he went?" When Lynley didn't reply, she added, "Sir?"

"I . . ." Lynley hesitated, studying the road ahead. "Tessa's right. He's gone to London."

"How can you be certain of that?"

"Because I think I saw him, Havers. At the Yard."

"So he *did* go to turn her in. I suppose she knew all along that he would."

"No. I don't think so."

Havers offered a new thought. "Well, then there's Ezra."

Lynley flashed her a smile. "William in his jimjams in the middle of the road ripping up Ezra's watercolours while Ezra curses him to hell and back? We *could* have a motive for murder there. I don't think an artist would take lightly to having someone rip up his work."

Havers opened her mouth, stopped. She reflected for a moment. "But it wasn't his pyjamas."

"Yes, it was."

"It wasn't. It was his dressing gown. Remember? Nigel said his legs reminded him of a gorilla. So what was he doing in his dressing gown? It was still light out. It wasn't time for bed."

"Changing for dinner, I dare say. He's up in his room, looks out the window, sees Ezra trespassing, and comes charging into the yard."

"I suppose that could be it."

"What else?"

"Exercising, perhaps?"

"Deep knee bends in his underwear? That's hard to picture."

"Or . . . perhaps with Olivia?"

Lynley smiled. "Not if everything we've heard about him is true. William sounds to me like a strictly after-marriage man. I don't think he'd try any funny business with Olivia beforehand."

"What about Nigel Parrish?"

"What about him?"

"Walking the dog back to the farm out of the goodness of his heart, like a card-carrying member of the RSPCA? Doesn't that whole story seem a bit off to you?"

"It does. But do you really think Parrish would want to get his hands dirty with a bit of William Teys' blood? Not to mention his head rolling across the stall floor."

"To be honest, he seems the type to faint at the sight."

They laughed, a first shared communication. It dropped almost immediately into an uncomfortable silence at the sudden realisation that they could become friends.

* * *

The decision to go to Barnstingham Mental Asylum grew out of Lynley's belief that Roberta held all the cards in the current game they were playing: the identity of the murderer, the motive behind the crime, and the disappearance of Gillian Teys. He'd stopped an hour out of York to make the arrangements by telephone, and now, pulling the car to a stop on the gravel drive in front of the building, he turned to Barbara.

"Cigarette?" He offered his gold case.

"No, sir. Thank you."

He nodded, glanced at the imposing building, then back at her. "Rather wait here, Sergeant?" he asked as he lit his cigarette with the silver lighter. He took a few moments about replacing all the impedimenta of his habit.

She watched him with speculative eyes. "Why?"

He shrugged casually. Too casually, she noted. "You look fagged out. I thought you might want a bit of a rest."

Fagged out. It was his public-school-fop act. She'd begun to notice how he used it occasionally to serve the need of the moment. He'd dropped it earlier. Why was he picking it up now?

"If we're talking about exhaustion, Inspector, *you* look just about ready to drop. What's up?"

He examined himself in the mirror at her words, his cigarette dangling from his lips, his eyes narrowed against the smoke, part Sam Spade, part Algernon Moncrieff. "I *do* look a sight." He busied himself about his appearance for a moment: straightening his tie, examining his hair, brushing at nonexistent lint on the lapels of his jacket. She waited. Finally he met her eyes. The fop, as well as the other personae, was gone. "The farm upset you a bit yesterday," he said frankly. "I have an idea that what we'll find in here is going to be a hell of a lot worse than the farm."

For a moment she couldn't take her eyes from his, but she pressed her hand to the door and flung it open. "I can *deal* with it, sir," she said abruptly and got out into the brisk autumn air.

* * *

"We've kept her confined," Dr. Samuels was saying to Lynley as they walked down the transverse passage that ran straight through the building from east to west.

Barbara followed behind them, relieved to find that Barnstingham was not exactly what she had pictured when she first heard the words *mental asylum*. It was really not very hospital-like at all, an English baroque building laid out on cross-axes. They had entered through a front hall that rose two storeys, with fluted pilasters standing on plinths against the walls. *Light* and *colour* were the operative words here, for the room was painted a calming shade of peach, the decorative plasterwork was white, the ankle-thick carpeting was merely a shade off rust, and while the portraits were dark and moody, of the Flemish school, their subjects managed to look suitably apologetic about the fact.

All this was a relief, for when Lynley had first mentioned the need to see Roberta, to come to this place, Barbara had become quite faint, that old insidious panic setting in. Lynley had seen it, of course. Damn the man. He didn't miss a trick.

Now that she was inside the building, she felt steadier, a feeling that improved once they left the great central hall and began their journey down the passage. Here conviviality expressed itself in soothing Constable landscapes and vases of fresh flowers and quiet voices in the air. The sound of music and singing came from a distance.

"The choir," Dr. Samuels explained. "Here, it's just this way."

Samuels himself had been a secondary source of both surprise and relief. Outside the walls of the hospital, Barbara wouldn't have known he was a psychiatrist. *Psychiatrist* somehow conjured up images of Freud: a bearded Victorian face, a cigar, and those speculative eyes. But Samuels had the look of a man who was more at home on horseback or hiking across the moors than probing disturbed psyches. He was well-built, loose limbed, and clean shaven, with a tendency, Barbara guessed, to be less than patient with anyone whose intelligence did not match his own. He was probably the devil on a tennis court as well.

She'd begun to feel quite at ease with the hospital when Dr. Samuels opened a narrow door—funny how it had been concealed by some panelling—and led them into the new wing of the building. This was the locked ward, looking and smelling exactly as

Barbara had supposed a locked ward would. The carpeting was a very dark, serviceable brown. The walls were the colour of sun-baked sand, unadorned and broken only by doors into which small windows were set at eye level. The air was filled with that medicinal smell of antiseptics and detergents and drugs. And it was cut by a low moaning that seemed to come from nowhere and everywhere. It could have been the wind. It could have been anything.

Here it is, she told herself. The place for psychos, for girls who decapitate daddies, for girls who murder. Lots of things are murder, Barb.

"There's been absolutely nothing since her original statement," Dr. Samuels was saying to Lynley. "She's not catatonic. She's merely said what she intends to say, I think." He glanced at the clipboard he was carrying. " 'I did it. I'm not sorry.' On the day the body was found. She's not spoken since."

"There's no medical cause? She's been examined?"

Dr. Samuels' lips tightened in offence. It was clear that this Scotland Yard intrusion bordered on insult, and if he had to impart information, it would be minimal at best.

"She's been examined," he said. "No seizure, no stroke. She can speak. She chooses not to."

If he was bothered by the clipped nature of the doctor's response, Lynley didn't let it show. He was used to encountering attitudes like the psychiatrist's, attitudes proclaiming that the police were antagonists to be thwarted rather than allies to be helped. He slowed his steps and told Dr. Samuels about Roberta's cache of food. This, at least, caught the man's attention. When he next spoke, his words walked the line between frustration and deeper thought.

"I don't know what to tell you, Inspector. The food could, as you guess, be a compulsion. It could be a stimulus or a response. It could be a source of gratification or a form of sublimation. Until Roberta's willing to give us something to go on, it could be damn well anything."

Lynley shifted to another area. "Why did you take her from the Richmond police? Isn't that a bit irregular?"

"Not when the responsible party's signed her in," Dr. Samuels replied. "We're a private hospital."

"The responsible party. Was that Superintendent Nies?"

Samuels shook his head impatiently. "Not at all. We don't take people at random from the police." He scanned Roberta's chart. "It was . . . let me see where . . . Gibson, Richard Gibson. He names himself as her closest relative. He's the one who got the court to agree and filled out the paperwork."

"Richard Gibson?"

"That's the name on the form, Inspector," Samuels replied tersely. "He's signed her in for treatment pending the trial. She's in therapy daily. There's no progress yet, but that isn't to say there never will be any."

"But why would Gibson—" Lynley was speaking more to himself than the other two, but Samuels went on, perhaps in the assumption that he was being addressed.

"She's his cousin, after all. And the sooner she's better, the sooner the trial. That is, unless she's proven incompetent to stand trial at all."

"And in that case," Lynley finished, his eyes fixed grimly on the doctor's face, "she's in for life, isn't she?"

"Until she recovers." Samuels led them up to a heavy, locked door. "She's just in here. It's unfortunate that she has to be alone, but considering the circumstances. . . ." He gestured with his hands, unlocked the door, and swung it open. "Roberta, you've visitors," he said.

He'd chosen Prokofiev—*Romeo and Juliet*—and the music had begun almost immediately when he started the car. Thank God, Barbara thought brokenly. Thank God. Let the music of violins, cellos and violas drive thought away, drive memory away, drive everything completely, irreversibly away so that there is no existence but that of audition, so that she needn't think of the girl in the room and, even more frightening, of the man in the car.

Even staring steadfastly ahead, she could still see his hands on the wheel, could see the gold hair on them—lighter even than the hair on his head—could see each finger, note its movement, as he guided the car back to Keldale.

When he leaned forward to make an adjustment in the sound, she could see his profile. He was very lightly tanned. Gold and brown. Skin, hair, and eyes. Straight, classical nose. The firm line of jaw. A face that spoke clearly of tremendous inner strength, of resources of character that she couldn't comprehend.

How had he done it?

She'd been by a window, not looking out but rather staring fixedly at the wall, a lummox of a girl nearly six feet tall who must have weighed well over fifteen stone. She sat on a stool, her back hunched over in an arc of defeat, and she rocked.

"Roberta, my name is Thomas Lynley. I've come to talk to you about your father."

The rocking continued. The eyes looked at nothing, saw nothing. If she heard at all, she gave absolutely no sign.

Her hair was filthy, foul-smelling. It was pulled back from her broad, moon-shaped face with an elastic band, but greasy tendrils had escaped imprisonment and hung forward stiffly, kissing on her neck the pockets of flesh that encased in their folds the incongruous ornament of a single, slender gold chain.

"Father Hart came to London, Roberta. He's asked us to help you. He says he knows you didn't hurt anyone."

Nothing. The broad face was expressionless. Suppurating pimples covered cheeks and chin. Bloated skin stretched over layers of fat that had long ago erased whatever definition her features might have had. She was dough-like, grey and unclean.

"We've been talking to a great many people in Keldale. We've seen your cousin Richard, and Olivia, and Bridie. Bridie cut her hair, Roberta. She's made quite a mess of it, unfortunately, in an effort to look like the Princess of Wales. Her mother was quite upset about it. She said how good you always were to Bridie."

No response. Roberta was dressed in a too-short skirt that revealed white, flabby thighs upon which the flesh, dotted by red pustules, quivered when she rocked. There were hospital slippers on her feet, but they were too small, and her sausage toes hung out, their uncut nails curling round them.

"We've been to the house. Have you read all those books? Stepha Odell said that you'd read them all. We were amazed at how many you have. We saw the pictures of your mother, Roberta. She was lovely, wasn't she?"

Silence. Her arms hung at her sides. Her enormous breasts strained against the cheap material of her blouse. Its buttons struggled to hold the thin garment closed as the pressure of the rocking continued, each movement causing the flesh to heave to and fro in a rebarbative pavane.

"I think this may be a bit difficult for you to hear, Roberta, but we saw your mother today. Do you know that she lives in York? You have another brother and sister there. She told us how much your father loved you and Gillian."

The movement ceased. The face neither acknowledged nor changed, but the tears began. They were silent, ugly rivers of mute pain dipping and plunging through the crevices of fat, climbing the peaks of acne. With the tears came the mucus. It began its descent from her nose in a slimy cord, touched her lips, and crawled onto her chin.

Lynley squatted before her. He removed a snowy handkerchief from his pocket and wiped her face clean. He took her pulpy, lifeless hand in his own and pressed it firmly.

"Roberta." There was no response. "I'll find Gillian." He stood, folded the elegant, monogrammed linen square, and returned it to his pocket.

What had Webberly said? Barbara thought. *There's a lot you might learn from working with Lynley.*

And now she knew. She couldn't look at him. She couldn't meet his eyes. She knew what would be there and the thought of its existence in this man she had been determined to believe was an absolute fop of an upper-class snob chilled her entirely.

He was supposed to be the man who danced in nightclubs, who dispensed sexual favours, laughter, and good cheer, who moved effortlessly in a gilt-edged world of money and privilege. But he was not supposed to be—never supposed to be—the man she had seen today.

He'd stepped neatly out of the mould she'd created and destroyed it without a backward glance. She *had* to fit him back into it somehow. If she didn't, the fires within her that for so many years had kept her alive would be swiftly extinguished. And then, she knew well, she would die in the cold.

That was the thought that carried her to Keldale, longing

to fly from his presence. But when the Bentley made the final turn into the village, she knew immediately that there would be no quick escape. For Nigel Parrish and another man were having a violent quarrel upon the bridge, directly in the path of the car.

9

ORGAN MUSIC SEEMED to be blasting from the very trees. It swelled to crescendoes, faded, and roared out again: a baroque combination of chords, rests, and flourishes that made Lynley think that at any moment the phantom himself would come swinging down from the opera chandeliers. At the appearance of the Bentley, the two men parted, the one shouting a final violent imprecation at Nigel Parrish before he stalked off in the direction of the high street.

"I think I'll have a word with our Nigel," Lynley remarked. "No need for you to come, Havers. Go have a bit of a rest."

"I can certainly—"

"That's an order, Sergeant."

Damn him. "Yes, sir."

Lynley waited until Havers had disappeared into the lodge before he walked back across the bridge to the strange little cottage that sat on the far side of the common. It was, he thought, a more than curious structure. The front of the building was trellissed by late roses. Unrestrained, they spread out like an encroaching wilderness towards the narrow windows on either side of the door. They climbed the wall, crowned the lintel majestically, and travelled upward to begin their glory on the roof. They were a solid blanket of disturbing colour—bloodred—and they flooded the air with a scent so rich as to be virtually miasmal. The entire effect was one step short of obscene.

Nigel Parrish had already retreated inside, and Lynley followed him, pausing in the open doorway to survey the room. The source of the music that continued to soar round them was a speaker system that beggared belief. Enormous amplifiers sat in all four corners, creating at the centre a vortex of sound. Other than an organ, a tape recorder, a receiver, and a turntable, there was nothing in the room save a threadbare carpet and a few old chairs.

Parrish switched off the tape recorder that had been the source of the sound. He rewound the tape, removed it from the machine, and replaced it in its container. He took his time about it all, giving every movement a precision which told Lynley that he knew very well that the other man was standing at the door. It was nonetheless a nice performance.

"Mr. Parrish?"

A start of surprise. A swift turn. A welcoming smile breaking over the features. But he couldn't hide the fact that his hands were shaking. As Lynley saw this, so apparently did Parrish, for he stuffed them into the pockets of his tweed trousers.

"Inspector! A social call, I hope? Sorry you had to come upon that little scene with Ezra."

"Ah. So that was Ezra."

"Yes. Honey-haired, honey-tongued little Ezra. Dear boy thought 'artistic licence' gave him access to my back garden to study the light on the river. Can you imagine such cheek? Here I was fine-tuning my psyche with Bach when I glanced out the window and saw him setting up shop. Blast his pretty little heart."

"It's a bit late in the afternoon to be setting up for a painting," Lynley remarked. He wandered to the window. Neither the river nor the garden could be seen from the room. He reflected on the nature of Parrish's lie.

"Well, who knows what goes on in the minds of these great magicians of the paintbrush," Parrish said lightly. "Didn't Whistler paint the Thames in the middle of the night?"

"I'm not sure Ezra Farmington's in Whistler's league." Lynley watched Parrish take out a packet of cigarettes and struggle to light one with fingers that wouldn't cooperate. He crossed the room and offered the flame of his lighter.

Parrish's eyes met his and then hid themselves behind a thin veil of smoke. "Thanks," he said. "Beastly little scene. Well, I haven't welcomed you to Rose Cottage. A drink? No? I hope you don't mind if I indulge." He disappeared into an adjoining room. Glass rattled. There was a long pause followed by the sounds of bottles and glassware again. Parrish emerged, a respectable inch of whisky in a tumbler. His second or third, Lynley speculated.

"Why do you drink at the Dove and Whistle?"

The question caught Parrish off guard. "Do sit down, Inspector. I need to, and the thought of you towering over me like Nemesis himself makes me positively limp with fear."

It was an excellent stall tactic, Lynley thought. But two could play at that game. He walked over to the stereo and took his time over an inventory of Parrish's tapes: a considerable collection of Bach, Chopin, Verdi, Vivaldi, and Mozart, with an adequate representation of modernists as well. Parrish indulged a wide range of musical tastes, he concluded. He crossed the room to one of the heavy, stuffed chairs and meditated on the black oak beams that spanned the ceiling.

"Why do you live in this village in the middle of nowhere? A man with your musical taste and talent would obviously be happier in a more cosmopolitan environment, wouldn't he?"

Parrish laughed shortly. He smoothed a hand over his perfectly combed hair. "I think I like the other question better. Have I choice on which one to answer?"

"The Holy Grail is only round the corner. But you walk to the other end of the village on—what was it?—your tired old legs to drink in the other pub on St. Chad's Lane. What's the attraction?"

"Absolutely nothing. Well, I could say it's Hannah, but I doubt if you'd believe me. The truth is I prefer the Dove's atmosphere. There's something unholy about getting roaring drunk just opposite a church, isn't there?"

"Avoiding someone at the Holy Grail?" Lynley asked.

"Avoiding . . . ?" Parrish's eyes slipped from Lynley to the window. A full-headed rose was kissing the glass with enormous lips. The petals had begun to curl back. Stigma, style, anther, and filament had blackened. It should have been picked. It would die soon. "Good heavens, no. Whom would I avoid? Father Hart, perhaps? Or the dear, deceased William? He and the priest used to tipple a few once or twice a week there."

"You didn't care much for Teys, did you?"

"No, not much. Holier-than-thous have never been in my line. I don't know how Olivia abided the man."

"Perhaps she wanted a father for Bridie."

"Perhaps. God knows the child could use some parental influence. Even dour old William was probably better than nothing. Liv is hopeless with her. I'd take it on myself, but to be frank, I don't much care for children. And I don't like ducks at all."

"But you're close to Olivia anyway?"

Parrish's eyes showed nothing. "I went to school with her husband. Paul. What a man *he* was! Rip-roaring, good-time Paul."

"He died four years ago, is that correct?"

Parrish nodded. "Huntington's chorea. At the end he didn't even recognise his wife. It was horrible. For everyone. Changed everyone's life to see him die that way." He blinked several times and gave his attention to his cigarette and then to his fingernails. They were well manicured, Lynley noted. The man went on with another bright smile. It was his defensive weapon, his way of denying any emotion that might seep through the surface of his thin-shelled indifference. "I suppose the next question is where was *I* on the fatal night? I'd love to trot out an alibi for you, Inspector. In bed with the village tart would be nice. But I'm afraid that I didn't know our blessed William would encounter an axe that evening, so I sat here playing my organ. Quite alone. But I must clear myself, mustn't I? So I suppose I should say that anyone who heard me could verify the story."

"Like today perhaps?"

Parrish ignored the question and finished off his drink. "Then when I was done, I skipped off to bed. Again, unfortunately, very much alone."

"How long have you lived in Keldale, Mr. Parrish?"

"Ah. Back to the original thought, are we? Let me see. It must be nearly seven years."

"Before that?"

"Before that, Inspector, I lived in York. I was a music teacher at a prep school. And no, if you're going to go delving into my past for tasty little items, I was not dismissed. I left by choice. I wanted the country. I wanted some peace." His voice rose slightly on the last word.

Lynley got to his feet. "Let me give you some now. Good evening to you."

As he left the cottage, the music resumed—muted this time—but not before the discordant noise of glass breaking on stone told him the manner in which Nigel Parrish celebrated his departure.

"I hope you don't mind, but I've booked you into Keldale Hall for dinner," Stepha Odell said. She cocked her bright head to one side and regarded Lynley thoughtfully. "Yes, I think I did just the right thing. You look as if you need that tonight."

"Am I becoming gaunt before your eyes?"

She closed a ledger and shelved it behind the reception desk. "Not at all. The food's excellent, of course, but that isn't why I've booked you there. The hall is one of our biggest diversions. It's run by the local eccentric."

"You have everything here, don't you?"

She laughed. "All the pleasures that life affords, Inspector. Would you like a drink, or are you still on duty?"

"I wouldn't say no to a pint of Odell's."

"Good." She led him into the lounge and busied herself behind the bar. "Keldale Hall is run by the Burton-Thomas family. I use that last word quite loosely, of course. Mrs. Burton-Thomas has half a dozen or more young people working for her, and she stubbornly insists that they all call her auntie. It's part of the cloud of eccentricity in which she likes to move, I should imagine."

"Sounds a Dickensian group," Lynley remarked.

She pushed his ale across the bar and pulled a smaller one for herself. "Just wait till you meet them. And meet them you shall, for Mrs. Burton-Thomas always takes dinner with her guests. When I rang her to book you in, she was beside herself with the idea of Scotland Yard dining at her table. No doubt she'll poison someone just to see you at work. The pickings are going to be rather slim, however. She said she has only two couples there now: an American dentist and two 'hoochiesmoochie types,' to use her expression."

"It sounds just the kind of evening I'm longing for." He walked to the window, glass in hand, and looked down the winding lane that was Keldale Abbey Road. He couldn't see much of it, for it curved to the right and disappeared into the dusk.

Stepha came to join him. They didn't speak for some moments. "I expect you've seen Roberta," she said gently at last.

He turned, thinking to find her watching him, but she wasn't. Instead her eyes were on the glass of ale she held. She turned it slowly in the palm of her hand, as if all her concentration were centred on its balance and the total necessity of not spilling a drop. "How did you know?"

"She was quite tall as a child. I remember. Almost as tall as Gillian. A big girl." With a hand dampened by the moisture of the glass, she brushed a few hairs from her brow. Her fingers left a misty streak on her skin. She rubbed it off impatiently. "It happened quite slowly, Inspector. First she was just filled out—chubby, I suppose. Then she was . . . what you saw today." The shudder that passed through her body spoke volumes. And as if she realised what her reaction implied, she went on. "That's horrible of me, isn't it? I have rather a despicable aversion to ugliness. Frankly, I don't much like that about myself."

"But you didn't answer me."

"I didn't? What did you ask?"

"How you knew I'd seen Roberta."

A dull flush crept into Stepha's cheeks. She shifted her weight from one foot to the other and looked so ill-at-ease that Lynley was sorry he had pressed her.

"It doesn't matter," he said.

"It's just that . . . you look a bit different than you did this morning. More weighted down. And there are lines at the corners of your mouth." The flush deepened on her beautiful skin. "They weren't there before."

"I see."

"So I wondered if you'd seen her."

"But you knew without asking."

"Yes, I suppose I did. And I wondered how you can bear to look at the ugliness of other people's lives as you do."

"I've done it for some years. One gets used to it, Stepha." The big man strangled as he sat at his desk, the dirty girl dead with the needle in her arm, the savage mutilation of a young man's corpse. Did one ever really get used to man's dark side?

Her eyes met his with surprising directness. "But surely it must be like looking at hell."

"A bit."

"Then have you never wanted to run from it? Run away madly in the other direction? Never? Not once?"

"One can't run forever."

She turned from him, moving her eyes back to the window. "I can," she murmured.

A sharp rap on the door caused Barbara to stub out her third cigarette. She looked around in a panic, opened the window, and rushed to the lavatory, where she flushed the incriminating evidence down the toilet. A second rap and Lynley's voice called her name.

She went to the door. He hesitated, glancing over her shoulder curiously before he spoke. "Ah, Havers," he said. "Apparently Miss Odell has seen fit to find us a more edible repast this evening. She's booked us into Keldale Hall." He consulted his watch. "In an hour."

"What?" Barbara cried out in involuntary horror. "I haven't . . . I can't . . . I don't think . . ."

Lynley raised an eyebrow. "Please don't go all Helen on me and say you've nothing to wear, Havers."

"But I haven't!" she protested. "You go alone. I'll get something at the Dove and Whistle."

"Considering your reaction to last night's fare, do you think that's wise?"

A blow below the belt. Blast him. "I don't care much for chicken. I never have."

"Wonderful. I understand the cook at the hall is a bit of a gourmet. I doubt if anything with feathers will even put in an appearance. Unless, of course, Hannah's waiting on tables."

"But I simply can't—"

"It's an order, Havers. In an hour." He turned on his heel.

Damn him! She slammed the door loud enough to signal her

displeasure. Wonderful! What an evening to look forward to: fumbling aimlessly with sixteen pieces of silverware; wineglasses everywhere; waiters and waitresses removing knives and forks before one even had a chance to decide what to do with them. Chicken and peas at the Dove and Whistle sounded like heaven compared to that.

She stomped to the wardrobe and yanked it open. Divine. Now what *shall* it be for an evening of mingling elegantly with society? The brown tweed skirt and matching pullover? The jeans and hiking boots? What about the blue suit, to remind him of Helen? Ha! Who could ever remind him of Helen, with her impeccable wardrobe, her well-cut hair, her manicured hands, her lyrical voice?

She yanked a white wool shirtwaist from the wardrobe and tossed it onto the rumpled bed. It really was almost amusing. Would people actually think she was his date? Apollo taking Medusa to dine? How would he handle the stares and the gibes?

One hour later, as good as his word, he knocked on her door. She looked in the mirror, her stomach churning. Oh God, the dress was *awful*. She resembled a white-garbed barrel with legs. She jerked open the door and glared at him furiously. He was dressed to the absolute teeth.

"Do you always carry clothes like that around with you?" she demanded, incredulous.

"Just like the Boy Scouts." He smiled. "Shall we go?"

He escorted her gallantly down the stairs and into the night, where he opened the car door for her and tucked her within the tooled leather comfort of the Bentley. The born gentleman, she thought derisively. On automatic pilot. Get him into his Lord of the Manor outfit and forget Scotland Yard.

As if he read her mind, he turned to her before starting the car. "Havers, I'd like to give the case a rest for the evening."

What on earth would they have to talk about if the murder of Teys was going to be taboo? "All right," she replied, brusquely.

He nodded and turned the ignition key. The big car purred to life. "I love this part of England," he said as they set off down Keldale Abbey Road. "You haven't been told that I'm an unabashed Yorkist, have you?"

"A Yorkist?"

"The War of Roses. We're deep in their country now. Sheriff Hutton's not far from here and Middleham's practically within shouting distance."

"Oh." Wonderful. A discourse on history. Her entire knowledge of the War of Roses began and ended with the conflict's name.

"Naturally, I know one's really obliged to think badly of the Yorks. They *did*, after all, do away with Henry VI." He tapped his fingers reflectively against the wheel. "Except I can never help thinking that there was a justice in that. Pomfret and all. Richard II being murdered by his very own cousin. Killing Henry seems to have closed the circle of the crime."

She pleated the white dress between her fingers and sighed, defeated. "Look, sir, I'm no good at this sort of thing. I . . . well, I'd do much better at the Dove and Whistle. If you'd please just—"

"*Barbara.*" He pulled abruptly to the verge. He was looking at her, she knew, but she stared ahead into the darkness and counted the moths that danced in the car's headlamps. "Would you just for an evening be what you are? *Whatever* you are."

"What's that supposed to mean?" God, how shrewish she sounded.

"It means that you may drop the act. Or at least that I wish you would."

"What act?"

"Just be what you are."

"How dare you—"

"Why do you pretend not to smoke?" he interrupted.

"Why do *you* pretend to be such a public school fop?" She hadn't intended the words to be so shrill. At first, as if evaluating her comment, he didn't respond.

There was silence. Then he threw back his head and laughed. "Touché. Shall we call a truce for the rest of the evening and go on despising each other with the dawn?"

She glared at him a moment, then, in spite of herself, smiled. She knew she was being manipulated, but it didn't seem to matter. "All right," she said reluctantly. But she noticed that neither of them had answered the other's question.

* * *

They were welcomed into Keldale Hall by a woman who put to rest every sartorial fear of Barbara's that Lynley had not been able to assuage. She was dressed in a moth-eaten skirt of indeterminate colour, a gypsy blouse decorated with stars, and a beaded shawl that she had slung round her shoulders like an Indian blanket. Her grey hair was gathered tightly into two elastic bands, one on each side of her neck, and to complete the ensemble she had perched an elaborate tortoiseshell Spanish comb on the top of her head.

"Scotland Yard?" she asked and looked Lynley over with a critical eye. "God, they didn't package 'em that way when I was young." She laughed uproariously. "Come in! We're a small party tonight, but you've saved me from murder."

"How's that?" Lynley asked, ushering Barbara ahead of him.

"I've an American couple that I'd love to kill. But we'll leave that. You'll understand soon enough. We're gathered in here." She led them across the massive stone hall, scented with the assorted meats that were roasting in the kitchen nearby. "I haven't breathed a word that you're Scotland Yard," she confided loudly, shouldering her beadwork back into place. "When you meet the Watsons, you'll know why." On through the dining room, where candlelight was casting shadows on the walls. A linen-covered table was set with china and silver. "The other couple are newlyweds. Londoners. I like 'em. Don't paw each other in public the way so many newlyweds do. Very quiet. Very sweet. I expect they don't like to draw attention to themselves because the man's crippled. Wife is a lovely little creature, though."

Barbara heard Lynley's swift intake of breath. Behind her, his steps slowed and then stopped altogether. "Who are they?" he asked hoarsely.

Mrs. Burton-Thomas turned around at the entrance to the oak hall. "Name of Allcourt-St. James." She threw open the door. "Here's more company for us!" she announced.

Barbara was intensely aware of the photographic quality of the scene. A fire burned brilliantly, hissing as the flames devoured the coal. Comfortable chairs were gathered round it. At the far end of the room, touched by shadows, Deborah St. James was bent over a piano, leafing through a family album with delight. She looked up with a smile. The men rose to their feet. And the picture froze.

"*Lord,*" Lynley whispered—prayer, curse, resignation.

At his tone, Barbara looked at him, and it came with a sudden jolt of recognition. How ridiculous that she hadn't seen it before. Lynley was in love with the other man's wife.

"Hi there! That's one heckuva nice-lookin' suit," Hank Watson said. He extended his hand to Lynley. It was fat, slightly sweaty, like shaking hands with a warm, uncooked fish. "Dentistry," he announced. "Here for the ADA convention in London. Tax write-off to the s-k-y. This is JoJo, my wife."

Somehow the introductions were muddled through.

"Champagne before dinner is my rule," Mrs. Burton-Thomas said. "Before breakfast as well, if I have *my* way. Danny, bring the juice!" she shouted, in the general direction of the doorway, and a few moments later a girl came into the room, burdened with an ice bucket, champagne, and glasses.

"What line-a work you in, fella?" Hank asked Lynley as the glasses went around. "I thought Si here was some sort-a college professor type. Gave me the jumping hee-haws when he said he was a dead-body man."

"Sergeant Havers and I work for Scotland Yard," Lynley responded.

"Say-hey, JoJo-bean. Did you hear that, woman?" He looked at Lynley with new interest. "You here on the baby gig?"

"The baby gig?"

"Three-year-old case. Guess the trail's kinda cold now." Hank winked in the direction of Danny, who was putting the bottle of champagne into the bucket of ice. "Dead baby in the abbey? *You* know."

Lynley didn't know anything, didn't want to know anything. He couldn't have answered if his life depended upon it. He found that he didn't know what to do with himself, where to cast his eyes, what to say. He was only conscious of Deborah.

"We're here on the decapitation gig," Havers responded politely, miraculously.

"De-cap-i-ta-tion?" Hank crowed. "This is one jumping area of the country! Don't you think so, Bean?"

"Sure is," his wife said, nodding in solemn affirmation. She fingered the long strand of white beads she wore and looked hopefully in the direction of the silent St. Jameses.

Hank hunched forward in his chair, dragging it closer to Lynley's. "Well, give us the poop!" he demanded.

"I beg your pardon?"

"The p-o-o-p. The verified, certified poop." Hank slapped the arm of Lynley's chair. "Who did it, fella?" he demanded.

It was too much. The appalling little man screwing his face up in excitement was too much to bear. He was wearing a saffron polyester suit, a matching shirt in a floral print, and round his neck hung a heavy gold chain with a medallion that danced on the thick hair of his chest. A diamond the size of a walnut glittered on his finger, and he flashed white teeth made even whiter by his burnt sienna tan. His bulbous nose flexed its nostrils blackly.

"We're not entirely sure," Lynley replied seriously. "But you fit the description."

Hank stared at him, bug-eyed. "*I* fit the description?" he croaked. Then he peered at Lynley closely and broke into a grin. "*Damn* you Brits! I just can't get the hang of your humour! But I'm gettin' better, right, Si?"

Lynley finally looked at his friend and found him smiling. Amusement danced in St. James' eyes. "Absolutely," Si replied.

As they drove in the darkness back to the lodge, Barbara studied Lynley furtively, realising that until this evening it had been entirely unthinkable to her that a man such as he could ever have been unsuccessful in love. Yet here on the outskirts of the village was the undeniable evidence of that fact: Deborah.

There had been at the hall a horrified moment with the three of them staring at one another before she had come forward, a tentative smile on her face, a hand outstretched in greeting.

"Tommy! Whatever are you doing in Keldale?" Deborah St. James had asked.

He'd been at an absolute loss. Barbara saw it and intervened. "An investigation," she replied.

Then the horrible little American had thrown himself into their midst—it was a merciful intervention, really—and the other three began to breathe evenly once more.

Still, St. James had remained in his place by the fire, greeting his friend politely but making no other movement, his eyes for the most part following his wife. If he was concerned about Lynley's unexpected arrival, if jealousy stirred in him at the man's blatant feelings, his face betrayed nothing.

Of the two, Deborah had been more obviously distressed. Her colour was high. Her hands had clasped and unclasped repeatedly in her lap. Her eyes had moved restlessly between the two men, and she hadn't concealed her relief when Lynley suggested their departure at the earliest opportunity after the meal's conclusion.

Now he was pulling the car in front of the lodge and switching off the ignition. He leaned back and rubbed his eyes. "I feel as if I could sleep for a year. How do you suppose Mrs. Burton-Thomas is going to get rid of that dreadful dentist?"

"Arsenic?"

He laughed. "She'll have to do something. He was talking as if staying another month were the dearest thing to his heart. What an appalling man!"

"Not exactly the sort one wants to run into on a honeymoon," she admitted. She wondered if he would pick up the conversational thread, if he would say anything about St. James and Deborah and the awkward coincidence that had flung them into his path. Indeed, she wondered further if he would say anything at all about how he had come to position himself on the worst possible side of this unusual love triangle.

Instead of replying, however, he got out of the car and slammed the door. Barbara watched him shrewdly as he came to her side. Not a ripple appeared on the surface of his calm. He was in firm control. If anything at all, the fop was back.

The lodge door opened and a square of light framed Stepha Odell. "I thought I heard your car," she said. "You've a visitor, Inspector."

Deborah gazed at her reflection in the mirror. He'd said absolutely nothing since coming into their room, merely walking over to the fire and sitting in the chair, the brandy glass in his hand. She'd watched him, not sure what to say, afraid to penetrate the wall of his sudden isolation. *Don't go that way, Simon,* she'd wanted to shout. *Don't cut yourself off from me. Don't go back to that darkness.* But how could she say it and risk having Tommy thrown up in her face?

She ran the water into the bathroom basin and dismally watched its flow. What was he thinking, alone in that room? Was he haunted by Tommy? Did he wonder if she closed her eyes when they made love so she could dream of him? He never once had asked. He never once had questioned. He simply accepted whatever she said, whatever she gave. So what could she say or give to him now, with her past and Tommy's between them?

She splashed her face repeatedly, dried it, turned off the water, and forced herself to walk back into the bedroom. Her heart sank when she saw that he'd gone to bed. His heavy leg brace lay on the floor near the chair, and his crutches leaned against the wall next to the bed. The room was dark. But in the dying light of the fire she saw that he was still awake, sitting up in fact, with the pillows behind him, watching the glow of the embers.

She walked to the bed and sat down. "I'm in a welter," she said.

He felt for her hand. "I know. I've been sitting here trying to think how I might help you. But I don't know what to do."

"I hurt him, Simon. I never intended to, but it happened all the same, and I can't seem to forget it. When I see him, I feel so responsible for his pain. I want to make it go away. I . . . I suppose *I'd* feel better then. Less guilty about it all."

He touched her cheek and traced the line of her jaw. "If it were only that easy, my love. You can't make it go away. You can't help him. He's got to do it alone, but it's hard because he's in love with you. And the fact that you're wearing a wedding ring doesn't change that, Deborah."

"Simon—"

He wouldn't let her finish. "What bothers me is seeing the effect he has on you. I see your guilt. I want to take it away, and I don't know how. I wish that I did. I don't like to see you feeling so wretched."

She searched his face, finding comfort and peace in the fa-

miliar battle of its lines and angles. Utterly unhandsome. A catalogue of agonies lived through and conquered and lived through
again. Her heart swelled with love for him. Her throat tightened
with the emotion's sudden intensity.

"Have you actually been sitting in this darkness worried about
me? How like you, Simon."

"Why do you say that? What did you think I was doing?"

"Tormenting yourself with . . . things in the past."

"Ah." He drew her into his arms, resting his cheek on the top
of her head. "I won't lie to you, Deborah. It's not easy for me,
knowing that Tommy was your lover. If it had been some other
man, I could have attributed to him all sorts of faults to convince
myself that he wasn't worthy of you. But that's not the case, is
it? He is a good man. He does deserve you. And no one knows
that better than I."

"So you are haunted by it. I thought as much."

"Not haunted. Not at all." His fingers moved lightly down
her hair to caress her throat and slip the nightdress from her
shoulders. "I was at first. I'll admit that. But frankly, the very
first time we made love, I realised that I never had to think of
you and Tommy again. If I didn't want to. And now," she could
feel his smile, "every time I look at you, I'm reminded most
decidedly of the present, not the past. And then, I find that I want
to undress you, breathe the fragrance of your skin, kiss your
mouth and breasts and thighs. In fact, the distraction's becoming
quite a problem in my life."

"In mine as well."

"Then perhaps, my love," he whispered, "we should concentrate all our energies on seeking a solution." Her hand slid under
the covers. He caught his breath at her touch. "That's a good
beginning," he admitted and brought his mouth to hers.

10

THE VISITOR WAS Superintendent Nies. He was waiting in the lounge, three empty pint glasses on a table nearby and a cardboard carton at his feet. He was standing, not sitting, a man wary and watchful and never relaxed. His lips thinned at the sight of Lynley, and his nostrils pinched as if he smelled something foul. He was contempt personified.

"You wanted *everything*, Inspector," he snapped. "Here it is." He gave the carton a sharp kick, not so much to move it as to direct the other man's attention to it.

No one stirred. It was as if the raw hatred behind Nies' words immobilised them all. Next to her, Barbara felt Lynley's tension tightening his muscles like a whipcord. His face, however, was without expression as he took the measure of the other man.

"This *is* what you wanted, isn't it?" Nies persisted nastily. He picked up the carton, dumping its contents onto the carpet. "I expect, when you ask for everything, that you do mean everything, Inspector. Something about you tells me you're a man of your word. Or were you hoping that I'd send it all with someone else so you might avoid having any further chats with me?"

Lynley's eyes dropped to the objects on the floor. A woman's clothing, by their appearance.

"Perhaps you've had too much to drink," he suggested.

Nies took a step forward. Blood rushed to his face. "You'd like to think that, wouldn't you? You'd like to see me giving it over to drink, in my cups with flaming regret for having you in the nick for a few days over Davenport's death. Not exactly the digs his precious lordship was used to, were they?"

Barbara had never recognised so acutely one man's need to strike another or the atavistic savagery that often drove that need to completion. She saw it in Nies now, in his posture, in his hands with their talon-like fingers halfway drawn into a fist, in the cords that stood out on his neck. What she couldn't understand was Lynley's reaction. After the initial flash of tension, he'd become unnaturally unperturbed. That seemed to be the source of Nies' increasing rage.

"Have you solved this case, Inspector?" Nies sneered. "Made any arrests? No, of course not. Not without having all the facts. So let me give you a few and save you a little time. Roberta Teys killed her father. She chopped off his miserable head, sat herself down, and waited to be discovered. And no bloody evidence you can dig out of the blue is *ever* going to prove this case otherwise. Not for Kerridge. Not for Webberly. Not for anyone. But you have a fine time digging for it, laddie. You'll get nothing more from me. Now, get out of my way."

Nies shoved past them, flung open the outer door, and stormed to his car. It roared into life. He ground the gears viciously and was gone.

Lynley looked at the two women. Stepha was very pale, Havers was stoic, but both clearly expected some kind of response from him. He found he couldn't make one. Whatever devils were driving Nies' behaviour, he didn't care to discuss them. He longed to hang labels on the man: *paranoid, psychopath, madman* came to mind. But he knew too well what it felt like to be brought to the breaking point through sheer endeavour and exhaustion during a case. Lynley could see that Nies was a hair's-breadth from breaking under the stress of the Scotland Yard scrutiny of his competence. So if it gave the man even a moment's relief to rail wildly about their run-in five years ago, he was more than happy to give Nies free rein.

"Would you get the Teys file from my room, Sergeant?" he asked Havers. "You'll find it on the chest of drawers."

Havers gawked at him. "Sir, that man just—"

"It's on the chest of drawers," Lynley repeated. He crossed the room to the heap of garments on the floor, picked up the dress, and laid it like a collapsed tent across the couch. It was a pale pastel print with a white sailor collar and long sleeves that ended in upturned white cuffs.

The left sleeve of the garment was heavily stained with a solid mass of brown. Another solid mass formed an irregular pool from thighs to knees. The bottom of the skirt was speckled with it. Blood.

He fingered the material and recognised the texture without looking to see if a label revealed it: a delicate lawn.

Shoes had been part of the package as well: large black high-heeled pumps with mud encrusted along the ridge where left sole met shoe body. These too were flecked with the same brown substance. Petticoat and underclothes completed the lot.

"That's her church dress," Stepha Odell said and added tonelessly, "she had two. One for winter and one for spring."

"Her best dress?" Lynley asked.

"As far as I know."

He was beginning to understand the villagers' stubborn refusal to believe that the girl had committed the crime. With each new piece of information, it made less and less sense. Havers returned with the file, her face without expression. Before he began leafing through it, he was convinced that the information he wanted wouldn't be there. It wasn't.

"Damn the man," Lynley muttered fruitlessly and looked at Havers. "He's given us no analysis of the stains."

"He'd have to have done them, wouldn't he?" Havers asked.

"He's done them. But he has no intention of giving them to us. Not if that would make our job easier." Lynley uttered an oath beneath his breath and swept the garments back into their cardboard container.

"What's to do?" Havers asked.

Lynley knew the answer. He needed St. James: the mechanical precision of his highly trained mind; the quick, clean certainty of his finely wrought skill. He needed a laboratory where tests could be made and a forensic expert he could trust who would make them. It was a maddening, circular sort of problem because in any direction the trail curved unquestionably back to St. James.

He regarded the open carton at his feet and gave himself the ephemeral pleasure of cursing the man from Richmond. Webberly was wrong, he thought. I'm the last person he should have involved in this. Nies reads the London condemnation too clearly. He sees in me his single serious mistake.

He considered his options. He could turn the case over to another DI: MacPherson could certainly come sailing into Keldale and have the matter taken care of within two days. But MacPherson was caught up in the Ripper murders. It would be inconceivable to move him from the one case where his expertise was so desperately needed simply because Nies couldn't come to terms with his past. He could telephone Kerridge in Newby Wiske. Kerridge, after all, was Nies' superior officer. But to have Kerridge involved, chomping at the bit to make up for the Romanivs in any way he could, was even more absurd. Besides, Kerridge didn't have the paperwork, the results of the lab tests, the depositions. All he had was an overwhelming hatred of Nies and an inability to get along with the man. The entire situation was an irritating, howling, political maelstrom of thwarted ambition, error, and revenge. He was sick of it.

A glass was placed before him on the table. He looked up into Stepha's serene eyes. "A bit of Odell's is called for, I think."

He laughed shortly. "Sergeant," he said, "would you care to indulge?"

"No, sir," she replied, and just when he thought she would go on in her former, exasperating I'm-on-duty manner, she added, "but I could do with a smoke, if you don't mind."

He handed her his gold case and silver lighter. "Have as many as you like."

She lit her cigarette. "Got all dressed up to chop off Dad's head? It doesn't make sense."

"The dress does," Stepha said.

"Why?"

"Because it was Sunday. She was ready for church."

Lynley and Havers looked up, realising simultaneously the import of Stepha's words. "But Teys was killed on Saturday night," Havers said.

"So Roberta must have got up as usual on Sunday morning, put her church clothes on, and waited for her father." Lynley eyed the dress heaped in the carton. "He wasn't in the house, so she probably assumed he was somewhere on the farm. She wouldn't worry, of course, because he'd be back in time to take her to church. He probably never missed church in his life. But when he didn't show up, she began to get worried. She went out to look for him."

"And she found him in the barn," Havers concluded. "But the blood on her dress—how do you think it came to be there?"

"I'd guess she was in shock. She must have picked up the body and cradled it in her lap."

"But he had no head! How could she—"

Lynley went on. "She lowered the body back down to the floor and, still in shock, sat there until Father Hart came and found her."

"But then why say she killed him?"

"She never said that," Lynley replied.

"What do you mean?"

"What she said was, 'I did it. I'm not sorry.' " Lynley's voice held a note of decision.

"That sounds like a confession to me."

"Not necessarily." He ran his fingers round the edges of the stain on the dress and tested the spacing of the spatters on the skirt. "But it does sound like something."

"What?"

"That Roberta knows quite well who murdered her father."

Lynley awoke with a jolt. Early morning light filtered into the room in delicate bands that streaked across the floor to the bed. A chill breeze blew back the curtains and carried upon it the pleasant sounds of waking birds and the distant cries of sheep. But none of this touched his awareness. He lay in the bed and knew only depression, overwhelming desperation, and the burning of desire. He longed to turn on his side and find her there, her wealth of hair spread across the bedclothes, her eyes closed in sleep. He longed to arouse her to wakefulness, his mouth and tongue feeling the subtle, familiar changes in her body that betrayed her desire.

He flung back the covers. *Madness*, he thought. He began pulling on clothing mindlessly, furiously, any article that first came to hand. Escape was the exigency.

He grabbed an Aran sweater and ran from the room, thundering down the stairs and out into the street. There, he finally noticed the time. It was half past six.

A heavy mist lay on the dale, swirling delicately round the edges of buildings and blanketing the river. To his right the high street was shuttered, abandoned. Not even the greengrocer was stirring his boxes out onto the pavement. Sinji's windows were darkened, the Wesleyan chapel was barred, and the tea room looked back at him with blank disinterest.

He walked to the bridge, wasted five minutes restlessly tossing pebbles into the river, and was finally distracted by the sight of the church.

On its hillock, St. Catherine's looked peacefully down upon the village, the very exorcist he needed for the demons of his past. He began to walk towards it.

It was a proud little church. Surrounded by trees and an ancient, crumbling graveyard, it lifted its splendid Norman exterior to the sky. Its apse housed a semi-circle of stained glass windows, while its bell tower at the opposite end played host to a whispering band of doves. For a moment he watched them rustling at the edges of the roof, then he walked up the gravel path to the lychgate. He entered, and the peace of the graveyard settled round him.

Idly, he began to wander among the graves, looking at tombstones made barely legible by the ravages of time. The yard was overgrown with weeds and grass, dampened by morning mist. Gravestones bent into thick vegetation. Moss flourished on surfaces that never saw sun, and trees sheltered final resting places of people long forgotten.

A curious group of twisting Italian cypresses arched over a few toppled tombstones some distance from the church. Their contortions were mystifying, oddly humanoid, as if they were attempting to protect the graves beneath them. Intrigued, he walked in their direction and saw her.

How completely like her to have rolled up the legs of her faded blue jeans, to have removed her shoes and plunged barefoot into the tall, damp growth so as to capture the graves in the best angle and light. How like her as well to be utterly oblivious to her surroundings: oblivious to the streak of mud that snaked from ankle to calf, to the torn crimson leaf that had somehow become tangled in her hair, to the fact that he stood less than ten yards away and drank in her every movement and longed quite hopelessly for her to be again what she once had been in his life.

The low ground fog hid and revealed in alternate patches. The early sunlight weakly dappled the stones. An inquisitive bird watched with bright eyes from a grave nearby. He was only dimly aware of this, but he knew that with her camera she would capture it all.

He looked for St. James. Surely the man would be sitting somewhere nearby, fondly watching his wife work. But he was nowhere in sight. She was very much alone.

He felt immediately as if the church had betrayed him with its early promise of comfort and peace. *It's no good, Deb*, he thought as he watched her. *Nothing makes it go away. I want you to leave him. Betray him. Come back to me. It's where you belong.*

She looked up, brushed her hair off her face, and saw him. He knew from her expression that he might as well have said everything aloud. She read it at once.

"Oh, Tommy."

Of course she wouldn't pretend, wouldn't fill the awkward moment with amusing chatter that, Helen-like, would serve to get them through the encounter. Instead she bit her lip, looking very much as if he had struck her, and turned back to her tripod, making unnecessary adjustments.

He walked to her side. "I'm so sorry," he said. She continued to fumble uselessly with her equipment, her head bent, her hair hiding her face. "I can't get past it. I try to see my way clear, but it's just no good." Her face was averted. She seemed to be examining the pattern of the hills. "I tell myself that it's ended the right way for us all, but I don't believe that. I still want you, Deb."

She turned to him then, her face quite white, her eyes gleaming with tears. "You *can't*. You've got to let that go."

"My mind accepts that, but nothing else does." A tear escaped and descended her cheek. He put out his hand to wipe it away but remembered himself and dropped his arm to his side. "I woke up this morning so desperate to make love with you again that I thought if I didn't get out of the room at once I should begin clawing at the walls in pure, adolescent frustration. I thought the church would be a balm to me. What I didn't think was that you would be wandering round its graveyard at dawn." He looked at her equipment. "What are you doing here? Where's Simon?"

"He's still at the hall. I . . . I woke up early and came out to see the village."

It didn't ring true. "Is he ill?" he asked sharply.

She scanned the branches of the cypresses. A shallowness in Simon's breathing had immediately awakened her shortly before six. He was lying so still that for one horrifying moment she thought he was dying. He was drawing in each breath carefully, and she knew all at once that his only thought had been not to awaken her. But when she reached for his hand, his fingers closed bruisingly round her own. "Let me get your medicine," she whispered, and had done so, and then had watched his determined face as he battled to be master of the pain. "Can you . . . for an hour, my love?" It was the part of his life that brooked no companion. It was the part of his life she could never share. She had left him.

"He had . . . there was some pain this morning."

Lynley felt the full impact of Deborah's words. He understood so well everything that they implied. "Christ, there's no escaping it, is there?" he asked bitterly. "Even *that's* part of the miserable account."

"No!" Raw horror tore her voice. "Don't say that! Don't you *ever!* Don't you do that to yourself! It isn't your fault!" Having spoken so quickly, really without thinking of the impression that her words would have upon Lynley, it was suddenly as if she had said too much—far more than she had intended to say—and she went back to fumbling with her camera, taking it apart this time, detaching lens from body and body from tripod, putting everything away.

He watched her. Her movements were jerky, like an old-time motion picture run at the wrong speed. Perhaps sensing this and realising what her discomfort revealed, she stopped what she was doing, her head bent, one hand at her eyes. Her hair was caught in a shaft of sunlight. It was the colour of autumn. Summer's death.

"Is he still at the hall? Did you leave him there, Deb?" It wasn't that he wanted to know but that she needed to tell him. Even now he couldn't let that need go unanswered.

"He wanted . . . it was the pain. He doesn't want me to see it. He thinks he's protecting me if he makes me leave." She looked up at the sky, as if for some sort of sign. The delicate muscles worked in her throat. "Being cut out like this. It's so hard. I *hate* it."

He understood. "That's because you love him."

She stared at him for a moment before she replied. "I do. I do love him, Tommy. He's half of myself. He's part of my soul." She put a tentative hand on his arm, a mere whisper of a touch. "I want you to find someone to love you like that. It's what you need. It's what you deserve. But I . . . I can't be that someone for you. I don't even want to be."

His face blanched at her words. His spirit despaired at the finality behind them. Seeking composure, he found a distraction in the grave at their feet. "Is this the source of your morning's inspiration?" he asked lightly.

"Yes." She deliberately matched her tone to his. "I've heard so much about the baby in the abbey that I thought I'd have a peek at its grave."

" 'As Flame to Smoke,' " he read. "Bizarre epitaph for a child."

"I'm rather attached to Shakespeare," a thin voice said behind them. They swung around. Father Hart, looking like a spiritual gnome in his cassock and surplice, stood on the gravel path a few feet away, hands folded demurely over his stomach. He'd managed to come upon them noiselessly, like an apparition taking its form from the mist.

"Left to my own devices, I always think Shakespeare's just the thing for a grave. Timeless. Poetic. He gives life and death meaning." He patted the pockets of his cassock and brought out a packet of Dunhills, lighting one absently and pinching the match between his fingers before pocketing it. It was a dream-like movement, as if he were unaware that he was doing it at all.

Lynley noticed the yellowed pallour of his skin and the rheumy quality of his eyes. "This is Mrs. St. James, Father Hart," he said gently. "She's taking photographs of your most famous grave."

Father Hart stirred from his reverie. "Most famous . . . ?" Puzzled, he looked from man to woman before his eyes fell on the grave and clouded. His cigarette burned, ignored, between his stained fingers. "Oh, yes. I see." He frowned. "What a horrible thing to have done to an infant, leaving it out naked in the cold to die. I needed special permission to bury the poor thing here."

"Special permission?"

"She was unbaptized. But I call her Marina." He blinked quickly, moving on to other things. "But if it's famous graves that you've come to see, Mrs. St. James, then what you really want is the crypt."

"Sounds like something from Edgar Allan Poe," Lynley remarked.

"Not at all. It's a holy place." The priest dropped his cigarette to the path and crushed it out. He stooped unselfconsciously for the extinguished butt, put it into his pocket, and began to walk in the direction of the church. Lynley picked up Deborah's camera equipment, and they followed.

"It's the burial place of St. Cedd," Father Hart was saying. "Do come in. I was just getting ready for daily Mass but I'll show it to you first." He unlocked the doors of the church with an enormous key and motioned them inside. "Weekday Mass is a bit of a bygone now. No one much bothers unless it's a Sunday. William Teys was my only consistent daily attendant, and with William gone . . . well, I've found myself more often than not saying Mass in an empty church during the week."

"He was a close friend of yours, wasn't he?" Lynley asked.

The priest's hand wavered over the light switch. "He was . . . like a son."

"Did he ever talk to you about the trouble he had sleeping? About his need for sleeping pills?"

The hand wavered again. The priest hesitated. It was too long a pause, Lynley decided, and adjusted his position in the dim light to see the old man's face more clearly. His eyes were on the light switch but his lips moved as if in prayer.

"Are you all right, Father Hart?"

"I . . . yes, fine. I just . . . so often the memory of him." The priest pulled himself up with an effort, like someone drawing the scattered pieces of a puzzle into one disjointed pile. "William was a good man, Inspector, but a troubled spirit. He . . . he never spoke to me about having difficulty sleeping, but it doesn't surprise me at all to hear it."

"Why?"

"Because unlike so many troubled souls who drown themselves in alcohol or escape their difficulties some other way, William always faced them head on and did the best he could. He was strong and decent, but his burdens were tremendous."

"Burdens like Tessa leaving and Gillian running away?"

On the second name, the priest's eyes closed. He swallowed with difficulty: it was a rasping sound. "Tessa hurt him. But Gillian devastated him. He was never the same once she'd gone."

"What was she like?"

"She . . . she was an angel, Inspector. Sunshine." The shaking hand moved quickly to the lights and switched them on, and the priest gestured towards the church. "Well. What do you think of it?"

It was decidedly not the expected interior of a village church. Village churches tend to be small, square, purely functional affairs with an absence of colour, line, or beauty. This was none of that. Whoever had built it had cathedrals in mind, for two great pillars at the west end had been intended to bear a more tremendous weight than that of St. Catherine's roof.

"Ah, so you've noticed," Father Hart murmured, following the direction of Lynley's gaze from pillars to apse. "This was to have been the site of the abbey; St. Catherine's was to have been the great abbey church. But a conflict among the monks resulted in the other location by Keldale Hall. It was a miracle."

"A miracle?" Deborah asked.

"A real miracle. If they'd built the abbey here, where the remains of St. Cedd are, it would all have been destroyed in the time of Henry VIII. Can you imagine destroying the very church where St. Cedd lay buried?" The priest's voice managed to convey his complete revulsion. "No, it was an act of God that brought about the disagreement among the monks. And since the foundation for this church was already laid and the crypt complete, there was no reason to disinter the body of the saint. So they left him here with just a small chapel." He moved with painful slowness to a stone stairway that led from the main aisle down into darkness. "It's just this way," he beckoned them.

The crypt was a second tiny church deep within the main church of St. Catherine's. It was a vault, arched in Norman style, and pillared with columns that had meagre ornamentation. At its far end, a simple stone altar was adorned with two candles and a crucifix, and along its sides stones from an earlier version of the church—crossheads and cross shafts and pieces from vesicular windows—lay preserved for posterity. It was a damp and musty place, poorly lit and smelling of loam. Green mould clung to the walls.

Deborah shivered. "Poor man. It's so cold here. One would think he might prefer to be buried somewhere in the sun."

"He's safer here," the priest answered. He moved reverently to the altar rail, knelt, and spent the next few moments in meditation.

They watched him. His lips moved and then he paused for a moment as if in communion with an unknown god. His prayer completed, he smiled angelically and got to his feet.

"I speak to him daily," Father Hart whispered, "because we owe him everything."

"Why is that?" Lynley asked.

"He saved us. The village, the church, the life of Catholicism here in Keldale." As he spoke, the priest's face began to glow.

Lynley thought fleetingly of Montressor and restrained himself from looking for the mortar and bricks. "The man himself or the relics?" he asked.

"The man, his presence, his relics, all of it." The priest flung out his arms and encompassed the crypt, and his voice rose in zealous jubilation. "He gave them courage to keep their faith, Inspector, to remain true to Rome, during the terrible days of the Reformation. The priests hid *here* then. The stairway was covered with a false floor, and the village priests remained in hiding for years. But the saint was with them all the time, and St. Catherine's *never* fell to the Protestants." There were tears in his eyes. He fumbled for his handkerchief. "You . . . I'm . . . please excuse me. When I talk about Cedd . . . to be so privileged to have his relics here. To be in communion with him. I'm not quite sure you could understand."

To be on a first-name basis with an early Christian saint was obviously too much for the old man. Lynley sought a diversion. "The confessionals above look like Elizabethan carvings," he said kindly. "Are they?"

The man wiped his eyes, cleared his throat, and gave them a shaky smile. "Yes. They weren't originally intended for confessionals. That's why they have such a secular theme. One doesn't generally expect to see young men and women entwined in dance on the wood carving in a church, but they're lovely, aren't they? I think the light in that part of the church is too poor for the penitents to see the doors clearly. I expect some of them think it's a depiction of the Hebrews left on their own while Moses went up to Sinai."

"What *does* it depict?" Deborah asked as they followed the little priest up the stairs and into the larger church once again.

"A pagan bacchanal, I'm afraid," he replied. He smiled apologetically as he said it, bid them good morning, and disappeared through a carved door near the altar.

They watched it close behind him. "What an odd little man. How do you know him, Tommy?"

Lynley followed Deborah out of the church into the light. "He brought us all the information on the case. He found the body." He told her briefly about the murder, and she listened as she always had, her soft green eyes never moving from his face.

"Nies!" she cried when he had completed the tale. "How dreadful for you! Tommy, how completely unfair!"

It was like her, he thought, to cut to the quick of the matter, to see beneath the surface to the issue that plagued him at the heart of the case.

"Webberly thought my presence might make him more cooperative, God knows how," he said drily. "Unfortunately, I seem to be having the opposite effect on the man."

"But how awful for you! After what Nies put you through in Richmond, why did they assign you to this case? Couldn't you have turned it down?"

He smiled at her white-faced indignation. "We're not usually given that option, Deb. May I drive you back to the hall?"

She responded in an instant. "Oh no, you don't need to. I've—"

"Of course. I wasn't thinking." Lynley set down her camera case and bleakly watched the doves grooming and settling themselves on the bell tower of the church. Her hand touched his arm.

"It isn't that," she said gently. "I've a car just over there. You probably didn't notice it."

Now he saw the blue Escort parked under a chestnut that was blanketing the ground with crisp, autumn leaves. He picked up her case and carried it to the car. She followed some paces behind.

She unlocked the boot and watched as he put the case inside. She took more time than was necessary to arrange it in a safe travelling position for the short mile back to the hall. And then, because it could no longer be avoided, she looked at him.

He was watching her, making a passionate study of her features as if she were about to vanish forever and all he would have left was the image in his mind.

"I remember the flat in Paddington," he said. "Making love to you there in the afternoon."

"I haven't forgotten that, Tommy."

Her voice was tender. For some reason that did nothing but hurt him further. He looked away. "Will you tell him you saw me?"

"Of course I will."

"And what we talked about? Will you tell him of that?"

"Simon knows how you feel. He's your friend. So am I."

"I don't want your friendship, Deborah," he said.

"I know. But I hope you will someday. It'll be there when you do."

He felt her fingers on his arm again. They tightened, then loosened in farewell. She opened the car door, slipped inside, and was gone.

Alone, he walked back towards the lodge, feeling the cloak of desolation settle more firmly round his shoulders. He had just reached the Odell house when the garden door opened and a little figure hurtled determinedly down the steps. She was followed moments later by her duck.

"You wait there, Dougal!" Bridie shouted. "Mummy put your new food in the shed yesterday."

The duck, unable to navigate the steps anyway, sat patiently waiting as the child tugged open the shed door and disappeared inside. She was back in a moment, lugging a large sack behind her. Lynley noticed that she wore a school uniform, but it was badly rumpled and not particularly clean.

"Hello, Bridie," he called.

Her head darted up. Her hair, he noticed, had been managed somewhat more expertly since yesterday's fiasco. He wondered who had done it.

"Got to feed Dougal," she said. "Got to go to school today as well. I hate school."

He joined her in the yard. The duck watched his approach warily, one brown eye on him and the other on the promised breakfast. Bridie poured a gargantuan portion onto the ground and the duck flapped his wings eagerly.

"Okay, Dougal, here you go," Bridie said. She lifted the bird lovingly from the steps and placed him on the damp ground, watching fondly as he plunged headfirst into the food. "He likes breakfast best," she confided to Lynley, taking an accustomed place on the top step. She rested her chin on her knees and gazed adoringly at the mallard. Lynley joined her on the step.

"You've fixed your hair quite nicely," he commented. "Did Sinji do it for you?"

She shook her head, eyes still on duck. "Nope. Aunt Stepha did it."

"Did she? She did a very nice job."

"She's good at stuff like that," Bridie acknowledged in a tone that indicated there were other things that Aunt Stepha was not at all good at. "But now I have to go to school. Mummy wouldn't let me go yesterday. She said it was 'too humiliating for words.' " Bridie tossed her head scornfully. "It's my hair, not hers," she added, practically.

"Well, mothers have a way of taking things a bit personally. Haven't you noticed?"

"She could've taken it the way Aunt Stepha did. *She* just laughed when she saw me." She hopped off the steps and filled a shallow pan with water. "Here, Dougal," she called. The duck ignored her. There was a chance the food might be taken away if he did not eat it all as fast as he could. Dougal was a duck who never took chances. Water could wait. Bridie rejoined Lynley. Companionable, they watched as the duck gorged himself. Bridie sighed. She was inspecting the scuffed tops of her shoes and she rubbed at them ineffectually with a dirty finger. "Don't know why I have to go to school anyway. William never did."

"Never?"

"Well . . . not after he was twelve years old. If Mummy'd married William I wouldn't've had to go to school. Bobba didn't go."

"Ever?"

Bridie adjusted her information. "William never made her go after she was sixteen. I don't know what I'll do if I have t' wait till I'm sixteen. Mummy'll make me go. She wants me to go to university, but I don't want to."

"What would you rather do?"

"Take care of Dougal."

"Ah. Not that he doesn't look like the picture of complete health, Bridie, but ducks don't live forever. It's always nice to have something to fall back on."

"I can always help Aunt Stepha."

"At the lodge?"

She nodded. Dougal had finished his breakfast and was now beak deep into the water pan. "I tell Mummy that, but it's no use. 'I don't want you spending your life at that lodge.' " She did a disconcertingly fair imitation of Olivia Odell's distracted voice. She shook her head darkly. "If William and Mummy had married, it would all be different. I could leave school and do all my learning at home. William was awfully clever. He could have taught me. He would have. I know it."

"How do you know it?"

"'Cause he always would read to me and Dougal." The duck, hearing his name, waddled contentedly back to them in his peculiar, lopsided fashion. "Mostly Bible stuff, though." Bridie polished one shoe on the back of her sock. "I don't much like the Bible. Old Testament especially. William said it was because I didn't understand it, and he told Mummy I ought to have religious 'structions. He was real nice and explained stories to me, but I didn't understand 'em very well. It's mostly 'cause no one ever got in trouble for their lies."

"How's that?" Lynley sought fruitlessly through his own limited religious instruction for successful biblical liars.

"Everybody was always lying with other people. Least, that's what the stories said. And no one ever got told it was wrong."

"Ah. Yes. Lying." Lynley studied the mallard, who was examining his shoelaces with a knowing beak. "Well, things are a bit symbolic in the Bible," he said breezily. "What else did you read?"

"Nothing. Just the Bible. I think that's all William and Bobba ever read. I tried to like it, but I didn't. I didn't tell William that 'cause he was trying to be nice, and I didn't want to be rude. I think he was trying to get to know me," she added wisely. " 'Cause if he married Mummy, I'd be round all the time."

"Did you want him to marry your Mummy?"

She scooped the bird up and placed it on the step between them. With a level, dispassionate look at Lynley, Dougal began grooming his shining feathers.

"Daddy read to me," Bridie said in answer. Her voice was a shade lower and her concentration on her shoe tops was total. "And then he went away."

"Went away?" Lynley wondered if this was a euphemism for his death.

"He went away one day." Bridie rested her cheek on her knee, pulled the bird to her side, and stared at the river. "He didn't even say goodbye." She turned and kissed the duck's smooth head. He pecked at her cheek in return. "I would've said goodbye," she whispered.

"Would you use the word *angel* or *sunshine* to describe someone who drank, swore, and ran around like mad?" Lynley asked.

Sergeant Havers looked up from her morning eggs, stirred sugar into her coffee, and thought about it. "I suppose it depends on your definition of rain, doesn't it?"

He smiled. "I suppose so." He pushed his plate away from him and regarded Havers thoughtfully. She wasn't looking half bad this morning: there was a hint of colour on her eyelids, cheeks, and lips, and her hair had a noticeable curl to it. Even her clothes had distinctly improved, for she wore a brown tweed skirt and matching pullover which, even if they weren't exactly the best colour for her skin tone, at least were a marked improvement over yesterday's ghastly blue suit.

"Why the question?" she asked.

"Stepha described Gillian as wild. A drinker."

"Who ran around like mad."

"Yes. But Father Hart said she was sunshine."

"That *is* peculiar."

"He said Teys was devastated when she ran away."

Havers knotted her thick eyebrows and, without thinking about how the action redefined their relationship, poured Lynley a second cup of coffee. "Well, that does explain why her photos are gone, doesn't it? He'd devoted his life to his children and look at his reward for the effort. One of the two vanishes into the night."

The last four words struck a chord in Lynley. He rummaged through the file on the table between them and brought out the picture of Russell Mowrey that Tessa had given them.

"I'd like you to take this round the village today," he said.

Havers took the photograph, but her expression was quizzical. "But you said he was in London."

"Now, yes. Not necessarily three weeks ago. If Mowrey was here then, he would have had to ask someone for directions to the farm. Someone would have had to see him. Concentrate on the high and the patrons of the pubs. You might go to the hall as well. If no one's seen him—"

"We're back to Tessa, then," she finished.

"Or someone else with a motive. There seem to be several."

Madeline Gibson answered the door to Lynley's knock. He'd climbed his way over two quarrelling children in the war-torn front garden, manoeuvred past a broken tricycle and a dismembered doll, and avoided a plate of congealing fried eggs on the front steps. She surveyed all this with a bored glance and adjusted an emerald green peignoir over high, pointed breasts. She wore nothing under it and made no secret of the fact that he couldn't have arrived at a more inconvenient time.

"Dick," she called, her sultry eyes on Lynley, "put it back in your trousers. It's Scotland Yard." She gave him a lazy smile and held the door open wider. "Do come in, Inspector." She left him in the tiny entryway among the toys and the dirty clothes and strolled to the stairwell. "Dick!" she called again. She turned, folded her arms across her breasts, and kept her eyes on Lynley. A smile played over her features. A well-formed knee and thigh showed themselves between the folds of thin satin.

There was movement above them, a man's mumbling, and Richard Gibson appeared. He clattered noisily to the bottom of the stairs and caught sight of his wife. "Jesus Christ, put on some clothes, Mad," he said.

"You didn't want them on five minutes ago," she replied, looked him over with a knowing smile, and made her way deliberately—revealing as much of her slim body as possible—up the stairs.

Gibson watched her with wry amusement. "You should see what she's like when she *really* wants it," he confided. "She's just teasing now."

"Ah. Yes. I see."

The farmer laughed through his nose. "At least it keeps her happy, Inspector. For a while." He scrutinised the chaos of the cottage and added, "Let's go out in front."

Lynley thought the front garden was even less appealing a place for their encounter than the malodorous cottage, but he held his tongue and followed the other man.

"Go in to your mother," Gibson ordered his two wrangling children. With his foot, he pushed the plate to the edge of the front step. In a moment, the family's mangy cat appeared from the tangle of dry and dying bushes and began to devour the remains of the eggs and toast. It was the greedy, surreptitious eating of a scavenger, and it reminded Lynley of the woman upstairs.

"I saw Roberta yesterday," he said to Gibson. The other man had sat down on the step and was lacing his work shoes tightly.

"How was she? Any improvement?"

"No. When we first met, you didn't mention the fact that you'd signed Roberta into the asylum, Mr. Gibson."

"You didn't ask, Inspector." He finished with the boots and

got to his feet. "Did you expect me to leave her with the police in Richmond?"

"Not especially. Have you arranged for a solicitor as well?"

Gibson, Lynley saw, wasn't a man who expected the police to concern themselves with the legal representation of confessed murderesses. The question surprised him. His eyelids quivered and he spent a moment tucking his flannel shirt into his blue jeans. He took his time about answering.

"A solicitor? No."

"Intriguing that you'd make arrangements to have her put into hospital but not make arrangements for her legal interests. Convenient as well, wouldn't you say?"

A muscle worked in Gibson's jaw. "No, I wouldn't say."

"Can you explain yourself, then?"

"I don't think I need to explain myself to you," Gibson said tersely. "But it seems to me that Bobby's mental problems were a wee bit more pressing than her legal ones." His swarthy skin had darkened.

"Indeed. And if she's found incompetent to stand trial—as no doubt she will be—you're in a good position, aren't you?"

Gibson faced him. "By God, I am, yes," he retorted angrily. "Free to take the damn farm, free to have the damn house, free to screw my damn wife on the dining room table if I want. And all without Bobby hulking about. That's what you want to hear, isn't it, Inspector?" He thrust his face forward belligerently, but when Lynley offered no reaction to this aggression, he backed away. His words, however, were no less angry. "I've just about had it with people believing I'd hurt Bobby, with people believing Madeline and I would be only too happy to see her put away for life. You think I don't know that's what everyone believes? You think Madeline doesn't know it?" He laughed bitterly. "No, I *didn't* get her a solicitor. I got one myself. And if I can get her certified mentally incompetent, I intend to do so. Do you think that's worse than seeing she ends up in prison?"

"So you think she did kill her father?" Lynley asked.

Gibson's shoulders sagged. "I don't know what to think. All I know is Bobby's not the same girl that I knew when I left Keldale. *That* girl wouldn't have hurt a fly. But this new girl . . . she's a stranger."

"Perhaps that has to do with Gillian's disappearance."

"*Gillian?*" Gibson laughed incredulously. "I'd say Gilly's leaving was a relief to all concerned."

"Why?"

"Let's just say Gilly was advanced for her years, shall we?" He glanced back at the house. "Let's just say she'd have made Madeline look like the Virgin Mary. Am I making myself clear?"

"Perfectly. Did she seduce you?"

"You *are* direct, aren't you? Give me a fag and I'll tell you about it." He lit the cigarette that Lynley offered from his case and looked off into the fields that began just across the unpaved street. Beyond them, the trail to High Kel Moor weaved into the trees. "I was nineteen years old when I left Keldale, Inspector. I didn't want to leave. God knows that was the last thing I wanted to do. But I knew if I didn't, there'd be hell to pay eventually."

"But you slept with your cousin Gillian before you left?"

Gibson snorted. "Hardly. *Slept* isn't exactly the word I'd use with a girl like Gilly. She wanted control and she had it, Inspector. She could do things to a man . . . better than a high-class tart. She made me crazy just about four times a day."

"How old was she?"

"She was twelve when she first locked her eyes on me in an uncousinly fashion, thirteen the first time she . . . performed. Then for the next two years, she drove me wild."

"Are you telling me you left to escape her?"

"I'm hardly that noble. I left to escape William. It was only a matter of time before he caught her going at me. I didn't want that to happen to either of us. I wanted it to end."

"Why did you never just speak to William about it?"

Gibson's eyes widened. "As far as he was concerned, neither of those girls could do anything wrong. How was I supposed to tell him that Gilly, the proverbial apple of his eye, was rubbing up to me like a cat in heat and taking me on like a whore? He'd never have believed it. Half the time, I didn't myself."

"She left Keldale a year after you, didn't she?"

He tossed his cigarette into the street. "That's what they tell me," he replied.

"Did you ever see her again?"

Gibson's eyes slid away. "I never did," he replied. "And it was a blessing."

Marsha Fitzalan was a bent, withered woman with a face that reminded Lynley of the kind on American dolls carved from apples: it was a mass of delicate wrinkles that traced a pattern across her cheeks up to her eyes. These were blue. They danced in her face with interest and amusement and told anyone who looked at her that the body was indeed old but the heart and the mind had not changed from youth.

"Good morning," she smiled, and then with a look at her watch, "or nearly afternoon. You're Inspector Lynley, aren't you? I thought you might be by sooner or later. I've lemon pie made."

"For the occasion?" Lynley asked.

"Indeed," she replied. "Come in."

Although she lived in one of the council houses on St. Chad's Lane, its appearance couldn't have been more different from the Gibsons'. The front garden was planted, parterre-like, with neat patterns of flowers: in the spring there would be alyssum and primrose, snapdragons and geraniums. They had been trimmed back for the coming of winter, the soil turned over lovingly round each plant. On two of the stepping stones leading to the door, birdseed had been fashioned into small, accessible piles, and a set of metal wind chimes hung near a window, its six notes still managing to be heard over the din of the Gibson children next door.

The contrast to the Gibsons' small cottage continued indoors, where the smell of potpourri in the air reminded Lynley of long afternoons spent in his grandmother's bedroom at Howenstow. The tiny sitting room was comfortably if inexpensively furnished and two of its walls were lined from floor to ceiling with books. A small table under the single window was covered by a collection of photographs, and several needlepoint tapestries hung above an ancient television set.

"Will you come into the kitchen, Inspector?" Marsha Fitzalan asked. "I know it's dreadful to entertain in the kitchen, but I've always been far more comfortable there. My friends tell me it's because I grew up on a farm, and the life of a farm always centres itself in the kitchen, doesn't it? I suppose I never got over that. Here, please sit at the table. Coffee and pie? You do look hungry. I imagine you're a bachelor. Bachelors never eat as well as they should, do they?"

Again there was the memory of his grandmother, that unmistakable security of unconditional love. As he watched her busily putting together a tray, her hands sure and unshaking, Lynley knew for a certainty that Marsha Fitzalan held the answer.

"Can you tell me about Gillian Teys?" he asked.

Her hands stopped. She turned to him with a smile. "Gilly?" she said. "What a pleasure that shall be. Gillian Teys was the loveliest creature I've ever known."

11

She returned to the table and placed the tray between them. It was an unnecessary nicety. The kitchen was so tiny that only a few steps were needed to move across the room, yet still she preserved the semblance of gentility and countered the claustrophobia of poverty by using the tray. It was covered with a piece of old lace upon which rested fine bone china. Both plates were chipped, but the cups and saucers had somehow managed the years unscathed.

Autumn leaves in a pottery jug served to decorate the plain pine table, and onto its surface Marsha Fitzalan set everything out carefully: plates, cutlery, and linen. She poured the steaming coffee into their cups and added sugar and milk to her own before she began to speak.

"Gilly was exactly like her mother. I taught Tessa as well. Of course, it betrays my age dreadfully to admit to that. But there you have it. Nearly everyone in the village passed through my classroom, Inspector." Her eyes twinkled as she added, "Except Father Hart. He and I are of the same generation."

"I should never have guessed," Lynley said solemnly.

She laughed. "Why is it that truly charming men always know when a woman is fishing for a compliment?" She dug into her pie enthusiastically, chewed appreciatively for a few moments, and then continued. "Gillian was the mirror image of her mother. She had that same lovely blonde hair, those beautiful eyes, and that same wonderful spirit. But Tessa was a dreamer and Gillian was a bit more of a realist, I should say. Tessa's head was always in the clouds. She was all romance. I think that's why she chose to marry so young. She was determined that life was all about being swept off one's feet by a tall, dark hero, and William Teys certainly fit the image."

"Gillian wasn't worried about being swept off her feet?"

"Oh no. I don't think the thought of men ever entered Gilly's head. She wanted to be a teacher. I can remember her coming by in the afternoons, curling up on the floor with a book. How she loved the Brontës! That child must have read *Jane Eyre* six or seven times by her fourteenth birthday. She, Jane, and Mr. Rochester were all rather intimate acquaintants, as I recall. And she loved to talk about everything she read. But it wasn't just chatter. She talked about characters, motivations, meanings. She would say, 'I shall have to know these things when I'm a teacher, Miss Fitzalan.' "

"Why did she run away?"

The old woman studied the bronze leaves in the jug. "I don't know," she replied slowly. "She was such a good child. There was never a problem that she couldn't seem to solve with that quick mind of hers. I honestly don't know what happened."

"Could she have been involved with a man? Perhaps someone she was running after?"

Miss Fitzalan dismissed the idea with a movement of her hand. "I don't believe Gillian was interested in men yet. She was a bit slower to mature than the other girls were."

"What about Roberta? Was she much like her sister?"

"No, Roberta was like her father." She stopped suddenly and frowned. *"Was.* I don't want to talk about her in the past tense like that. But she seems to have died."

"She does, doesn't she?"

The woman looked as if she appreciated his concurring with her. "Roberta was big like her father, very solid and silent. People will tell you she had no personality at all, but that's not true. She was simply excruciatingly shy. She had her mother's romantic disposition, her father's taciturnity. And she lost herself in books."

"Like Gillian?"

"Yes and no. She read like Gillian, but she never spoke about what she read. Gillian read to learn. Roberta, I think, read to escape."

"Escape what?"

Miss Fitzalan fussily straightened the lace that covered the old tray. Her hands, Lynley saw, were spotted with age. "The knowledge of being deserted, I should guess."

"By Gillian or her mother?"

"By Gillian. Roberta worshipped Gillian. She never knew her mother. You can imagine what it must have been like having Gilly for an older sister: so lovely, so lively, so intelligent. Everything Roberta wasn't and wished she could be."

"Jealousy?"

She shook her head. "She wasn't jealous of Gilly. She loved her. I should think it hurt Roberta dreadfully when her sister left. But unlike Gillian, who would have talked about her pain—Lord knows, Gilly talked about anything and everything—Roberta internalised it. I remember, in fact, the poor child's skin after Gilly left. Funny that I would still remember that."

Lynley thought of the girl he had seen in the asylum and was not surprised that the teacher would remember the condition of Roberta's skin. "Acne?" he asked. "She would have been young for that."

"No. She broke out into the most dreadful rash. I know it was nerves, but when I spoke to her about it, she blamed it on Whiskers." Miss Fitzalan dropped her eyes and toyed with her fork, making delicate patterns in the crumbs on her plate. Lynley waited patiently, convinced there was more. Finally she went on. "I felt so inadequate, Inspector, such a failure as a friend and as a teacher that she couldn't talk to me about what had happened to Gilly. But she just couldn't talk, so she blamed it all on being allergic to her dog."

"Did you speak to her father about it?"

"Not at first. William had been so crushed by Gillian's running off that he wasn't the least bit approachable. For weeks it seemed the only person he would talk to at all was Father Hart. But in the end, frankly, I felt I owed it to Roberta. After all, the child was only eight years old. It wasn't her fault that her sister had run away. So I went out to the farm and told William I was worried about her, especially considering the pathetic story she'd made up about the dog." She poured herself more coffee and sipped it as she brooded over that long-ago visit. "Poor man. I certainly needn't have worried about his reaction. I think he must have felt terribly guilty about having ignored Roberta, because he drove to Richmond directly and bought three or four different kinds of lotion to put on her skin. It may well have been that all the poor girl needed was her father's attention, because the rash went away after that."

But nothing else did, Lynley thought. In his mind he saw the lonely little girl in the gloomy farmhouse, surrounded by the ghosts and voices of the past, living her life in grim sterility, taking her nourishment from books.

Lynley unlocked the back door and let himself into the house. It was unchanged, as cold and airless as it had been before. He went through the kitchen to the sitting room, where Tessa Teys smiled at him tenderly from her corner shrine, looking young and infinitely vulnerable. He imagined Russell Mowrey raising his head from his excavation and seeing that lovely face framed in a gap in the fence. It was easy to see why Mowrey had fallen in love. It was easy to see why he would be in love still.

Not a thousand ships but one enraged husband, Lynley thought. *Is it possible, Tessa? Or did you see your world shatter in one afternoon and know you couldn't bear to build it again?*

He turned from the shrine and ran up the stairs. No, the answer had to be in the house. It had to be Gillian.

He went first to her bedroom, but its vacuity told him nothing. The bed stared up at him wordlessly, its covering unblemished. The rug held no footprints leading back into the past. The wallpaper covered no long-held secrets. It was as if a young girl had never lived in the room, had never breathed her liveliness and spirit into the air. And yet something . . . Something of Gillian lingered, something he had seen, something he could feel.

He walked to the window and looked, unseeing, at the barn. *She was wild, ungoverned. She was an angel, sunshine. She was a cat in heat. She was the loveliest creature I've ever seen.* It was as if there were no real Gillian at all, but only a kaleidoscope that, juggled before viewing, appeared different to each person who gazed into it. He longed to believe that the answer was in the room, but when he turned from the window, he saw nothing but furniture, wallpaper, and rug.

How could someone be wiped so completely out of the life of the family in which she had lived for sixteen years? It was inconceivable. Yet it had been done. Or had it?

He walked to Roberta's room. Gillian couldn't have faded from her sister's life so completely. The love was there. The bond was strong. Everyone, at least, no matter what they had said about Gillian, agreed upon that. His gaze roamed from window to wardrobe to bed. He considered this last: it was her hiding place for food, why not for Gillian as well?

Steeling himself to the sight and the smell of the putrefaction, Lynley pulled back the mattress. The stench rose like an undulating wave.

He glanced about, looking for a way to make the job at hand easier but finding nothing that would do. The light in the room was poor, and, unpleasant as it would be, there was nothing for it but to drag the entire mattress off and rip the box spring apart. Grunting with the effort, he jerked mattress and bedding onto the floor and then went to the window. He threw it open and stood for a moment sucking in the fresh air before turning back to the bed. He climbed onto the box spring and planned his attack, ignoring his queasiness. *Come on, old boy. Isn't this why you got into police work? Buck up, now. Give it one big pull.*

He did so, and the rotting material—that thin layer of sanity —came apart in his hands, exposing the madness beneath it. Mice scattered in all directions, leaving diminutive tracks through the decaying fruit. One sow-like rodent nursed her litter of clutching, blind offspring in a bed of women's dirty underclothes. And an angry cloud of moths, disturbed from their slumber, burst out into the light, flinging themselves upwards into Lynley's face.

Startled, he reeled back, managed to keep from crying out, and quickly made his way to the bathroom, where he took a moment to splash water on his face. He looked at himself in the mirror and laughed soundlessly. *Good thing you skipped lunch. After that, you may well skip eating for the rest of your life.*

He sought a towel on which to dry his face. There was none

on the rack, but he caught a glimpse of a dressing gown hanging on the back of the bathroom door. He swung it shut. Its broken hasp lock grated against the frame like a shriek. He dried his face on the hem of the garment, fingered the lock meditatively, and after a moment, a new thought triggered, he left the room.

The box of keys was where he had seen it before, far in the back on the top shelf of Teys' wardrobe. He took it out and dumped it onto the bed. Teys would have put Gillian's things in a trunk somewhere. In the attic, perhaps. And the keys would be here. He searched through them fruitlessly. They were all door keys, the old-fashioned key-hole variety, a strange collection of rusting, metallic mementoes. He threw them back into their box in disgust and cursed the blind determination of the man who had wiped one daughter's existence off the face of the earth.

Why? he wondered. What kind of anguish was it that had driven William Teys to deny the existence of the child he so loved? What could she possibly have done to bring him to such an act of destruction? And at the same time provoke her sister to such an impotent yet desperate act of preservation as the simple hiding of a photograph.

He knew what came next. *The attic's a blind, old boy. Back to her bedroom. You know it's there. Maybe not in the mattress, but you know it's there.* He shuddered at the thought of what other surprises waited like spectres in that sepulchral room.

As he was gathering his shattered defences for another assault, the sound of whistling, joyful and unrestrained, came to him from outside. He went to the window.

A young man was walking down the trail from High Kel Moor, an easel over his shoulder and a wooden case in his hand. It was time, Lynley decided, to meet Ezra.

His first thought was that the other man was not as young as he looked from a distance. It must have been the hair, Lynley thought, which was a rich, deep blond and worn much longer than was the current fashion. Up close, Ezra looked very much what he was: a man somewhere in his thirties, wary about this meeting with the detective from Scotland Yard. The wariness came through in the careful stance; it also came through in the swiftly veiled eyes, the kind of eyes that changed colour with the clothing he wore. They were deep blue now, as was the man's shirt, which was streaked with paint. He had stopped whistling the moment he saw Lynley come out of the house and climb nimbly over the pasture wall.

"Ezra Farmington?" he said pleasantly.

Farmington halted. His features put Lynley in mind of the Delacroix painting of Frederic Chopin. Here were the same sculpted lips; the shadow of a cleft in the chin; the dark brows—much darker than the hair; the nose that was dominant but not detractive.

"That's right," he said, noncommittally.

"Doing some painting on the moor today?"

"Yes."

"Nigel Parrish tells me you do light studies."

The name got a reaction. The eyes became guarded. "What else does Nigel tell you?"

"That he saw William Teys run you off his property. You seem to be making free use of it now."

"With Gibson's permission." The words were terse.

"Indeed? He didn't mention it." Lynley gazed serenely in the direction of the trail. It was steep and rocky, ill-maintained, not the place for a country hike. An artist would have to be most sincere about his endeavours to bother climbing up to the high moor at all. He turned back to the other man. The afternoon breeze that rustled through the pasture ruffled Farmington's blond hair appealingly so that the sun struck its highlights. Lynley began to understand why he wore it long. "Mr. Parrish tells me that Teys destroyed some of your work."

"Does he also tell you what the hell *he* was doing out here that night?" Farmington demanded. "No, blast his eyes, I'll be *damned* if he does."

"According to him, he was bringing Teys' dog back to the farm."

The artist's face mirrored his disbelief. "Bringing the *dog* back to the farm? What a laugh!" He savagely drove the pointed legs of his easel into the soft earth. "Nigel really knows how to manipulate the facts, doesn't he? Let me guess what he told you. That Teys and I were having a bloody fine row in the middle of the road when up he popped, innocently walking the poor, blind dog home." Farmington ran one hand through his hair in agitation. His body was so tense that Lynley wondered if he would start swinging his fists. "Christ, that man will drive me to do something mad."

Lynley lifted an eyebrow in interest. The other man read the expression.

"And I suppose *that* is a confession of guilt, Inspector? Well, I suggest you trot back to Nigel and ask him what *he* was doing wandering down Gembler Road that night. Believe me, that dog could have found his way back from Timbuktu, if he'd wanted to." He laughed. "That dog was a damn sight smarter than Nigel. Not that that means much."

Lynley wondered at the source of Farmington's anger. The passion was real, without doubt. Yet it was out of all proportion to the subject at hand. The man was like a taut bowstring upon which undue pressure was being exterted. An ounce more, and he would snap.

"I saw your work at Keldale Lodge. The way you painted the abbey put me in mind of Wyeth. Was that deliberate?"

Ezra relaxed a tightly balled fist. "That was done years ago. I was floundering for style. I didn't trust my instincts so I copied everyone else's. I'm surprised Stepha still has it hanging."

"She said you did it to pay for your board one autumn."

"That's right. I paid for most everything like that in those days. If you look hard enough, you'll see my crap hanging in every shop in town. I even bought toothpaste that way." It was a derisive statement, an indication of contempt, but directed at himself, not at Lynley.

"I like Wyeth," Lynley went on. "There's a simplicity to his work that I find refreshing. I like simplicity. The clarity of line and image. Details."

Farmington folded his arms. "Are you always this obvious, Inspector?"

"I try to be," Lynley responded with a smile. "Tell me about your argument with William Teys."

"And if I refuse?"

"You may, of course. But I'd wonder why. Have you something to hide, Mr. Farmington?"

Farmington shifted on the balls of his feet. "I've nothing to hide. I was on the moor that day and came down towards dark. Teys must have seen me from a window. Hell, I don't know. He caught up with me here on the road. We had it out."

"He destroyed some of your work."

"It was crap anyway. It didn't matter."

"I was always under the impression that artists like to have control over their own creations rather than give it to other people. Wouldn't you agree?" Lynley immediately saw that he'd struck tender flesh, for Farmington stiffened involuntarily. His eyes moved to the low sun in the sky. He didn't respond immediately.

"I'd agree," he said finally. "Yes, by God, I'd agree."

"Then when Teys took it upon himself—"

"*Teys?*" Ezra laughed. "I didn't care what Teys did. I told you, what he'd destroyed was pure crap anyway. Not that he'd have known the difference. Any man who'd play Souza full blast for an evening's entertainment hasn't got a whole lot of taste, as far as I'm concerned."

"Souza?"

"The god-awful stars-and-stripes piece. Christ, you'd think he was entertaining a house full of flag waving Americans. And then to have the cheek to howl at me for disturbing his peace by tiptoeing across his land to get to the trail. I laughed at him. That's when he went for my paintings."

"What did Nigel Parrish do while all this was going on?"

"Nothing. Nigel had seen what he'd come to see, Inspector. He'd done his bit of sleuthing. He could rest an easy man that night."

"And on other nights?"

Farmington picked up his easel. "If there's nothing more, I'll be on my way."

"No, there *is* one thing more."

Farmington pivoted to face him. "What?" he demanded.

"What were you doing the night William Teys died?"

"I was at the Dove and Whistle."

"And after time was called?"

"Home in bed. Sleeping it off. Alone." He tossed his hair off his face. It was an odd, distinctly feminine gesture. "Sorry I didn't take Hannah with me, Inspector. She'd be quite an alibi, but I've never gone in for the whips and chains routine." He climbed over the rock wall and strode angrily down the road.

"It was, as they say in American detective films, a total bust." Sergeant Havers tossed the photograph onto the table in the Dove and Whistle and dropped wearily into a chair opposite him.

"Which means, I suppose, that no one has ever seen Russell Mowrey in this lifetime?"

"And unless we can believe in reincarnation, no one has ever seen him at all. Tessa, however, was widely recognised. A few lifted eyebrows. A few pointed questions."

"What was your response?"

"I was suitably vague, murmuring a lot of interesting Latin adages to get me through difficult moments. I was fine until I tried out *caveat emptor*. Somehow it didn't have that ring of authority the other phrases had."

"Would you care to drown your disappointment in a drink, Sergeant?" he asked.

"Just tonic water," she responded and, seeing his expression, added, "really. I don't drink much, sir. Honest," with a smile.

"I've spent a rather fascinating day," Lynley told her when he returned with her drink. "An encounter with Madeline Gibson, all hotly deshabille in an emerald negligee with absolutely nothing at all underneath."

"The life of a policeman is rotten," Havers noted.

"And Gibson upstairs at the absolute ready. I was a welcome guest."

"I can imagine."

"I've learned the most today about Gillian, however. She was a sunshine angel, a cat in heat, or the loveliest creature ever seen. It depends who's reporting the details. Either the woman's a chameleon or some of these people are taking considerable trouble to make it look that way."

"But why?"

"I don't know. Unless, of course, they have a vested interest in keeping her as mysterious as possible." He swallowed the rest of his ale and leaned back in his chair, stretching his tired muscles. "But the real atmosphere today was at Gembler Farm, Havers."

"Why's that?"

"I was hot on the trail of Gillian Teys. Picture it, please. Something told me it was all in Roberta's room. So I threw myself into the investigation with a passion, ripped off the top of her mattress' box spring, and fairly lost myself on the spot." He described the sight.

Havers made a grimace of distaste. "Glad I missed that."

"Oh, have no fear. I was far too discomposed to put the bed back together. So I shall need your assistance tomorrow. Shall we say directly after breakfast?"

"Sod you." She grinned.

It was obviously teatime when they arrived at the cottage on the corner of Bishop Furthing Road. It was a late tea, however, probably sliding itself right into dinner, for Constable Gabriel Langston answered the door, holding tightly in his hand a plate weighted down with a variety of food. Cold chicken legs, cheese, fruit, and cake jockeyed for position on a brown pottery dish.

Langston seemed very young for a policeman but aptly named Gabriel, for he was slightly built, with thinning yellow hair the consistency of spun glass, baby-smooth skin, and features that looked undeveloped, as if the bones were too soft beneath them.

"I sh-sh-should've s-seen you at once," he stammered, blushing heavily on cheeks and neck. "Wh-when you ar-arrived. But I was to-told you'd c-come to m-me if you n-needed anything."

"Nies told you, no doubt," Lynley guessed. The other man nodded awkwardly and gestured them into his home.

The table was laid out for one and the constable hastily set his meal down on it, wiped his hand on his trousers, and extended it to Lynley. "N-nice to m-meet you b-both. S-sorry about . . ." He blushed darker and gestured helplessly at his mouth as if there were something he could have done about his speech impediment. "T-tea?" he said eagerly.

"Thank you. I'd love a cup. What about you, Sergeant?"

"Yes, thank you," Havers replied.

The man nodded in obvious relief, smiled, and disappeared

into an undersized kitchen off the room in which they stood. The cottage, they could see, was strictly a one-person affair, not much more than a bed-sitting room. But it was conscientiously clean—swept, polished, and dusted. Only the faint odour of wet dog marred it. The source of this lay on a chewed and stringy rag rug, toasting himself before a single bar electric fire set into a small stone fireplace. He was a white highland terrier, and he lifted his chin, blinked at them seriously, and yawned, revealing a long pink tongue. This done, he turned his nose happily back to the electric blaze.

Langston returned with a tray in his hands and another terrier at his heels. This was a livelier version of the first, for it threw itself upon Lynley in excited greeting.

"H-here, *down!*" Langston ordered as sharply as his gentle voice would allow. The dog obeyed reluctantly, then scampered across the room to join the other in a heap by the fire. "Th-they're g-good lads, Inspector. S-sorry."

Lynley waved off the apology as Langston poured the tea. "Go on with your meal, Constable. Havers and I are out prowling a bit late this evening. We can talk while you eat."

Langston didn't look as if he believed this was possible, but he dug into his food with a shy duck of his head.

"I understand that Father Hart rang you directly after he found William Teys' body," Lynley began. When the man nodded eagerly, he went on. "Roberta was still there when you arrived?" Another nod. "Did you bring Richmond in immediately? Why was that?" Lynley regretted the question the moment he asked it. Stupid clod, he thought, wondering what it would be like for the man to have to agonise his way through questioning witnesses, especially those like Father Hart who seemed to float between two distinct planes of existence.

Langston was staring at his plate, attempting to formulate an answer.

"I expect that was the quickest way to go about it," Havers offered. Langston nodded gratefully.

"Did Roberta speak to anyone at all?" Langston shook his head. "Not to you? Not to anyone from Richmond?" Again, the negative. Lynley glanced at Havers. "Then she only spoke to Father Hart." He considered the situation. "Roberta was sitting on the overturned pail, the axe was nearby, the dog was under

Teys. But the weapon used to slit the dog's throat was missing. Is that correct?" A nod. Langston bit into his third chicken leg, his eyes on Lynley. "What happened to the dog?"

"I . . . b-buried h-him."

"Where?"

"Out the b-back."

Lynley leaned forward. "Behind this cottage? Why? Did Nies tell you to do so?"

Langston swallowed, rubbed his hands on his trousers. He looked miserably at his two companions by the fire and, seeing themselves the focus of his attention, they wagged their tails supportively. "I . . ." It was embarrassment rather than his speech that stopped him this time. "I love d-dogs," he said. "D-didn't want th-them to burn old Wh-Whiskers. He . . . was a p-pal o' the l-lads."

"Poor man," Lynley murmured when they were on the street again. Darkness was falling quickly. Somewhere a woman's voice rose, calling to a child. "No wonder he brought in Richmond."

"What could have possessed him, becoming a police constable?" Havers demanded as they crossed to the lodge.

"I expect he never thought he'd come across a murder. At least not one like this. Who would expect it in a place like Keldale? God knows before this, Langston's most serious duty was probably patrolling the village and checking shop doors to see they were locked at night."

"Then what's next?" Havers asked. "We won't have the dog till the morning."

"True." Lynley flipped open his watch. "That gives me twelve hours to talk St. James into abandoning his honeymoon for the thrill of the chase. What do you think, Havers? Have we a chance?"

"Will he have to choose between the dead dog and Deborah?"

"Afraid so."

"I think we'll need a miracle, sir."

"I'm good at that," Lynley said grimly.

It would have to be the white shirtwaist again. Barbara took it out of the wardrobe and looked at it critically. A different belt and it wouldn't look bad. Or perhaps a scarf at the throat. Had she brought a scarf? Even one for the head could be tied someway to give a touch of colour, to change the outfit somehow, to make it look a bit different. Humming beneath her breath, she rummaged through her things. They were tossed into the chest of drawers in a heap, but she found what she was looking for easily enough. A scarf of red and white checks. A bit like a tablecloth, but it couldn't be helped.

She went to the mirror and saw her reflection with a start of pleased surprise. The country air had whipped colour into her cheeks and her eyes had sparkle to them. It was being useful that did it, she decided.

She had enjoyed her day in the village alone. It was the first time a DI had allowed her to do something all by herself. It was the first time a DI had assumed she had brains. She felt bolstered by the experience and realised how much her confidence had been destroyed by her humiliating return to uniform. What a horrible time that had been in her life: the seething anger boiling over into incomprehensible rage, the festering sore of unhappiness, the knowledge of being evaluated by others as not good enough, not up to snuff.

Snuff: the image of Jimmy Havers' little pig eyes looked back at her from the mirror. Her eyes were his. She turned from the glass.

Everything was going to be better now. She was on her way, and nothing could stop her. She would sit for the inspector's exam again. She would pass this time. She knew it.

She stepped out of her tweed skirt, struggled out of the pullover, and kicked off her shoes. Of course, no one had given her any information about Russell Mowrey, but everyone had taken her quite seriously in her questioning. Everyone had seen her for what she was: a representative of New Scotland Yard. A fine representative: competent, intelligent, insightful. It was what she had needed. Now she could really be part of the case.

She completed her dressing, tied the scarf jauntily round her throat, and descended the stairs to meet Lynley.

He was in the lounge, standing before the watercolour of the abbey, lost in thought. Behind the bar, Stepha Odell watched him. They might have been part of a painting themselves. The woman stirred first.

"A drink before you leave, Sergeant?" she asked pleasantly.

"Thank you, no."

Lynley turned. "Ah, Havers," he said, absently rubbing his temples. "Are you ready for another assault on Keldale Hall?"

"Quite," she replied.

"Then we're off." He nodded a detached goodnight to the other woman and, hand on Barbara's elbow, guided her from the room. "I've been meditating on our best approach," he said once they were in the car. "You'll have to keep that dreadful American couple engaged in conversation long enough for me to have a word with St. James. Can you do that? I hate to abandon anyone to such a fate, but if good old Hank hears me, I have the most appalling suspicion that he'll demand to be part of the case himself."

"No problem, sir," Barbara replied. "I'll keep him enthralled."

He glanced at her suspiciously. "How?"

"I'll have him talk about himself."

In response, Lynley laughed, suddenly looking younger and far less fatigued. "That should do it, all right."

"Now lookit, Barbie," Hank said with a wink, "if it's investigating you and Tom are up to in this burg, then you oughta get yourselfs hooked up in *this* place for a nighter two. Whatsay, JoJo-bean? This place j-u-m-p-s after dark, huh?"

They were taking their postprandial drinks in the oak hall. Hank, wearing blinding white trousers, an embroidered south-of-the-border shirt open to the waist, and the requisite gold chain, leered at Barbara knowingly. He stood as if hoping to become at one with the garlands and cherubs of the carved chimneypiece. One hand was resting on a stylised stone primrose, the fingers curling round a generous measure of brandy: his third or fourth. The other hand was at his waist, the thumb cocked into the loop of his trousers. It was quite a pose.

His wife sat in a high-backed chair, directing her mournfully apologetic gaze alternately between Deborah and Barbara. Lynley and St. James, Barbara noted with satisfaction, had managed to effect a disappearance in the direction of the stone hall almost immediately after dinner, and Mrs. Burton-Thomas had dozed off noisily on a well-padded couch nearby. Barbara reflected upon the uneven quality of Mrs. Burton-Thomas' snores and decided the woman was faking it. She couldn't blame her. Hank had been holding forth for a good quarter hour.

Barbara cast a quick look at Deborah to see how she was dealing with her husband's sudden desertion of her to Hank's clutches. The other woman's face, crossed by fire and shadow, was tranquil, but when she felt Barbara's eyes on her, a mischievous smile touched her lips for an instant. She knows perfectly well what's happening, Barbara decided, and liked Deborah for the generosity implied behind her acceptance of the fact.

As Hank was opening his mouth to continue his description of the after-dark j-u-m-p-s at Keldale Hall, Lynley and St. James rejoined them by the fire.

"Now you gotta get the pitcher here," Hank was continuing. "I go to the window two nights ago to shut out that damned screeching. Ever hear peacocks make such a ruckus, Debbie?"

"*Peacocks?*" Deborah asked. "Good heavens, Simon, it wasn't the baby in the abbey at all! Did you lie to me?"

"I was obviously misled," St. James replied. "It sounded remarkably like a baby to me. Are you telling me we warded off evil for nothing?"

"Like a *baby?*" Hank demanded, incredulous. "You must be lost in the throes of l-u-v, Si. That was a peacock screeching fit to beat the band." He sat down, knees spread apart, his arms resting on his chunky thighs. "So I go to the window to either shut the thing or give the old heave-ho to a shoe and kill that damn bird. I'm one helluva shot. Did I tell you that? No? Well, we got this alley in Laguna, see, where the queers hang out." He waited to see if he would once again have to explain the denizens of Laguna Beach to his audience, but they were caught in the grip of his pictorial pun. He went on happily. "And I get puhlenty of practice heaving shoes out at them, lemme tell you. Whatsay, Bean? Truth or not?"

"Truth, honey," JoJo replied. "He can hit *anything*," she swore to the others.

"I have no doubt," Lynley said grimly.

Hank flashed his capped teeth. "So, here I am at the window, ready to heave it, see, when what I notice is a heckuva lot more 'an some bird."

"Someone else screeching?" Lynley enquired.

"Hell no. The bird was there all right, but I got an eyefull-a something else!" He waited for them to ask what it was. There was polite silence. "Okay, okay!" He laughed. He lowered his voice. "Danny and that fella, whatsisname, Ira . . . Hezekiah . . ."

"Ezra?"

"Yep! And they are liplocked like I never s-e-e-n. Whew! 'You two gonna come up for air?' I yell." He howled appreciatively.

Polite smiles all around. JoJo gazed from one face to another like a puppy eager to be loved.

"Only, this is the best part." Hank lowered his voice again. "What we got on our hands isn't Danny at all. But it's Ezra all right." He smiled triumphantly. Their complete attention was his at last.

"More brandy, Deborah?" St. James asked.

"Thank you."

Hank squirmed forward in his seat. "But he's gettin' it on with *Angelina*! Can you *see* it?" He barked with laughter and pounded his knee. "This Ezra's busier than a rooster in a hen-house, fellas. I don't know what he's got, but he sure likes spreading it around!" He slurped at his drink. "I made a few pointed remarks to Angelina in the A.M., but that girl is *deep*. Not a twitch of the e-y-e. I'm telling you, Tom, if it's action you're looking for, you oughta get yourself down *here*." He sighed with satisfaction and fingered his heavy gold chain. "L-u-v. Wonderful thing, huh? Nothing messes with the mind like l-u-v. Bet you can attest to *that*, Si, huh?"

"I've been distraught for years," St. James acknowledged.

Hank brayed. "Cotcher heart pretty young, did she?" He pointed a knowing finger at Deborah. "After him for a while, huh?"

"Since childhood," she replied smoothly.

"*Childhood!*" Hank crossed the room to slosh more brandy into his glass. Mrs. Burton-Thomas snored loudly as he passed her. "You two're school sweethearts like me and the Bean, I'll bet. Remember it, Bean? A little you-know-what in the back of the Chevy. You got drive-in movies here?"

"I think that's a phenomenon endemic to your country," St. James replied.

"Say what?" Hank shrugged and fell back into his seat. Brandy splashed out onto his white trousers. He ignored it. "So you met in school?"

"No. We were formally introduced at my mother's house." St. James and Deborah exchanged innocent glances.

"Hey, she set you two up, I bet. The Bean and I met on a blind date, too! We got something in common, Si."

"Actually, I was born in his mother's house," Deborah added politely. "But I grew up mostly in Simon's house in London."

Hank's face fell. These were dangerous waters. "Did you catch that, Bean? You two related? Cousins or something?" Visions of hemophiliacs languishing behind closed doors clearly danced in his head.

"Not at all. My father is Simon's . . . well, what would you call Dad?" She turned to her husband. "Footman, servant, butler, valet?"

"Father-in-law," St. James replied.

"Did you catch that, Bean?" Hank said in awe. "This is *some* romance."

It was sudden, unexpected. She was trying to adjust. Lynley's was turning out to be such a multifaceted character, like a diamond cut by a master jeweller, that in every situation a new surface glittered that she had never seen before.

In love with Deborah. All right, certainly. That was understandable. But in love with the daughter of St. James' *servant*? Barbara struggled to assimilate the information. How had it ever happened to him? she wondered. He had always seemed to be in such complete control of his life and his destiny. How had he ever *allowed* it to happen?

She now saw his peculiar behavior at St. James' wedding in an entirely new light. Not anxious to be rid of *her* as soon as he could, but anxious to be away from a source of considerable pain: the nuptial happiness of a woman he loved with another man.

At least she understood now why of the two men Deborah had chosen St. James. Obviously, she'd never even been given a choice, for Lynley would never have allowed himself to speak to her of love. To do this would ultimately have led him to speak of marriage, and Lynley would never marry the daughter of a servant. It would shake his family tree to its very roots.

Yet he certainly must have wanted to make Deborah his wife, and how he must have suffered, watching St. James placidly break the ridiculous code of social behaviour that held Lynley immobilised.

What had St. James said? *Father-in-law.* In four short syllables he had coolly wiped away every class distinction that might ever have separated him from his wife.

No wonder she loves him, Barbara realised suddenly.

She glanced warily at Lynley as they drove back to the lodge. What must it be like for him, knowing that he had lacked the courage to tell Deborah that he wanted her, knowing that he'd put his family and his title before his love? How he must hate himself! What regret he must feel! How horribly lonely he must really be!

He felt her looking at him. "You did nice work today, Sergeant. Especially at the hall. Keeping Hank at bay for a quarter of an hour shall get you a citation, rest assured."

She felt absurdly warmed by the praise. "Thank you, sir. St. James agreed to help?"

"He did indeed."

He did indeed, Lynley thought. He let out his breath sharply in self-derision and tossed the file onto the bedside table. He dropped his spectacles on top of it, rubbed his eyes, and adjusted the pillows behind his back.

Deborah had spoken to her husband. Lynley could see that. They'd already discussed what his response would be when he was asked to assist. It was a simple one: "Of course, Tommy. What can I do?"

How like both of them! How like Deborah to have seen in their conversation that morning all of his concerns about the case. How like her to have paved the way for him to ask St. James' help. And how like St. James to have agreed without hesitation, for any hesitation would have aroused the guilt that always lay like a dangerous, wounded tiger between them.

He leaned back against the pillows and closed his eyes wearily, allowing his mind in its exhaustion to drift back to the past. He gave himself to the bewitching visions of a former happiness that remained unclouded by grief or pain.

> The lovely Thais by his side,
> Sate like a blooming Easter bride,
> In flow'r of youth and beauty's pride.
> Happy, happy, happy pair!
> None but the brave deserves the fair.

Dryden's words came from nowhere, unbidden and unwanted. He swallowed them down and demanded that they recede into his mind, an effort that took every ounce of his concentration and prevented him from hearing the door open and the footsteps cross to the bed. He was quite unaware, in fact, of the presence in the room until a cool hand touched his cheek gently. His eyes flew open.

"I think you need an Odell's, Inspector," Stepha whispered.

12

Nonplussed, he stared at her. He waited for his smooth persona to click into place, for the arrival of that illusory man who laughed and danced and had a quick-witted answer for everything. But nothing happened. Stepha's appearance in his room, materialising for all he knew out of nowhere, seemed to have destroyed his only line of defence, and all that was left in his repertoire of engaging behaviours was the ability to meet, without wavering, her beautiful eyes.

He needed to give reality to the moment, to make her something he hadn't dreamt up from the mist of his dispirited memory, so he reached out and touched the fall of her hair. *Soft*, he thought wonderingly.

She caught his hand and kissed the palm, the wrist. Her tongue lightly traced the length of his fingers. "Let me love you tonight. Let me drive away the shadows."

She spoke on the merest breath of a whisper, and he wondered if her voice were a part of the dream. But her smooth hands played across his cheeks and jaw and throat, and when she bent to him and he tasted the sweetness of her mouth, felt the caress of her tongue, he knew she was part of a searing reality, a present calmly laying siege to the castellated walls of his past.

He wanted to flee from the onslaught, to escape to that haven of bliss-charged remembrance that had kept him well armoured in the year that had passed, a year during which all desire had been absent, all longing dead, all life incomplete. But she allowed no evasion, and as she purposefully destroyed the ramparts that shielded him, he felt once again not a sweet liberation but that terrifying need to possess another person, body and soul.

He *couldn't*. He wouldn't allow it to happen. He desperately sought out last, shattered defences, uselessly willing back into being an insensate creature who no longer lived. In its place was reborn—quiet and vulnerable—the man who had been there, inside, all along.

"Tell me about Paul."

She raised herself on one elbow, touched her finger to his lips, traced their shape. The light struck her hair, her shoulders, her breasts. She was fire and cream, scented almost imperceptibly with the sweetness of Devon violets.

"Why?"

"Because I want to know about you. Because he was your brother. Because he died."

Her eyes moved from his. "What did Nigel say?"

"That Paul's death changed everyone."

"It did."

"Bridie said that he went away, that he never said goodbye."

Stepha lowered herself next to him, into his arms. "Paul killed himself, Thomas," she whispered. Her body trembled on the words. He held her closer. "Bridie's not been told. We say he died of Huntington's, and he did, in a way. It was Huntington's that killed him. Have you ever seen people with the disease? St. Vitus' dance. They've no control over their bodies. They twitch and stagger and leap and fall. And then their minds go at the last. But not Paul. By *God*, not Paul." Her voice caught. She drew in a breath. His hand found its way to her hair and he pressed his lips to the top of her head.

"I'm sorry."

"He had just enough mind left to know that he no longer recognised his wife, no longer knew the name of his child, no longer had any control over his body. He had just enough mind left to decide it was time for him to die." She swallowed. "I helped him. I had to. He was my twin."

"I didn't know that."

"Nigel didn't tell you?"

"No. Nigel's in love with you, isn't he?"

"Yes." She answered without artifice.

"Did he come to Keldale to be near you?"

She nodded. "We were all at university together: Nigel, Paul, and I. I might have married Nigel at one time. He was less mad then, less angry. I'm the source of his madness, I'm afraid. But I'll never marry now."

"Why not?"

"Because Huntington's is a hereditary disease. I'm a carrier. I don't want to pass it on to a child. It's bad enough seeing Bridie every day and thinking every time she stumbles or drops something that she's got the bloody disease herself. I don't know what I'd do if I had a child of my own. Probably drive myself mad with worry."

"You don't have to have children. Or you could adopt."

"Men say that, of course. Nigel does all the time. But there's no point to marriage as far as I'm concerned if I can't have my own child. My own healthy child."

"Was the baby in the abbey a healthy child?"

She drew herself up to look at him. "On duty, Inspector? An odd time and place for it, wouldn't you say?"

He smiled wryly. "Sorry. Reflex action, I'm afraid." And then he added, unrepentant, "Was she?"

"Wherever did you hear about the baby in the abbey? No, don't tell me. Keldale Hall."

"I understand it was a bit of a legend come true."

"Of sorts. The legend—fanned by the Burton-Thomases at every opportunity—is that sometimes one can hear a baby cry from the abbey at night. The reality, I'm afraid, is much as you'd expect. It's a trick of wind when it's blowing with just the right force from the north through a crack in the wall between the north transept and nave. It happens several times a year."

"How do you know?"

"When we were teenagers, my brother and I camped there for a fortnight one spring until we'd tracked the sound down. Of course, we didn't disappoint the Burton-Thomases by telling them the truth. But to be honest, even that wind doesn't sound a great deal like a baby."

"And the real baby?"

"Ah, back to that, are we?" She rested her cheek on his chest. "I don't know much about it. It was just over three years ago. Father Hart found her, managed to stir up a great deal of local outrage about her, and it fell to Gabriel Langston to sort it all out. Poor Gabriel. He never was able to discover anything at all. The furor died down after a few weeks. There was a funeral that everyone of conscience attended and that was the end of it, I'm afraid. It was all rather grim."

"And you were glad when it was over?"

"I was. I don't like grimness. I don't want it in my life. I want life filled with laughter and wild, crazy joy."

"Perhaps you're afraid of feeling anything else."

"I am. But I'm mostly afraid of ending up lost like Olivia, of loving someone so much and then having that person ripped out of my life. I can't bear to be near her any longer. After Paul died, she went into a fog bank and never emerged. I don't want to be like that. Ever." She spoke the last word on a hard note of anger, but when she raised her head, her eyes shone with tears. "Please. Thomas," she whispered, and his body responded with the quicksilver flame of desire.

He pulled her to him roughly, felt her heat and passion, heard her cry of pleasure, felt the shadows drift away.

"What about Bridie?"

"What do you mean?"

"She's like a little lost soul. Just Bridie and that duck."

Stepha laughed. She curled on her side, her smooth back a pleasant pressure against him. "Bridie's special, isn't she?"

"Olivia seems oddly detached from her. It's as if Bridie's growing up without parents at all."

"Liv wasn't always that way. But Bridie's like Paul. So exactly like. I think it hurts Olivia even to see her. She's not really over Paul yet. I doubt she ever will be."

"Then why on earth was she going to remarry?"

"For Bridie's sake. Paul was a very strong father. Olivia seems to have felt duty bound to replace him with someone else. And William was eager to be the replacement, I suppose." Her voice was growing sleepy. "I don't quite know what she thought it was going to be like for herself. But I think she was more interested in getting Bridie under control. It would have worked well, too. William was very good to Bridie. So was Roberta."

"Bridie says you are as well."

She yawned. "Does she? I fixed her hair, poor little pumpkin. I'm not certain I'm good at anything else."

"You chase ghosts away," he whispered. "You're very good at that." But she was asleep.

He awoke to find the reality this time. She lay, child-like, curled with her knees drawn up, with both of her fists under her chin. She was frowning with her dream, and a strand of hair was caught between her lips. He smiled at the sight.

A glance at his watch told him it was nearly seven. He bent and kissed her bare shoulder. She awoke at once, coming fully awake in an instant, not the least bit confused about where she was. She raised her hand, touching his cheek, pulling him down to her.

He kissed her mouth, then her neck, and heard the delicate change in her breathing that signalled her pleasure when he reached her breast. His hand slid the length of her body. She sighed.

"Thomas." He lifted his head. Her cheeks were flushed, her eyes bright. "I must go."

"Not just yet."

"Look at the time."

"In a moment." He bent to her, felt her hands in his hair.

"You . . . I . . . Oh Lord." She laughed as she realised how her body was betraying her.

He smiled. "Go if you must, then."

She sat up, kissed him a last time, and crossed to the bathroom. He lay there, filled with a contentment that he had thought was entirely lost to him, and listened to the familiar noises she made. He found himself wondering how he'd survived the last year of isolation. Then she was returning to him, smiling, running his hairbrush through her tangled hair. She reached for her grey dressing gown and began to put it on, lifting one arm gracefully as she did so.

And it was in that movement in the early morning light that he saw the unmistakable evidence on her body that she had borne a child.

Barbara finally got up when she heard Lynley's door open and close softly. She'd been lying on her side, her eyes fixed desperately upon a single spot on the wall, her teeth grinding together so fiercely that her entire jaw ached. She had willed conscious feeling into absolute death for the last seven hours, ever since the first moment when she'd heard them together in his room.

She walked now to the window on legs that felt numb. She stared stonily out into the Keldale morning. The village seemed lifeless, a place without colour or sound. How appropriate, she thought.

The real agony was the bed: the unmistakable, rhythmic creaking of his bed. It went on and on until she wanted to scream, to pound her fists against the wall to bring it to an end. But the silence that fell just as suddenly was worse. It beat against her eardrums in angry pulsations that she finally came to recognise as the pounding of her heart. And then the bed again, endlessly. And the woman's muffled cry.

She put a dry, hot hand onto the windowpane and felt with listless surprise the damp, cool glass. Her fingers slipped, left streaks. She examined them meticulously.

So much for his unrequited love for Deborah, Barbara thought acidly. Christ, I must have been absolutely out of my mind! When had he ever been more than what he'd been last night: a real stud, a bona fide bull, a hard, hot stallion of a man who had to prove his virility between the legs of every woman he met.

Well, you proved it last night, Inspector. Took her directly up to heaven three or four times, didn't you? You've got solid gold talent, all right.

She laughed soundlessly, mirthlessly. It was a pleasure, really, to discover that he was just what she'd always assumed him to be: an alley cat on the prowl for any female in heat, cleverly disguised under a refulgent veneer of upper-class breeding. But what a thin veneer it was after all! Scratch the surface of the man and the truth oozed out.

The bath began running noisily in the next room, a rushing of water that sounded to Barbara like a burst of applause. She stirred, turned from the window, and made her decision about how to face the day.

"We're going to have to take the house apart one room at a time," Lynley said.

They were in the study. Havers had gone to the bookshelves and was sullenly flipping through a dog-eared Brontë. He watched her. Other than monosyllabic, expressionless replies to every remark he'd made at breakfast, she had said nothing at all. The fragile thread of communication they had established between them seemed to be utterly broken. To make matters worse, she'd returned to her hideous light blue suit and ridiculous, coloured tights.

"Havers," he said sharply. "Are you listening to me?"

Her head turned with slow insolence. "To every word . . . Inspector."

"Then start with the kitchen."

"One of the two places where a little woman belongs."

"What's that supposed to mean?"

"Not a thing." She left the room.

His eyes followed her, perplexed. What in God's name had got into the woman? They had been working so well together, but now she was acting as if she could hardly wait to throw it all away and return to uniform. It made no sense. Webberly was offering her a chance to redeem herself. Given that, why would she deliberately attempt to prove justifiable every prejudice held against her by the other DIs at the Yard? He muttered an oath and summarily dismissed her from his thoughts.

St. James would be in Newby Wiske by now, the corpse of the dog wrapped in a polystyrene shroud in the boot of the Escort and Roberta's clothing in a cardboard carton on the rear seat. He would perform the autopsy, supervise the tests, and report the results with his usual efficiency. Thank God. St. James' involvement would ensure that at least something in the case was handled correctly.

Chief Constable Kerridge of the Yorkshire Constabulary had been only too delighted to hear that Allcourt-St. James would be coming to use their well-equipped lab. Anything, Lynley thought, to put another nail in Nies' coffin. He shook his head in disgust, went to William Teys' desk, and opened the top drawer.

It held no secrets. There were scissors, pencils, a wrinkled map of the county, a typewriter ribbon, and a roll of tape. The map caused a flurry of short-lived interest and he unfolded it eagerly: perhaps it marked out a careful search for Teys' older daughter. But it was unmarred by any cryptogrammic message that indicated the location of a missing girl.

The other drawers were as devoid of pertinent facts as the first: a pot of glue, two boxes of unused Christmas cards, three packets of photographs taken on the farm, account books, records of lambing, a roll of ageing breath mints. But nothing of Gillian.

He leaned back in the chair. His eyes fell on the bookstand and the Bible it held. Struck by a thought, he opened it to the previously marked page. "And Pharaoh said unto Joseph, 'Forasmuch as God hath showed thee all this, there is none so discreet and wise as thou art. Thou shalt be over my house, and according unto thy word shall all my people be ruled: only in the throne will I be greater than thou.' And Pharaoh said unto Joseph, 'See, I have set thee over all the land of Egypt.' And Pharaoh took off his ring from his hand, and put it on Joseph's hand, and arrayed him in vestures of fine linen, and put a gold chain about his neck; and he made him to ride in the second chariot which he had; and they cried before him, 'Bow the knee': and he made him ruler over all the land of Egypt."

"Seeking guidance from the Lord?"

Lynley looked up. Havers was leaning against the study door, her shapeless body silhouetted sharply by the morning light, her face a blank.

"Have you finished the kitchen?" he asked.

"Thought I'd take a break." She sauntered into the room. "Got a smoke on you?"

He handed her his cigarette case absently and went to the bookshelves, running his eyes over them, seeking a volume of Shakespeare. He found it and began looking.

"Is Daze a redhead, Inspector?"

It took a moment for the odd question to strike him. When he looked up, Havers was back at the door, running her fingers meditatively against the wood, apparently indifferent to whatever answer he might give. "I beg your pardon?"

She flipped open the cigarette case and read its inscription. " 'Darling Thomas. We'll always have Paris, won't we? Daze.' " Coldly, she met his eyes. It was then that he noticed how pale she was, how the skin beneath her eyes was dark with fatigue, how the gold case shook in her hand. "Aside from her rather hackneyed use of Bogart, is she a redhead?" Havers repeated. "I only ask because you seem to prefer them. Or is the truth that anyone will do?"

Horrified, Lynley realised too late what the change in her was and his own responsibility for having brought it about. There was nothing he could say. There was no quick answer he could give. But he could tell at once that none was necessary, for she had every intention of continuing without his response.

"Havers—"

She held up a hand to stop him. She was deathly white. Her features looked flat. Her voice was tight. "You know, it's really poor form not to go to the woman's room for your trysts, Inspector. I'm surprised you didn't know that. With *your* experience I should think that a little social nicety like that would be the last thing you'd forget. Of course, it's just a small lapse, and it probably doesn't really bother a woman at all, not when it's compared with the ecstatic experience of fucking you."

He recoiled from the brutal ugliness that her tone gave the word. "I'm sorry, Barbara," he said.

"Why be sorry?" She forced a guttural laugh. "No one thinks about listeners in the heat of passion. I know *I* never do." She gave a brittle smile. "And it certainly was the old heat of passion last night, wasn't it? I couldn't believe it when you two started banging away on a second go. And so *soon*! Lord, you barely gave it a rest."

He watched her move to the shelf and run a finger along the spine of a book. "I didn't know you could hear us. I apologise, Barbara. I'm terribly sorry."

She swung back to him quickly. "Why be sorry?" she repeated, her voice louder this time. "You aren't on duty twenty-four hours a day. And besides, it's not really your fault, is it? How were you to know Stepha would howl like a banshee?"

"Nonetheless, it was never my intention to hurt your feelings—"

"You haven't hurt my feelings at all!" She laughed shrilly. "Where on earth did you get an idea like *that*? Let's say you've merely piqued my interest. As I listened to you sending Stepha to the moon—was it three times or four?—I wondered if Deborah used to howl as well."

It was a wild shot in the dark, but the barb had gone home. He knew that she saw it, for her face blazed with triumph. "That's hardly your concern, is it?"

"Of course not! I know that! But during your second session with Stepha—it *was* at least an hour, wasn't it?—I couldn't help thinking about poor old Simon. He must have to struggle like hell to follow *your* act."

"You've certainly done your homework, Havers. I'll say that much for you. And when you take off the gloves, you do shoot to kill. Or am I mixing my metaphors?"

"Don't you patronise me. Don't you dare!" she shouted. "Just who the hell do you think you are?"

"Your superior officer, for a start."

"Oh, that's right, Inspector. Now's the time to pull rank. Well, what shall I do? Shall I get to work in here? Don't *mind* if I'm not quite up to par. I didn't *sleep* well last night." She pulled a book angrily from the shelf. It toppled to the floor. He could see she was struggling not to cry.

"Barbara—" She continued to pull books down, to turn the pages savagely, to drop them to the floor. They were mildewed and damp, filling the air with the unpleasant odour of neglect. "*Listen* to me. You've done good work so far. Don't be foolish now."

She pivoted, trembling. "What's *that* supposed to mean?"

"You have a chance to be back in CID. Don't throw it away because you're angry with me."

"I'm not angry with you! I don't give a *shit* about you."

"Of course not. I didn't mean to imply that you did."

"We both know why I was assigned to you anyway. They wanted a woman on the case and they knew I was *safe*." She spat the word out. "The minute this is over, I'm back on the street."

"What are you talking about?"

"Come on, Inspector, I'm not stupid. I've looked in a few mirrors."

He was astonished at the implication behind her words. "Do you think you've been brought back to CID because Webberly believes I'd take any other female officer to bed?" She didn't respond. "Is that what you think?" he repeated. The silence continued. "*Dammit*, Havers—"

"It's what I know!" she shouted. "But what Webberly doesn't know is that *any* blonde or brunette is safe with you these days, not just pigs like me. It's redheads you've a taste for, redheads like Stepha, replacements for the one that you've lost."

"That has *nothing* to do with this conversation!"

"It has everything to do with it! If you weren't so desperate to have Deborah back, you wouldn't have spent half the night pounding Stepha into pulp and we wouldn't be having this whole, bleeding discussion!"

"Then let's drop it, shall we? I've apologised. You've made your feelings and beliefs—bizarre as they are—absolutely clear. I think we've said enough."

"Oh, that's damned convenient to call *me* bizarre," she cried bitterly. "What about *you*? You won't marry a woman because her father's in service, you watch your very own friend fall in love with her instead, you spend the rest of your life racked with misery over it, and then you decide to call *me* bizarre."

"Your facts aren't quite straight," he said icily.

"Oh, I've got all the facts I need. And when I string them together, *bizarre* is just the word I'd use to describe them. Fact one: you're in love with Deborah St. James, and don't bother to deny it. Fact two: she's married to someone else. Fact three: you obviously had a love affair with her, which leads us inescapably to fact four: you *damn* well could have married her but you chose not to and you're going to pay for that stupid, narrow-minded upper-class decision for the rest of your bleeding, goddamn life!"

"You seem to have a great deal of confidence in my fatal attraction for women. Any woman who sleeps with me is only too willing to become my wife. Is that correct?"

"Don't you laugh at me!" she shrieked, her eyes squeezed shut in rage.

"I'm not laughing at you. I'm also not spending another moment discussing this with you." He started for the door.

"Oh that's it! Run away! That's just what I'd expect of you, Lynley! Go have it off with Stepha again! Or what about Helen? Does she pop a red wig on so you can get it up? Does she let you call her *Deb*?"

He felt anger like a current shooting through his veins. He drove himself towards calm by looking at his watch. "Havers, I'm going to Newby Wiske to see the results of St. James' tests. That gives you about—shall we say—three hours to tear this house apart and find me something—*anything*, Havers—that leads me to Gillian Teys. Since you have such a remarkable ability to gather facts out of thin air, that should prove to be no problem whatsoever for you. If, however, you have nothing to report within three hours, consider yourself sacked. Is that clear?"

"Why not sack me right now and have done with it then?" she shrilled.

"Because I like to look forward to my pleasures." He walked over to her, took his cigarette case from her limp hand. "Daze is a blonde," he said.

She snorted. "I find *that* hard to believe. Does she wear a red wig for those intimate moments?"

"I don't know." He turned the cigarette case over in his hand so that the old ornate *A* engraved on its cover was face up. "But it's an interesting question. If my father were still alive, I'd ask him. This was his. Daze is my mother." He picked up the volume of Shakespeare and left.

Barbara stared after him, motionless, waiting for the pounding of her blood to stop, slowly coming to terms with the terrible enormity of what she had done.

You've done good work so far. . . . You have a chance to be back on CID. Don't throw it away because you're angry with me.

And isn't that exactly what she had done? The need to rage

at him, to castigate him, to rail against his attraction to a beautiful woman had overcome every good intention that she had
ever possessed in setting to work on the case. What in God's
name had come over her?

Was she jealous? Had there been one insane moment when
she had been so foolish as to think that Lynley might ever look
at her and not see her for what she truly was: a plain, dumpy
woman, angry at the world, bitter and friendless and terribly
alone? Had she possibly harboured a secret hope that he might
come to care for her? Is that what had driven her to attack him
this morning? The thought was patently absurd.

It couldn't be. It wasn't possible. She knew enough about him
not to be *that* ignorant.

She felt drained. It was this house, she decided. It was having
to come and work in this dwelling place of ghouls. Five minutes
here and she was ready to snap and snarl, to climb the walls, to
tear wildly at her hair.

She went to the study door and looked across the sitting room
to Tessa's shrine. The woman smiled at her kindly. But wasn't
there just a touch of victory in her eyes? Wasn't it as if Tessa
had known all along that she could do nothing but fail once she
walked into this house and felt its silence and chill?

Three hours, he'd said. Three hours to find the secret of Gillian
Teys.

She laughed bitterly at the thought, tasting the sound in the
empty air. He knew that she would fail, that he would have the
enjoyment of sending her back to London, back to uniform, back
to disgrace. So what was the point of trying at all? Why not leave
now rather than give him the pleasure?

She threw herself down on the sitting-room couch. Tessa's
image watched her sympathetically. But . . . what if she could
find Gillian? What if, where Lynley himself had failed, she was
able to succeed? Would it really matter then if he sent her back
to the streets? Wouldn't she know, once and for all, that she was
good for something, that she could have been part of a working
team?

It was a thought. She picked idly at the worn upholstery of
the couch. The sound of her fingers scratching at the threads
was the only noise in the house. Except for the rustling and

burrowing of mice at the edge of her consciousness, like a half-formed thought.

She looked at the stairway reflectively.

They sat at a table in the corner of the Keys and Candle, Newby Wiske's central and most thriving pub. Most of the lunch-time crowd had thinned out and, aside from themselves, only the regulars remained, hunched over the bar to nurse pints of bitters.

They pushed their plates to one side of the table, and Deborah poured the coffee that had just been placed before them. Outside, the cook and the dishwasher dumped rubbish into the bin, arguing loudly over the merits of a three-year-old who would be running at Newmarket and upon whom the cook had evidently invested a considerable sum of his most recent week's wages.

St. James ministered to his coffee with his usual amount of sugar. Lynley spoke after the fourth teaspoonful was dumped absently into the cup.

"Does he count?"

"Not that I've ever noticed," Deborah replied.

"St. James, that's appalling. How can you stand it?"

"Just sugaring 'o'er the devil himself,' " his friend replied. He pulled the test results towards him. "I need to do something to recover from the smell of that dog. You owe me for this one, Tommy."

"In spades. What do you have?"

"The animal bled to death from a wound in the neck. It appeared to have been inflicted with a knife the blade of which was five inches long."

"Not a pocketknife, then."

"I should guess a kitchen knife. A butcher knife. Something along that line. Did forensics see to all the knives on the farm?"

Lynley fingered through the material from the file he had brought with him. "Apparently. But the knife in question was nowhere to be found."

St. James looked thoughtful. "That's intriguing. It almost suggests . . ." He paused, brushing aside the idea. "Well, they have the girl admitting to killing her father, they have the axe sitting right there on the floor—"

"With no fingerprints on it," Lynley interjected.

"Given. But unless the RSPCA wants to make a case for cruelty to animals, there's no real necessity to have the weapon that killed the dog."

"You're starting to sound like Nies."

"Perish the thought." St. James stirred his coffee and was about to apply more sugar to it when, with a beatific smile, his wife moved the bowl out of his reach. He grumbled good-naturedly and continued his conversation. "However, there was something else. Barbiturates."

"*What?*"

"Barbiturates," St. James repeated. "They showed up in the drug screen. Here." He passed the toxicology report across the table.

Lynley read it, amazed. "Are you telling me the dog was drugged?"

"Yes. The amount of residual drug that showed up in the tests indicates that the animal was unconscious when his throat was slit."

"Unconscious!" Lynley scanned the report and tossed it down on the table. "Then he couldn't have been killed to silence him."

"Hardly. He wouldn't have been making a sound."

"Was there enough barbiturate to kill him? Had someone attempted to kill him with the drug and then, having botched it, decided to take a knife to the poor creature?"

"That's possible, I suppose. Except that with everything you've told me about the case, it doesn't make much sense."

"Why not?"

"Because this unknown person would have had to get into the house first, get the drug, administer it to the dog, wait for it to do the trick, realise that it wasn't going to kill him, go back for a knife, and finish the job off. What was the dog doing all this time? Cooperatively waiting to have his throat slit? Wouldn't he have been barking, raising the devil?"

"Wait. You're too far ahead of me. Why would the person have to go into the house for the drug?"

"Because it was the very same drug that William Teys had

taken, and he kept his sleeping pills in the house, not in the barn, I should think."

Lynley assimilated this. "Perhaps someone brought it with him."

"Perhaps. I suppose the person could have administered it to the dog, waited for it to take effect, slit the dog's throat, and waited for Teys to come out to the barn."

"Between ten and midnight? What would Teys be doing in the barn between ten and midnight?"

"Looking for the dog?"

"Why? Why the barn? Why not in the village where the dog always went? Why look for him at all, in fact? Everyone says that the dog wandered freely. Why would he have suddenly been worried about him on this one night?"

St. James shrugged. "What Teys was up to is a moot point, if your attention is fixed on finding the killer of the animal. Only one person could have killed that dog—Roberta."

Outside the pub, St. James spread the tent-like dress over the boot of Lynley's car, oblivious of the curious stares of a group of elderly tourists who passed, in pursuit of pictorial souvenirs, cameras slung round their necks. He pointed to the stain on the inside elbow of the left sleeve, to the pool-like stain between waist and knees, and to the same substance on the right, white cuff.

"All of these test as the dog's blood, Tommy." He turned to his wife. "My love, will you demonstrate? As you did in the lab? On this bit of lawn?"

Deborah cooperatively dropped to her knees, resting back on her heels. Her rich, umber dress billowed out and spread on the ground like a mantle. St. James moved behind her.

"A willing dog would make this easier to imagine, but we'll do our best. Roberta—who had access to her father's sleeping pills, I should guess—would have given the dog the drug earlier. In his dinner, perhaps. She would have had to make sure the animal stayed in the barn. It wouldn't have done to have had the creature keel over in the village somewhere. Once the dog was unconscious, she would kneel down on the ground just as Deborah has done. Only that particular posture could give us the stains in the precise places they appear on her dress. She would lift the dog's head and hold it in the crook of her arm." He gently bent Deborah's arm to demonstrate. "Then, with her right hand, she would cut the dog's throat."

"That's insane," Lynley said hoarsely. *"Why?"*

"Wait a moment, Tommy. The dog's head is turned away from her. She drives the knife into his throat, which results in the pool of blood on the skirt of her dress. She pulls the knife upward with her right hand until the job is done." He pointed to specific areas on Deborah's dress. "We have blood on the elbow where the head was cradled, blood on the skirt where it poured from the neck, and blood on the right sleeve and cuff from where she drove the knife in and continued the path of the slash." St. James touched his wife's hair lightly. "Thank you, my love." He helped her to her feet.

Lynley walked back to the car and examined the dress. "Frankly, it doesn't make a great deal of sense. Why on earth would she do it? Are you saying the girl dressed herself up on a Saturday night in her best Sunday clothes, calmly went out to the barn, and slit the throat of a dog she'd loved since childhood?" He looked up. *"Why?"*

"I can't answer that. I can't tell you what she was thinking, only what she had to have done."

"But couldn't she have gone out to the barn, found the dog dead, and, in her panic, picked him up, cradled him, and got the blood all over herself then?"

There was a fractional pause. "Possibly. But unlikely."

"But it's possible. It *is* possible?"

"Yes. But unlikely, Tommy."

"What scenario do *you* have then?"

Deborah and St. James exchanged uneasy glances in which Lynley saw that they had discussed the case and were of a mutual opinion they were reluctant to share. "Well?" he demanded. "Are you saying that Roberta killed her dog, that her father came to the barn and discovered the deed, that they got into a tremendous row, and then she beheaded him?"

"No, no. It's quite possible that Roberta didn't kill her father at all. But she was definitely present when it happened. She had to have been."

"Why?"

"Because his blood is all over the bottom of her dress."

"Perhaps she went to the barn, found his body, and fell to her knees in shock."

St. James shook his head. "That idea doesn't wash."

"Why not."

He pointed to the garment on the back of the car. "Look at the pattern. Teys' blood is in splatters. You know what that means as well as I. It only got there one way."

Lynley was silent for a moment. "She was standing by when it happened," he concluded.

"She had to have been. If indeed she didn't do it herself, then she was standing right there when someone else did."

"Is she protecting someone, Tommy?" Deborah asked, seeing the expression on Lynley's face.

He didn't reply at once. He was thinking of patterns: patterns of words, patterns of images, patterns of behaviours. He was thinking of what a person learns, and when he learns it, and when it emerges into practical use. He was thinking of knowledge and how it ultimately, inevitably combines with experience and points to what is incontrovertible truth.

He roused himself to answer the question with one of his own. "St. James, what would you do, how far would you go, to save Deborah?" It was a dangerous query. It's risk was deadly. These were waters, perhaps, best left unexplored.

" 'Forty thousand brothers?' Is that where we are with it now?" St. James' voice was unchanged, but the angles of his face were a warning, finely drawn and grim.

"How far would you go?" Lynley insisted.

"Tommy, don't!" Deborah put out her hand, a gesture to stop him from going any further, to stop him from doing irreparable damage to the delicate crystal of their friable peace.

"Would you hold back the truth? Would you lay down your life? How far would you go to save Deborah?"

St. James looked at his wife. The colour had completely drained from her face; her sprinkling of freckles danced across her nose; her eyes were haunted with tears. And he understood. This was no grappling in an Elsinore grave, but the question primeval.

"I'd do anything," he replied, his eyes on his wife. "By God, yes, I would. I'd do anything."

Lynley nodded. "People generally do, don't they, for the ones they love most."

He chose Tchaikovsky: Symphony No. 6, *Pathetique*. He smiled as the swelling of the first movement filled the car. Helen would never have allowed it.

"Darling Tommy, absolutely *not!*" she would have protested. "Let's not drive our mutual depression right into suicide!" Then she would have resolutely rooted through all of his tapes to find something suitably uplifting: invariably Strauss, played at full volume with Helen making her usual assortment of amusing remarks over the din. "Just picture them, Tommy, flitting through the woods in their little tutus. It's positively religious!"

Today, however, the heavy theme of *Pathetique* with its relentless exploration of man's spiritual suffering suited his mood. He couldn't remember the last time he had felt so burdened by a case. It felt as if a tremendous weight, having nothing whatsoever to do with the responsibility of getting to the bottom of the matter, were pressing upon his heart. He knew the source. Murder—its atavistic nature and ineffable consequences—was a hydra. Each head, ruthlessly cut off in an effort to reach the "prodigious dog-like body" of culpability, left in its place two heads more venomous than the last. But unlike so many of his previous cases, in which mere rote sufficed to see him sear his way to the core of evil—stopping the flow of blood, allowing no further growth, and leaving him personally untouched by the encounter—this case spoke to him far more intimately. He knew instinctively that the death of William Teys was merely one of the heads of the serpent, and the knowledge that eight others waited to do battle with him—and, more than that, that he had not even come to know the true nature of the evil he faced— filled him with a sense of trepidation. But he knew himself well enough to know that there was more to his desolation and despair than the death of a man in a Keldale barn.

There was Havers to be dealt with. But beyond Havers, there was the truth. For underneath her bitter, unfounded accusations, her ugliness and hurt, the words she spoke rang with veracity. Had he not indeed spent the last year of his life fruitlessly seeking a replacement for Deborah? Not in the way Havers had suggested, but in a way far more dishonest than an inconsequential coupling in which two bodies meet, experience momentary pleasure, and separate to lead their individual lives, untouched and unchanged by the encounter. That, at least, was an expression of some sort, a giving of the moment no matter how brief. But for the last year of his life, he had given nothing to anyone.

Behind his behaviour, wasn't the reality that he had maintained his isolated celibacy this last, long year not because of Deborah but because he had become high priest in a religion of one: a celebrant caught up in devotion to the past? In this twisted religion, he had held up every woman in his life to unforgiving scrutiny and had found each one wanting in comparison to Deborah, not the real Deborah but a mystical goddess who lived only in his mind.

He saw now that he had not wished to forget the past, that he had done everything instead to keep it alive, as if his intention had always been to make it, not Deborah, his bride. He was sick at heart.

With the sickness came the realisation that there were facts to be faced about Stepha as well. But he could not bring himself to them. Not yet.

As the final movement of the symphony came to a close, he turned down the winding road from the moors into Keldale. Autumn leaves flew from under the car's wheels, leaving a cloud of red, gold, and yellow billowing behind him, promising winter. He pulled in front of the lodge and spent a moment gazing at the windows, numbly wondering how and when he was going to piece together the fragments of his life.

Havers must have been watching for him from the lounge, for she came to the door as soon as he switched off the car's ignition. He groaned and steeled himself to another confrontation, but she gave him no chance to make preliminary remarks.

"I've found Gillian," she announced.

13

SHE HAD SOMEHOW survived the morning. The dreadful row with Lynley followed by the horrors of Roberta's bedroom had served to wear down her anger and wretchedness, abrading them both into a dull detachment. She knew he was going to sack her anyway. She certainly deserved it. But before he did, she would prove to him that she could be a decent DS. In order to do that, however, there was this one last meeting to get through, this one last opportunity to show her stuff.

She watched Lynley's eyes roam over the unusual collection of items spread out on one of the tables in the lounge: the album containing the defaced family pictures, a dog-eared and well-thumbed novel, the photograph from Roberta's chest of drawers, the additional one of the two sisters, and a collection of six yellowed newspaper pages, all folded and shaped to the identical size, seventeen by twenty-two inches.

Lynley absently felt in his pocket for his cigarettes, lit one, and sat down on the couch. "What is this, Sergeant?" he asked.

"I think these are the facts on Gillian," she responded. Her voice was carefully modulated, but a slight quaver in it caught his attention. She cleared her throat to hide it.

"You're going to need to enlighten me, I'm afraid," he said. "Cigarette?"

Her fingers itched to feel the cylinder of tobacco; her body ached for the soothing smoke. But she knew, if she lit one, it would betray her shaking hands. "No, thank you," she replied. She took a breath, kept her eyes on his noncommittal face, and went on. "How does your man Denton line your chest of drawers?"

"With some sort of paper, I should guess. I've never noticed."

"But it isn't newspaper, is it?" She sat down opposite him, squeezing her hands into fists in her lap, feeling the sharp crescent pain of nails biting palms. "It wouldn't be, because the newsprint would come off on your clothes."

"True."

"So I was intrigued when you mentioned that Roberta's drawers were lined with newspapers. And I remembered Stepha saying that Roberta used to come every day for the *Guardian*."

"Until Paul Odell died. Then she stopped."

Barbara pushed her hair back behind her ears. It was quite unimportant, she told herself, if he didn't believe her, if he laughed at the conclusions she had drawn after nearly three hours in that horrible room. "Except that I don't think the reason she stopped coming for the *Guardian* had anything to do with Paul Odell. I think it was Gillian."

His eyes drifted to the newspapers and Barbara saw him take in what she herself had noticed: that Roberta had lined her drawers with the classified section. Moreover, although there were six pieces of newspaper on the table, they were duplicates of only two pages of the *Guardian*, as if something memorable had appeared in a single issue, and Roberta had collected that day's edition from the villagers to keep as souvenirs.

"The personal column," Lynley murmured. "By God, Havers, Gillian sent her a message."

Barbara pulled one of the sheets towards her and ran her finger down the column. " 'R. Look at the advert. G,' " she read. "I think that's the message."

"Look at the advertisement? What advertisement?"

She reached for a representation of the second saved page. "This one, I think."

He read it. Dated nearly four years previously, it was a small, square announcement of a meeting in Harrogate, a panel discussion involving a group from an organisation called Testament House. The members of the panel were listed, but Gillian Teys was not among them. Lynley looked up, his brown eyes frankly quizzical.

"You've lost me, Sergeant."

Her eyebrows lifted in surprise. "Aren't you familiar with Testament House? Never mind, I keep forgetting that you haven't been in uniform in years. Testament House is run out of Fitzroy Square by an Anglican priest. He used to teach at university but evidently one day one of his students asked him why he wasn't bothering to practise what he preached—feeding the hungry and clothing the naked—and he decided that was something in his life that he ought to address. So he started Testament House."

"Which is?"

"An organisation that collects runaways. Teenaged prostitutes—both male and female—drug abusers of every colour and shape, and everyone else under the age of twenty-one who's hanging about aimlessly in Trafalgar or Piccadilly or in any of the stations just waiting to be preyed on by a pimp or a whore. He's been doing it for years. The uniformed police all know him. We always took kids to him."

"He's the Reverend George Clarence that's listed here, I take it?"

She nodded. "He goes out on fund-raising tours for the organisation."

"Do I understand you to mean that you believe Gillian Teys was picked up by this group in London?"

"I . . . Yes, I do."

"Why?"

It had taken her ages to find the advertisement, ages longer to decipher its significance, and now everything—most especially her career, she admitted—depended upon Lynley's willingness to believe. "Because of this name." She pointed to the third on the list of panelists.

"Nell Graham?"

"Yes."

"I'm completely in the dark."

"I think *Nell Graham* was the message Roberta was waiting for. She faithfully searched the paper each day for years, waiting to see what had happened to her sister. *Nell Graham* told her. It meant Gillian had survived."

"Why Nell Graham? Why not," he glanced at the other names, "Terence Hanover, Caroline Paulson, or Margaret Crist?"

Havers picked up the battered novel from the table. "Because none of those were born of one of the Brontës." She tapped the book. "*The Tenant of Wildfell Hall* is about Helen Huntington, a woman who breaks the social code of her time and leaves her alcoholic husband to start a new life. She falls in love with a man who knows nothing about her past, who knows only the name she has chosen for herself: Helen Graham, *Nell* Graham, Inspector." She finished and waited in agony for his response.

When it came, nothing could have surprised her more, could have disarmed her more quickly. "*Bravo*, Barbara," he said softly, his eyes lit and a smile breaking over his face. He leaned forward earnestly. "What's your theory on how she came to be involved with this group?"

The relief was so tremendous that Barbara found she had begun trembling from head to toe. She took a ragged breath and somehow found her voice. "My . . . I suspect that Gillian had enough money to get to London but that ran out fairly soon. They may have picked her up off the street somewhere or in one of the stations."

"But wouldn't they return her to her father?"

"That's not how Testament House works. They encourage the kids to go home or at least to phone their parents and let them know they're all right, but no one is forced to do it. If they choose to stay at Testament, they just have to obey the rules. No questions asked."

"But Gillian left home at sixteen. If she is this Nell Graham, she would have been twenty-three when she was on this panel in Harrogate. Does it make sense that she would have stayed with Testament House for all those years?"

"If she had no one else, it makes perfect sense. If she wanted a family, they were her best bet. At any rate, there's only one way we can know for sure—"

"Talk to her," he finished promptly. He got to his feet. "Get your things together. We'll leave in ten minutes." He rooted through the file and took out the photograph of Russell Mowrey and his family. "Give this to Webberly when you get to London," he said as he scribbled a message on the back.

"When I get to London?" Her heart sank. He was giving her the sack then. He'd as much as promised that after their encounter at the farm. It was, indeed, all she could expect.

Lynley looked up, all business. "You found her, Sergeant. You can bring her back to Keldale. I think Gillian's the only way we're going to get through to Roberta. Don't you agree?"

"I . . . What about . . ." She stopped herself, afraid to believe the meaning behind his words. "You don't want to phone Webberly? Have someone else . . . ? Go there yourself?"

"I've too many things to see to here. You can see to Gillian. If Nell Graham *is* Gillian. Hurry up. We've got to get to York so you can catch the train."

"But . . . how should I? What approach should I use? Should I simply—"

He waved her off. "I trust your judgement, Sergeant. Just bring her back as quickly as you can."

She unclenched her hands, aware of the numbing relief sweeping over her. "Yes, sir," she heard her voice whisper.

He tapped his fingers against the steering wheel and regarded the house cresting its smooth slope of lawn. By driving like the devil, he had managed to get Havers on the three o'clock train for London and now he sat in front of the Mowrey home, trying to decide how best to approach the woman inside. Wasn't the truth, after all, better than the silence? Had he not at least learned that?

She met him at the door. The wary glance that she cast back over her shoulder told him he was far less welcome than when they had previously met. "My children are just home from school," she said in explanation and stepped outside, pulling the door shut behind her. She drew her cardigan firmly round her slender body. It was like the body of a child. "Have you . . . Is there word about Russell?"

He reminded himself that he couldn't have expected her to ask about her daughter. Tessa, of all people, had said goodbye to the past, had made a surgical cut and walked away cleanly. "You need to involve the police, Mrs. Mowrey."

She paled. "He couldn't. He didn't."

"You must telephone the police."

"I can't. I *can't*," she whispered fiercely.

"He's not with his relatives in London, is he?" She shook her head briefly, once, and kept her face averted. "Have they heard from him at all?" Again, the same response. "Then isn't it best to find out where he is?" When she didn't reply, he took her arm and led her gently towards the drive. "Why did William keep all those keys?"

"What keys?"

"There was a box of them on the shelf in his wardrobe. But there are no keys anywhere in the rest of the house. Do you know why?"

She bent her head, put a hand to her brow. "Those. I'd forgotten," she murmured. "I . . . It was because of Gillian's tantrum."

"When was this?"

"She must have been seven. No, she was nearly eight. I remember because I was pregnant with Roberta. It was one of those situations that come up out of nowhere and are blown all out of proportion, the kind that families laugh about later when the children are grown. I remember William said at dinner, 'Gilly, we'll read from the Bible tonight.' I was sitting there—daydreaming probably—and expected her to say, 'Yes, Papa,' as she always did. But she decided that she wouldn't read the Bible that night, and William decided just as definitely that she would. She became absolutely hysterical about it, ran to her room and locked the door."

"And then?"

"Gilly had never disobeyed her father before. Poor William simply sat there, astonished. He didn't seem to know how to handle it."

"What did you do?"

"Nothing that helped particularly, as I recall. I went to Gilly's room, but she wouldn't let me in. She'd only scream that she wouldn't read the Bible any longer and that no one could make her. Then she threw things at the door. I . . . I went back down to William." She looked at Lynley with an expression that combined both perplexity and admiration as she went on. "You know, William never scolded her. That wasn't his way. But he later took the keys from all the doors. He said if the house had burned down that night and he hadn't been able to get to Gilly because she'd locked her door, he would never have forgiven himself."

"Did they go back to reading the Bible after that?"

She shook her head. "He never asked Gilly to read the Bible after that."

"Did he read it with you?"

"No. Just alone."

A girl had come to the door as they spoke, a piece of bread in her hand and a thin line of jam traced across her upper lip. She was small like her mother but with her father's dark hair and intelligent eyes. She watched them curiously.

"Mummy," she called. Her voice was sweet and clear. "Is anything wrong? Is it Daddy?"

"No, darling," Tessa called back hastily. "I'll be in in a moment." She turned to Lynley.

"How well did you know Richard Gibson?" he asked her.

"William's nephew? As well as anyone could have known Richard, I suppose. He was a quiet boy but immensely likable, with a wonderful sense of humour, as I recall. Gilly quite adored him. Why do you ask?"

"Because William left the farm to him, not to Roberta."

Her brow furrowed. "But why not to Gilly?"

"Gillian ran away from home when she was sixteen, Mrs. Mowrey. No one ever heard from her again."

Tessa drew in a breath. It was sharp and quick, like the reaction to an unexpected blow. Her eyes fixed themselves on Lynley.

"No," she said. It was not so much denial as disbelief.

He continued. "Richard had been gone for a time as well. To the fens. There's a chance that Gillian followed him there and then perhaps went on to London."

"But why? Whatever happened? What could have happened?"

He considered how much to tell her. "I've got the impression," he said, spacing the words delicately, "that she was involved with Richard somehow."

"And William found out? If that's the case, he would have torn Richard limb from limb."

"Suppose he did find out and Richard knew what his reaction would be. Would that be enough for Richard to leave the village?"

"I should think so. But it doesn't explain why William left the farm to him and not to Roberta, does it?"

"It was apparently a bargain he'd struck with Gibson. Roberta would continue to live there for her lifetime with Richard and his family, but the land would go to the Gibsons."

"But certainly Roberta would marry someday. It hardly seems fair. Surely William would have wanted the land to remain in the immediate family, to be passed on to his grandchildren, if not to Gilly's children, then to Roberta's."

Even as she spoke, Lynley realised what a vast chasm the nineteen years of her absence had caused. She knew nothing of Roberta, nothing of the girl's hidden storehouse of food, nothing of her vacant, rocking catatonia. Roberta was just a name to her mother, a name who would marry, have children, grow old. She was not at all real. She did not actually exist.

"Did you never think about them?" he asked her. She looked down at her feet, employing in the act an intensity that suggested all of her concentration was centred on the smooth, rusty suede of her shoes. When she didn't reply, he persisted. "Did you never wonder how they were, Mrs. Mowrey? Did you never imagine what they looked like or how they'd grown up?"

She shook her head once, sharply. And when she answered him at last, in a voice so controlled that it spoke volumes on the emotion she had spent on the subject, she kept her eyes on the minster in the distance. "I couldn't let myself do that, Inspector. I knew they were safe. I knew they were well. So I let them die. I had to if I wanted to survive. Can you understand?"

A few days ago, he would have said no. And that would have been the truth of the matter. But that was not the case now. "Yes," he replied. "I do understand." He nodded to her in farewell and walked back to his car.

"Inspector—" He turned, his hand on the door handle. "You know where Russell is, don't you?"

She read the answer in his face, but she listened instead to the lie. "No," he responded.

* * *

Ezra Farmington lived directly across from the Dove and Whistle in the council house that abutted against Marsha Fitzalan's. Like hers, its front garden was planted and cared for, but with less detailed concern, as if the man had started out with the best of intentions, but they, along with the plants, had become the worse for wear. Bushes were thriving but overgrown, weeds were assaulting the flower beds, dead annuals needed to be uprooted and discarded, and a small patch of lawn was looking long enough to be considered a potential source of fodder.

Farmington was not at all pleased to see him. He opened the door to Lynley's knock and placed his body squarely in the frame. Over his shoulder Lynley saw that the other man had been going through his work, for dozens of watercolours were spread upon the sitting room couch and scattered on the floor. Some were torn into shreds, others were crumpled into tight, angry balls, still others were abandoned to meet their fate under foot. It was a haphazard purging of artistic effort, however, because the artist himself was more than halfway drunk.

"Inspector?" Farmington asked with deliberate politeness.

"May I come in?"

The man shrugged. "Why not?" He opened the door wider and gestured Lynley inside with a lackadaisical sweep. " 'Scuse the mess. Just cleaning out the crap."

Lynley stepped over several paintings. "From four years ago?" he asked blandly.

It was the right choice of time. Farmington's face told him so in the sudden flare of nostrils and the movement of lips.

"What's that s'posed to mean?" He was just on the edge of slurring his words, and, perhaps noticing this himself, he sought control visibly.

"What time was it when you and William Teys argued?" Lynley asked, ignoring the man's question.

"Time?" Ezra shrugged. "No idea. Drink, Ins . . . Inspector?" He smiled glassily and stiffly crossed the room to pour himself a tumbler of gin. "No? You don't mind if I . . . ? Thank you." He gulped back a mouthful, coughed, and laughed, swiping at his mouth so savagely with his wrist that the movement was as good as a blow. "Pulin' wimp. Can' even handle a drink."

"You were coming down from High Kel Moor. That's not a walk you would make in the dark, is it?"

"Course not."

"And you heard music from the farmhouse?"

"Ha!" He waved his glass at Lynley. "Whole screamin' *band*, In . . . spector. Thought I was in the middle of a flipping parade."

"Did you see only Teys? No one else?"

"Are we counting sweet Nigel bringing the doggie home?"

"Aside from Nigel."

"Nope." He lifted his glass and drained it. "Course, Roberta was proba'ly inside the house changing the records, poor fat slob. She wasn't much good for anything else. 'Cept," his bleary eyes twinkled, "swinging an axe and sending Papa into the great beyond." He laughed at his comment. "Like Lizzie Borden!" he added and laughed louder still.

Lynley wondered why the man was being deliberately repugnant, wondered what was motivating him to go to such great lengths to develop and then display a side of his character so ugly as to be intolerable. Hatred and anger were the foundation here and a contempt so virulent that it was like a third person in the room. Farmington was obviously a talented man and yet a man blindly bent upon destroying the single creative force that gave his life meaning.

As he clutched at himself with callous nonchalance and stumbled in the direction of the lavatory, Lynley looked at the paintings he left behind and saw the source of the man's despair in the studies the artist could not bring himself to destroy.

They were done from every possible angle, in charcoal, pencil, pastels, and paint. They chronicled movement, passion, and desire, and bore witness to the anguish of the artist's soul. They were all of Stepha Odell.

When Lynley heard the man's returning footsteps, he forced his eyes from the work and his mind away from the implication. Instead, he made himself look at Farmington and in doing so he saw the other man clearly for the first time: womanizer and hypocrite, using past pain as an excuse for present behavior. He saw that Farmington was at best his own mirror image, his second self, the man, indeed, he could choose to become.

* * *

From King's Cross Station, Barbara took the Northern Line to Warren Street. Fitzroy Square was only a few minutes' walk from there. She spent that time meditating on a plan of attack. It was clear that Gillian Teys was involved in this situation up to her neck, but that was going to be extremely difficult to prove. If she was smart enough to disappear from sight for eleven years, certainly she was smart enough to have a cast iron alibi for the night in question. It seemed to Barbara that the best approach—if indeed Gillian was Nell Graham and if she could be located using the scant information they had—was to give her no choice, arrest her if necessary, in order to get her back to Keldale that night. She thought about everything that had been said about Gillian: about her delinquent behavior, her sexual licence, and her ability to hide both under an exterior of angelic refinement. There was only one way to deal with someone that clever. Be tough, be aggressive, be absolutely ruthless.

Fitzroy Square—a tidily renovated patch of Camden Town—was an unusual spot to find a home for stray teenagers. Twenty years before, when the square had still been a postwar rectangle of sagging buildings, grubby pavements, and empty window-boxes, a home for the flotsam and jetsam of London life would be what one would expect to find. But now, when the entire face of the square was crisp and new, when the lovely green in the centre was carefully fenced off against vagrants, when every building was freshly painted and every burnished door gleamed in the fading light of the day, it was hard to believe that society's forgotten and unwanted, frightened and pained still lived here.

Number 11 was the home of Testament House, a Georgian building whose front was covered with scaffolding. A rubbish bin overflowing with plaster, empty paint tins, cardboard cartons, and dropcloths gave evidence to the fact that Testament House was joining its neighbours in an architectural renaissance. The front door stood open, and from within came the sound of music, not the rowdy rock-and-roll one might have expected from a gathering place for runaway teenagers, but the delicate strains of classical guitar and the kind of quiet that spoke of an audience held spellbound. However, those on this week's kitchen duty were not taking part in the recital above stairs, Barbara guessed, for even outside the air was rich with the aroma of tomato sauce and spices, sure indication of the evening's fare.

She walked up the two steps and entered the building. The long hallway was covered with an old red runner, worn so thin in places that the wood of the floor beneath showed through. Walls were bare of decoration save bulletin boards that held employment information, messages received, and announcements posted. A schedule of classes at the university on Gower Street was given the most prominent position, with large cardboard arrows pointing to it encouragingly. Nearby clinics, drug programs, and Planned Parenthood offices were advertised for inhabitants, and the telephone number of a suicide hotline was printed repeatedly on tear-off sheets at the bottom of the board. Most of them, Barbara noted, were gone.

"Hello," a voice called cheerfully. "Need some help?"

Barbara turned to find a plump middle-aged woman leaning over the reception counter, pushing a pair of hornrimmed spectacles to the top of her clipped grey hair. Her smile was welcoming, but it faded immediately when her eyes fell upon the warrant card that Barbara produced. Above them, the intricate music continued.

"Is there some sort of trouble?" the woman asked. "I suppose you want Mr. Clarence."

"No," Barbara replied. "That may not be necessary. I'm looking for this young woman. Her name is Gillian Teys, but we think she may be using the name Nell Graham." She handed over the photograph, a gesture she knew would be unnecessary, for the moment she had said the name the other woman's expression had altered and revealed.

Nonetheless, she looked at the photograph cooperatively. "Yes, this is Nell," she said.

In spite of having been so certain, Barbara felt a surge of triumph. "Can you tell me how to locate her? It's quite important that I find her as soon as possible."

"She's not in trouble, is she?"

"It's important that I find her," Barbara said again.

"Oh yes, of course. I suppose you can't tell me. It's only that . . ." The woman fingered her chin nervously. "Let me get Jonah," she said impulsively. "This is his concern."

Before Barbara could reply, the woman was running up the stairs. In a moment the guitar music stopped abruptly to a storm of protesting voices and then laughter. That was followed by the sound of footsteps. The hushed voice of the receptionist was met by a man's response.

When he came into sight on the stairway, Barbara saw that he was the musician, for he carried a fine guitar over his shoulder. He was far too young to be the Reverend George Clarence, but he wore clerical garb and his marked resemblance to the founder of Testament House indicated to Barbara that this must be the man's son. For here were the same chiselled features, the same broad expanse of forehead, the same quick glance that assimilated and evaluated within an instant. Even his hair was the same, parted on the left, with an unruly tuft that no comb could discipline. He was not a big man, probably no more than five feet eight inches tall, and his build was slight. But there was something about the way he held his body that indicated the presence of an inner core of strength and self-confidence.

He strode down the hall and extended his hand. "Jonah Clarence," he said. His grip was firm. "Mother tells me you're looking for Nell."

Mrs. Clarence had removed her spectacles from their perch on the top of her head. She chewed on the earpiece unconsciously as she listened to their conversation, her brow creased and her eyes moving back and forth between them as they spoke.

Barbara handed him the photograph. "This is Gillian Teys," she said. "Her father was murdered three weeks ago in Yorkshire, and she's going to have to come with me for some questioning."

Clarence greeted the statement with no strong visible reaction beyond what appeared to be an inability to take his eyes from Barbara's face. But he made himself do so, made himself look at the picture. Then his eyes met his mother's. "It's Nell."

"Jonah," she murmured. "My dearest . . ." Her voice was laced with compassion.

Clarence handed the photograph back to Barbara but spoke to his mother. "It had to happen one day, didn't it?" he said. His tone was coloured by emotion.

"Darling, shall I . . . Do you want to . . ."

He shook his head. "I was just about to leave anyway," he said, and looked at Barbara. "I'll take you to Nell. She's my wife."

Lynley gazed at the painting of Keldale Abbey and wondered why he had been so blind to its message. The painting's beauty lay in its utter simplicity, its devotion to detail, its refusal to distort or romanticise the crumbling ruin, to make it anything other than what it was: a vestige of time dead, being devoured by time to come.

Skeletal walls arched against a desolate sky, straining to lift themselves out of the inevitable end that waited for them on the ground below. They fought against flora: ferns that grew stubbornly out of barren crevices; wildflowers that bloomed on the edge of transept walls; grass that grew thickly and mingled with wild parsley on the very stones where monks had once knelt in prayer.

Steps led to nowhere. Curving stairways that once had carried the devoted from cloister to parlour, from day room to court, now sank into moss-covered oblivion, submitting to changes that did not make them ignoble, but merely moulded them into a different shape and a purpose changed.

Windows were gone. Where long ago stained glass had proudly enclosed presbytery and quire, nave and transept, nothing remained but gaping holes, gazing sightlessly out onto a landscape which rightfully proclaimed that it alone had ascendancy in the battle with time.

How did one really define the remains of Keldale Abbey? Was it the plundered ruin of a glorious past or a tumbling promise of what the future could be? Wasn't it all, Lynley thought, in the definition?

He stirred at the sound of a car stopping at the lodge, of doors opening and the murmur of voices, of uneven footsteps approaching. He realised that darkness was falling in the lounge and switched on one of the lamps just as St. James entered the room. He was alone, as Lynley had known he would be.

They faced each other across a short expanse of inoffensive carpeting, across a virtual chasm created and maintained by one man's guilt and another man's pain. They both knew and recognised these components of their history, and, as if to escape them,

Lynley went behind the bar and poured each of them a whisky. He crossed the room and handed it to his friend.

"Is she outside?" he asked.

"She's gone to the church. Knowing Deborah, to have one last look at the graveyard, I expect. We're off tomorrow."

Lynley smiled. "You've been braver than I. Hank would have driven me off within the first five minutes. Are you fleeing to the lakes?"

"No. To York for a day, then back to London. I'm to be in court to testify on Monday morning. I need a bit of time to complete a fibre analysis before then."

"Rotten luck to have had so few days."

"We've the rest of our lives. Deborah understands."

Lynley nodded and looked from St. James to the windows in which they saw themselves reflected, two men so entirely different from each other, who shared an afflicted past and who could, if he chose, share a full, rich future. It was all, he decided, in the definition. He tossed back the rest of his drink.

"Thank you for your help today, St. James," he said finally, extending his hand. "You and Deborah are wonderful friends."

Jonah Clarence drove them to Islington in his delapidated Morris. It wasn't a very long drive, and he was quiet for every moment of it, his hands on the wheel showing white knuckles that betrayed his distress.

They lived on a peculiar little street called Keystone Crescent, directly off Caledonian Road. Blessed with two take-away food stores at its head—exuding the multi-cultural odours of frying eggs rolls, falafel, and fish and chips—and a butcher shop at its foot on Pentonville Road, it was located in an area of town that was arguing between industrial and residential. Dressmaking factories, car hire firms, and tool companies gave way to streets which were trying very hard to become fashionable.

Keystone Crescent was just that, a crescent lined on one side with concave and on the other with a convex terrace of houses. All were fenced by identical wrought iron, and where once diminutive gardens had bloomed, concrete paving provided additional parking for cars.

The buildings were sooty brick, two storeys tall, topped by

dormer windows and a thin scalloping of ornamentation at the roofline. Each building had its own basement flat, and while some of the houses had recently been refurbished in keeping with the neighbourhood effort towards chic, the one in front of which Jonah Clarence parked his car was definitely shabby, white-washed and decorated with green woodwork at one time, but grimy now, with two unlidded dustbins standing in front of it.

"It's this way," he said tonelessly.

He opened the gate and led her down a set of narrow, steep steps to the door of a flat. Unlike the building itself, which was in sad disrepair, the door was sturdy, freshly painted, with a brass knob gleaming in its centre. He unlocked and opened it, gesturing Barbara inside.

She saw at once that a great deal of care had gone into the decorating of the little home, as if the occupants wanted to drive a very firm wedge between the exterior grubbiness of the building and the crisp, clean loveliness of what existed within it. Walls were freshly painted; floors were covered with colourful rugs; white curtains hung in windows which housed a splendour of plants; books, photograph albums, a humble stereo system, a collection of phonograph records, and three pieces of antique pewter occupied a low shelving unit that ran along one wall. There were few pieces of furniture, but each one had been clearly selected for its workmanship and beauty.

Jonah Clarence set his guitar carefully down on a stand and went to the bedroom door. "Nell?" he called.

"I was just changing, darling. Out in a moment," a woman's voice replied cheerfully.

He looked at Barbara. She saw that his face had become grey and ill. "I'd like to go in—"

"No," Barbara said. "Wait here. Please, Mr. Clarence," she added when she read his determination to go to his wife.

He sat down on a chair, moving painfully, as if he had aged years in their brief twenty-minute acquaintance. He fixed his eyes on the door. Behind it, brisk movement accompanied light-hearted humming, a lilting rendition of "Onward Christian Soldiers." Drawers opened and closed. A wardrobe door creaked. There was a pause in the humming as footsteps approached. The song finished, the door opened, and Gillian Teys returned from the dead.

She looked exactly like her mother, but her blonde hair was quite short, almost like a boy's, and gave her the appearance of being ten years old, something that carried over to her manner of dress. She wore a plaid, pleated skirt, a dark blue pullover, and black shoes and knee socks. She might have been on her way home from school.

"Darling, I—" She froze when she saw Barbara. "Jonah? Is something . . . ?" Her breathing seemed to stop. She groped for the doorknob behind her.

Barbara took a step forward. "Scotland Yard, Mrs. Clarence," she said crisply. "I'd like to ask you some questions."

"Questions?" Her hand went to her throat. Her blue eyes darkened. "What about?"

"About Gillian Teys," her husband replied. He hadn't moved from his chair.

"Who?" she asked in a low voice.

"Gillian Teys," he repeated evenly. "Whose father was murdered in Yorkshire three weeks ago, Nell."

She backed into the door stiffly. "No."

"Nell—"

"No!" Her voice grew louder. Barbara took another step forward. "Stay away from me! I don't know what you're talking about! I don't know any Gillian Teys!"

"Give me the picture," Jonah said to Barbara, rising. She handed it to him. He walked to his wife, put his hand on her arm. "This is Gillian Teys," he said, but she turned her face from the photograph he held.

"I don't know, I don't know!" Her voice was high with terror.

"Look at it, darling." Gently, he turned her face towards it.

"No!" She screamed, tore herself from his grasp and fled into the other room. Another door slammed. A bolt was shot home.

Wonderful, Barbara thought. She pushed past the young man and went to the bathroom door. There was silence within. She rattled the handle. *Be tough, be aggressive.* "Mrs. Clarence, come out of there." No reply. "Mrs. Clarence, you need to listen to me. Your sister Roberta is charged with this murder. She's in Barnstingham Mental Asylum. She hasn't said a word in three weeks other than to claim to having murdered your father. Decapitated your father, Mrs. Clarence." Barbara rattled the handle again. "*Decapitated*, Mrs. Clarence. Did you hear me?"

There was a choked whimper from behind the door, the sound of a terrified, wounded animal. An anguished cry followed. "I left it for you, Bobby! Oh God, did you lose it?"

Then every tap in the bathroom was turned on full force.

14

CLEAN. *Clean!* HAVE to do it. Have to get it. Fast, fast, *fast!* It will happen *now* if I don't get clean. Shouting, pounding, shouting, pounding. Ceaseless, endless. Shouting, pounding. But they'll both go away—God, they *must* go away—once I'm clean, clean, clean.

Water hot. Very hot. Steam gushing forth in clouds. Feel it on my face. Breathe it deeply to be clean.

"Nell!"

No, no, no!

Cupboard handles slippery. Get it open. Pull it open. Get the shaking hands to find them, hidden safely under towels. Stiff, hard brushes. Wooden backs, metal bristles. Good brushes, strong brushes. Brushes make me clean.

"Mrs. Clarence!"

No, no, no!

Ugly breathing, tortured breathing. Fills the room, pounds in ears. Stop it, stop it! Hands at head can't stop the echo, fists on face can't kill the sound.

"Nellie, please. Open the door!"

No, no, no! No doors open now. No escape can come that way. Only one way to escape it. And that's clean, clean, clean. Shoes off first. Kick them off. Shove them quickly out of sight. Socks come next. Hands don't work. Tear it! Fast, fast, fast!

"Mrs. Clarence, do you hear me? Are you listening to what I'm saying?"

Can't hear, can't see. Won't hear, won't see. Clouds of steam to fill me up. Clouds of steam to burn and sear. Clouds of steam to make me clean!

"Is that what you want to happen, Mrs. Clarence? Because that's *exactly* what's going to happen to your sister if she continues not to speak. For life, Mrs. Clarence. For the rest of her life."

No! Tell them no! Tell them nothing matters now. Can't think, can't act. Just hurry up, water. Hurry up and make me clean. Feel it on my hands. No, it's still not hot enough! Can't feel, can't see. Never, never be clean.

She called his name Moab, father of Moabites unto this day. She called his name Ben-ammi, father of the children of Ammon unto this day. The smoke of the country went up as the smoke of a furnace. They went up out of Zoar and dwelled in the mountain. For they were afraid.

"How is it locked? Is it a bolt? A key? How?"

"I just . . ."

"Pull yourself together. We're going to have to break it."

"No!"

Pounding, pounding, loud, relentless. Make them, *make* them go away!

"Nell, Nell!"

Water all over. Can't feel it, can't see it, won't be hot enough to make me clean, clean, clean! Soap and brushes, soap and brushes. Rub hard, hard, hard. Slip and slither, slip and slither. Make me clean, clean, clean!

"It's either that or call for help. Is that what you want? The whole bloody police force breaking down the door?"

"Shut up! Look at what you've done to her! Nell!"

Bless me father. I have sinned. Understand and forgive. Brushes digging, brushes digging, brushes *dig* to make me clean.

"You don't have any choice! This is a police matter, not some marital squabble, Mr. Clarence."

"What are you doing? Damn you, stay away from that phone!"

Pounding, pounding.

"Nell!"

Reader, I married him a quiet wedding we had: he and I, the parson and clerk, were alone present when we got back from church I went into the kitchen of the manor house where Mary was cooking the dinner and John cleaning the knives and I said Mary I have been married to Mr. Rochester this morning.

"Then you have exactly two minutes to get her out of there or you're going to have more police than you've ever laid eyes on crawling through this place. Is that clear?"

You *are* some little cat. Not again! Not so soon! God, Gilly, God!

Gilly's dead, Gilly's dead. But Nell is clean, clean, clean. Scrub her hard, dig in deep, make her clean, clean, clean!

"I've got to come in, Nell. Do you hear me? I'm going to break the lock. Don't be frightened."

Come on, Gilly girl. I want *nothing* serious tonight. Let's laugh and be wild and be absolutely mad. We'll have drinks, dance till dawn. We'll find men and go to Whitby. We'll take wine. We'll take food. We'll dance nude on the abbey walls. They can try to catch us, Gilly. We'll be absolutely wild.

Pounding louder now. Pounding hard, hard, hard! Bursting ears, bursting heart. Rub her skin all clean.

"That's not going to work, Mr. Clarence. I'm going to have to—"

"No! Shut up, damn you!"

Late at night. I said goodbye. Did you hear me? Did you see me? Did you find it where I left it? Bobby, did you find it? Did you finditfinditfindit?

Shrieking wood, splintering wood. Never safe anymore. One last chance before Lot finds me. One last chance to make me clean.

"Oh *God*! Oh my God, Nell."

"I'm going to phone for an ambulance."

"No! Just leave us alone!"

Hands gripping. Hands sliding. Water pink and rich with blood. Arms holding. Someone crying. Wrapping warm and holding near.

"Nellie. Oh God. *Nell.*"

Pressed against him. Hear him sobbing. Is it over? Am I clean?

"Bring her out here, Mr. Clarence."

"Go away! Leave us alone!"

"I can't do that. She's accessory in a murder. You know that as well as I. If nothing else, her reaction to all this should have—"

"She *isn't*! She couldn't be! I was with her!"

"You don't expect me to believe that, do you?"

"Nell! I won't let them. I won't let them!"

Weeping, weeping. Aching tears. Body racked with pain and sorrow. Make it end. Make it end. "Jonah—"

"Yes, darling. What is it?"

"Nell's dead."

"So he broke down the door," Havers said.

Lynley rubbed his throbbing forehead. The last three hours had given him an appalling headache. The conversation with Havers was making it worse. "And?"

There was a pause.

"Havers?" he demanded. He knew that his voice was abrupt, that it would sound like anger instead of the fatigue that it was. He heard her catch her breath. Was she crying?

"It was . . . She had . . ." She cleared her throat. "It was a bath."

"She'd taken a *bath*?" He wondered if Havers was aware of the fact that she was making no sense. Good God, what had happened?

"Yes. Except . . . she'd used brushes on herself. They were metal brushes. She was bleeding."

"God in heaven," he muttered. "Where is she, Havers? Is she all right?"

"I wanted to phone for an ambulance."

"Why didn't you, for God's sake?"

"Her husband . . . he was . . . It was my fault, Inspector. I thought that I should be tough with her. I . . . It was my fault." Her voice broke.

"Havers, for God's sake. Pull yourself together."

"There was blood. She'd used the brushes all over her body. He wrapped her up. He wouldn't let go of her. He was crying. She said she was dead."

"Christ," he whispered.

"I went to the phone. He came after me. He—"

"Are you all right? Are you hurt?"

"He pushed me outside. I fell. I'm all right. I . . . It was my fault. She came out of the bedroom. I remembered everything we'd said about her. It seemed best to be firm with her. I didn't think. I didn't realise she would—"

"Havers, listen to me."

"But she locked herself in. There was blood in the water. It was so hot. There was steam. . . . How could she have stood the water that hot?"

"Havers!"

"I thought I could do something right. This time. I've destroyed the case, haven't I?"

"Of course not," he replied, although he was absolutely unconvinced that she hadn't blown their chances right into oblivion. "Are they still at their flat?"

"Yes. Shall I get someone from the Yard?"

"No!" He thought rapidly. The situation could not possibly have been any worse. To have found the woman after all these years and then to have this happen was infuriating. He knew quite well that she represented their only hope of reaching the bottom of the case. No matter the reality that insinuated itself from the pages of Shakespeare, only Gillian could give it substance.

"Then what shall I—"

"Go home. Go to bed. I'll handle this."

"*Please*, sir." He could hear the despair in her voice. He couldn't help it, couldn't stop it, couldn't worry about it now.

"Just do as I say, Havers. Go home. Go to bed. Do *not* ring the Yard, and do *not* return to that flat. Is that clear?"

"Am I—"

"Then get a train back here in the morning."

"What about Gillian?"

"I'll worry about Gillian," he said grimly and hung up the telephone.

He gazed down at the book in his lap. He'd spent the last four hours dredging up from his memory every single exposure he'd had to Shakespeare. It was limited. His interest in the Elizabethans had been historical, not literary, and more than once during the evening he had cursed the educational path he had taken all those years ago at Oxford, wishing for expertise in an area that, at the time, had hardly seemed relevant to his interests.

He had found it at last, however, and now he read and reread the lines, trying to wring a twentieth century meaning from the seventeeth century verse.

> One sin, I know, another doth provoke.
> Murder's as near to lust as flame to smoke.

He gives life and death meaning, the priest had said. So what did the words of the Prince of Tyre have to do with an abandoned grave in Keldale? And what did a grave have to do with the death of a farmer?

Absolutely nothing, his intellect insisted. Absolutely everything, his intuition replied.

He snapped the book closed. It was imprisoned in Gillian: the meaning and the truth. He picked up the telephone and dialled.

It was after ten when she trudged down the ill-lit street in Acton. Webberly had been surprised to see her, but the surprise had faded when he opened the envelope Lynley had sent. He glanced at the message, turned it over, and picked up the phone. After barking an order for Edwards to come at once, he dismissed her without a question as to why she had suddenly appeared in London without Lynley. It was quite as if she didn't exist for him. And she didn't, did she? Not any longer.

Who gives a shit, she thought. Who bloody cares what happens? It was inevitable. Fat, stupid little pig, snorting around trying to play the detective. Thought you knew everything about Gillian Teys, didn't you? Heard her humming in the next room and even then you weren't smart enough to figure it out.

She looked up at the house. The windows were dark. Mrs. Gustafson's television blared from next door, but not a sign of life glimmered from the interior of the building in front of which she stood. If its inhabitants were disturbed by the neighbourhood noise, there was no indication. There was nothing.

Nothing. That's really it, isn't it, she thought. *There's nothing inside, not a single thing and especially not the one thing that you want to be in there. All these years you've been incubating a chimera, Barb. And what a bloody waste it's been.*

She steeled herself against the thought, refused to accept it, and unlocked the door. In the quiet house, the smell assailed her, a smell of unwashed bodies, of trapped cooking odours, of dead air, of ponderous despair. It was foul and unhealthy, and she welcomed it. She breathed it in deeply, finding it fitting, finding it just.

She closed the door behind her and leaned against it, letting her eyes adjust to the darkness. *Here it is, Barb. It all began here. Let it bring you back to life.*

She put her handbag down on the splintered table next to the door and forced herself towards the stairs. But as she reached them, her eyes were caught by a flash of light from the sitting room. She walked to the door curiously to find the room empty, the flash only a brief flicker of a passing car's lights hitting the glass of the picture. His picture. Tony's picture.

She was drawn into the room, and she sat in her father's chair, which, along with her mother's, faced the shrine. Tony's face grinned its impish grin at her; his wiry body twisted with life.

She was weary and numb, but she forced herself to keep her eyes on the picture, forced herself back to the deepest reaches of her memory where Tony still lay, wizened and gaunt, in a narrow white hospital bed. He was branded into her consciousness as he always would be, tubes and needles sprouting from him every-where, his fingers plucking spasmodically at the covers. His thin neck no longer supported a head that appeared by contrast to have grown immense. His eyelids were heavy, crusted and closed. His cracked lips bled.

"Coma," they had said. "It's nearly time now."

But it hadn't been. Not yet. Not until he'd opened his eyes, managed a fleeting elf's smile, and murmured, "I'm not scared when you're here, Barbie. You won't leave me, will you?"

He might have actually spoken to her in the sitting room's darkness, for she felt it all again as she always did: the swelling of grief and then—blasting it away like a breath from hell—the rage. That single reality that was keeping her alive.

"I won't leave you," she swore. "I'll *never* forget."

"Lovey?"

She cried out in surprise, brought back to the shattering present.

"Lovey? Is that you?"

Past the pounding of her heart, she forced her voice to sound pleasant. No problem, really, after so many years of practice. "Yes, Mum. Just having a sit."

"In the dark, lovey? Here, let me turn on the light so—"

"No!" Her voice rasped. She cleared her throat. "No, Mum. Just leave it off."

"But I don't like the dark, lovey. It . . . it frightens me so."

"Why are you up?"

"I heard the door open. I thought it might be . . ." She moved into Barbara's line of vision, a ghostly figure in a stained pink dressing gown. "Sometimes I think he's come back to us, lovey. But he never will, will he?"

Barbara got to her feet abruptly. "Go back to bed, Mum." She heard the roughness of her voice, and she tried unsuccessfully to modulate it. "How's Dad?" She took her mother's bony arm and firmly led her from the sitting room.

"He had a good day today. We thought about Switzerland. You know, the air is so fresh and pure there. We thought Switzerland would be the nicest place next. Of course, back so soon from Greece, it doesn't seem quite right to go off again, but he thinks it sounds a good idea. Will you like Switzerland, lovey? Because if you don't think you'll like it, we can always choose someplace else. I want you to be happy."

Happy? *Happy!* "Switzerland's fine, Mum."

She felt her mother's bird-claw hand grip her arm tightly. They started up the stairs. "Good. I thought you'd like it. I think Zurich would be the best place to begin. We'll do a tour this time, with a hired car. I long to see the Alps."

"Sounds fine, Mum."

"Dad thought so, lovey. He even went to Empress Tours to get me the brochures."

Barbara's steps slowed. "Did he see Mr. Patel?"

Her mother's hand fluttered on her arm, "Oh, I don't know, lovey. He didn't mention Mr. Patel. I'm certain he would have said something if he had."

They reached the top of the stairs. Her mother paused at the door to her bedroom. "He's such a new man when he goes out for a bit in the afternoon, lovey. *Such* a new man."

Barbara's stomach turned on the thought of what her mother might mean.

Jonah Clarence opened the bedroom door softly, an unnecessary precaution, for she was awake. She turned her head at the sound of his movement and smiled wanly at her husband.

"I've made you some soup," he said.

"Jo—" Her voice was so small, so weak, that he went hurriedly on.

"It's just the tinned stuff from the pantry. I've some bread and butter here as well." He placed the tray on the bed and helped her into a sitting position. At the movement, several of the deeper cuts began to bleed again. He took a towel and pressed it firmly against her skin, a movement not only to stem the flow of the blood but also to block out the memory of what had happened to their lives that evening.

"I don't—"

"Not now, darling," he said. "You need to eat something first."

"Will we talk then?"

His eyes moved from her face. Slashes covered her hands, her arms, her breasts, her stomach, her thighs. At the sight, he felt such a burden of anguish that he wasn't sure he could answer her. But she was watching him, her beautiful eyes trusting, filled with love, waiting for his reply.

"Yes," he whispered. "We'll talk then."

She smiled tremulously, and he felt his heart wrench. He put the tray across her lap, but when she tried to spoon the soup, he saw that her weakness had become so pronounced that no effort would make it possible for her to feed herself. Gently, he took the spoon from her and began to help her eat, a slow process in which every bit swallowed seemed an individual act of triumph.

He wouldn't let her talk. He was too afraid of what she might say. Instead he soothed her with whispered words of love and encouragement and wondered who she was and what kind of terrible grief she had brought into his life.

They had been married for less than a year, but it seemed to him that they had always been together, that they had been meant for each other from the moment when his father brought her to Testament House from King's Cross Station—a solemn little waif of a girl who looked twelve years old. She's all eyes, he had thought when he saw her. But when she smiled, she was sunlight. He knew within the first few weeks that he loved her, but it took nearly ten years to make her his own.

During that time, he had been ordained, had made his decision to be part of his father's work, had laboured like Jacob in pursuit of a Rachel he could never be certain of winning. Yet that thought had not discouraged him. Like a crusader, he had set on a quest, and Nell was his Grail. No one else would do.

Except she's not Nell, he thought. I don't know who she is. And the worst of it is, I'm not certain I want to know.

He had always seen himself as a man of action, one of courage, a man powered by the force of his inner convictions, yet still, intimately, a man of peace. All that had died tonight. The sight of her in the bath—mindlessly lacerating her flesh, staining the water with her blood—had demolished that carefully constructed facade in two short minutes: the time it had taken to pull her, frail and screaming, from the tub, to try frantically to stop the bleeding, to throw the shouting police officer from their flat.

In two short minutes, he had become not the cheek-turning, sincere minister of God that had long been his guise, but a maniacal stranger who could have killed, without impunity, anyone seeking to harm his wife. He was shaken to the core, even more so when he considered that, in protecting her from enemies, he couldn't think of how he was going to protect Nell from herself.

Except she's not Nell, he thought.

She was finished eating, had been finished, in fact, for several minutes and lay back against the pillows. They were stained with her blood. He got to his feet.

"Jo—"

"I'm going to get something for the cuts. I'll just be a moment."

He tried not to see the gruesome condition of the bathroom as he rooted in the cupboard. The tub looked and smelled as if they had been butchering livestock in it. Blood was everywhere, in every crevice and crack. His hands weakened as he grabbed the bottle of hydrogen peroxide. He felt faint.

"Jonah?"

He took several deep breaths and went back to the bedroom. "Delayed reaction." He tried to smile, clutched the bottle so tightly he thought it might break in his hands, and sat on the edge of the bed. "Mostly surface cuts," he said conversationally. "We'll see what it looks like in the morning. If they're bad, we'll go to hospital then. How does that sound?"

He didn't wait for a response. Rather, he washed the abrasions with the chemical and continued speaking determinedly. "I thought we might go to Penzance this weekend, darling. It would be good to get away for a few days, don't you think so? I was talking to one of the kids about a hotel down there that she'd stayed at as a child. If it's still there, it should be wonderful. A view of St. Michael's Mount. I thought we'd take the train down and hire a car when we got there. Or bicycles. Would you like to hire bicycles, Nell?"

He felt her hand on his cheek. At the touch, his heart swelled, and he knew he was horribly close to tears. "Jo," she whispered. "Nell's dead."

"Don't say that!" he returned fiercely.

"I've done terrible things. I can't bear for you to know. I thought I was safe from them, that I'd run from them right into forever."

"No!" He continued mindlessly, passionately to see to her wounds.

"I love you, Jonah."

That stopped him. His face sank into his hands. "What do I call you?" he whispered. "I don't even know who you are!"

"Jo, Jonah, my love, my only love—"

Her voice was a torment he could barely endure, and when she reached out for him, he was broken and ran from the room, slamming the door firmly, and irrevocably, behind him.

He stumbled to a chair, hearing his own breathing tear at the air, feeling wedges of panic drive themselves into his stomach and groin. He sat, staring unseeing at the material objects that comprised their home, and desperately pushed away from him the one piece of information that was at the core of his terror.

Three weeks ago, the police sergeant had said. He had lied to her, an immediate response rising from the horror of her incomprehensible allegation. He had not been in London with his wife at that time but rather at a four-day conference in Exeter, followed by two additional days of fund-raisers for Testament House. Nell was supposed to have gone with him but at the last moment had begged off with flu. So she said. Had she been ill? Or had she seen it as an opportunity to travel to Yorkshire?

"No!" The word came out involuntarily, from between his teeth. Despising himself for even considering the question for a moment, Jonah willed his breathing to calm, willed his muscles to relax.

He reached for his guitar, not to play it but to reaffirm its reality and to reestablish the meaning it had in his life, for he had been sitting on the back stairs of Testament House, in the semi-darkness, playing strains of the music he loved when she first spoke to him.

"That's so nice. D'you think anyone could learn?" She came to crouch next to him on the step, her eyes on his fingers as they moved expertly among the strings, and she smiled, a child's smile, lit with pleasure.

It had been simple to teach her to play, for she was a natural mimic: something seen or heard was never forgotten. Now she played as often to him as he did to her, not with his assurance or passion but with a melancholy sweetness that long ago should have told him what he didn't want to face now.

He stood abruptly. To assure himself, he opened book after book and saw the name, *Nell Graham*, written in each volume in her neat script. To show ownership, he wondered, or to convince herself?

"No!"

He picked up a photograph album from the bottom shelf and hugged it to his chest. It was a document of Nell, a verification of the fact that she was real, that she had no other life but the one she shared with him. He didn't even need to open the album to know what lay within its pages: a pictorial history of the love they shared, of the memories that were an integral part of the tapestry of their lives being woven together. In a park, on a trail, dreaming quietly at dawn, laughing at the antics of birds on the beach. All of these bore testimony, were illustrations of Nell's life and the things she loved.

His eyes drifted, for more assurance, to her plants in the window. The African violets had always reminded him the most of her. The beautiful flowers poised themselves delicately, precariously, at the tips of their stalks. The heavy green leaves protected and surrounded them. They were plants that looked as if they could never survive in the rigours of the London weather, but in spite of their appearance, they were deceptive plants really, plants of remarkable strength.

Looking at them, he knew at last and fought fruitlessly to deny it. Tears, long in coming, broke the surface and a sob escaped him. He made his way back to the chair, fell into it, and wept inconsolably.

It was then that he heard the knocking at the door.

"Go away!" he sobbed.

The knocking persisted.

"Go away!"

There was no other sound. The knocking continued. Like the voice of his conscience. It would never end.

"Damn you, go away!" he screamed and threw himself at the door. He flung it open.

A woman stood there. She wore a neat black suit and a white silk blouse with a froth of lace at her throat. She carried a black shoulder bag and a leatherbound book. But it was her face that riveted his attention. It was calm, clear-eyed, and masked by tenderness. She might have been a missionary. She might have been a vision. But she extended her hand and made it clear that she was real.

"My name is Helen Clyde," she said quietly.

Lynley chose a corner. Candles flickered some distance away, but where he was darkness shrouded the church. The building smelled vaguely of incense, but more strongly of age, of guttering candles, of the burnt ends of matches, of dust. It was utterly peaceful. Even the doves, who had been stirred into momentary rustling upon his approach, had fallen back into stillness, and no night wind made tree branches creak and scratch against the windows.

He was alone. His only companions were the youths and maidens, entwined Grecian urn-like in a soundless eternal dance of truth and beauty on the doors of the Elizabethan confessionals nearby.

His heart felt heavy and sore. It was an old story, a Roman

legend from the fifth century, but as real at this moment as it had been to Shakespeare when he used it as the foundation for his drama. The Prince of Tyre went to Antioch, pursuing a riddle and marriage to a princess. But he came away with nothing, fleeing for his life.

Lynley knelt. He thought about prayer, but nothing came.

He knew he was near the body of the hydra, but the knowledge gave him neither triumph nor satisfaction. Instead, he wanted to flee from the final confrontation with the monster, knowing now that, although the heads were destroyed and the trunk well seared, he could not hope to emerge unscathed from the encounter.

" 'Fret not thyself because of evil-doers.' " It was an insubstantial, disembodied, wavering voice. It came out of nowhere, tremulous and uncertain, and it hovered mistily in the frigid air. It was some moments before Lynley located its black-robed source.

Father Hart knelt at the foot of the altar. He was bent over double, his forehead pressed to the floor. " 'Neither be thou envious against the workers of iniquity. For they shall be cut down like the grass, and wither as the green herb. Trust in the Lord and do good; so shalt thou dwell in the land, and verily thou shall be fed. Delight thyself also in the Lord: and he shall give thee the desires of thine heart. Commit thy way unto the Lord; Trust also in him, and he shall bring it to pass. Evil-doers shall be cut off; But those that wait upon the Lord, they shall inherit the earth. For yet a little while and the wicked shall not be.' "

Lynley listened to the words, anguished, and tried to deny their meaning. As a hush swept over the darkened church once more—broken only by the priest's stertorous breathing—he sorted through himself, trying to find the detachment he needed to carry him, disinterested, to the end of the case.

"Have you come to confess?"

He started at the voice. Unseen to him, the priest had materialised from the dark. Lynley stood. "No, I'm not a Catholic," he replied. "I was just gathering my thoughts."

"Churches are good places for that, aren't they?" Father Hart smiled. "I always stop for a prayer before locking up for the night. I always check first, as well, to make sure no one is still inside. It wouldn't do to be locked up in St. Catherine's in this kind of cold, would it?"

"No," Lynley agreed. "It wouldn't do at all." He followed the little priest to the end of the aisle and out into the night. Clouds obscured moon and stars. The other man was merely a shadow, without form or feature. "How well do you know *Pericles*, Father Hart?"

The priest didn't answer at first as he fumbled with his keys and locked the church door. "*Pericles?*" he repeated musingly. He moved past the other man, out into the graveyard. "It's Shakespeare, isn't it?"

" 'As flame to smoke.' Yes, it's Shakespeare."

"I . . . well, I suppose I know it fairly well."

"Well enough to know why Pericles fled from Antiochus? Why Antiochus wanted to have him killed?"

"I . . ." The priest groped in his pockets. "I don't think I quite remember all the details of the play."

"You remember enough, I daresay. Good night, Father Hart," Lynley replied and left the graveyard.

He descended the hillock by the gravel path, his footsteps sounding unnaturally loud in the nighttime peace. On the bridge, he paused to gather his thoughts, and he leaned against its stone side, surveying the village. To his right, Olivia Odell's house was dark, and woman and child slept in innocent safety within. Across the street, organ music floated eerily from Nigel Parrish's cottage on the edge of the common. To his left the lodge awaited his entry, and beyond that the high street curved in the direction of the pub. From where he stood, he couldn't see St. Chad's Lane with its council houses. But he could imagine them. Not wanting to do that, he returned to the lodge.

He'd been gone less than an hour, but he knew as soon as he walked in the door that, during his absence, Stepha had returned. The building held its breath, waiting for him to discover and know. His feet felt like lead.

He wasn't entirely sure where Stepha's rooms would be, but his instinct told him that they were somewhere on the ground floor of the old building, past the reception desk, in the direction of the kitchen. He went through the door.

As he did so, he had his answers, palpably alive in the atmosphere that surrounded him. He could smell the cigarette smoke. He could almost taste the liquor in the air. He could hear the laughter, the whispered passion, the delight. He could feel the hands drawing him relentlessly forward. All that was left was to see the truth.

He knocked on the door. There was immediate quiet.

"Stepha?"

Movement within, hurried and suppressed. Stepha's soft laugh hung in the air. At the last moment, he nearly stopped himself, but then he turned the knob, to enter and to know.

"Perhaps now *you* can give me an alibi that sticks," laughed Richard Gibson, giving the woman a proprietary slap on her naked thigh. "I don't think the inspector believed my little Madeline for a moment."

15

LADY HELEN SAW him as they made their way over the crowded pedestrian walkway from the arrivals platform. It had been a harrowing enough two hours on the train, one moment afraid that Gillian might go all to pieces in any one of a dozen appalling ways; the next moment desperately trying to rouse Sergeant Havers from whatever black pit of humour she had decided to inhabit. The entire experience had filled Lady Helen with such anxiety that the very sight of Lynley, brushing his blond hair back off his forehead against the breeze of a departing train, made her nearly weak with relief. People in the crowded station bustled and pushed round him. But still he looked as if he were quite alone. He raised his head. Their eyes met and her steps slowed momentarily.

Even at this distance, she could see the difference in him. The smoky darkness under his eyes. The tension in the set of his head and shoulders, the deepening lines round nose and mouth. He was Tommy still, but somehow not quite Tommy at all. There could be only one reason for it: Deborah.

He'd seen her in Keldale. His face told Lady Helen as much. And for some reason—in spite of the year that had passed since he'd broken his engagement to Deborah, in spite of the hours that she'd spent with him since then—Lady Helen found that she couldn't bear the thought of him talking about seeing her. She desperately wanted to avoid giving him an opportunity to do so. It was craven. She despised herself for it. And she didn't at that moment care to reflect upon why it had suddenly become so crucial that Tommy never speak to her of Deborah again.

He appeared to have been reading her thoughts—how typical of him, really—for he gave her that brief, quirky smile of his and walked to meet them at the foot of the stairs.

"How absolutely wonderful to see you, Tommy," she said. "I spent half the journey—when I wasn't frantically eating every pastry that wandered by—terrified that you'd be stuck in Keldale and we'd have to hire a car and drive wildly about the moors in best Earnshaw fashion, trying to find you. Well, it's all ended for the best, hasn't it, and I needn't have given in to my craving for week-old *pain au chocolat* in order to dull my anxiety. The food is absolutely appalling on the train, isn't it?" She tightened her arm round Gillian protectively. It was an instinctive gesture, for, although she knew the young woman had nothing to fear from Lynley, the last twelve hours had bonded Gillian to her and now she found herself reluctant to hand the young woman over. "Gillian, this is Inspector Lynley," she murmured.

A tentative smile touched Gillian's lips. Then she dropped her eyes. Lynley began to extend his hand to her, but Lady Helen shook her head in warning. At that, his glance slid to the young woman's hands. The angry red scoring that covered them was ugly but not as deep or serious as the abrasions that covered her neck, breasts, and thighs, hidden by the dress that Lady Helen had carefully selected for her to wear.

"I've the car just outside," he said.

"Thank God," Lady Helen declared. "Lead me to it this moment before my feet suffer irreparable damage from these ghastly shoes. They *are* fetching, aren't they? But the agony I endure hobbling about in them simply beggars belief. I keep asking myself why I'm such a slave to fashion." She airly dismissed the question as unanswerable. "I'm even willing to put up with five minutes of the most melancholy Tchaikovsky in your collection just to get off my feet."

He smiled. "I'll remember that, old duck."

"Darling, I haven't the slightest doubt of it." She turned to Sergeant Havers, who had plodded wordlessly behind them since they had disembarked. "Sergeant, I need to pop into the ladies' and undo the damage I did to my make-up by burying my face in that last pastry just before that dreadful tunnel. Will you take Gillian out to the car?"

Havers looked from Lady Helen to Lynley. "Of course," she replied impassively.

Lady Helen watched the pair walk off before she spoke again. "I'm really not sure which one of them is the worse for wear, Tommy."

"Thank you for last night," he said in answer. "Was it awful for you?"

She took her eyes off the departing women. "Awful?" The terrible desolation in Jonah Clarence's face; the sight of Gillian lying vacant-eyed, scarcely covered by a bloodied sheet, her wounds still seeping slow crimson where the self-inflicted damage was most severe; the blood on the floor and the walls of the bathroom and deep in the grout where it would never come clean; the smashed door and the brushes with bits of flesh still adhering to their horrifying metal bristles.

"I'm sorry for putting you through it," Lynley said. "But you were the only one I could trust to manage it. I don't know what I would have done had you not been at home when I phoned."

"I'd only just got in. I have to admit that Jeffrey wasn't at all pleased at the manner in which our evening ended."

Lynley's reaction played at the corners of his mouth and eyes, equal parts amusement and surprise. "Jeffrey Cusick? I thought you threw him over."

She laughed lightly and took his arm. "I tried, darling Tommy. I *did* try. But Jeffrey is quite determined to prove that, whether I realise it or not, he and I *are* on the path to true love. So he was working on advancing us a bit further towards the journey's end last night. It *was* romantic. Dinner in Windsor on the bank of the Thames. Champagne cocktails in the garden of the Old House. You would have been proud of me. I even remembered that Wren built it, so all these years of your seeing to my education haven't been in vain."

"But I hardly thought you'd be throwing it away on Jeffrey Cusick."

"Not throwing it away at all. He's a lovely man. Really. Besides, he was only too helpful in assisting me with my dressing."

"I've no doubt of that," Lynley remarked drily.

She laughed at his grim expression. "Not that way. Jeffrey would never take advantage. He's far too . . . too . . ."

"Fish-like?"

"Spoken like the most petulant Oxonian, Tommy," she declared. "But to be *dreadfully* honest, he is the teeniest bit like a cod. Well, what can one expect? I've never in my life known a Cambridge man to get caught in the throes of passion."

"Was he wearing his Harrovian tie when I phoned?" Lynley asked. "For that matter, was he wearing *anything*?"

"Tommy, how vicious! But, let me think." She tapped her cheek thoughtfully. Her eyes twinkled up at him as she pretended to consider his question at some length. "No, I'm afraid we were both fully clothed when you phoned. And after that, well, there simply wasn't time. We rushed desperately to my wardrobe and began looking for something that would do. What do you think? Is it a success?"

Lynley eyed the beautifully tailored black suit and matching accessories. "You look like a Quaker on the path to hell," he said soberly. "Good Lord, Helen, is that really a *Bible*?'

She laughed. "Doesn't it just *do*?" She examined the leather volume in her hand. "Actually, it's a collection of John Donne, given to me by darling Grandfather on my seventeenth birthday. I may actually open it someday."

"What would you have done if she had asked you to read a few verses to her to get her through the night?"

"I can sound positively biblical when I want to, Tommy. A few *thee*s and *thou*s, a few *lay*s and *beget*s and . . . What is it?" He had stiffened at her words. She felt the sudden rigidity in his arm.

Lynley was looking at his car parked outside the station doors. "Where's her husband?"

She regarded him curiously. "I don't know. He's vanished. I went directly in to see Gillian, and later, when I came out of the bedroom, he'd gone. I spent the night there, of course, and he never returned."

"How did Gillian react to that?"

"I'm . . ." Lady Helen considered how best to answer the question. "Tommy, I'm not even certain that she's aware that he's gone. This sounds a little strange, I'm sure, but I think he's ceased to exist for her. She hasn't mentioned his name to me."

"Has she said anything?"

"Only that she left something for Bobby."

"The message in the newspaper, no doubt."

Lady Helen shook her head. "No. I have the distinct impression that it was something at the house."

Lynley nodded pensively and asked a final question. "How did you talk her into coming, Helen?"

"I didn't. She'd already made up her mind, and I credit that to Sergeant Havers, Tommy, although from the way she's been acting, I think she believes that I performed some sort of loaves and fishes in the Clarence flat. *Do* speak to her, won't you? She's been positively monosyllabic since I rang her this morning, and I think she's blaming herself for everything that's happened."

He sighed. "That sounds just like Havers. Christ, what I don't need is one more thing to have to deal with in this *bloody* case."

Lady Helen's eyes widened fractionally. Rarely, if ever, did he give vent to anger. "Tommy," she said hesitantly, "while you were in Keldale, did you happen to . . . Is it . . ." She didn't want to speak of it. She *wouldn't* speak of it.

He flashed her his crooked smile. "Sorry, old duck." He dropped his arm round her shoulders and squeezed affectionately. "Did I mention how damnably good it is to have you here?"

He hadn't said anything to her. He hadn't so much as acknowledged her beyond a cursory nod. But then, why should he? Now that her little ladyship was there to save the day—just as she'd managed to do last night—there was no reason for them to communicate at all.

She might have known that Lynley would use one of his mistresses rather than someone from the Yard. Wasn't that typical of him? An ego so enormous that he had to make certain his London women would jump to his bidding in spite of his catting about in the country. Wonder if her ladyship will still jump through hoops when she finds out about Stepha, Barbara thought. And just look at her with her perfect skin, perfect posture, perfect breeding—as if her ancestors spent the last two hundred years throwing out the rejects, leaving them on hillsides like unacceptable Spartan babies in order to arrive at the eugenic masterpiece that was Lady Helen Clyde. *But not quite good enough to keep his lordship faithful, are we, sweetheart?* Barbara smiled inwardly.

She observed Lynley from the rear seat. *Had another big night with little Stepha, I'll bet.* Of course he had. Since he hadn't had to worry about how much the woman howled, he probably banged happily away at her for hours on end. And now here was her precious ladyship to be serviced tonight. Well, he could handle it. He could rise to the challenge. Then he could move right on to give Gillian a treat. No doubt that anaemic little husband of hers would be only too happy to give the reins over to a *real* man.

And weren't they both handling the little bitch with kid gloves! One couldn't really blame her ladyship for that approach. She didn't have all the facts on Gillian Teys. But what was Lynley's excuse? Since when did an accessory to murder get the red carpet treatment from CID?

"You're going to find Roberta very much changed, Gillian," he was saying.

Barbara listened to the words with incredulity. What was he doing? What was he talking about? Was he actually preparing her to see her sister when both of them knew damn well she'd seen her only three weeks ago when they'd killed William Teys?

"I understand," Gillian responded in a very small, nearly inaudible voice.

"She's been placed in the asylum as a temporary measure," Lynley continued gently. "It's a question of mental competence arising out of her admission to the crime and her unwillingness to speak."

"How did she . . . Who . . . ?" Gillian hesitated, then gave up the effort. She seemed to shrink into her seat.

"Your cousin Richard Gibson had her committed."

"Richard?" Her voice grew even smaller.

"Yes."

"I see."

No one spoke. Barbara waited impatiently for Lynley to begin questioning the woman, and she couldn't understand his obvious reluctance to do so. *What* was he doing? He was making the kind of solicitous conversation that one generally made with the victim of a crime, not with its perpetrator!

Furtively, Barbara examined Gillian. Good God, she was manipulative, right to the bitter end. A few minutes in the bathroom last night and she had the whole lot of them right where she wanted. How long had she been trotting out *that* little routine?

Her eyes moved back to Lynley. Why had he brought her back on the case today? There could be only one reason, really: to put her in her place once and for all, to humiliate her with the knowledge that even an amateur like her sweet ladyship had more expertise than Havers the pig. And then to condemn her, forever, to the street.

Well, the message was received, Inspector. Now all she longed for was a return to London and to uniform, leaving Lynley and his lady to sweep up the shards of the mess she had made.

She'd worn her hair in two long, blonde braids. That's why she looked so young that first night in Testament House. She spoke to no one, instead taking a quiet measure of the group, deciding whether they were worthy of her trust. The decision once made, she said only her name: Helen Graham, Nell Graham.

But hadn't he known from the first that it wasn't really her name? Perhaps the slight hesitation before her response when someone addressed her had betrayed her. Perhaps it was the wistful look in her eyes when she said it herself. Perhaps it was her tears when he first entered her body and whispered *Nell* in the darkness. At any rate, hadn't he always known—somewhere in his heart—that it wasn't her name?

What had drawn him to her? At first, it was the child-like innocence with which she embraced the life at Testament House. She was so eager to learn, and then so passionately involved in the purpose of the community. After that it was her purity he so admired, the purity which allowed her to lead a new life, unaffected by personal animosities in a world where she had simply decided that such ugliness would never exist. Then it was her devotion to God—not the breast-beating, ostentatious piety of the religious reborn but a calm acceptance of a power greater than her own—that touched him. And last, it was her steadfast faith in his ability to do anything, her words of encouragement when he felt despair, her abiding love when he needed it most.

As I do now, Jonah Clarence thought.

In the last twelve hours he had looked deeply, unforgivingly, at his own behaviour and had come to see it for what it was: unremitting cowardice. He had left wife and home, running to an unknown destination, fleeing so that he wouldn't have to face what he was afraid to know. Yet what was there to fear when Nell—whoever she was—could be nothing more or less than the lovely creature who stood by his side, who listened, rapt, to his words, who held him in her arms at night? There could be no dark monster in her past for him to dread. There could be only what she was and always had been.

This was the truth. He knew it. He could feel it. He believed it. And when the door to the mental hospital opened, he stood up quickly and strode across the central hall to meet his wife.

Lynley felt, rather than saw, the hesitation in Gillian's footsteps as they entered the hospital. At first he attributed it to her understandable trepidation about seeing her sister after so many years. But then he saw that her gaze was fixed on a young man who came across the lobby in their direction. Curious, Lynley turned to Gillian to speak, only to see on her face an expression of unmitigated dread.

"Jonah," she gasped, taking a step backwards.

"I'm sorry." Jonah Clarence reached out as if to touch her but stopped. "Forgive me. I'm sorry, Nell." His eyes were burnt out, as if he hadn't slept in days.

"You *mustn't* call me that. Not any longer."

He ignored her words. "I spent the night sitting on a bench

in King's Cross, trying to sort it all out, trying to decide if you could love a man who was too much of a coward to stay with his wife when she needed him most."

She reached out, touched his arm. "Oh, Jonah," she said. "Please. Go back to London."

"Don't ask that of me. It would be too easy."

"Please. I beg you. For me."

"Not without you. I won't do that. Whatever you feel you must do here, I'll be here as well." He looked at Lynley. "May I stay with my wife?"

"It's up to Gillian," Lynley replied and noticed the manner in which the young man involuntarily recoiled at the name.

"If you want to stay, Jonah," she whispered.

He smiled at her, touched her cheek lightly, and looked up from her face only when the sound of voices from the transverse passage signalled Dr. Samuels' approach. The man carried a stack of file folders which he handed to a female colleague before swiftly crossing towards them.

He eyed the entire group, unsmiling. If he was grateful for the appearance of Roberta Teys' sister and the possibility of progress that her presence implied, he gave no indication.

"Inspector," he said by way of greeting. "Is a group this large absolutely necessary?"

"It is," Lynley responded evenly and hoped the man had the good sense to take a close look at Gillian's condition before he raised a storm of protest and threw them all out.

A pulse beat in the psychiatrist's temple. It was obvious that he was unused to anything short of fawning courtesy and that he was caught between a desire to put Lynley summarily in his place and a wish to carry on with the planned meeting between the two sisters. His concern for Roberta won out.

"This is the sister?" Without waiting for an answer, he took Gillian's arm and devoted his attention to her as they started down the passageway towards the locked ward. "I've told Roberta that you're coming to see her," he said quietly, his head bent to hers, "but you must prepare yourself for the fact that she may not respond to you. She probably won't, in fact."

"Has she . . ." Gillian hesitated, seemed unsure how to proceed. "Has she still said nothing?"

"Nothing at all. But these are the very early stages of therapy, Miss Teys, and—"

"Mrs. Clarence," Jonah interjected firmly.

The psychiatrist stopped, swept his eyes over Jonah Clarence. A spark shot between them, suspicion and dislike.

"Mrs. Clarence," Samuels corrected himself, his eyes steadily on her husband. "As I was saying, Mrs. Clarence, these are the earliest stages of therapy. We've no reason to doubt that your sister will someday make a full recovery."

The use of the modifier was not lost on Gillian. "Someday?" Her arm encircled her waist in a gesture very like her mother's.

The psychiatrist appeared to be evaluating her reaction. He answered in a way that indicated that her single-word response had communicated far more than she realised.

"Yes, Roberta is very ill." He put his hand on her elbow and guided her through the door in the panelling.

They walked through the locked ward, the only noise among them the muffled sounds of their footsteps on the carpeting and the occasional cry of a patient from behind the closed doors. Near the end of the corridor, a narrow door was recessed into the wall, and Samuels stopped before it, opening it and switching on the light to reveal a small, cramped room. He motioned them inside.

"You're going to find yourselves crowded in here," he warned, his tone of voice indicating how little he regretted the fact.

It was a narrow rectangle, no larger than a good-sized broom closet, which in fact it once had been. One wall was completely covered by a large mirror, two speakers hung at either end, and a table and chairs were set up in the middle. It was claustrophobic and pungent with the smell of floor wax and disinfectant.

"This is fine," Lynley said.

Samuels nodded. "When I fetch Roberta, I shall switch these lights out, and you'll be able to see through the two-way mirror into the next room. The speakers will allow you to hear what's being said. Roberta will see only the mirror, but I've told her that you will be present behind it. We couldn't have her in the room otherwise, you understand."

"Yes, of course."

"Fine." He smiled at them grimly as if he sensed their apprehension and was glad to see that they—like himself—were not anticipating that the upcoming interview would be a diverting lark. "I'll be in the next room with Gillian and Roberta."

"Is that necessary?" Gillian asked hesitantly.

"Considering the circumstances, yes, I'm afraid it is."

"The circumstances?"

"The murder, Mrs. Clarence." Samuels surveyed them all one last time and then buried his hands deeply in the pockets of his trousers. His eyes were on Lynley. "Shall we deal in legalities?" he asked brusquely.

"That isn't necessary," Lynley said. "I'm well aware of them."

"You know that nothing she says—"

"I know," Lynley repeated.

He nodded sharply. "Then I'll fetch her." He spun smartly on one heel, switched out the lights, and left the room, closing the door behind him.

The lights from the room beyond the mirror gave them some illumination, but their close little cell was alive with shadows. They seated themselves on the unforgiving wooden chairs and waited: Gillian with her legs straight out in front of her, staring passionately down at the scarred tips of her fingers; Jonah with his chair next to hers, cradling its wooden back protectively; Sergeant Havers slumped down, brooding on the darkest corner of the room; Lady Helen next to Lynley, observing the unspoken communication between husband and wife; and Lynley himself, lost in deep contemplation from which he was roused by the touch of Lady Helen's hand squeezing his own.

Bless her, he thought, returning the pressure. She knew. She always knew. He smiled at her, so glad that she was with him with her clear-eyed sanity in a world that would shortly go mad.

Roberta was very much as she had been. She entered the room between two white-clad nurses, dressed as she had been dressed before: in the too-short skirt, the ill-fitting blouse, the flip-flopping slippers that barely sufficed to give her feet protection. She had, however, been bathed in anticipation of the interview, and her thick hair was clean and damp, pulled back and fastened at her neck with a piece of scarlet yarn, an incongruous note of colour in the otherwise monochromatic room. The room itself was inoffensive and barren, devoid of decoration save for a trio of chairs and a waist-high metal cabinet. Nothing hung on the walls. There was no distraction, no escape.

"Oh, Bobby," Gillian murmured when she saw her sister through the glass.

"There are three chairs here in the room, as you can see, Roberta." Samuels' voice came to them without distortion over the speakers. "In a moment I'm going to ask your sister to join us. Do you remember your sister Gillian, Roberta?"

The girl, seated, began to rock. She gave no reply. The two nurses left the room.

"Gillian's come up from London. Before I fetch her, however, I'd like you to look round the room and accustom yourself to it. We've never met in here before, have we?"

The girl's dull eyes remained where they had been, fixed on a point on the opposite wall. Her arms hung, inanimate, at her sides, lifeless, pulpy masses of fat and skin. Samuels, undisturbed by her silence, let it continue while he placidly watched the girl. Two interminable minutes dragged by in this way before he got to his feet.

"I shall fetch Gillian now, Roberta. I'm going to be in the room while you meet with her. You're quite safe."

The last declaration seemed entirely unnecessary, for if the hulking girl felt fear—felt anything at all—she gave no sign.

In the observation room, Gillian got to her feet. It was a hesitant movement, unnatural, as if she were being propelled upward and forward by a force other than her own free will.

"Darling, you know you don't have to go in there if you're afraid," her husband said.

She did not reply but rather, with the back of her hand upon which the heavy scoring from the metal brushes stood out like cutaneous veins, she stroked his cheek. She might have been saying goodbye to him.

"Ready?" Samuels asked when he opened the door. His sharp glance made a rapid assessment of Gillian, cataloguing her potential weaknesses and strengths. When she nodded, he went on crisply. "There's nothing to worry about. I'll be in there and several orderlies are within calling distance should she need to be quickly subdued."

"You act as if you believe that Bobby could really hurt someone," Gillian said and preceded him to the next room without waiting for a response.

The others watched, waiting for a reaction from Roberta when the door opened and her sister entered. There was none. The big square body continued to rock.

Gillian hesitated, her hand on the door. "Bobby," she said clearly. Her tone was quiet, but matter-of-fact, the way a parent might speak to a recalcitrant child. Receiving no response, the young woman took one of the three chairs and placed it in front of her sister, directly in her line of vision. She sat down. Roberta gazed through her to the spot on the wall. Gillian looked towards the psychiatrist, who had pulled his chair to one side, out of Roberta's vision. "What should I—"

"Talk about yourself. She can hear you."

Gillian fingered the material of her dress. She dragged her eyes up to her sister's face. "I've come up from London to see you, Bobby," she began. Her voice quavered, but as she proceeded, it gathered strength. "That's where I live now. With my husband. I was married last November." She looked at Samuels, who nodded encouragingly. "You're going to think it's so funny, but I married a minister. It's hard to believe that a girl with such a strong Catholic background would marry a minister, isn't it? What would Papa ever say if he knew?"

The plain face offered neither acknowledgement nor interest. Gillian might have been speaking to the wall. She licked her dry lips and stumbled on. "We have a flat in Islington. It's not a very large flat, but you'd like it. Remember how I loved plants? Well, I've lots in the flat because the kitchen window gets just the right kind of sun. Remember how I could never get plants to grow in the farmhouse? It was too dark."

The rocking continued. The chair on which Roberta sat groaned with her weight.

"I have a job, as well. I work at a place called Testament House. You know that place, don't you? It's where runaways go to live sometimes. I do all sorts of work there, but I like counselling the kids the best. They say I'm easy to talk to." She paused. "Bobby, won't you talk to me?"

The girl's breathing sounded drugged, her heavy head hung to one side. She might have been asleep.

"I like London. I never thought I would, but I do. I expect it's because that's where my dreams are. I . . . I'd like to have a baby. That's one of my dreams. And I'd . . . I think I'd like to write a book. There are all sorts of stories inside me, and I want to write them down. Like the Brontës. Remember how we read the Brontës? They had dreams as well, didn't they? I think it's important to have dreams."

"It's not going to work," Jonah Clarence said brusquely. The moment his wife had left the room, he had seen the trap, had understood that her entry into her sister's presence was a return to a past in which he had played no part, from which he could not save her. "How long does she have to stay in there?"

"As long as she wants." Lynley's voice was cool. "It's in Gillian's hands."

"But anything can happen. Doesn't she understand that?" Jonah wanted to jump up, fling open the door, and drag his wife away. It was as if her mere presence in the room—trapped with the horrible, whale-like creature that was her sister—were enough to contaminate and destroy her forever. *"Nell!"* he said fiercely.

"I want to talk to you about the night I left, Bobby," Gillian went on, her eyes on her sister's face, waiting for the slightest flicker that would indicate comprehension and recognition, that would allow her words to stop. "I don't know if you remember it. It was the night after my sixteenth birthday. I . . ." It was too much. She couldn't. She fought onward. "I stole money from Papa. Did he tell you that? I knew where he kept it, the extra money for the house, so I took it. It was wrong, I know that, but I . . . I needed to leave. I needed to go away for a while. You know that, don't you?" And then again, seeking reassurance, *"Don't* you?"

Was the rocking faster now, or was it so only in the imagination of the watchers?

"I went to York. It took me all night. I walked and hitchhiked. I just had that rucksack, you know the one I used to carry my school books in, so I only had one change of clothes with me. I don't know what I was thinking about, running away like that. It seems crazy now, doesn't it?" Gillian smiled briefly at her sister. She could feel her heart hammering. It was becoming quite difficult to breathe. "I got to York at dawn. I'll never forget the sight of the morning light hitting the Minster. It was beautiful. I wanted to stay there forever." She stopped, put her hands firmly into her lap. The deep scratches showed. It couldn't be helped. "I stayed in York that entire day. I was so frightened, Bobby. I'd never even been away from home for a night by myself, and I wasn't sure I wanted to go on to London. I thought it might be easier if I went back to the farm. But I . . . I couldn't. I just couldn't."

"What's the point of this?" Jonah Clarence demanded. "How is all this supposed to help Roberta?"

Wary, Lynley glanced at him, but the man settled himself again. His face was rigid, every muscle tight.

"So I caught the train that night. There were so many stops, and at every one of them, I thought that I would be questioned. I thought that Papa might have sent the police after me, or come after me himself. But nothing happened. Until I got to King's Cross."

"You don't need to tell her about the pimp," Jonah whispered. "What's the point?"

"There was a nice man at King's Cross who bought me something to eat. I was so grateful to him. He was such a gentleman, I thought. But while I was eating and he was telling me about a house he had where I could live, another man came into the cafeteria. He saw us. He came up and said, 'She's coming with me.' I thought he was a policeman, that he would make me go home again. I started to cry. I hung on to my friend. But he shook me off and ran out of the station." She paused, caught in the memory of that night. "This new man was very different. His clothes were old, a bit shabby. But his voice was kind. He said his name was George Clarence, that he was a minister, and that the other man had wanted to take me to Soho to . . . to take me to Soho," she repeated firmly. "He said he had a house in Camden Town where I could stay."

Jonah remembered it all so vividly: the ancient rucksack, the frightened girl, the scuffed shoes and tattered jeans she wore. He remembered his father's arrival and the conversation between his parents. The words "pimp from Soho . . . didn't even understand . . . looks like she hasn't slept at all . . ." echoed in his mind. He remembered watching her from the breakfast table where he'd been dividing his time between scrambled eggs and cramming for a literature test. She wouldn't look at anyone. Not then.

"Mr. Clarence was very good to me, Bobby. I was like part of his family. I . . . I married his son Jonah. You'd love Jonah. He's so gentle. So good. When I'm with him, I feel as if nothing could ever . . . nothing ever again," she concluded.

It was enough. It was what she had come to do. Gillian looked at the psychiatrist beseechingly, waiting for direction from him, for his nod of dismissal. He merely watched her from behind the protection of his spectacles. They winked in the light. His face told her nothing, but his eyes were very kind.

"There. That's it. It's done nothing," Jonah concluded decisively. "You've brought her up here to this all for nothing. I'm taking her home." He began to get to his feet.

"Sit down," Lynley said, his voice making it clear that the other man had no choice in the matter.

"Bobby, talk to me," Gillian begged. "They say you killed Papa. But I know that you couldn't have. You didn't look like . . . There was no *reason*. I know it. Tell me there was no reason. He took us to church, he read to us, he made up games we could play. Bobby, you didn't kill him, did you?"

"It's important to you that I didn't kill him, isn't it?" Dr. Samuels said quietly. His voice was like a feather floating gently in the air between them.

"Yes," Gillian responded immediately, although her eyes were on her sister. "I put the key under your pillow, Bobby. You were awake! I talked to you! I said 'Use it tomorrow' and you understood. Don't tell me you didn't understand. I *know* you did."

"I was too young. I didn't understand," the doctor said.

"You had to understand! I told you I'd put a message in the *Guardian*, that it would say *Nell Graham*, remember? We loved that book, didn't we? She was so brave and strong. It was the way we both wanted to be."

"But I wasn't strong, was I?" the doctor queried.

"You were! You didn't look like . . . You were supposed to come to Harrogate! The message told you to come to Harrogate, Bobby! You were sixteen. You could have come!"

"I wasn't like you at sixteen, Gillian. How could I have been?" The psychiatrist hadn't moved in his chair. His eyes travelled between the two sisters, waiting for a sign, reading the underlying messages in body movements, posture, and tone of voice.

"You didn't have to be! You weren't supposed to be! All you had to do was come to Harrogate. Not to London, just to Harrogate. I would have taken you from there. But when you didn't come, I thought—I *believed*—that you were all right. That nothing . . . that you were fine. You weren't like Mummy. You were fine."

"Like Mummy?"

"Yes, like Mummy. I was like her. Just exactly like. I could see it in the pictures. But you weren't. So that made you fine."

"What did it mean, to be like Mummy?" the doctor asked.

Gillian stiffened. Her mouth formed the single word *no* three times in rapid succession. It was too much to bear. She couldn't go on.

"Was Bobby like Mummy in spite of what you believed?"

No!

"Don't answer him, Nell," Jonah Clarence muttered. "You don't have to answer him. You're not the patient here."

Gillian looked at her hands. She felt the burden of guilt heavy upon her shoulders. The sound of her sister's ceaseless rocking filled the air, the sound of tortured breathing, the beating of her own heart. She felt that she couldn't go on. She knew she couldn't turn back.

"You know why I left, don't you?" she said hollowly. "It was because of the present on my birthday, the special present, the one . . ." Her hand went to her eyes. It shook. She controlled herself. "You must tell them the truth! You must tell them what happened! You can't let them lock you away for the rest of your life!"

Silence. She *couldn't*. It was in the past. It had all happened to someone else. Besides, the little eight-year-old who had followed her round the farm, who had watched her every movement with eyes shining with adoration, was dead. This gross, obscene creature before her was not Roberta. There was no need to go further. Roberta was gone.

Gillian lifted her head. Roberta's eyes had shifted. They had moved to her, and in that movement Gillian saw that she had indeed broken through where the psychiatrist had failed these last three weeks. But there was no triumph in that knowledge. There was only condemnation. There was only facing, one last time, the immutable past.

"I didn't understand," Gillian said brokenly. "I was only four or five years old. You weren't even born then. He said it was special. A kind of friendship fathers always had with their daughters. Like Lot."

"Oh no," Jonah whispered.

"Did he read the Bible to you, Bobby? He read it to me. He came in at night and sat on my bed and read the Bible to me. And as he read it—"

"No, no, *no!*"

"—his hand would find me underneath the covers. 'Do you like that, Gilly?' he would ask me. 'Does it make you happy? It makes Papa very happy. It's so nice. So soft. Do you like it, Gilly?' "

Jonah pounded his right fist against his forehead. With his left arm he hugged himself tightly across his chest up to his shoulder. *"Please,"* he moaned.

"I didn't know, Bobby. I didn't understand. I was only five years old and then it was dark in the room. 'Turn over,' he would say, 'Papa will rub your back. Do you like that? Where do you like it best? Here, Gilly? Is it special here?' And then he'd take my hand. 'Papa likes it there, Gilly. Rub Papa there.' "

"Where was Mummy?" the doctor asked.

"Mummy was asleep. Or in her room. Or reading. But it really didn't matter because this was special. This was something fathers share with daughters. Mummy mustn't know. Mummy wouldn't understand. She didn't read the Bible with us so she wouldn't understand. And then she left. I was eight years old."

"And then you were alone."

Gillian shook her head numbly. Her eyes were wide, tearless. "Oh no," she said in a small, torn voice. "I was Mummy then."

At her words, a cry escaped Jonah Clarence's lips. Lady Helen looked at Lynley immedeiately and covered his hand with her own. It turned, grasping her fingers tightly.

"Papa set up all her pictures in the sitting room so I could see her every day. 'Mummy's gone,' he said and made me look at them all so I could see how pretty she was and how much I had sinned in being born in the first place to drive her away. 'Mummy knew how much Papa loved you, Gilly, so she left. You must be Mummy to me now.' I didn't know what he meant. So he showed me. He read the Bible. He prayed. And he showed me. But I was too little to be a proper Mummy to him. So he . . . I did other things. He taught me. And I . . . was a very good student."

"You wanted to please him. He was your father. He was all you had."

"I wanted him to love me. He said he loved me when I . . . when we . . . 'Papa loves it in your mouth, Gilly.' And afterwards we prayed. We always prayed. I thought God would forgive me for making Mummy run away if I became a good enough Mummy to Papa. But God never forgave me. He didn't exist."

Jonah's head sank to the table, cradled in his arms, and he began to weep.

Gillian finally looked at her sister again. Roberta's eyes were on her, although her face remained without expression. The rocking had stopped.

"So I did things, Bobby, things I didn't understand because Mummy was gone and I needed . . . I wanted my Mummy again. And I thought the only way to get Mummy back was to be her myself."

"Is that what you did when you were sixteen?" Dr. Samuels asked softly.

"He came to my room. It was late. He said it was time to become Lot's daughter, the real way, the way the Bible said, and he took off his clothes."

"He'd never done that before?"

"Never all his clothes. Not like that. I thought he wanted . . .

what I usually . . . But he didn't. He . . . spread my legs and . . . 'You're . . . I can't breathe, Papa. You're too heavy. Please, don't. I'm afraid. Oh it hurts, it hurts!' "

Her husband swayed to his feet, scraping his chair back viciously on the linoleum floor. He staggered to the window. "It never happened!" he cried against it. "It couldn't! It didn't! You're my *wife!*"

"But he put his hand over my mouth. He said, 'We can't wake Bobby, darling. Papa loves *you* best. Let Papa show you, Gilly. Let Papa inside. Like Mummy. Like a real Mummy. Let Papa inside.' And it hurt. And it hurt. And I *hated* him."

No!" Jonah screamed. He threw open the door. It crashed against the wall. He ran from the room.

Then Gillian began to cry. "I was just a shell. I wasn't a person. What did it matter what he did to me? I became what he wanted, what *anyone* wanted. That's how I lived. Jonah, that's how I *lived!*"

"Pleasing everyone?" the doctor asked.

"People love looking into mirrors. So that's what I was. That's what he made me. Oh God, I hated him. I *hated* him!" She buried her face in her hands and wept as the grief overcame her, tortured tears held in check for eleven long years. The others sat motionless, listening to her weeping. After long, painful minutes she raised her ravaged face to her sister's. "Don't let him kill you, Bobby. Don't let him do it. For God's sake, tell them the truth!"

There was no response. There was absolutely nothing. Only the unbearable sound of Gillian's personal torment. Roberta was motionless. She might have been deaf.

"Tommy," Lady Helen whispered. "I can't bear this. She's done it for *nothing.*"

Lynley stared into the next room. His head was pounding, his throat ached, his eyes burned. He wanted to find William Teys, find him alive, and tear the man savagely limb from limb. He had never known such rage, such sickness. He felt Gillian's anguish overcome him like a disease.

But her weeping had lessened. She was getting to her feet. She was walking unevenly, numbly, to the door. Her hand reached for the knob. She turned it, pulled it open. Her presence had been useless after all. It was over.

"Did he make you have the naked parade, Gilly?" Roberta asked.

16

As if under water, Gillian turned slowly from the door at the sound of her sister's husky voice. "Tell me," she whispered. She walked back to her chair, moved it closer to the other, and sat down.

Roberta's eyes, heavy-lidded under their protective folds of fat, were fixed but unfocused on her sister. Her lips worked convulsively. The fingers of one hand flexed. "It was music. Loud. He would take off my clothes." And then the girl's voice altered. It became honey-toned, insinuatingly persuasive, chillingly male. "*Pretty baby. Pretty baby* and *Time to march, pretty baby. Time to march for Papa.* And he would . . . it was in his hand . . . *Watch what Papa does while you march, pretty baby.*"

"I left the key for you, Bobby," Gillian said brokenly. "When he fell asleep that night in my bed, I went to his room and I found the key. What happened to it? I *left* it for you."

Roberta struggled with information buried so long beneath the weight of her childhood terrors. "I didn't . . . didn't know. I locked the door. But you never said why. You never said to keep the key."

"Oh God." Gillian's voice was anguished. "Are you saying that you locked the door at night but in the day you left the key in the keyhole? Bobby, is that what you mean?"

Roberta drew her arm across her damp face. It was like a shield, and behind its protection she nodded. Her body heaved with a repressed cry. "I didn't *know*."

"So he found it and took it away."

"He put it in his wardrobe. All the keys were there. It was locked. I couldn't get it. *Don't need keys, pretty baby. Pretty baby march for Papa.*"

"When did you march?"

"Daytime, nighttime. *Come here, pretty baby, Papa wants to help you march.*"

"How?"

Roberta's arm dropped. Her face was quickly shuttered. Her fingers picked and pulled at her lower lip.

"Bobby, *tell* me how," Gillian insisted. "Tell me what he did."

"I love Papa. I love Papa."

"Don't say that!" She reached out, grabbed her sister's arm. "Tell me what he did to you!"

"Love. *Love* Papa."

"Don't say that! He was evil!"

Roberta shrank from the word. "No. *I* was evil."

"How?"

"What I made him . . . he couldn't help . . . he prayed and prayed and couldn't help . . . you weren't there . . . *Gilly knew what I wanted. Gilly knew how to do me. You're no good, pretty baby. March for Papa. March on Papa.*"

" 'March *on* Papa'?" Gillian gasped.

"Up and down in one place. Up and down. *That's nice, pretty baby. Papa big between your legs.*"

"Bobby. *Bobby.*" Gillian averted her face. "How old were you?"

"Eight. *Mmmmm, Papa likes to feel all over. Likes to feel and feel and feel.*"

"Didn't you tell anyone? Wasn't there anyone?"

"Miss Fitzalan. I told. But she didn't . . . she couldn't . . ."

"She didn't *do* anything? She didn't *help*?'

"She didn't understand. I said whiskers . . . his face when he rubbed me. Didn't understand. *Did you tell, pretty baby? Did you try to tell on Papa?*"

"Oh God, she *told* him?"

"*Gilly never told. Gilly never told on Papa. Very bad, pretty baby. Papa needs to punish you.*"

"How?"

Roberta gave no answer. Instead, she began to rock, began to return to the place she had inhabited so long.

"You were only eight years old!" Gillian began to cry. "Bobby, I'm sorry! I didn't know! I didn't think he would. You didn't look like me. You didn't look like Mummy."

"Hurt Bobby in the bad place. Not like Gilly. Not like Gilly."

"Not like Gilly?"

"Turn over, pretty baby. Papa has to punish you."

"Oh my God!" Gillian fell to her knees, took her sister into her arms. She sobbed against her breast, but the girl did not respond. Instead, her arms hung limply at her sides and her body tensed as if the proximity of her sister was frightening or distasteful. "Why didn't you come to Harrogate? Didn't you see the message? Why didn't you come? I thought you were all right! I thought he left you alone! Why didn't you come?"

"Bobby died. Bobby died."

"Don't say that! You're alive. Don't let him kill you now!"

Roberta shrank back, freeing herself fiercely. "Papa never kill, Papa never kill, Papa never kill!" Her voice grew high with panic.

The psychiatrist leaned forward in his chair. "Kill what, Roberta?" he asked quickly, and pressed the advantage. "What did Papa never kill?"

"Baby. Papa didn't kill the baby."

"What did he do?"

"Found me in the barn. Cried and prayed and cried."

"Is that where you had the baby? In the barn?"

"No one knew. Fat and ugly. No one knew."

Gillian's eyes were transfixed in horror, not on her sister's face, but on the psychiatrist. She rocked on her heels, a hand at her mouth, biting down on her fingers as if to keep from screaming. "You were pregnant? Bobby! He didn't know you were pregnant?"

"No one knew. Not like Gilly. Fat and ugly. No one knew."

"What happened to the baby?"

"Bobby died."

"What happened to the baby?"

"Bobby died."

"What happened to the baby!" Gillian's voice rose to a scream.

"Did you kill the baby, Roberta?" Dr. Samuels asked.

Nothing. She began to rock. It was a rapid movement, as if she were hurtling back into madness.

Gillian watched her, watched the panic that drove her and the unassailable armour of psychosis that protected her. And she knew. "Papa killed the baby," she asserted numbly. "He found you in the barn, he cried and prayed, read the Bible for guidance, and then he killed the baby." She touched her sister's hair. "What did he do with it?"

"Don't know."

"Did you ever see it?"

"Never saw the baby. Boy or girl. Don't know."

"Is that why you didn't come to Harrogate? Were you pregnant then?"

The rocking slowed to a stop. It was affirmation.

"Baby died. Bobby died. It didn't matter. *Papa sorry, pretty baby. Papa never hurt again. Pretty baby march for Papa. Papa never hurt again.*"

"He didn't have intercourse with you again, Roberta?" Dr. Samuels asked. "But everything else stayed the same?"

"Pretty baby march for Papa."

"Did you march for Papa, Roberta?" the doctor continued. "After the baby, did you march for him?"

"Marched for Papa. Had to march."

"Why? Why did you have to?"

She looked about furtively, an odd smile of twisted satisfaction dancing on her face. And then began to rock. "Papa happy."

"It was important that Papa be happy," Dr. Samuels said reflectively.

"Yes, yes. *Very* happy. Happy Papa won't touch . . ." She cut the words off. The rocking increased in intensity.

"No, Bobby," Gillian said. "Don't you leave. You mustn't leave now. You marched for Papa to keep him happy so that he wouldn't touch someone. Who?"

In the darkened observation room, the terrible realisation cut like a sword's swath down Lynley's spine. The knowledge had been there before him all along. A nine-year-old girl being schooled in the Bible, being read the Old Testament, learning the lessons of Lot's daughters.

"Bridie!" he said savagely and understood everything at last.

He could have told the rest of the story himself, but he listened instead to the purgation of a tortured soul.

"Papa wanted Gilly not a cow like Roberta."

"Your father wanted a child, didn't he?" Dr. Samuels asked. "He needed a child's body to arouse him. Like Gillian's. Like your mother's."

"Found a child."

"And what happened?"

Roberta pressed her cracked lips together as if to stop herself from speaking. The corners of her mouth were spotted with blood. She gave a ragged cry and a flurry of words escaped as if of their own volition. "The Pharaoh put a chain on his neck and dressed him in fine linen and he ruled over Egypt and Joseph's brothers came to see him and Joseph said I am supposed to save your lives by a great deliverance."

Gillian spoke through her tears. "The Bible told you what to do, just as it always told Papa."

"Dress in linens. Wear a chain."

"What happened?"

"Got him in the barn."

"How did you do that?" Dr. Samuels' voice was low.

Roberta's face quivered. Her eyes filled with tears. They began to spill down her acne-covered cheeks. "Tried twice. Didn't work. Then . . . Whiskers," she replied.

"You killed Whiskers to get your father to the barn?" the doctor asked.

"Whiskers didn't know. Gave him pills. Papa's pills. He was asleep. Cut . . . cut his throat. Called for Papa. Papa ran. Knelt by Whiskers." She began to rock furiously, cradling her bloated body, accompanying the movement with low, tuneless humming. She was in retreat.

"And then, Roberta?" the psychiatrist asked. "You can take the last step, can't you? With Gillian here?"

Rocking. Rocking. Savage and furious. Blindly determined. Her eyes on the wall. "Love Papa. Love Papa. Don't remember. *Don't remember.*"

"Of course you remember." The psychiatrist's voice was gentle but relentless. "The Bible told you what to do. If you hadn't done it, your father would have done to that little girl all the things he had done to you and Gillian through the years. He would have molested her. He would have sodomised her. He would have raped her. But you stopped him, Roberta. You saved that child. You dressed in fine linens. You put on the gold chain. You killed the dog. You called your father to the barn. He ran in, didn't he? He knelt down and—"

Roberta jumped off her chair. It flew across the room, striking the cabinet, and she went after it, moving like the wind. She picked it up, hurled it against the wall, dumped over the cabinet, and began to scream.

"I chopped off his head! He knelt down. He bent to pick up Whiskers. And I chopped off his head! I don't care that I did it! I wanted him to die! I wouldn't let him touch Bridie! He wanted to. He read to her just like he'd done to me. He talked to her just like he'd done to me. He was going to do it! I knew the signs! I killed him! I killed him and I don't care! I'm not sorry! He deserved to die!" Slumping to the floor, she wept into her hands, large grey dough-like hands that covered her face, but pinched and brutalised it even as they protected. "I saw his head on the floor. And I didn't care. And the rat came out of nowhere. And he sniffed at the blood. And he ate at the brains and I didn't *care*!"

With a strangled cry, Sergeant Havers leapt to her feet and staggered from the room.

Barbara crashed into the lavatory, fell blindly into a stall, and began to vomit. The room swam round her. She was so ragingly hot that she was sure she would faint, but she continued, instead, to vomit. And as she retched—painfully, spasmodically—she knew that what was spewing forth from her body was the turbid mass of her own despair.

She clung to the smooth porcelain bowl, fought for breath to redeem her, and vomited. It was as if she had never seen life clearly until the last two hours and, suddenly faced with its filth, she had to get away from it, had to get it out of her system.

In that dark, stifling room the voices had come to her relentlessly. Not just the voices of the sisters who had lived the nightmare, but the voices of her own past and of the nightmare that remained. It was too much. She could no longer live with it; she could no longer bear it.

I can't, she sobbed inwardly. Tony, I can't any longer! God forgive me, but I can't!

Footsteps entered the room. She stuggled to pull herself together but the illness continued and she knew she would have to endure the further humiliation of being mortally ill in front of the fashionable competence of Lady Helen Clyde.

Water was turned on. More footsteps. The stall door opened and a damp cloth was pressed to the back of her neck, folded quickly, and then wiped across her burning cheeks.

"Please. No! Go away!" She was sick again and, what was even more despicable, she began to cry. "I can't!" she wept. "I can't! Please. *Please!* Leave me alone!"

A cool hand pushed her hair off her face and supported her forehead. "Life's rotten, Barb. And the hell of it is that it doesn't get much better," Lynley's voice said.

Horrified, she spun around. But it was Lynley, and in his eyes the compassion she had seen before: in his treatment of Roberta, in his conversation with Bridie, in his questioning of Tessa. And she suddenly saw what it was that Webberly had known she could learn from Lynley—the source of his strength, the centre of what she knew quite well was tremendous personal courage. It was that quiet compassion, nothing else, that finally broke her.

"How could he?" she sobbed. "If it's your child . . . you're supposed to love, not hurt. Not let him die. Never let him die! And that's what they did!" Her voice spiralled hysterically and all the time Lynley's dark eyes were on her face. "I hate . . . I can't . . . They were supposed to *be* there for him. He was their son! They were supposed to love him and they didn't. He was sick for four years, the last year in hospital. They wouldn't even go to see him! They said they couldn't bear it, that it hurt too much. But I went. I went every day. And he asked for them. He asked why Mum and Dad wouldn't come to see him. And I lied. I went every day and I lied. And when he died, he was all alone. I was in school. I didn't get there in time. He was my little brother! He was only ten years old! And all of us—*all* of us—let him die alone."

"I'm so sorry," Lynley said.

"I swore that I would *never* let them forget what they'd done. I asked his teachers for the letters. I framed the death certificate. I made the shrine. I kept them in the house. I closed the doors and the windows. And every *single* day I made sure they had to sit there and stare at Tony. I drove them mad! I *wanted* to do it! I destroyed them. I destroyed myself!''

She put her head down on the porcelain and wept. She wept for the hate that had filled her life, for the guilt and the jealousy that had been her companions, for the loneliness that she had brought upon herself, for the contempt and disgust that she had directed towards others.

At the last, when Lynley wordlessly took her into his arms, she wept against his chest, mourning most of all the death of the friendship that could have lived between them.

Through the transom windows in Dr. Samuels' orderly office, they could see the the rose garden. It was designed in plots and descending terraces, the plants segregated by colour of flower and type. A few bushes still had blooms on them, despite the lateness of the year, the cold nights, the rare frost in the mornings. Soon, however, the heavy blossoms would die. Gardeners would cut the bushes back for a dormant winter. But they would renew themselves in the spring, and the circle of life would continue.

They watched the little party wander on the gravel paths among the plants. They were a study in contrasts: Gillian and her sister, Lady Helen and Sergeant Havers, and far behind them the two nurses, their forms hidden beneath the long capes they wore against the wind-blown afternoon.

Lynley turned from the sight and saw Dr. Samuels watching him thoughtfully from behind his desk, his intelligent face carefully devoid of expression.

"You knew she'd had a baby," Lynley said. "From her admission physical, I should guess."

"Yes."

"Why didn't you tell me?"

"I didn't trust you," Samuels replied and added, "then. Whatever fragile bond I could hope to develop with Roberta by keeping that to myself was far more important than sharing the information with you and running the risk of your blurting it out to her." He tempered his words. "It was, after all, privileged information."

"What's going to happen to them?" Lynley asked.

"They're going to survive."

"How can you know that?"

"They're beginning to understand that they were his victims. That's the first step." Samuels took off his spectacles and polished them on the interior of his jacket. His lean face was tired. He had heard it all before.

"I don't understand how they survived this long."

"They coped."

"How?"

The doctor gave a final glance to his spectacles and put them back on. He adjusted their position carefully. He'd worn them for years, and deep, painful indentations had been created on either side of his nose from their pressure. "For Gillian it appears to have been what we call dissociation, a way of subdividing the self so that she could pretend to have or be those things which she couldn't really have or couldn't really be."

"Such as?"

"Normal feelings, for one. Normal relationships for another. She called it being a mirror, just reflecting the behaviour of those round her. It's a defence. It protected her from feeling anything about what was happening to her."

"How?"

"She wasn't a 'real person,' so nothing her father did could really touch or hurt her."

"Everyone in the village describes her in an entirely different way."

"Yes. That's the behaviour. Gillian simply mirrored them. Taking it to its furthest extreme, it becomes multiple personalities, but she seems to have prevented that from occurring. In itself, that's remarkable, considering what she went through."

"What about Roberta?"

The psychiatrist frowned. "She didn't cope as well as Gillian," he admitted.

Lynley gave a last glance out the window and returned to his seat, a worn upholstered chair: resting place, no doubt, for hundreds of tormented psyches. "Is that why she ate?"

"As a way of escaping? No, I don't think so. I'd say it was more an act of self-destruction."

"I don't understand."

"The abused child feels he or she has done something wrong and is being punished for it. Roberta may well have eaten because the abuse led her to despise herself—her 'wickedness'—and destroying her body was a scourging. That's one explanation." The doctor hesitated.

"And the other?"

"Hard to say. It could be that she tried to stop the abuse the only way she knew how. Short of suicide, what better way than to destroy her body, to make herself as un-Gilly-like as possible. That way, her father wouldn't want her sexually."

"But it didn't work."

"Unfortunately, no. He merely turned to perversions to arouse himself, making her part of it. That would feed his need for power."

"I feel as if I'd like to tear Teys apart," Lynley said.

"I feel that way all the time," the doctor responded.

"How could anyone . . . I don't understand it."

"It's a deviant behaviour, a sickness. Teys was aroused by children. His marriage to a sixteen-year-old girl—not a voluptuous, womanly sixteen-year-old, but a late-maturing sixteen-year-old—would have been a glaring sign to anyone looking for aberrant behaviour. But he was able to mask it well with his devotion to religion and his persona of the strong, loving father. That's so typical, Inspector Lynley. I can't tell you how typical it is."

"And no one ever knew? I can't believe it."

"If you consider the situation, it's easy to believe. Teys projected a very successful image in his community. At the same time, his daughters were tricked into self-blame and secrecy. Gillian believed *she* had been responsible for her mother's desertion of her father and was making reparation for that by, in Teys' words, 'being a mummy' to him. Roberta believed that Gillian had pleased her father and that she was supposed to do the same. And both of them, of course, were taught from the Bible—Teys' careful selection of passages and his twisted interpretations of them—that what they were doing was not only right but written by the hand of God as their duty as his daughters."

"It makes me sick."

"It *is* sick. He was sick. Consider his sickness: He chose a child to be his bride. That was safe. He was threatened by the adult world and in the person of this sixteen-year-old girl, he saw someone who could arouse him with her childlike body and, at the same time, gratify his need for the self-respect that a marriage would give him."

"Then why did he turn to his children?"

"When Tessa—this childlike bride of his—produced a baby, Teys had frightening and irrefutable evidence that the creature who had been arousing him and upon whose body he had taken such gratification was not a child at all, but a woman. And he was threatened by women, I should guess, the feminine representation of the entire adult world that he feared."

"She said he stopped sleeping with her."

"I've no doubt of that. If he had slept with her and failed to perform, imagine his humiliation. Why risk that kind of failure when there in his house was a helpless infant from whom he could get immense pleasure and satisfaction?"

Lynley felt his throat close. *"Infant?"* he asked. "Do you mean . . ."

Dr. Samuels took the measure of Lynley's reaction and nodded in sad recognition of an outrage he himself had felt for many years. "I should think that the abuse of Gillian began in infancy. She remembers the first incident when she was four or five, but Teys was unlikely to have waited that long unless his religion was providing him with self-control for those years. It's possible."

His religion. Each piece was falling into place more tidily than the last, but as each did, Lynley felt an anger that needed free rein. He controlled it with an effort. "She'll stand trial."

"Eventually. Roberta's going to recover. She'll be found competent to stand trial." The doctor turned in his chair to watch the group in the garden. "But you know as well as I, Inspector, that no jury in the world is going to convict her of anything when the truth is told. So perhaps we can believe that there will be a form of justice after all."

The trees that towered above St. Catherine's Church cast long shadows on the exterior of the building so that, even though it was still light outside, the interior was dim. The deep reds and purples from stained glass windows poured forth bloody pools of light which faded slowly on the cracked tile floor, and votive candles flickered under statues who watched his movement in the aisle. The air within the building was heavy and dead, and as Lynley made his way to the Elizabethan confessional, he shivered.

He opened the door, went inside the booth, knelt, and waited. The darkness was complete, the tranquillity absolute. A suitable ambience for meditating upon one's sins, Lynley thought.

A grill was moved in the darkness. A gentle voice murmured incantations to a nonexistent god. Then, "Yes, my child?"

At the last moment, he wondered if he would be able to do it. But he found his voice.

"He came to you here," Lynley said. "This was the place where he confessed his sins. Did you absolve him, Father? Did you make some sort of mystical configuration in the air that told William Teys he was free of the sin of abusing his children? What did you tell him? Did you give him your blessing? Did you release him from the confessional, his soul purged once more, to go home to his farm and begin it again? Is that how it was?"

In response, he only heard breathing, harsh and rapid, that told him a living creature was on the other side of the grill.

"And did Gillian confess? Or was she too frightened? Did you talk to her about what her father did to her? Did you try to help her?"

"I . . ." The voice sounded as if it were coming from a great distance. "Understand and forgive."

"That's what you told her? Understand? Forgive? What about Roberta? Was she supposed to understand and forgive as well? Was a sixteen-year-old girl supposed to learn to accept the fact that her father raped her, made her pregnant, that he then murdered her child? Or was that *your* idea, Father?"

"I didn't know about the baby. I didn't know! I didn't *know!*" The voice was frantic.

"But you knew once you found it in the abbey. You damn well knew. You chose *Pericles*, Father Hart. You damn *well* knew."

"He . . . he never confessed to that. Never!"

"And what would you have done if he had? What exactly

would his penance have been for the murder of his child? And it was murder. You know it was murder."

"No. No!"

"William Teys carried that baby from Gembler Farm to the abbey. He couldn't wrap it in anything because anything he used might have been traced back to him. So he carried it naked. And it died. You knew when you saw it whose baby it was, how it got to the abbey. You chose *Pericles* for the epitaph. *Murder's as near to lust as flame to smoke.* You damn well knew."

"He said . . . after that . . . he swore he was cured."

"*Cured?* A miraculous recovery from sexual deviance, nicely engineered by the death of his infant child? Is that what you thought? Is that what you wanted to think? He was recovered, all right. His idea of recovery was that he'd stopped raping Roberta. But listen to me, Father, because this is on your conscience and by God you shall hear me, he stopped *nothing* else."

"No!"

"You know it's the truth. He was addicted. The only problem was that he needed a fresh young fix for his habit. He needed Bridie. And you were going to let it happen."

"He swore to me—"

"He *swore?* On what? The Bible that he used to make Gillian believe she had to give her body to her father? Is that what he swore on?"

"He stopped confessing. I didn't know. I—"

"You knew. From the moment he started on Bridie, you knew. And when you went to the farm and saw what Roberta had done, the real truth came crashing right down, didn't it?"

There was a stifled sob. And then growing out of it a keening of grief that rose like the wail of Jacob and broke on the utterance of three nearly incoherent words. *"Mea . . . mea culpa!"*

"Yes!" Lynley hissed. "Through *your* fault, Father."

"I couldn't . . . it was the silence of the confessional. It's a holy oath."

"There is no oath more important than life. There is no oath more important than the ruin of a child. You saw that, didn't you, when you went to the farm? You knew that it was finally time to break the silence. So you wiped off the axe, you got rid of the knife, and you came to Scotland Yard. You knew the real truth would come out that way, the truth *you* lacked the courage to reveal."

"Oh God, I . . . understand and forgive." The whisper was broken.

"Not for this. Not for twenty-seven years of physical abuse. For two ruined lives. For the death of their dreams. There is *no* understanding. There is *no* forgiveness. By God, not for this." He shoved open the door of the confessional and left.

Behind him a querulous voice rose in agonising prayer. " 'Fret not thyself because of evildoers . . . they shall soon be cut down like the grass . . . trust in the Lord . . . he shall give thee the desires of thy heart . . . evildoers shall be cut off . . .' "

Scarcely able to breathe, Lynley flung open the church door and stepped out into the air.

Lady Helen was leaning against the edge of a lichened sarcophagus, watching Gillian, who stood at the small, distant grave under the cypress trees, her cropped blonde head bent in contemplation or prayer. She heard Lynley's footsteps but did not stir, not even when he joined her and she felt the sure, steady pressure of his arm against her own.

"I saw Deborah," he said at last.

"Ah." Her eyes remained on Gillian's slight form. "I thought you might see her, Tommy. I hoped you wouldn't but I did think you might."

"You knew they were here in Keldale. Why didn't you tell me?"

Still she looked away from him, but for a moment she lowered her eyes. "What was there to say, really? We'd said it already. So many times." She hesitated, wanting to let it go, to let the subject die between them once and for all. But the backward abysm of time that constituted the many years of their friendship would not allow her to do so. "Was it dreadful for you?" she made herself ask.

"At first."

"And then?"

"Then I saw that she loves him. As you did once."

A regretful smile touched her lips briefly. "Yes. As I did once."

"Where did you find the strength to let St. James go, Helen? How on earth did you survive it?"

"Oh, I muddled through somehow. Besides, you were always there for me, Tommy. You helped me. You were always my friend."

"As you've been mine. My very best friend."

She laughed softly at that. "Men say that about their dogs, you know. I'm not sure I ought to be flattered by the appellation."

"But *are* you?" he asked.

"Most decidedly," she replied. She turned to him then and searched his face. The exhaustion was there as it had been before, but the weight of sorrow was lessened. Not gone, that would not happen quickly, but dissolving and leading him out of the past. "You're beyond the worst of it now, aren't you?"

"I'm beyond the worst. I think, in fact, I'm ready to go on." He touched the fall of her hair and smiled.

The lych-gate opened and over Lynley's shoulder Lady Helen saw Sergeant Havers coming into the graveyard. Her steps slowed momentarily when she saw them talking tranquilly together, but she cleared her throat as if in warning of her intrusion and strode towards them quickly, her shoulders squared.

"Sir, you've a message from Webberly," she said to Lynley. "Stepha had it at the lodge."

"A message? What sort?"

"His usual cryptogram, I'm afraid." She handed the paper to him. " 'ID positive. London verifies. York informed last P.M.,' " she recited. "Does it make sense to you?"

He read the message over, folded the paper, and looked bleakly off through the graveyard to the hills beyond. "Yes," he replied, but the words were not coming easily to him, "it makes perfect sense."

"Russell Mowrey?" Havers asked perceptively. When he nodded, she went on. "So he did go to London to turn Tessa in to Scotland Yard. How strange. Why not turn her in to the York police? What could Scotland Yard—"

"No. He'd gone to London to see his family, just as Tessa guessed. But he never made it further than King's Cross Station."

"King's Cross Station?" Havers repeated.

"That's where the Ripper got him, Havers. His picture was on the wall in Webberly's office."

* * *

He went to the lodge alone. He walked down Church Street and stood for a moment on the bridge as he had done only the night before. The village was hushed, but, as he took a final look at Keldale, a door slammed nearby. A little red-haired girl hurtled down the back steps of her house and darted to a shed. She disappeared, emerging moments later, dragging a large sack of feed on the ground.

"Where's Dougal?" he called.

Bridie looked up. Her curly hair trapped the sunlight, burning an autumn contrast against the bright green pullover—several sizes too large—that she wore. "Inside. He has a stomachache today."

Lynley wondered idly how one diagnosed a stomachache in a mallard and wisely thought better of asking. "Why are you feeding him, then?" he asked.

She pondered the question, scratching her left leg with the top of her right foot. "Mummy says I ought to. She's been keeping him warm all day and she says she thinks he can eat something now."

"Sounds like a good nurse."

"She is." She waved a grubby hand at him and disappeared into the house, a small package of life with her dreams intact.

He walked across the bridge and into the lodge. Behind the reception desk, Stepha stood up, her lips parted to speak.

"It was Ezra Farmington's baby that you had, wasn't it?" he asked her. "He was part of the wild, crazy laughter you wanted after your brother died, wasn't he?"

"Thomas—"

"Wasn't he?"

"Yes."

"Do you watch when he and Nigel torment each other over you? Are you amused when Nigel drinks himself blind at the Dove and Whistle, hoping to catch you spending time with Ezra at his house across the street? Or do you escape the whole conflict with Richard Gibson's help?"

"That's really unfair."

"Is it? Do you know that Ezra doesn't believe he can paint

any longer? Are you interested, Stepha? He's destroyed his work. The only pieces left are his paintings of you."

"I can't help him."

"You won't help him."

"That's not true."

"You won't help him," Lynley repeated. "For some reason, he still wants you. He wants the child as well. He wants to know where it is. He wants to know what you did with it, who has it. Have you even bothered to tell him if it's a boy or girl?"

She dropped her eyes. "She's . . . she was adopted by a family in Durham. That's the way it had to be."

"And that's to be his punishment, I take it?"

Her eyes flew up. "For what? Why would I punish him?"

"For stopping the laughter. For insisting on having something more with you. For being willing to take chances. For being all the things you're too afraid to be."

She didn't reply. There was no need for her to do so when he could read the answer so clearly on her face.

She had not wanted to go to the farm. The scene of so many of her childhood terrors, the farm was a place she wished to bury in the past. All she had wanted to see was the baby's grave. That done, she was ready to leave. The others, this group of kind strangers who had come into her life, did not question her. Rather, they bundled her into the large, silver car and drove her out of Keldale.

She had no idea where they were taking her, and she didn't much care. Jonah was gone. Nell was dead. And whoever Gillian was remained to be discovered. She was simply a shell. There was nothing else left.

Lynley glanced at Gillian in the mirror. He wasn't sure what would happen. He wasn't sure that it was the right thing to do. He was working on instinct, a blind instinct which insisted that something good had to rise, like a phoenix triumphant, from the ashes of the day.

He knew that he was looking for meaning, that he couldn't

accept the senselessness of Russell Mowrey's death in King's Cross Station at the hands of an unknown killer. He raged against it, against its vile brutality, against its diabolical ugliness, against its terrible waste.

He *would* give meaning to it all. He would not accept that these fragmented lives could not somehow conjoin, could not reach across the chasm of nineteen years and find peace at last.

It was a risk. He didn't care. He would take it. It was six o'clock when he pulled in front of the house in York.

"I'll just be a moment," he said to the others in the car and reached for his door handle.

Sergeant Havers touched his shoulder. "Let me, sir. Please."

He hesitated. She watched him.

"Please," she repeated.

He glanced at the closed front door of the house, knowing that he couldn't possibly face the responsibility of putting the matter into Havers' incapable hands. Not here. Not now. Not with so much at stake.

"Havers—"

"I can do it," she replied. "Please. Believe me."

He saw then that she was giving him the final say over her future, that she was allowing him to be the one to decide whether she would stay in CID or return once and for all to the street. It was represented in the matter before them.

"Sir?"

He wanted desperately to refuse her permission, to tell her to stay where she was in the car, to condemn her to the pavements she had walked in uniform. But none of that had been Webberly's plan. He understood that now, and as he looked at her trusting, resolute face, he saw that Havers—reading his intention in their destination—had built the funeral pyre herself and was perfectly determined to strike the match that would put to the test the promise of the phoenix.

"All right," he finally replied.

"Thank you, sir." She got out of the car and went to the front door. It was opened. She stepped inside the house. And the waiting began.

He had never thought of himself much as a praying man, but as he sat in the car in the growing darkness and the minutes passed, he knew what it was to pray. It was to will goodness out of evil, hope out of despair, life out of death. It was to will dreams into existence and spectres into reality. It was to will an end to anguish and a beginning to joy.

Gillian stirred in the back seat. "Whose house—" Her voice died as the door flew open and Tessa ran outside, hesitating on the front path, peering towards the car. "Mummy." Gillian said it on a breath. She said nothing else. She got out of the car slowly and stared at the woman as if she were an apparition, clinging to the door for support. "Mummy?"

"Gilly! Oh my God, *Gilly*!" Tessa cried and began coming towards her.

It was all Gillian needed. She ran up the slope into her mother's arms, and they entered the house together.